Appropriately enough, this first volume of the ALPHA series covers a roster of writers from A to Z. Specifically, Aldiss to Zelazny—although this coincidence in alphabet is merely incidental to the fact that both these gentlemen, and the several others represented in this anthology, all write superb science fiction.

Two criteria were used in the selecting of these stories—literary merit and importance to the *genre*. The result is that the variety of subjects is matched only by the richness and diversity of their handling—brilliant, frightening, clever, bizarre, powerful, witty, funny —and several steps in-between.

This is wonderful reading by any standards—and a positive feast for s.f. cognoscenti.

ALPHA ONE

Edited by

ROBERT SILVERBERG

BALLANTINE BOOKS • NEW YORK
An Intext Publisher

SBN 345-02014-6-095

ACKNOWLEDGMENTS

Poor Little Warrior, by Brian W. Aldiss. Copyright © 1958 by Fantasy House, Inc. Reprinted by permission of the author's agents, Scott Meredith Literary Agency, Inc.

The Moon Moth, by Jack Vance. Copyright © 1961 by Galaxy Publishing Corporation. Reprinted by permission of the author's agents, Scott Meredith Literary Agency, Inc.

Testament of Andros, by James Blish. Copyright © 1953 by Columbia Publications, Inc. Reprinted by permission of the author and his agent, Robert P. Mills, Ltd.

A Triptych, by Barry Malzberg. Copyright © 1969 by Mercury Press, Inc. Reprinted by permission of the author.

For A Breath I Tarry, by Roger Zelazny. Copyright © 1966 by Ultimate Publishing Co., Inc. Reprinted by permission of the author and his agent, Henry Morrison, Inc.

Game for Motel Room, by Fritz Leiber. Copyright © 1963 by Mercury Press, Inc. Reprinted by permission of the author and his agent, Robert P. Mills, Ltd.

Thus We Frustrate Charlemagne, by R. A. Lafferty. Copyright © 1966 by Galaxy Publishing Corporation. Reprinted by permission of the author and his agent, Virginia Kidd.

The Man Who Came Early, by Poul Anderson. Copyright © 1956 by Fantasy House, Inc. Reprinted by permission of the author's agents, Scott Meredith Literary Agency, Inc.

The Time of His Life, by Larry Eisenberg. Copyright © 1968 by Mercury Press, Inc. Reprinted by permission of the author.

The Doctor, by Ted Thomas. Copyright © 1967 by Damon Knight. Reprinted by permission of the author and his agent, Robert P. Mills, Ltd.

Time Trap, by Charles L. Harness. Copyright © 1948 by Street & Smith Publications, Inc. Reprinted by permission of the author's agents, Scott Meredith Literary Agency, Inc.

The Pi Man, by Alfred Bester. Copyright © 1959 by Fantasy House, Inc. Reprinted by permission of the author and his agent, Robert P. Mills, Ltd.

The Last Man Left in the Bar, by C. M. Kornbluth. Copyright © 1957 by Royal Publications, Inc. Reprinted by permission of Robert P. Mills, Ltd.

The Terminal Beach, by J. G. Ballard. Copyright © 1964 by Nova Publications, Ltd. Reprinted by permission of the author's agents, Scott Meredith Literary Agency, Inc.

First Printing: September, 1970

Cover art by John Lindner

Printed in the United States of America

BALLANTINE BOOKS, INC.
101 Fifth Avenue, New York, N. Y. 10003

Table of Contents

INTRODUCTION

Alpha is, aside from the first letter of the Greek alphabet, a term that denotes excellence and primacy in a variety of disciplines: in nuclear physics, for example, it is the name of a particle of unusually large mass and charge. It seemed a useful label to attach to this volume, the first of an intended series of collections of science fiction stories.

The Alpha series of anthologies will center on no particular theme except that of literary quality. The presence in any one volume of a cluster of stories bearing other thematic resemblance—as in this volume, where there are four or five time-travel stories—will be purely coincidental. I propose to cull the files of the science fiction magazines for stories that an educated and sophisticated reader will find stimulating, and to assemble them in books of roughly equal size that will appear once a year over the next few years. Some of the stories will be fifteen or twenty years old and richly in need of restoration to print. Others will be quite recent: the literary level of the science fiction short story has undergone an extraordinary transformation in the past few years, a fact that demands recognition here.

So much for policy. Herewith, *Alpha One. Alpha Two* is already in preparation. When the series is complete, some volumes hence, it should provide an exciting cumulative view of a field in which some of the most vigorous and inventive fiction of our times has been produced.

ROBERT SILVERBERG

ALPHA ONE

POOR LITTLE WARRIOR

Brian W. Aldiss

Herewith a relatively early work by the celebrated author of *The Hand Reared Boy* and *Barefoot in the Head*—showing that even at the outset of his career Aldiss' work was marked by style, wit, panache, and a certain cheerful somberness. The story of the safari into the Mesozoic has been written many times, but rarely with the force and liveliness of imagination displayed here.

Claude Ford knew exactly how it was to hunt a brontosaurus. You crawled heedlessly through the mud among the willows, through the little primitive flowers with petals as green and brown as a football field, through the beauty-lotion mud. You peered out at the creature sprawling among the reeds, its body as graceful as a sock full of sand. There it lay, letting the gravity cuddle it nappy-damp to the marsh, running its big rabbit-hole nostrils a foot above the grass in a sweeping semicircle, in a snoring search for more sausage reeds. It was beautiful: here horror had reached its limits, come full circle and finally disappeared up its own sphincter. Its eyes gleamed with the liveliness of a week-dead corpse's big toe, and its compost breath and the fur in its crude aural cavities were particularly to be recommended to anyone who might otherwise have felt inclined to speak lovingly of the work of Mother Nature.

But as you, little mammal with opposed digit and .65 self-loading, semi-automatic, dual-barrelled, digitally-computed, telescopically-sighted, rustless, high-powered rifle gripped in your otherwise-defenseless paws, slide along under the bygone willows, what primarily attracts you is the thunder lizard's hide. It gives off a smell as deeply resonant as the bass note of a piano. It makes the elephant's epidermis look like a sheet of crinkled lavatory paper. It is gray as the Viking seas, daft-deep as cathedral foundations. What contact possible to bone could allay the fever of that flesh? Over it scamper—you can see them from here!—the little brown lice that live in those gray walls and canyons, gay as ghosts, cruel as crabs. If one of them jumped on you, it would very likely break your back. And when one of those parasites stops to cock its leg against one of the bronto's vertebrae, you can see it carries in its turn its own crop of easy-livers, each as big as a lobster, for you're near now, oh, so near that you can hear the monster's primitive heart-organ knocking, as the ventricle keeps miraculous time with the auricle.

Time for listening to the oracle is past: you're beyond the stage for omens, you're now headed in for the kill, yours or his; superstition has had its little day for today, from now on only this windy nerve of yours, this shaky conglomeration of muscle entangled untraceably beneath the sweat-shiny carapace of skin, this bloody little urge to slay the dragon, is going to answer all your orisons.

You could shoot now. Just wait till that tiny steam-shovel head pauses once again to gulp down a quarry-load of bulrushes, and with one inexpressibly vulgar bang you can show the whole indifferent Jurassic world that it's standing looking down the business end of evolution's six-shooter. You know why you pause, even as you pretend not to know why you pause; that old worm conscience, long as a baseball pitch, long-lived as a tortoise, is at work; through every sense it slides, more monstrous than the serpent. Through the passions: saying, here is a sitting duck, O Englishman! Through the intelligence: whispering that boredom, the kite hawk who never feeds, will settle again when the task is done. Through the nerves: sneering that when the adrenalin currents cease to flow the vomiting begins. Through the maestro behind the retina: plausibly forcing the beauty of the view upon you.

Spare us that poor old slipper-slopper of a word, *beauty;* holy mom, is this a travelogue, nor are we out of it? *"Perched now on this titanic creature's back, we see a round dozen—and, folks, let me stress that round—of gaudily plumaged birds, exhibiting between them all the color you might expect to find on lovely, fabled Copacabana Beach. They're so round because they feed from the droppings that fall from the rich man's table. Watch this lovely shot now! See the bronto's tail lift. . . . Oh, lovely, yep, a couple of hayricks-full at least emerging from his nether end. That sure was a beauty, folks, delivered straight from consumer to consumer. The birds are fighting over it now. Hey, you, there's enough to go round, and anyhow, you're round enough already. . . . And nothing to do now but hop back up onto the old rump steak and wait for the next round. And now as the sun sinks in the Jurassic west, we say 'Fare well on that diet' . . ."*

No, you're procrastinating, and that's a life work. Shoot the beast and put it out of your agony. Taking your courage in your hands, you raise it to shoulder level and squint down its sights. There is a terrible report; you are half stunned. Shakily, you look about you. The monster still munches, relieved to have broken enough wind to unbecalm the Ancient Mariner.

Angered (or is it some subtler emotion?), you now burst from the bushes and confront it, and this exposed condition is typical of the straits into which your consideration for yourself and others continually pitches you. Consideration? Or again something subtler? Why should you be confused just because you come from a confused civilization? But that's a point to deal with later, if there is a later, as these two hog-wallow eyes pupilling you all over from spitting distance tend to dispute. Let it not be by jaws alone, O monster, but also by huge hooves and, if convenient to yourself, by mountainous rollings upon me! Let death be a saga, sagacious, Beowulfate.

Quarter of a mile distant is the sound of a dozen hippos springing boisterously in gymslips from the ancestral mud, and next second a walloping great tail as long as

3

Sunday and as thick as Saturday night comes slicing over your head. You duck as duck you must, but the beast missed you anyway because it so happens that its coordination is no better than yours would be if you had to wave the Woolworth Building at a tarsier. This done, it seems to feel it has done its duty by itself. It forgets you. You just wish you could forget yourself as easily; that was, after all, the reason you had to come the long way here. *Get Away from It All,* said the time travel brochure, which meant for you getting away from Claude Ford, a husbandman as futile as his name with a terrible wife called Maude. Maude and Claude Ford. Who could not adjust to themselves, to each other, or to the world they were born in. It was the best reason in the as-it-is-at-present-constituted world for coming back here to shoot giant saurians—if you were fool enough to think that one hundred and fifty million years either way made an ounce of difference to the muddle of thoughts in a man's cerebral vortex.

You try and stop your silly, slobbering thoughts, but they have never really stopped since the coca-collaborating days of your growing up; God, if adolescence did not exist it would be unnecessary to invent it! Slightly, it steadies you to look again on the enormous bulk of this tyrant vegetarian into whose presence you charged with such a mixed death-life wish, charged with all the emotion the human orga(ni)sm is capable of. This time the bogeyman is real, Claude, just as you wanted it to be, and this time you really have to face up to it before it turns and faces you again. And so again you lift Ole Equalizer, waiting till you can spot the vulnerable spot.

The bright birds sway, the lice scamper like dogs, the marsh groans, as bronto sways over and sends his little cranium snaking down under the bile-bright water in a forage for roughage. You watch this; you have never been so jittery before in all your jittered life, and you are counting on this catharsis wringing the last drop of acid fear out of your system for ever. OK, you keep saying to yourself insanely over and over, your million-dollar, twenty-second century education going for nothing, OK, OK. And as you say it for the umpteenth time, the crazy head comes back out of the water like a renegade express and gazes in your direction.

Grazes in your direction. For as the champing jaw with its big blunt molars like concrete posts works up and down, you see the swamp water course out over rimless lips, lipless rims, splashing your feet and sousing the ground. Reed and root, stalk and stem, leaf and loam, all are intermittently visible in that masticating maw and, struggling, straggling or tossed among them, minnows, tiny crustaceans, frogs—all destined in that awful, jawfull movement to turn into bowel movement. And as the glump-glump-glumping takes place, above it the slimeresistant eyes again survey you.

These beasts live up to two hundred years, says the time travel brochure, and this beast has obviously tried to live up to that, for its gaze is centuries old, full of decades upon decades of wallowing in its heavyweight thoughtlessness until it has grown wise on twitterpatedness. For you it is like looking into a disturbing misty pool; it gives you a psychic shock, you fire off both barrels at your own reflection. Bang-gang, the dum-dums, big as pawpaws, go.

With no indecision, those century-old lights, dim and sacred, go out. These cloisters are closed till Judgment Day. Your reflection is torn and bloodied from them for ever. Over their ravaged panes nictitating membranes slide slowly upwards, like dirty sheets covering a cadaver. The jaw continues to munch slowly, as slowly the head sinks down. Slowly, a squeeze of cold reptile blood toothpastes down the wrinked flank of one cheek. Everything is slow, a creepy Secondary Era slowness like the drip of water, and you know that if you had been in charge of creation you would have found some medium less heartbreaking than Time to stage it all in.

Never mind! Quaff down your beakers, lords, Claude Ford has slain a harmless creature. Long live Claude the Clawed!

You watch breathless as the head touches the ground, the long laugh of neck touches the ground, the jaws close for good. You watch and wait for something else to happen, but nothing ever does. Nothing ever would. You could stand here watching for an hundred and fifty million years, Lord Claude, and nothing would ever happen here again. Gradually your bronto's mighty carcass, picked loving clean by predators, would sink into the slime, carried by its own weight deeper; then the waters would rise, and old Conqueror Sea come in with the leisurely air of a cardsharp dealing the boys a bad hand. Silt and sediment would filter down over the mighty grave, a slow rain with centuries to rain in. Old bronto's bed might be raised up and then down again perhaps half a dozen times, gently enough not to disturb him, although by now the sedimentary rocks would be forming thick around him. Finally, when he was wrapped in a tomb finer than any Indian rajah ever boasted, the powers of the Earth would raise him high on their shoulders until, sleeping still, bronto would lie in a brow of the Rockies high above the waters of the Pacific. But little any of that would count with you, Claude the Sword; once the midget maggot of life is dead in the creature's skull, the rest is no concern of yours.

You have no emotion now. You are just faintly put out. You expected dramatic thrashing of the ground, or bellowing; on the other hand, you are glad the thing did not appear to suffer. You are like all cruel men, sentimental; you are like all sentimental men, squeamish. You tuck the gun under your arm and walk round the dinosaur to view your victory.

You prowl past the ungainly hooves, round the septic white of the cliff of belly, beyond the glistening and how-thought-provoking cavern of the cloaca, finally posing beneath the switch-back sweep of tail-to-rump. Now your disappointment is as crisp and obvious as a visiting card: the giant is not half as big as you thought it was. It is not one half as large, for example, as the image of you and Maude is in your mind. Poor little warrior, science will never invent anything to assist the titanic death you want in the contraterrene caverns of your fee-fi-fo fumblingly fearful id!

Nothing is left to you now but to slink back to your timemobile with a belly full of anticlimax. See, the bright dung-consuming birds have already cottoned on to the

6

true state of affairs; one by one, they gather up their hunched wings and fly disconsolately off across the swamp to other hosts. They know when a good thing turns bad, and do not wait for the vultures to drive them off; all hope abandon, ye who entrail here. You also turn away.

You turn, but you pause. Nothing is left but to go back, no, but 2181 A.D. is not just the home date; it is Maude. It is Claude. It is the whole awful, hopeless, endless business of trying to adjust to an overcomplex environment, of trying to turn yourself into a cog. Your escape from it into *the Grand Simplicities of the Jurassic,* to quote the brochure again, was only a partial escape, now over.

So you pause, and as you pause, something lands socko on your back, pitching you face forward into tasty mud. You struggle and scream as lobster claws tear at your neck and throat. You try to pick up the rifle but cannot, so in agony you roll over, and next second the crab-thing is greedying it on your chest. You wrench at its shell, but it giggles and pecks your fingers off. You forgot when you killed the bronto that its parasites would leave it, and that to a little shrimp like you they would be a deal more dangerous than their host.

You do your best, kicking for at least three minutes. By the end of that time there is a whole pack of the creatures on you. Already they are picking your carcass loving clean. You're going to like it up there on top of the Rockies; you won't feel a thing.

THE MOON MOTH

Jack Vance

One of science fiction's specialties is the invention of alien societies, with as much richness
of detail and unexpectedness of juxtaposition as
the author can manage. Few writers handle this
aspect of the genre more deftly than California's
Jack Vance, who since the late 1940's has been
dazzling readers with his fertility of imagination
and suppleness of narrative technique. In 1961,
when this story first appeared, it went virtually
unnoticed, though such Vance novels as *The
Dying Earth* and *To Live Forever* had won him a
loyal audience. Its charm, grace, and cleverness
earn it a second outing in *Alpha*.

The houseboat had been built to the most ex-
acting standards of Sirenese craftmanship, which is to say,
as close to the absolute as human eye could detect. The
planking of waxy dark wood showed no joints, the fas-
tenings were platinum rivets countersunk and polished
flat. In style, the boat was massive, broad-beamed, steady
as the shore itself, without ponderosity or slackness of
line. The bow bulged like a swan's breast, the stem rising
high, then crooking forward to support an iron lantern.
The doors were carved from slabs of a mottled black-
green wood; the windows were many-sectioned, paned
with squares of mica, stained rose, blue, pale green, and
violet. The bow was given to service facilities and quar-
ters for the slaves; amidships were a pair of sleeping
cabins, a dining saloon, and a parlor saloon, opening
upon an observation deck at the stern.

Such was Edwer Thissell's houseboat, but ownership brought him neither pleasure nor pride. The houseboat had become shabby. The carpeting had lost its pile; the carved screens were chipped; the iron lantern at the bow sagged with rust. Seventy years ago the first owner, on accepting the boat, had honored the builder and had been likewise honored; the transaction (for the process represented a great deal more than simple giving and taking) had augmented the prestige of both. That time was far gone; the houseboat now commanded no prestige whatever. Edwer Thissell, resident on Sirene only three months, recognized the lack but could do nothing about it: this particular houseboat was the best he could get. He sat on the rear deck practicing the *ganga,* a zitherlike instrument not much larger than his hand. A hundred yards inshore, surf defined a strip of white beach; beyond rose jungle, with the silhouette of craggy black hills against the sky. Mireille shone hazy and white overhead, as if through a tangle of spider web; the face of the ocean pooled and puddled with mother-of-pearl luster. The scene had become as familiar, though not as boring, as the *ganga,* at which he had worked two hours, twanging out the Sirenese scales, forming chords, traversing simple progressions. Now he put down the *ganga* for the *zachinko,* this a small sound box studded with keys, played with the right hand. Pressure on the keys forced air through reeds in the keys themselves, producing a concertinalike tone. Thissell ran off a dozen quick scales, making very few mistakes. Of the six instruments he had set himself to learn, the *zachinko* had proved the least refractory (with the exception, of course, of the *hymerkin,* that clacking, slapping, clattering device of wood and stone used exclusively with the slaves).

Thissell practiced another ten minutes, then put aside the *zachinko.* He flexed his arms, wrung his aching fingers. Every waking moment since his arrival had been given to the instruments: the *hymerkin,* the *ganga,* the *zachinko,* the *kiv,* the *strapan,* the *gomapard.* He had practiced scales in nineteen keys and four modes, chords without number, intervals never imagined on the Home Planets. Trills, arpeggios, slurs; click-stops, and nasaliza-

9

tion; damping and augmentation of overtones; vibratos and wolf-tones; concavities and convexities. He practiced with a dogged, deadly diligence, in which his original concept of music as a source of pleasure had long become lost. Looking over the instruments, Thissell resisted an urge to fling all six into the Titanic.

He rose to his feet, went forward through the parlor saloon, the dining saloon, along a corridor past the galley and came out on the foredeck. He bent over the rail, peered down into the underwater pens where Toby and Rex, the slaves, were harnessing the dray-fish for the weekly trip to Fan, eight miles north. The youngest fish, either playful or captious, ducked and plunged. Its streaming black muzzle broke water, and Thissell, looking into its face felt a peculiar qualm: the fish wore no mask!

Thissell laughed uneasily, fingering his own mask, the Moon Moth. No question about it, he was becoming acclimated to Sirene! A significant stage had been reached when the naked face of a fish caused him shock!

The fish were finally harnessed; Toby and Rex climbed aboard, red bodies glistening, black cloth masks clinging to their faces. Ignoring Thissell, they stowed the pen, hoisted anchor. The dray-fish strained, the harness tautened, the houseboat moved north.

Returning to the afterdeck, Thissell took up the *strapan* —this a circular sound box eight inches in diameter. Forty-six wires radiated from a central hub to the circumference where they connected to either a bell or a tinkle-bar. When plucked, the bells rang, the bars chimed; when strummed, the instrument gave off a twanging, jingling sound. When played with competence, the pleasantly acid dissonances produced an expressive effect; in an unskilled hand, the results were less felicitous, and might even approach random noise. The *strapan* was Thissell's weakest instrument and he practiced with concentration during the entire trip north.

In due course the houseboat approached the floating city. The dray-fish were curbed, the houseboat warped to a mooring. Along the dock a line of idlers weighed and gauged every aspect of the houseboat, the slaves, and Thissell himself, according to Sirenese habit. Thissell, not yet accustomed to such penetrating inspection, found the scrutiny unsettling, all the more so for the immobility of the masks. Self-consciously adjusting his own Moon Moth, he climbed the ladder to the dock.

A slave rose from where he had been squatting, touched knuckles to the black cloth at his forehead, and sang on a three-tone phrase of interrogation: "The Moon Moth before me possibly expresses the identity of Ser Edwer Thissell?"

Thissell tapped the *hymerkin* which hung at his belt and sang: "I am Ser Thissell."

"I have been honored by a trust," sang the slave. "Three days from dawn to dusk I have waited on the dock; three nights from dusk to dawn I have crouched on a raft below this same dock listening to the feet of the Night-men. At last I behold the mask of Ser Thissell."

Thissell evoked an impatient clatter from the *hymerkin*. "What is the nature of this trust?"

"I carry a message, Ser Thissell. It is intended for you."

Thissell held out his left hand, playing the *hymerkin* with his right. "Give me the message."

"Instantly, Ser Thissell."

The message bore a heavy superscription:

EMERGENCY COMMUNICATION! RUSH!

Thissell ripped open the envelope. The message was signed by Castel Cromartin, Chief Executive of the Interworld Policies Board, and after the formal salutation read:

ABSOLUTELY URGENT the following orders be executed! Aboard *Carina Cruzeiro*, destination Fan, date of arrival January 10 U.T., is notorious assassin, Haxo Angmark. Meet landing with adequate authority, effect detention, and incarceration of this man. These instructions must be successfully implemented. Failure is unacceptable.

ATTENTION! Haxo Angmark is superlatively dangerous. Kill him without hesitation at any show of resistance.

11

Thissell considered the message with dismay. In coming to Fan as Consular Representative he had expected nothing like this; he felt neither inclination nor competence in the matter of dealing with dangerous assassins. Thoughtfully he rubbed the fuzzy gray cheek of his mask. The situation was not completely dark; Esteban Rolver, director of the spaceport, would doubtless cooperate, and perhaps furnish a platoon of slaves.

More hopefully, Thissell reread the message. January 10, Universal Time. He consulted a conversion calendar. Today, fortieth in the Season of Bitter Nectar—Thissell ran his finger down the column, stopped. January 10. Today.

A distant rumble caught his attention. Dropping from the mist came a dull shape: the lighter returning from contact with the *Carina Cruzeiro*.

Thissell once more reread the note, raised his head, studied the descending lighter. Aboard would be Haxo Angmark. In five minutes he would emerge upon the soil of Sirene. Landing formalities would detain him possibly twenty minutes. The landing field lay a mile and a half distant, joined to Fan by a winding path through the hills.

Thissell turned to the slave. "When did this message arrive?"

The slave leaned forward uncomprehendingly. Thissell reiterated his question, singing to the clack of the *hymerkin:* "This message: you have enjoyed the honor of its custody how long?"

The slave sang: "Long days have I waited on the wharf, retreating only to the raft at the onset of dusk. Now my vigil is rewarded; I behold Ser Thissell."

Thissell turned away, walked furiously up the dock. Ineffective, inefficient Sirenese! Why had they not delivered the message to his houseboat? Twenty-five minutes —twenty-two now . . .

At the esplanade Thissell stopped, looked right then left, hoping for a miracle: some sort of air-transport to whisk him to the spaceport, where with Rolver's aid, Haxo Angmark might still be detained. Or better yet, a second message canceling the first. Something, anything

. . . But aircars were not to be found on Sirene, and no second message appeared.

Across the esplanade rose a meager row of permanent structures, built of stone and iron and so proof against the efforts of the Night-men. A hostler occupied one of these structures, and as Thissell watched a man in a splendid pearl and silver mask emerged riding one of the lizard-like mounts of Sirene.

Thissell sprang forward. There was still time; with luck he might yet intercept Haxo Angmark. He hurried across the esplanade.

Before the line of stalls stood the hostler, inspecting his stock with solicitude, occasionally burnishing a scale or whisking away an insect. There were five of the beasts in prime condition, each as tall as a man's shoulder, with massive legs, thick bodies, heavy wedge-shaped heads. From their forefangs, which had been artificially lengthened and curved into near-circles, gold rings depended; the scales of each had been stained in diaper-pattern: purple and green, orange and black, red and blue, brown and pink, yellow and silver.

Thissell came to a breathless halt in front of the hostler. He reached for his *kiv*,* then hesitated. Could this be considered a casual personal encounter? The *zachinko* perhaps? But the statement of his needs hardly seemed to demand the formal approach. Better the *kiv* after all. He struck a chord, but by error found himself stroking the *ganga*. Beneath his mask Thissell grinned apologetically; his relationship with this hostler was by no means on an intimate basis. He hoped that the hostler was of sanguine disposition, and in any event the urgency of the occasion allowed no time to select an exactly appropriate instrument. He struck a second chord, and, playing as well as agitation, breathlessness, and lack of skill allowed, sang out a request: "Ser Hostler, I have immediate need of a swift mount. Allow me to select from your herd."

The hostler wore a mask of considerable complexity

---

*Kiv: five banks of resilient metal strips, fourteen to the bank, played by touching, twisting, twanging.

which Thissell could not identify: a construction of varnished brown cloth, pleated gray leather and high on the forehead two large green and scarlet globes, minutely segmented like insect eyes. He inspected Thissell a long moment, then, rather ostentatiously selecting his *stimic,** executed a brilliant progression of trills and rounds, of an import Thissell failed to grasp. The hostler sang, "Ser Moon Moth, I fear that my steeds are unsuitable to a person of your distinction."

Thissell earnestly twanged at the *ganga.* "By no means; they all seem adequate. I am in great haste and will gladly accept any of the group."

The hostler played a brittle cascading crescendo. "Ser Moon Moth," he sang, "the steeds are ill and dirty. I am flattered that you consider them adequate to your use. I cannot accept the merit you offer me. And"—here, switching instruments, he struck a cool tinkle from his *krodatch***—"somehow I fail to recognize the boon-companion and cocraftsman who accosts me so familiarly with his *ganga.*"

The implication was clear. Thissell would receive no mount. He turned, set off at a run for the landing field. Behind him sounded a clatter of the hostler's *hymerkin*— whether directed toward the hostler's slaves, or toward himself Thissell did not pause to learn.

The previous Consular Representative of the Home Planets on Sirene had been killed at Zundar. Masked as a Tavern Bravo he had accosted a girl beribboned for the Equinoctial Attitudes, a solecism for which he had been instantly beheaded by a Red Demiurge, a Sun Sprite, and a Magic Hornet. Edwer Thissell, recently graduated from the Institute, had been named his successor, and allowed

---

Stimic: three flutelike tubes equipped with plungers. Thumb and forefinger squeeze a bag to force air across the mouth-pieces; the second, third, and fourth little fingers manipulate the slide. The *stimic* is an instrument well adapted to the sentiments of cool withdrawal, or even disapproval.

**Krodatch*: a small square sound-box strung with resined gut. The musician scratches the strings with his fingernail, or strokes them with his fingertips, to produce a variety of quietly formal sounds. The *krodatch* is also used as an instrument of insult.

three days to prepare himself. Normally of a contemplative, even cautious, disposition, Thissell had regarded the appointment as a challenge. He learned the Sirenese language by subcerebral techniques, and found it uncomplicated. Then, in the *Journal of Universal Anthropology,* he read:

> The population of the Titanic littoral is highly individualistic, possibly in response to a bountiful environment which puts no premium upon group activity. The language, reflecting this trait, expresses the individual's mood, his emotional attitude toward a given situation. Factual information is regarded as a secondary concomitant. Moreover, the language is sung, characteristically to the accompaniment of a small instrument. As a result, there is great difficulty in ascertaining fact from a native of Fan, or the forbidden city Zundar. One will be regaled with elegant arias and demonstrations of astonishing virtuosity upon one or another of the numerous musical instruments. The visitor to this fascinating world, unless he cares to be treated with the most consummate contempt, must therefore learn to express himself after the approved local fashion.

Thissell made a note in his memorandum book: *Procure small musical instrument, together with directions as to use.* He read on.

> There is everywhere and at all times a plentitude, not to say, superfluity of food, and the climate is benign. With a fund of racial energy and a great deal of leisure time, the population occupies itself with intricacy. Intricacy in all things: intricate craftmanship, such as the carved panels which adorn the houseboat; intricate symbolism, as exemplified in the masks worn by everyone; the intricate half-musical language which admirably expresses subtle moods and emotions; and above all the fantastic intricacy of interpersonal relationships. Prestige, face, *mana,* repute, glory: the Sirenese word is *strakh.* Every

man has his characteristic *strakh,* which determines whether, when he needs a houseboat, he will be urged to avail himself of a floating palace, rich with gems, alabaster lanterns, peacock faïence, and carved wood, or grudgingly permitted an abandoned shack on a raft. There is no medium of exchange on Sirene; the single and sole currency is *strakh* . . .

Thissell rubbed his chin and read further.

Masks are worn at all times, in accordance with the philosophy that a man should not be compelled to use a similitude foisted upon him by factors beyond his control; that he should be at liberty to choose that semblance most consonant with his *strakh.* In the civilized areas of Sirene—which is to say the Titanic littoral—a man literally never shows his face; it is his basic secret.

Gambling, by this token, is unknown on Sirene; it would be catastrophic to Sirenese self-respect to gain advantage by means other than the exercise of *strakh.* The word "luck" has no counterpart in the Sirenese language.

Thissell made another note: *Get mask. Museum? Drama guild?*

He finished the article, hastened forth to complete his preparations, and the next day embarked aboard the *Robert Astroguard* for the first leg of the passage to Sirene.

The lighter settled upon the Sirenese spaceport, a topaz disk isolated among the black, green and purple hills. The lighter grounded, and Edwer Thissell stepped forth. He was met by Esteban Rolver, the local agent for Spaceways. Rolver threw up his hands, stepped back. "Your mask," he cried huskily. "Where is your mask?"

Thissell held it up rather self-consciously. "I wasn't sure—"

"Put it on," said Rolver, turning away. He himself wore a fabrication of dull green scales, blue-lacquered

16

wood. Black quills protruded at the cheeks, and under his chin hung a black and white checked pom-pom, the total effect creating a sense of sardonic supple personality.

Thissell adjusted the mask to his face, undecided whether to make a joke about the situation or to maintain a reserve suitable to the dignity of his post.

"Are you masked?" Rolver inquired over his shoulder.

Thissell replied in the affirmative and Rolver turned. The mask hid the expression of his face, but his hand unconsciously flicked a set of keys strapped to his thigh. The instrument sounded a trill of shock and polite consternation. "You can't wear that mask!" sang Rolver. "In fact—how, where, did you get it?"

"It's copied from a mask owned by the Polypolis museum," declared Thissell stiffly. "I'm sure it's authentic."

Rolver nodded, his own mask more sardonic-seeming than ever. "It's authentic enough. It's a variant of the type known as the Sea Dragon Conqueror, and is worn on ceremonial occasions by persons of enormous prestige: princes, heroes, master craftsmen, great musicians."

"I wasn't aware—"

Rolver made a gesture of languid understanding. "It's something you'll learn in due course. Notice my mask. Today I'm wearing a Tarn-Bird. Persons of minimal prestige—such as you, I, any other out-worlder—wear this sort of thing."

"Odd," said Thissell as they started across the field toward a low concrete blockhouse. "I assumed that a person wore whatever mask he liked."

"Certainly," said Rolver. "Wear any mask you like—if you can make it stick. This Tarn-Bird for instance. I wear it to indicate that I presume nothing. I make no claims to wisdom, ferocity, versatility, musicianship, truculence, or any of a dozen other Sirenese virtues."

"For the sake of argument," said Thissell, "what would happen if I walked through the streets of Zundar in this mask?"

Rolver laughed, a muffled sound behind his mask. "If you walked along the docks of Zundar—there are no streets—in any mask, you'd be killed within the hour. That's what happened to Benko, your predecessor. He

17

didn't know how to act. None of us out-worlders know how to act. In Fan we're tolerated—so long as we keep our place. But you couldn't even walk around Fan in that regalia you're sporting now. Somebody wearing a Fire-snake or a Thunder Goblin—masks, you understand —would step up to you. He'd play his *krodatch,* and if you failed to challenge his audacity with a passage on the *skaranyi,** a devilish instrument, he'd play his *hymerkin* —the instrument we use with the slaves. That's the ultimate expression of contempt. Or he might ring his duelling gong and attack you then and there."

"I had no idea that people here were quite so irascible," said Thissell in a subdued voice.

Rolver shrugged and swung open the massive steel door into his office. "Certain acts may not be committed on the Concourse at Polypolis without incurring criticism."

"Yes, that's quite true," said Thissell. He looked around the office. "Why the security? The concrete, the steel?"

"Protection against the savages," said Rolver. "They come down from the mountains at night, steal what's available, kill anyone they find ashore." He went to a closet, brought forth a mask. "Here. Use this Moon Moth; it won't get you in trouble."

Thissell unenthusiastically inspected the mask. It was constructed of mouse-colored fur; there was a tuft of hair at each side of the mouth-hole, a pair of featherlike antennae at the forehead. White lace flaps dangled beside the temples and under the eyes hung a series of red folds, creating an effect at once lugubrious and comic.

Thissell asked, "Does this mask signify any degree of prestige?"

"Not a great deal."

"After all, I'm Consular Representative," said Thissell. "I represent the Home Planets, a hundred billion people—"

"If the Home Planets want their representative to wear

___

*Skaranyi: a miniature bagpipe, the sac squeezed between thumb and palm, the four fingers controlling the stops along four tubes.

a Sea-Dragon Conqueror mask, they'd better send out a Sea-Dragon Conqueror type of man."

"I see," said Thissell in a subdued voice. "Well, if I must . . ."

Rolver politely averted his gaze while Thissell doffed the Sea-Dragon Conqueror and slipped the more modest Moon Moth over his head. "I suppose I can find something just a bit more suitable in one of the shops," Thissell said. "I'm told a person simply goes in and takes what he needs, correct?"

Rolver surveyed Thissell critically. "That mask—temporarily, at least—is perfectly suitable. And it's rather important not to take anything from the shops until you know the *strakh* value of the article you want. The owner loses prestige if a person of low *strakh* makes free with his best work."

Thissell shook his head in exasperation. "Nothing of this was explained to me! I knew of the masks, of course, and the painstaking integrity of the craftsmen, but this insistence on prestige—*strakh*, whatever the word is . . ."

"No matter," said Rolver. "After a year or two you'll begin to learn your way around. I suppose you speak the language?"

"Oh indeed. Certainly."

"And what instruments do you play?"

"Well—I was given to understand that any small instrument was adequate, or that I could merely sing."

"Very inaccurate. Only slaves sing without accompaniment. I suggest that you learn the following instruments as quickly as possible: the *hymerkin* for your slaves. The *ganga* for conversation between intimates or one a trifle lower than yourself in *strakh*. The *kiv* for casual polite intercourse. The *zachinko* for more formal dealings. The *strapan* or the *krodatch* for your social inferiors—in your case, should you wish to insult someone. The *gomapard** or the *double-kamanthil*** for ceremonials." He consid-

---

**Gomapard:* one of the few electric instruments used on Sirene. An oscillator produces an oboelike tone which is modulated, choked, vibrated, raised and lowered in pitch by four keys.

**Double-kamanthil: an instrument similar to the *ganga*, except the tones are produced by twisting and inclining a disk of resined leather against one or more of the forty-six strings.

ered a moment. "The *crebarin,* the water-lute, and the *slobo* are highly useful also—but perhaps you'd better learn the other instruments first. They should provide at least a rudimentary means of communication."

"Aren't you exaggerating?" suggested Thissell. "Or joking?"

Rolver laughed his saturnine laugh. "Not at all. First of all, you'll need a houseboat. And then you'll want slaves."

Rolver took Thissell from the landing field to the docks of Fan, a walk of an hour and a half along a pleasant path under enormous trees loaded with fruit, cereal pods, sacs of sugary sap.

"At the moment," said Rolver, "there are only four out-worlders in Fan, counting yourself. I'll take you to Welibus, our Commercial Factor. I think he's got an old houseboat he might let you use."

Cornely Welibus had resided fifteen years in Fan, acquiring sufficient *strakh* to wear his South Wind mask with authority. This consisted of a blue disk inlaid with cabochons of lapis-lazuli, surrounded by an aureole of shimmering snakeskin. Heartier and more cordial than Rolver, he not only provided Thissell with a houseboat, but also a score of various musical instruments and a pair of slaves.

Embarrassed by the largesse, Thissell stammered something about payment, but Welibus cut him off with an expansive gesture. "My dear fellow, this is Sirene. Such trifles cost nothing."

"But a houseboat—"

Welibus played a courtly little flourish on his *kiv.* "I'll be frank, Ser Thissell. The boat is old and a trifle shabby. I can't afford to use it; my status would suffer." A graceful melody accompanied his words. "Status as yet need not concern you. You require merely shelter, comfort, and safety from the Night-men."

"Night-men?"

"The cannibals who roam the shore after dark."

"Oh yes. Ser Rolver mentioned them."

"Horrible things. We won't discuss them." A shudder-

20

ing little trill issued from his *kiv.* "Now, as to slaves." He tapped the blue disk of his mask with a thoughtful forefinger. "Rex and Toby should serve you well." He raised his voice, played a swift clatter on the *hymerkin.* *"Avan esx trobu!"*

A female slave appeared wearing a dozen tight bands of pink cloth, and a dainty black mask sparkling with mother-of-pearl sequins.

"Fascu etz Rex ae Toby."

Rex and Toby appeared, wearing loose masks of black cloth, russet jerkins. Welibus addressed them with a resonant clatter of *hymerkin,* enjoining them to the service of their new master, on pain of return to their native islands. They prostrated themselves, sang pledges of servitude to Thissell in soft husky voices. Thissell laughed nervously and essayed a sentence in the Sirenese language. "Go to the houseboat, clean it well, bring aboard food."

Toby and Rex stared blankly through the holes in their masks. Welibus repeated the orders with *hymerkin* accompaniment. The slaves bowed and departed.

Thissell surveyed the musical instruments with dismay. "I haven't the slightest idea how to go about learning these things."

Welibus turned to Rolver. "What about Kershaul? Could he be persuaded to give Ser Thissell some basic instruction?"

Rolver nodded judicially. "Kershaul might undertake the job."

Thissell asked, "Who is Kershaul?"

"The third of our little group of expatriates," replied Welibus, "an anthropologist. You've read *Zundar the Splendid? Rituals of Sirene? The Faceless Folk?* No? A pity. All excellent works. Kershaul is high in prestige, and I believe visits Zundar from time to time. Wears a Cave Owl, sometimes a Star-wanderer or even a Wise Arbiter."

"He's taken to an Equatorial Serpent," said Rolver. "The variant with the gilt tusks."

"Indeed!" marveled Welibus. "Well, I must say he's earned it. A fine fellow, good chap indeed." And he strummed his *zachinko* thoughtfully.

Three months passed. Under the tutelage of Mathew Kershaul, Thissell practiced the *hymerkin,* the *ganga,* the *strapan,* the *kiv,* the *gompard,* and the *zachinko.* The *double-kamanthil,* the *krodatch,* the *slobo,* the water-lute, and a number of others could wait, said Kershaul, until Thissell had mastered the six basic instruments. He lent Thissell recordings of noteworthy Sirenese conversing in various moods and to various accompaniments, so that Thissell might learn the melodic conventions currently in vogue, and perfect himself in the niceties of intonation, the various rhythms, cross-rhythms, compound rhythms, implied rhythms, and suppressed rhythms. Kershaul professed to find Sirenese music a fascinating study, and Thissell admitted that it was a subject not readily exhausted. The quarter-tone tuning of the instruments admitted the use of twenty-four tonalities which multiplied by the five modes in general use, resulted in one hundred and twenty separate scales. Kershaul, however, advised that Thissell primarily concentrate on learning each instrument in its fundamental tonality, using only two of the modes.

With no immediate business at Fan except the weekly visits to Mathew Kershaul, Thissell took his houseboat eight miles south and moored it in the lee of a rocky promontory. Here, if it had not been for the incessant practicing, Thissell lived an idyllic life. The sea was calm and crystal-clear; the beach, ringed by the gray, green and purple foliage of the forest, lay close at hand if he wanted to stretch his legs.

Toby and Rex occupied a pair of cubicles forward, Thissell had the aftercabins to himself. From time to time he toyed with the idea of a third slave, possibly a young female, to contribute an element of charm and gaiety to the menage, but Kershaul advised against the step, fearing that the intensity of Thissell's concentration might somehow be diminished. Thissell acquiesced and devoted himself to the study of the six instruments.

The days passed quickly. Thissell never became bored with the pageantry of dawn and sunset; the white clouds and blue sea of noon; the night sky blazing with the twenty-nine stars of Cluster SI 1-715. The weekly trip to Fan broke the tedium. Toby and Rex foraged for food; Thissell visited the luxurious houseboat of Mathew Kershaul for instruction and advice. Then, three months after Thissell's arrival, came the message completely disorganizing the routine: Haxo Angmark, assassin, *agent provacateur,* ruthless and crafty criminal, had come to Sirene. *Effective detention and incarceration of this man!* read the orders. *Attention! Haxo Angmark superlatively dangerous. Kill without hesitation!*

Thissell was not in the best of condition. He trotted fifty yards until his breath came in gasps, then walked: through low hills crowned with white bamboo and black tree-ferns; across meadows yellow with grass-nuts, through orchards and wild vineyards. Twenty minutes passed, twenty-five minutes; with a heavy sensation in his stomach Thissell knew that he was too late. Haxo Angmark had landed, and might be traversing this very road toward Fan. But along the way Thissell met only four persons: a boy-child in a mock-fierce Alk-Islander mask; two young women wearing the Red-bird and the Green-bird; a man masked as a Forest Goblin. Coming upon the man, Thissell stopped short. Could this be Angmark?

Thissell essayed a strategem. He went boldly to the man, stared into the hideous mask. "Angmark," he called in the language of the Home Planets, "you are under arrest!"

The Forest Goblin stared uncomprehendingly, then started forward along the track.

Thissell put himself in the way. He reached for his *ganga,* then recalling the hostler's reaction, instead struck a chord on the *zachinko.* "You travel the road from the spaceport," he sang. "What have you seen there?"

The Forest Goblin grasped his hand-bugle, an instrument used to deride opponents on the field of battle, to summon animals, or occasionally to evince a rough and ready truculence. "Where I travel and what I see are the concern solely of myself. Stand back or I walk upon your face." He marched forward, and had not Thissell leapt aside the Forest Goblin might well have made good his threat.

23

Thissell stood gazing after the retreating back. Angmark? Not likely, with so sure a touch on the hand-bugle. Thissell hesitated, then turned and continued on his way.

Arriving at the spaceport, he went directly to the office. The heavy door stood ajar; as Thissell approached, a man appeared in the doorway. He wore a mask of dull green scales, mica plates, blue-lacquered wood and black quills—the Tarn-Bird.

"Ser Rolver," Thissell called out anxiously, "who came down from the *Carina Cruzeiro?*"

Rolver studied Thissell a long moment. "Why do you ask?"

"Why do I ask?" demanded Thissell. "You must have seen the spacegram I received from Castel Cromartin!"

"Oh yes," said Rolver. "Of course. Naturally."

"It was delivered only half an hour ago," said Thissell bitterly. "I rushed out as fast as I could. Where is Angmark?"

"In Fan, I assume," said Rolver.

Thissell cursed softly. "Why didn't you hold him up, delay him in some way?"

Rolver shrugged. "I had neither authority, inclination, nor the capability to stop him."

Thissell fought back his annoyance. In a voice of studied calm he said, "On the way I passed a man in rather a ghastly mask—saucer eyes, red wattles."

"A Forest Goblin," said Rolver. "Angmark brought the mask with him."

"But he played the hand-bugle," Thissell protested. "How could Angmark—"

"He's well acquainted with Sirene; he spent five years here in Fan."

Thissell grunted in annoyance. "Cromartin made no mention of this."

"It's common knowledge," said Rolver with a shrug. "He was Commercial Representative before Welibus took over."

"Were he and Welibus acquainted?"

Rolver laughed shortly. "Naturally. But don't suspect

24

poor Welibus of anything more venial than juggling his accounts; I assure you he's no consort of assassins."

"Speaking of assassins," said Thissell, "do you have a weapon I might borrow?"

Rolver inspected him in wonder. "You came out here to take Angmark barehanded?"

"I had no choice," said Thissell. "When Cromartin gives orders he expects results. In any event you were here with your slaves."

"Don't count on me for help," Rolver said testily. "I wear the Tarn-Bird and make no pretensions of valor. But I can lend you a power pistol. I haven't used it recently; I won't guarantee its charge."

"Anything is better than nothing," said Thissell.

Rolver went into the office and a moment later returned with the gun. "What will you do now?"

Thissell shook his head wearily. "I'll try to find Angmark in Fan. Or might be head for Zundar?"

Rolver considered. "Angmark might be able to survive in Zundar. But he'd want to brush up on his musicianship. I imagine he'll stay in Fan a few days."

"But how can I find him? Where should I look?"

"That I can't say," replied Rolver. "You might be safer not finding him. Angmark is a dangerous man."

Thissell returned to Fan the way he had come.

Where the path swung down from the hills into the esplanade a thick-walled *pisé-de-terre* building had been constructed. The door was carved from a solid black plank; the windows were guarded by enfoliated bands of iron. This was the office of Cornely Welibus, Commercial Factor, Importer and Exporter. Thissell found Welibus sitting at his ease on the tiled verandah, wearing a modest adaptation of the Waldemar mask. He seemed lost in thought, and might or might not have recognized Thissell's Moon Moth; in any event he gave no signal of greeting.

Thissell approached the porch. "Good morning, Ser Welibus."

Welibus nodded abstractedly and said in a flat voice, plucking at his *krodatch*. "Good morning."

Thissell was rather taken aback. This was hardly the

25

instrument to use toward a friend and fellow out-worlder, even if he did wear the Moon Moth.

Thissell said coldly, "May I ask how long you have been sitting here?"

Welibus considered half a minute, and now when he spoke he accompanied himself on the more cordial *crebarin*. But the recollection of the *krodatch* chord still rankled in Thissell's mind.

"I've been here fifteen or twenty minutes. Why do you ask?"

"I wonder if you noticed a Forest Goblin pass?"

Welibus nodded. "He went on down the esplanade—turned into that first mask shop, I believe."

Thissell hissed between his teeth. This would naturally be Angmark's first move. "I'll never find him once he changes masks," he muttered.

"Who is this Forest Goblin?" asked Welibus, with no more than casual interest.

Thissell could see no reason to conceal the name. "A notorious criminal: Haxo Angmark."

"Haxo Angmark!" croaked Welibus, leaning back in his chair. "You're sure he's here?"

"Reasonably sure."

Welibus rubbed his shaking hands together. "This is bad news—bad news indeed! He's an unscrupulous scoundrel."

"You knew him well?"

"As well as anyone." Welibus was now accompanying himself with the *kiv*. "He held the post I now occupy. I came out as an inspector and found that he was embezzling four thousand UMI's a month. I'm sure he feels no great gratitude toward me." Welibus glanced nervously up the esplanade. "I hope you catch him."

"I'm doing my best. He went into the mask shop, you say?"

"I'm sure of it."

Thissell turned away. As he went down the path he heard the black plank door thud shut behind him.

He walked down the esplanade to the mask-maker's shop, paused outside as if admiring the display: a hundred miniature masks, carved from rare woods and minerals,

26

dressed with emerald flakes, spider-web silk, wasp wings, petrified fish scales and the like. The shop was empty except for the mask-maker, a gnarled knotty man in a yellow robe, wearing a deceptively simple Universal Expert mask, fabricated from over two thousand bits of articulated wood.

Thissell considered what he would say, how he would accompany himself, then entered. The mask-maker, noting the Moon Moth and Thissell's diffident manner, continued with his work.

Thissell, selecting the easiest of his instruments, stroked his *strapan*—possibly not the most felicitous choice, for it conveyed a certain degree of condescension. Thissell tried to counteract this flavor by singing in warm, almost effusive, tones, shaking the *strapan* whimsically when he struck a wrong note: "A stranger is an interesting person to deal with; his habits are unfamiliar, he excites curiosity. Not twenty minutes ago a stranger entered this fascinating shop, to exchange his drab Forest Goblin for one of the remarkable and adventurous creations assembled on the premises."

The mask-maker turned Thissell a side-glance, and without words played a progression of chords on an instrument Thissell had never seen before: a flexible sac gripped in the palm with three short tubes leading between the fingers. When the tubes were squeezed almost shut and air forced through the slit, an oboelike tone ensued. To Thissell's developing ear, the instrument seemed difficult, the mask-maker expert, and the music conveyed a profound sense of disinterest.

Thissell tried again, laboriously manipulating the *strapan*. He sang, "To an out-worlder on a foreign planet, the voice of one from his home is like water to a wilting plant. A person who could unite two such persons might find satisfaction in such an act of mercy."

The mask-maker casually fingered his own *strapan*, and drew forth a set of rippling scales, his fingers moving faster than the eyes could follow. He sang in the formal style: "An artist values his moments of concentration; he does not care to spend time exchanging banalities with persons of at best average prestige." Thissell attempted to

27

insert a counter melody, but the mask-maker struck a new set of complex chords whose portent evaded Thissell's understanding, and continued: "Into the shop comes a person who evidently has picked up for the first time an instrument of unparalleled complication, for the execution of his music is open to criticism. He sings of homesickness and longing for the sight of others like himself. He dissembles his enormous *strakh* behind a Moon Moth, for he plays the *strapan* to a Master Craftsman, and sings in a voice of contemptuous raillery. The refined and creative artist ignores the provocation. He plays a polite instrument, remains noncommittal, and trusts that the stranger will tire of his sport and depart."

Thissell took up his *kiv*. "The noble mask-maker completely misunderstands me——"

He was interrupted by staccato rasping of the mask-maker's *strapan*. "The stranger now sees fit to ridicule the artist's comprehension."

Thissell scratched furiously at his *strapan:* "To protect myself from the heat, I wander into a small and unpretentious mask-shop. The artisan, though still distracted by the novelty of his tools, gives promise of development. He works zealously to perfect his skill, so much so that he refuses to converse with strangers, no matter what their need."

The mask-maker carefully laid down his carving tool. He rose to his feet, went behind a screen, and shortly returned wearing a mask of gold and iron, with simulated flames licking up from the scalp. In one hand he carried a *skaranyi,* in the other a scimitar. He struck off a brilliant series of wild tones, and sang: "Even the most accomplished artist can augment his *strakh* by killing seamonsters, Night-men, and importunate idlers. Such an occasion is at hand. The artist delays his attack exactly ten seconds, because the offender wears a Moon Moth." He twirled his scimitar, spun it in the air.

Thissell desperately pounded the *strapan*. "Did a Forest Goblin enter the shop? Did he depart with a new mask?"

"Five seconds have lapsed," sang the mask-maker in steady ominous rhythm.

Thissell departed in frustrated rage. He crossed the

square, stood looking up and down the esplanade. Hundreds of men and women sauntered along the docks, or stood on the decks of their houseboats, each wearing a mask chosen to express his mood, prestige and special attributes, and everywhere sounded the twitter of musical instruments.

Thissell stood at a loss. The Forest Goblin had disappeared. Haxo Angmark walked at liberty in Fan, and Thissell had failed the urgent instructions of Castel Cromartin.

Behind him sounded the casual notes of a *kiv*. "Ser Moon Moth Thissell, you stand engrossed in thought."

Thissell turned, to find beside him a Cave Owl, in a somber cloak of black and gray. Thissell recognized the mask, which symbolized erudition and patient exploration of abstract ideas; Mathew Kershaul had worn it on the occasion of their meeting a week before.

"Good morning, Ser Kershaul," muttered Thissell.

"And how are the studies coming? Have you mastered the C-Sharp Plus scale on the *gomapard*? As I recall, you were finding those inverse intervals puzzling."

"I've worked on them," said Thissell in a gloomy voice. "However, since I'll probably be recalled to Polypolis, it may be all time wasted."

"Eh? What's this?"

Thissell explained the situation in regard to Haxo Angmark. Kershaul nodded gravely. "I recall Angmark. Not a gracious personality, but an excellent musician, with quick fingers and a real talent for new instruments." Thoughtfully, he twisted the goatee of his Cave-Owl mask. "What are your plans?"

"They're nonexistent," said Thissell, playing a doleful phrase on the *kiv*. "I haven't any idea what masks he'll be wearing and if I don't know what he looks like, how can I find him?"

Kershaul tugged at his goatee. "In the old days he favored the Exo Cambian Cycle, and I believe he used an entire set of Nether Denizens. Now of course his tastes may have changed."

"Exactly," Thissell complained. "He might be twenty feet away and I'd never know it." He glanced bitterly across the esplanade toward the mask-maker's shop. "No one will tell me anything; I doubt if they care that a murderer is walking their docks."

"Quite correct," Kershaul agreed. "Sirenese standards are different from ours."

"They have no sense of responsibility," declared Thissell. "I doubt if they'd throw a rope to a drowning man."

"It's true that they dislike interference," Kershaul agreed. "They emphasize individual responsibility and self-sufficiency."

"Interesting," said Thissell, "but I'm still in the dark about Angmark."

Kershaul surveyed him gravely. "And should you locate Angmark, what will you do then?"

"I'll carry out the orders of my superior," said Thissell doggedly.

"Angmark is a dangerous man," mused Kershaul. "He's got a number of advantages over you."

"I can't take that into account. It's my duty to send him back to Polypolis. He's probably safe, since I haven't the remotest idea how to find him."

Kershaul reflected. "An out-worlder can't hide behind a mask, not from the Sirenese, at least. There are four of us here at Fan—Rolver, Welibus, you and me. If another out-worlder tries to set up housekeeping the news will get around in short order."

"What if he heads for Zundar?"

Kershaul shrugged. "I doubt if he'd dare. On the other hand—" Kershaul paused, then noting Thissell's sudden inattention, turned to follow Thissell's gaze.

A man in a Forest Goblin mask came swaggering toward them along the esplanade. Kershaul laid a restraining hand on Thissell's arm, but Thissell stepped out into the path of the Forest Goblin, his borrowed gun ready. "Haxo Angmark," he cried, "don't make a move, or I'll kill you. You're under arrest."

"Are you sure this is Angmark?" asked Kershaul in a worried voice.

"I'll find out," said Thissell. "Angmark, turn around, hold up your hands."

The Forest Goblin stood rigid with surprise and puzzlement. He reached to his *zachinko,* played an inter-rogatory arpeggio, and sang, "Why do you molest me, Moon Moth?"

Kershaul stepped forward and played a placatory phrase on his *slobo.* "I fear that a case of confused identity exists, Ser Forest Goblin. Ser Moon Moth seeks an out-worlder in a Forest Goblin mask."

The Forest Goblin's music became irritated, and he suddenly switched to his *stimic.* "He asserts that I am an out-worlder? Let him prove his case, or he has my retaliation to face."

Kershaul glanced in embarrassment around the crowd which had gathered and once more struck up an ingra-tiating melody. "I am sure that Ser Moon Moth—"

The Forest Goblin interrupted with a fanfare of *ska-ranyi* tones. "Let him demonstrate his case or prepare for the flow of blood."

Thissell said, "Very well, I'll prove my case." He stepped forward, grasped the Forest Goblin's mask. "Let's see your face, that'll demonstrate your identity!"

The Forest Goblin sprang back in amazement. The crowd gasped, then set up an ominous strumming and toning of various instruments.

The Forest Goblin reached to the nape of his neck, jerked the cord to his duel-gong, and with his other hand snatched forth his scimitar.

Kershaul stepped forward, playing the *slobo* with great agitation. Thissell, now abashed, moved aside, conscious of the ugly sound of the crowd.

Kershaul sang explanations and apologies, the Forest Goblin answered; Kershaul spoke over his shoulder to Thissell: "Run for it, or you'll be killed! Hurry!"

Thissell hesitated; the Forest Goblin put up his hand to thrust Kershaul aside. "Run!" screamed Kershaul. "To Welibus' office, lock yourself in!"

Thissell took to his heels. The Forest Goblin pursued him a few yards, then stamped his feet, sent after him a set of raucous and derisive blasts of the hand-bugle, while the crowd produced a contemptuous counterpoint of clacking *hymerkins.*

There was no further pursuit. Instead of taking refuge

31

in the Import-Export office, Thissell turned aside and after cautious reconnaissance proceeded to the dock where his houseboat was moored.

The hour was not far short of dusk when he finally returned aboard. Toby and Rex squatted on the forward deck, surrounded by the provisions they had brought back: reed baskets of fruit and cereal, blue-glass jugs containing wine, oil and pungent sap, three young pigs in a wicker pen. They were cracking nuts between their teeth, spitting the shells over the side. They looked up at Thissell, and it seemed that they rose to their feet with a new casualness. Toby muttered something under his breath; Rex smothered a chuckle.

Thissell clacked his *hymerkin* angrily. He sang, "Take the boat offshore; tonight we remain at Fan."

In the privacy of his cabin he removed the Moon Moth, stared into a mirror at his almost unfamiliar features. He picked up the Moon Moth, examined the detested lineaments: the furry gray skin, the blue spines, the ridiculous lace flaps. Hardly a dignified presence for the Consular Representative of the Home Planets. If, in fact, he still held the position when Cromartin learned of Angmark's winning free!

Thissell flung himself into a chair, stared moodily into space. Today he'd suffered a series of setbacks, but he wasn't defeated yet, not by any means. Tomorrow he'd visit Mathew Kershaul; they'd discuss how best to locate Angmark. As Kershaul had pointed out, another out-world establishment could not be camouflaged; Haxo Angmark's identity would soon become evident. Also, tomorrow he must procure another mask. Nothing extreme or vainglorious, but a mask which expressed a modicum of dignity and self-respect.

At this moment one of the slaves tapped on the door-panel, and Thissell hastily pulled the hated Moon Moth back over his head.

Early next morning, before the dawn-light had left the sky, the slaves sculled the houseboat back to that section of the dock set aside for the use of out-worlders. Neither Rolver nor Welibus nor Kershaul had yet arrived and Thissell waited impatiently. An hour passed, and Welibus brought his boat to the dock. Not wishing to speak to Welibus, Thissell remained inside his cabin.

A few moments later Rolver's boat likewise pulled in alongside the dock. Through the window Thissell saw Rolver, wearing his usual Tarn-Bird, climb to the dock. Here he was met by a man in a yellow-tufted Sand Tiger mask, who played a formal accompaniment on his *gomapard* to whatever message he brought Rolver.

Rolver seemed surprised and disturbed. After a moment's thought he manipulated his own *gomapard,* and as he sang, he indicated Thissell's houseboat. Then, bowing, he went on his way.

The man in the Sand Tiger mask climbed with rather heavy dignity to the float and rapped on the bulwark of Thissell's houseboat.

Thissell presented himself. Sirenese etiquette did not demand that he invite a casual visitor aboard, so he merely struck an interrogation on his *zachinko*.

The Sand Tiger played his *gomapard* and sang: "Dawn over the bay of Fan is customarily a splendid occasion; the sky is white with yellow and green colors; when Mireille rises, the mists burn and writhe like flames. He who sings derives a greater enjoyment from the hour when the floating corpse of an out-worlder does not appear to mar the serenity of the view."

Thissell's *zachinko* gave off a startled interrogation almost of its own accord; the Sand Tiger bowed with dignity. "The singer acknowledges no peer in steadfastness of disposition; however, he does not care to be plagued by the antics of a dissatisfied ghost. He therefore has ordered his slaves to attach a thong to the ankle of the corpse, and while we have conversed they have linked the corpse to the stern of your houseboat. You will wish to administer whatever rites are prescribed in the Outworld. He who sings wishes you a good morning and now departs."

Thissell rushed to the stern of his houseboat. There, near-naked and mask-less, floated the body of a mature man, supported by air trapped in his pantaloons.

Thissell studied the dead face, which seemed characterless and vapid—perhaps in direct consequence of the mask-wearing habit. The body appeared of medium stature and weight, and Thissell estimated the age as between forty-five and fifty. The hair was nondescript brown, the features bloated by the water. There was nothing to indicate how the man had died.

This must be Haxo Angmark, thought Thissell. Who else could it be? Mathew Kershaul? Why not? Thissell asked himself uneasily. Rolver and Welibus had already disembarked and gone about their business. He searched across the bay to locate Kershaul's houseboat, and discovered it already tying up to the dock. Even as he watched, Kershaul jumped ashore, wearing his Cave-Owl mask.

He seemed in an abstracted mood, for he passed Thissell's houseboat without lifting his eyes from the dock.

Thissell turned back to the corpse. Angmark, then, beyond a doubt. Had not three men disembarked from the houseboats of Rolver, Welibus, and Kershaul, wearing masks characteristic of these men? Obviously, the corpse of Angmark . . . The easy solution refused to sit quiet in Thissell's mind. Kershaul had pointed out that another out-worlder would be quickly identified. How else could Angmark maintain himself unless he . . . Thissell brushed the thought aside. The corpse was obviously Angmark.

And yet . . .

Thissell summoned his slaves, gave orders that a suitable container be brought to the dock, that the corpse be transferred therein, and conveyed to a suitable place of repose. The slaves showed no enthusiasm for the task and Thissell was forced to thunder forcefully, if not skillfully, on the *hymerkin* to emphasize his orders.

He walked along the dock, turned up the esplanade, passed the office of Cornely Welibus and set out along the pleasant little lane to the landing field.

When he arrived, he found that Rolver had not yet made an appearance. An over-slave, given status by a yellow rosette on his black cloth mask, asked how he might be of service. Thissell stated that he wished to dispatch a message to Polypolis.

There was no difficulty here, declared the slave. If Thissell would set forth his message in clear block-print it would be dispatched immediately.

Thissell wrote:

OUT-WORLDER FOUND DEAD, POSSIBLY ANGMARK. AGE 48, MEDIUM PHYSIQUE, BROWN HAIR. OTHER MEANS OF IDENTIFICATION LACKING. AWAIT ACKNOWLEDGMENT AND/OR INSTRUCTIONS.

He addressed the message to Castel Cromartin at Polypolis and handed it to the over-slave. A moment later he heard the characteristic sputter of trans-space discharge.

An hour passed. Rolver made no appearance. Thissell paced restlessly back and forth in front of the office. There was no telling how long he would have to wait: trans-space transmission time varied unpredictably. Sometimes the message snapped through in micro-seconds; sometimes it wandered through unknowable regions for hours; and there were several authenticated examples of messages being received before they had been transmitted.

Another half-hour passed, and Rolver finally arrived, wearing his customary Tarn-Bird. Coincidentally Thissell heard the hiss of the incoming message.

Rolver seemed surprised to see Thissell. "What brings you out so early?"

Thissell explained. "It concerns the body which you referred to me this morning. I'm communicating with my superiors about it."

Rolver raised his head and listened to the sound of the incoming message. "You seem to be getting an answer. I'd better attend to it."

"Why bother?" asked Thissell. "Your slave seems efficient."

"It's my job," declared Rolver. "I'm responsible for the accurate transmission and receipt of all space-grams."

35

"I'll come with you," said Thissell. "I've always wanted to watch the operation of the equipment."

"I'm afraid that's irregular," said Rolver. He went to the door which led into the inner compartment. "I'll have your message in a moment."

Thissell protested, but Rolver ignored him and went into the inner office.

Five minutes later he reappeared, carrying a small yellow envelope. "Not too good news," he announced with unconvincing commiseration.

Thissell glumly opened the envelope. The message read:

BODY NOT ANGMARK. ANGMARK HAS BLACK HAIR. WHY DID YOU NOT MEET LANDING. SERIOUS INFRACTION, HIGHLY DISSATISFIED. RETURN TO POLYPOLIS NEXT OPPORTUNITY.

CASTEL CROMARTIN

Thissell put the message in his pocket. "Incidentally, may I inquire the color of your hair?"

Rolver played a surprised little trill on his *kiv*. "I'm quite blond. Why do you ask?"

"Mere curiosity."

Rolver played another run on the *kiv*. "Now I understand. My dear fellow, what a suspicious nature you have! Look!" He turned and parted the folds of his mask at the nape of his neck. Thissell saw that Rolver was blond indeed.

"Are you reassured?" asked Rolver jocularly.

"Oh, indeed," said Thissell. "Incidentally, have you another mask you could lend me? I'm sick of this Moon Moth."

"I'm afraid not," said Rolver. "But you need merely go into a mask-maker's shop and make a selection."

"Yes, of course," said Thissell. He took his leave of Rolver and returned along the trail to Fan. Passing Welibus' office he hesitated, then turned in. Today Welibus wore a dazzling confection of green glass prisms and silver beads, a mask Thissell had never seen before.

36

Welibus greeted him cautiously to the accompaniment of a *kiv*. "Good morning, Ser Moon Moth."

"I won't take too much of your time," said Thissell, "but I have a rather personal question to put to you. What color is your hair?"

Welibus hesitated a fraction of a second, then turned his back, lifted the flap of his mask. Thissell saw heavy black ringlets. "Does that answer your question?" inquired Welibus.

"Completely," said Thissell. He crossed the esplanade, went out on the dock to Kershaul's houseboat. Kershaul greeted him without enthusiasm, and invited him aboard with a resigned wave of the hand.

"A question I'd like to ask," said Thissell; "What color is your hair?"

Kershaul laughed woefully. "What little remains is black. Why do you ask?"

"Curiosity."

"Come, come," said Kershaul with an unaccustomed bluffness. "There's more to it than that."

Thissell, feeling the need of counsel, admitted as much. "Here's the situation. A dead out-worlder was found in the harbor this morning. His hair was brown. I'm not entirely certain, but the chances are—let me see, yes, two out of three that Angmark's hair is black."

Kershaul pulled at the Cave-Owl's goatee. "How do you arrive at that probability?"

"The information came to me through Rolver's hands. He has blond hair. If Angmark has assumed Rolver's identity, he would naturally alter the information which came to me this morning. Both you and Welibus admit to black hair."

"Hm," said Kershaul. "Let me see if I follow your line of reasoning. You feel that Haxo Angmark has killed either Rolver, Welibus, or myself and assumed the dead man's identity. Right?"

Thissell looked at him in surprise. "You yourself emphasized that Angmark could not set up another outworld establishment without revealing himself! Don't you remember?"

"Oh, certainly. To continue. Rolver delivered a message to you stating that Angmark was dark, and announced himself to be blond."

"Yes. Can you verify this? I mean for the old Rolver?"

"No," said Kershaul sadly. "I've seen neither Rolver nor Welibus without their masks."

"If Rolver is not Angmark," Thissell mused, "if Angmark indeed has black hair, then both you and Welibus come under suspicion."

"Very interesting," said Kershaul. He examined Thissell warily. "For that matter, you yourself might be Angmark. What color is your hair?"

"Brown," said Thissell curtly. He lifted the gray fur of the Moon Moth mask at the back of his head.

"But you might be deceiving me as to the text of the message," Kershaul put forward.

"I'm not," said Thissell wearily. "You can check with Rolver if you care to."

Kershaul shook his head. "Unnecessary. I believe you. But another matter: what of voices? You've heard all of us before and after Angmark arrived. Isn't there some indication there?"

"No. I'm so alert for any evidence of change that you all sound rather different. And the masks muffle your voices."

Kershaul tugged the goatee. "I don't see any immediate solution to the problem." He chuckled. "In any event, need there be? Before Angmark's advent, there were Rolver, Welibus, Kershaul, and Thissell. Now—for all practical purposes—there are still Rolver, Welibus, Kershaul, and Thissell. Who is to say that the new member may not be an improvement upon the old?"

"An interesting thought," agreed Thissell, "but it so happens that I have a personal interest in identifying Angmark. My career is at stake."

"I see," murmured Kershaul. "The situation then becomes an issue between yourself and Angmark."

"You won't help me?"

"Not actively. I've become pervaded with Sirenese individualism. I think you'll find that Rolver and Welibus

38

will respond similarly." He sighed. "All of us have been here too long."

Thissell stood deep in thought. Kershaul waited patiently a moment, then said, "Do you have any further questions?"

"No," said Thissell. "I have merely a favor to ask you."

"I'll oblige if I possibly can," Kershaul replied courteously.

"Give me, or lend me, one of your slaves, for a week or two."

Kershaul played an exclamation of amusement on the *ganga*. "I hardly like to part with my slaves; they know me and my ways—"

"As soon as I catch Angmark you'll have him back."

"Very well," said Kershaul. He rattled a summons on his *hymerkin,* and a slave appeared. "Anthony," sang Kershaul, "you are to go with Ser Thissell and serve him for a short period."

The slave bowed, without pleasure.

Thissell took Anthony to his houseboat, and questioned him at length, noting certain of the responses upon a chart. He then enjoined Anthony to say nothing of what had passed, and consigned him to the care of Toby and Rex. He gave further instructions to move the houseboat away from the dock and allow no one aboard until his return.

He set forth once more along the way to the landing field, and found Rolver at a lunch of spiced fish, shredded bark of the salad tree, and a bowl of native currants. Rolver clapped an order on the *hymerkin,* and a slave set a place for Thissell. "And how are the investigations proceeding?"

"I'd hardly like to claim any progress," said Thissell. "I assume that I can count on your help?"

Rolver laughed briefly. "You have my good wishes."

"More concretely," said Thissell, "I'd like to borrow a slave from you. Temporarily."

Rolver paused in his eating. "Whatever for?"

"I'd rather not explain," said Thissell. "But you can be sure that I make no idle request."

Without graciousness Rolver summoned a slave and consigned him to Thissell's service.

On the way back to his houseboat, Thissell stopped at Welibus' office.

Welibus looked up from his work. "Good afternoon, Ser Thissell."

Thissell came directly to the point. "Ser Welibus, will you lend me a slave for a few days?"

Welibus hesitated, then shrugged. "Why not?" He clacked his *hymerkin;* a slave appeared. "Is he satisfactory? Or would you prefer a young female?" He chuckled rather offensively, to Thissell's way of thinking.

"He'll do very well. I'll return him in a few days."

"No hurry." Welibus made an easy gesture and returned to his work.

Thissell continued to his houseboat, where he separately interviewed each of his two new slaves and made notes upon his chart.

Dusk came soft over the Titanic Ocean. Toby and Rex sculled the houseboat away from the dock, out across the silken waters. Thissell sat on the deck listening to the sound of soft voices, the flutter and tinkle of musical instruments. Lights from the floating houseboats glowed yellow and wan watermelon-red. The shore was dark; the Night-men would presently come slinking to paw through refuse and stare jealously across the water.

In nine days the *Buenaventura* came past Sirene on its regular schedule; Thissell had his orders to return to Polypolis. In nine days, could he locate Haxo Angmark?

Nine days weren't too many, Thissell decided, but they might possibly be enough.

Two days passed, and three and four and five. Every day Thissell went ashore and at least once a day visited Rolver, Welibus, and Kershaul.

Each reacted differently to his presence. Rolver was sardonic and irritable; Welibus formal and at least superficially affable; Kershaul mild and suave, but ostentatiously impersonal and detached in his conversation.

Thissell remained equally bland to Rolver's dour jibes, Welibus' jocundity, Kershaul's withdrawal. And every day, returning to his houseboat he made marks on his chart.

The sixth, the seventh, the eighth day came and passed. Rolver, with rather brutal directness, inquired if Thissell wished to arrange for passage on the *Buenaventura*. Thissell considered, and said, "Yes, you had better reserve passage for one."

"Back to the world of faces," shuddered Rolver. "Faces! Everywhere pallid, fish-eyed faces. Mouths like pulp, noses knotted and punctured; flat, flabby faces. I don't think I could stand it after living here. Luckily you haven't become a real Sirenese."

"But I won't be going back," said Thissell.

"I thought you wanted me to reserve passage."

"I do. For Haxo Angmark. He'll be returning to Polypolis, in the brig."

"Well, well," said Rolver. "So you've picked him out."

"Of course," said Thissell. "Haven't you?"

Rolver shrugged. "He's either Welibus or Kershaul, that's as close as I can make it. So long as he wears his mask and calls himself either Welibus or Kershaul, it means nothing to me."

"It means a great deal to me," said Thissell. "What time tomorrow does the lighter go up?"

"Eleven twenty-two sharp. If Haxo Angmark's leaving, tell him to be on time."

"He'll be here," said Thissell.

He made his usual call upon Welibus and Kershaul, then returning to his houseboat, put three final marks on his chart.

The evidence was here, plain and convincing. Not absolutely incontrovertible evidence, but enough to warrant a definite move. He checked over his gun. Tomorrow, the day of decision. He could afford no errors.

The day dawned bright white, the sky like the inside of an oyster shell; Mireille rose through iridescent mists. Toby and Rex sculled the houseboat to the dock. The remaining three out-world houseboats floated somnolently on the slow swells.

One boat Thissell watched in particular, that whose owner Haxo Angmark had killed and dropped into the harbor. This boat presently moved toward the shore, and Haxo Angmark himself stood on the front deck, wearing a mask Thissell had never seen before: a construction of scarlet feathers, black glass, and spiked green hair.

Thissell was forced to admire his poise. A clever scheme, cleverly planned and executed—but marred by an insurmountable difficulty.

Angmark returned within. The houseboat reached the dock. Slaves flung out mooring lines, lowered the gangplank. Thissell, his gun ready in the pocket flap of his robes, walked down the dock, went aboard. He pushed open the door to the saloon. The man at the table raised his red, black and green mask in surprise.

Thissell said, "Angmark, please don't argue or make any—"

Something hard and heavy tackled him from behind; he was flung to the floor, his gun wrested expertly away.

Behind him the *hymerkin* clattered; a voice sang, "Bind the fool's arms."

The man sitting at the table rose to his feet, removed the red, black and green mask to reveal the black cloth of a slave. Thissell twisted his head. Over him stood Haxo Angmark, wearing a mask Thissell recognized as a Dragon-Tamer, fabricated from black metal, with a knife-blade nose, socketed-eyelids, and three crests running back over the scalp.

The mask's expression was unreadable, but Angmark's voice was triumphant. "I trapped you very easily."

"So you did," said Thissell. The slave finished knotting his wrists together. A clatter of Angmark's *hymerkin* sent him away. "Get to your feet," said Angmark. "Sit in that chair."

"What are we waiting for?" inquired Thissell.

"Two of our fellows still remain out on the water. We won't need them for what I have in mind."

"Which is?"

"You'll learn in due course," said Angmark. "We have an hour or so on our hands."

Thissell tested his bonds. They were undoubtedly secure.

Angmark seated himself. "How did you fix on me? I

admit to being curious . . . Come, come," he chided as Thissell sat silently. "Can't you recognize that I have defeated you? Don't make affairs unpleasant for yourself."

Thissell shrugged. "I operated on a basic principle. A man can mask his face, but he can't mask his personality."

"Aha," said Angmark. "Interesting. Proceed."

"I borrowed a slave from you and the other two outworlders, and I questioned them carefully. What masks had their masters worn during the month before your arrival? I prepared a chart and plotted their responses. Rolver wore the Tarn-Bird about eighty percent of the time, the remaining twenty percent divided between the Sophist Abstraction and the Black Intricate. Welibus had a taste for the heroes of Kan-Dachan Cycle. He wore the Chalekun, the Prince Intrepid, the Seavain most of the time: six days out of eight. The other two days he wore his South-Wind or his Gay Companion. Kersaul, more conservative, preferred the Cave Owl, the Star Wanderer, and two or three other masks he wore at odd intervals.

"As I say, I acquired this information from possibly its most accurate source, the slaves. My next step was to keep watch upon the three of you. Every day I noted what masks you wore and compared it with my chart. Rolver wore his Tarn-Bird six times, his Black Intricate twice. Kershaul wore his Cave Owl five times, his Star Wanderer once, his Quincunx once and his Ideal of Perfection once. Welibus wore the Emerald Mountain twice, the Triple Phoenix three times, the Prince Intrepid once, and the Shark-God twice."

Angmark nodded thoughtfully. "I see my error. I selected from Welibus' masks, but to my own taste—and as you point out, I revealed myself. But only to you." He rose and went to the window. "Kershaul and Rolver are now coming ashore; they'll soon be past and about their business—though I doubt if they'd interfere in any case; they've both become good Sirenese."

Thissell waited in silence. Ten minutes passed. Then Angmark reached to a shelf and picked up a knife. He looked at Thissell. "Stand up."

Thissell slowly rose to his feet. Angmark approached

43

from the side, reached out, lifted the Moon Moth from Thissell's head. Thissell gasped and made a vain attempt to seize it. Too late; his face was bare and naked.

Angmark turned away, removed his own mask, donned the Moon Moth. He struck a call on his *hymerkin*. Two slaves entered, stopped in shock at the sight of Thissell.

Angmark played a brisk tattoo, sang, "Carry this man up to the dock."

"Angmark," cried Thissell. "I'm maskless!"

The slaves seized him and in spite of Thissell's desperate struggles, conveyed him out on the deck, along the float and up on the dock.

Angmark fixed a rope around Thissell's neck. He said, "You are now Haxo Angmark, and I am Edwer Thissell. Welibus is dead, you shall soon be dead. I can handle your job without difficulty. I'll play musical instruments like a Night-man and sing like a crow. I'll wear the Moon Moth till it rots and then I'll get another. The report will go to Polypolis, Haxo Angmark is dead. Everything will be serene."

Thissell barely heard. "You can't do this," he whispered. "My mask, my face . . ." A large woman in a blue and pink flower mask walked down the dock. She saw Thissell and emitted a piercing shriek, flung herself prone on the dock.

"Come along," said Angmark brightly. He tugged at the rope, and so pulled Thissell down the dock. A man in a Pirate Captain mask coming up from his houseboat stood rigid in amazement.

Angmark played the *zachinko* and sang, "Behold the notorious criminal Haxo Angmark. Through all the outerworlds his name is reviled; now he is captured and led in shame to his death. Behold Haxo Angmark!"

They turned into the esplanade. A child screamed in fright; a man called hoarsely. Thissell stumbled; tears tumbled from his eyes; he could see only disorganized shapes and colors. Angmark's voice belled out richly: "Everyone behold, the criminal of the out-worlds, Haxo Angmark! Approach and observe his execution!"

Thissell feebly cried out, "I'm not Angmark; I'm Edwer Thissell; he's Angmark." But no one listened to him; there were only cries of dismay, shock, disgust at the sight of his face. He called to Angmark, "Give me my mask, a slave-cloth . . ."

Angmark sang jubilantly, "In shame he lived, in maskless shame he dies."

A Forest Goblin stood before Angmark. "Moon Moth, we meet once more."

Angmark sang, "Stand aside, friend Goblin; I must execute this criminal. In shame he lived, in shame he dies!"

A crowd had formed around the group; masks stared in morbid titilation at Thissell.

The Forest Goblin jerked the rope from Angmark's hand, threw it to the ground. The crowd roared. Voices cried, "No duel, no duel! Execute the monster!"

A cloth was thrown over Thissell's head. Thissell awaited the thrust of a blade. But instead his bonds were cut. Hastily he adjusted the cloth, hiding his face, peering between the folds.

Four men clutched Haxo Angmark. The Forest Goblin confronted him, playing the *skaranyi*. "A week ago you reached to divest me of my mask; you have now achieved your perverse aim!"

"But he is a criminal," cried Angmark. "He is notorious, infamous!"

"What are his misdeeds?" sang the Forest Goblin.

"He has murdered, betrayed; he has wrecked ships; he has tortured, blackmailed, robbed, sold children into slavery; he has——"

The Forest Goblin stopped him. "Your religious differences are of no importance. We can vouch however for your present crimes!"

The hostler stepped forward. He sang fiercely, "This insolent Moon Moth nine days ago sought to pre-empt my choicest mount!"

Another man pushed close. He wore a Universal Expert, and sang, "I am a Master Mask-maker; I recognize this Moon Moth out-worlder! Only recently he entered my shop and derided my skill. He deserves death!"

"Death to the out-world monster!" cried the crowd. A

wave of men surged forward. Steel blades rose and fell, the deed was done.

Thissell watched, unable to move. The Forest Goblin approached, and playing the *stimic* sang sternly, "For you we have pity, but also contempt. A true man would never suffer such indignities!"

Thissell took a deep breath. He reached to his belt and found his *zachinko*. He sang, "My friend, you malign me! Can you not appreciate true courage? Would you prefer to die in combat or walk maskless along the esplanade?"

The Forest Goblin sang, "There is only one answer. First I would die in combat; I could not bear such shame."

Thissell sang, "I had such a choice. I could fight with my hands tied, and so die—or I could suffer shame, and through this shame conquer my enemy. You admit that you lack sufficient *strakh* to achieve this deed. I have proved myself a hero of bravery! I ask, who here has courage to do what I have done?"

"Courage?" demanded the Forest Goblin. "I fear nothing, up to and beyond death at the hands of the Nightmen!"

"Then answer."

The Forest Goblin stood back. He played his *double-kamanthil*. "Bravery indeed, if such were your motives."

The hostler struck a series of subdued *gomapard* chords and sang, "Not a man among us would dare what this maskless man has done."

The crowd muttered approval.

The mask-maker approached Thissell, obsequiously stroking his *double-kamanthil*. "Pray Lord Hero, step into my nearby shop, exchange this vile rag for a mask befitting your quality."

Another mask-maker sang, "Before you choose, Lord Hero, examine my magnificent creations!"

A man in a Bright Sky Bird mask approached Thissell reverently. "I have only just completed a sumptuous houseboat; seventeen years of toil have gone into its fabrication. Grant me the good fortune of accepting and using this splendid craft; aboard waiting to serve you are alert slaves and pleasant maidens; there is ample wine in storage and soft silken carpets on the decks."

"Thank you," said Thissell, striking the *zachinko* with vigor and confidence. "I accept with pleasure. But first a mask."

The mask-maker struck an interrogative trill on the *gomapard*. "Would the Lord Hero consider a Sea-Dragon Conqueror beneath his dignity?"

"By no means," said Thissell. "I consider it suitable and satisfactory. We shall go now to examine it."

TESTAMENT OF ANDROS

James Blish

What you are about to read is either five stories in one, or one story refracted five ways; the author knows which, and he may tell those who ask him, but since he chose not to state his position explicitly in his story, I see no merit in doing so for him. With or without benefit of such footnotes, this is a powerful and disturbing work —enigmatic at first, but irresistible and incantatory, and close to the top of its author's form, which is saying a great deal.

James Blish has written *A Case of Conscience*, *Black Easter*, and many other science fiction novels and stories. He, his wife, and several cats now live in England.

Beside the dying fire lie the ashes.
There are voices in them. Listen:

1

My name is Theodor Andresson. I will write my story if you wish. I was at one time Resident in Astrophysics at Krajputnii, which I may safely describe as the greatest center of learning in the Middle East, perhaps of the entire Eastern Hemisphere. Later—until the chain of incidents which brought me to this *Zucht-Haus*—I was professor emeritus in radio-astronomy at Calimyrna University, where I did the work leading to the discovery of the solar pulsation cycle.

I am sure that this work is not credited to me; that is of no importance. I would like it clearly understood that I am not making this record for your benefit, but for mine. Your request means nothing to me, and your pretense of interest in what I may write cannot deceive me. My erstwhile colleagues in the so-called sciences were masters of this kind of pretense; but they, too, were unable to prevent me from penetrating the masquerade at the end. How then does a simple doctor hope to succeed where the finest charlatanry has failed?

And what is allocation of credit—of what importance is priority of discovery before the inexorability of the pulsation cycle? It will work to its new conclusion without regard for your beliefs, my colleagues', or mine. Neither the pretended solicitude nor the real metal bars with which you have surrounded me will matter after that.

I proceed, therefore, to the matter at hand. My position at Calimyrna in that remote time before the cycle was discovered, befit my age (eighty-four years) and the reputation I had achieved in my specialty. I was in excellent health, though subject occasionally to depressions of spirit, readily ascribable to my being in a still-strange land and to those scars inflicted upon me in earlier times.

Despite these fits of moodiness, I had every reason to be happy. My eminence in my field afforded me the utmost satisfaction; despite poverty and persecution in youth, I had won through to security. I had married Marguerita L——, in her youth and mine the toast of twelve continents, not only for her beauty but for her voice. I can still hear now the sound of her singing as I heard it for the first time—singing, on the stage of La Scala in Moscow, the rapturous quartet from the second act of Wagner's *Tristan et Messalina*.

It is quite true—I admit it immediately and calmly—that there were certain flaws in my world, even at Calimyrna. I do not mean the distractions which in old age replace, in the ordinary man, the furies of youth, but rather certain faults and fissures which I found in the world outside myself.

Even a man of my attainments expects at some time

to grow old, and to find that process changing the way in which he looks at the world around him. There comes a time, however, when even the most rational of men must notice when these changes exceed the bounds of reason—when they begin to become extraordinary, even sinister. Shall I be specific? Consider, then—quite calmly —the fact that Marguerita did not herself grow old.

I passed into my eighth decade without taking more than perfunctory notice. I was deeply involved in the solar work we were then carrying on at Calimyrna. I had with me a young graduate student, a brilliant fellow of about thirty, who assisted me and who made certain original contributions of his own to the study. His name, and you will recognize it, was Mario di Ferruci. Calimyrna had completed its thousand-inch radio-telescope, the largest such antenna anywhere in the world—except for the 250-foot Manchester instrument. This was at once put to work in the search for so-called radio stars— those invisible bodies, many of them doubtless nearer to Earth than the nearest visible star, which can be detected only by their emission in the radio spectrum.

Completion of the thousand-inch freed the 600-inch paraboloid antenna for my use in solar work. The smaller instrument had insufficient beam-width between half-power points for the critical stellar studies, but it was more suitable for my purpose.

I had in mind at that time a study of the disturbed sun. Hagen of the Naval Research Laboratory had already done the definitive study on the sun in its quiet state. I found myself more drawn to what goes on in the inferno of the sunspots—in the enormous, puzzling catastrophes of the solar flares—the ejection of immense radioactive clouds from the sun's interior high into its atmosphere.

It had already become clear that the radio-frequency emission from the disturbed sun was not, and could not be, thermal in origin, as in the RF emission of the quiet sun. The equivalent temperature of the disturbed sun in selected regions at times rises to billions of degrees, rendering the whole concept of thermal equivalency meaningless.

That the problem was not merely academic impressed me from the first. I have, if you will allow me the term, always had a sense of destiny, of *Schicksal,* an almost Spenglerian awareness of the pressure of fate against the retaining walls of human survival. It is not unique in me; I lay it to my Teutonic ancestry. And when I first encountered the problem of the disturbed sun, something within me felt that I had found destiny itself.

For here, just *here* was the problem in which destiny was interested, in which some fateful answer awaited the asking of the omnipotent question. I felt this from the moment when I had first opened Hagen's famous paper—NRL Report 3504—and the more deeply I became interested in the sun as an RF radiator, the more the sensation grew.

Yet how to describe it? I was eighty-four, and this was early in 1976; in all those preceding years I had not known that the mortal frame could sustain such an emotion. Shall I call it a sensation of enormous unresolvable dread? But I felt at the same time an ecstasy beyond joy, beyond love, beyond belief; and these transports of rapture and terror did not alternate as do the moods of an insane man, but occurred simultaneously—they were one and the same emotion.

Nor did the solar flares prove themselves unworthy of such deep responses. Flares have been observed in many stars. Some of them have been major outbursts, as indeed they would have to be to be visible to us at all. That such a flare could never occur on our own sun, furthermore, could not be said with certainty, for flares are local phenomena—they expend their energy only on one side of a star, not in all directions like a nova—and we had already seen the great detonation of July 29, 1948 on our own sun, which reached an energy level one hundred times the output of the quiet sun, which showed that we did not dare to set limits to what our own sun might yet do.

It was here, however, that I ran into trouble with young di Ferruci. He persistently and stubbornly refused to accept the analogy.

"It's penny-dreadful," he would say, as he had said

51

dozens of times before. "You remind me of Dr. Richardson's stories—you know, the ones he writes for those magazines, about the sun going nova and all that. Whenever it's cloudy at Palomar he dreams up a new catastrophe."

"Richardson is no fool," I would point out. "Other suns have exploded. If he wants to postulate that it could happen to ours, he has every right to do so."

"Sure, Dr. Andresson, in a story," di Ferruci would object. "But as a serious proposition it doesn't hold water. Our sun just isn't the spectral type that goes nova; it hasn't ever even approached the critical instability percentage. It can't even produce a good flare of the Beta Centauri type."

"I don't expect it to go nova. But it's quite capable of producing a major flare, in my opinion. I expect to prove it."

Di Ferruci would shrug, as he always did. "I wouldn't ride any money on you, Dr. Andresson. But I'll be more than interested in what the telescope shows—let's see what we have here right now. The thermocouple's been calibrated; shall I cut in the hot load?"

At this point—I am now reporting a particular incident, although it, too, was frequently typical of these conversations—I became aware that Marguerita was in the observatory. I swung sharply around, considerably annoyed. My wife is innocent of astronomical knowledge, and her usually ill-timed obtrusions upon our routine—although I suppose they were of the desire to "take an interest" in her husband's profession—were distracting.

Today, however, I was not only annoyed, but stunned. How had I failed to notice this before—I, who pride myself on the acuity of my observation? What stood before me was a young woman!

How shall I say how young? These things are relative. We had married when she was thirty-six and I was forty-four; a difference of eight years is virtually no difference during the middle decades, though it is enormous when both parties are young. Marguerita had been in no sense a child at the time of our marriage.

Yet now, as I was finding, a spread as small as eight

years can again become enormous when the dividing-line of old age insensibly approaches. And the difference was even greater than this—for now Marguerita, as she stood looking down at our day's three-dimensional graph of solar activity, seemed no older to me than the day on which I had first met her: a woman, tall, graceful, lithe, platinum-haired, and with the somber, smoldering, unreadable face of Eve—and yet compared to me now a child in truth.

"Good afternoon, Mrs. Andresson," di Ferruci said, smiling.

She looked up and smiled back. "Good afternoon," she said. "I see you're about to take another series of readings. Don't let me interrupt you."

"That's quite all right; thus far it's routine," di Ferruci said. I glanced sidewise at him and then back to my wife. "We'd just begun to take readings to break up the monotony of the old argument."

"That's true," I said. "But it would be just as well if you didn't drop in on us unexpectedly, Marguerita. If this had been a critical stage—"

"I'm sorry," she said contritely. "I should have phoned, but I'm always afraid that the telephone will interrupt you, too. When I'm here I can hope to see whether or not you're busy—and you can see who's calling. The telephone has no eyes."

She touched the graph, delicately. This graph, I should explain, is made of fourteen curves cut out in cardboard, and assembled so that one set of seven curved pieces is at right angles to the other set. It expresses the variation in intensity of RF emanation across the surface of the sun at the ten-centimeter wavelength, where our readings commonly are taken; we make a new such model each day. It shows at a glance, by valley or peak, any deviation from the sun's normal output, thus helping us greatly in interpreting our results.

"How strange it looks today," she said. "It's always in motion, like a comber racing toward the shore. I keep expecting it to begin to break at the top."

Di Ferruci stopped tinkering with the drive clock and sat down before the control desk, his blue-black helmet of hair—only a little peppered by his memories of the Inchon landing—swiveling sharply toward her. I could not see his face. "What an eerie notion," he said. "Mrs. Andresson, you and the doctor'll have me sharing your presentiments of doom any minute now."

"It isn't a question of presentiments," I said sharply. "You should be aware by now, Mario, that in the RF range the sun is a variable star. Does that mean nothing to you? Let me ask you another question: How do you explain Eta Carina?"

"What's Eta Carina?" Marguerita said.

I did not know quite how to begin answering her, but di Ferruci, who lacked my intimate knowledge of her limitations, had no such qualms.

"It's a freak—one of the worst freaks of the past ten years," he said eagerly. "It's a star that's gone nova three times. The last time was in 1972, about a hundred years after the previous explosion. Before that it had an outburst in the 1600's, and it may have blown up about 142 A.D., too. Each time it gains in brightness nearly one hundred thousand times—as violent a stellar catastrophe as you can find anywhere in the records." He offered the data to her like a bouquet, and before I could begin to take offense, swung back upon me again. "Surely, doc, you don't maintain that Eta Carina is a flare star?"

"All stars are flare stars," I said, looking steadily at him. His eyes were in shadow. "More than that; all stars are novas, in the long run. Young stars like our sun are variable only in the radio spectrum, but gradually they become more and more unstable, and begin to produce small flares. Then come the big flares, like Beta Centauri outburst; then they go nova; and then the cycle begins again."

"Evidence?"

"Everywhere. The process goes on in little in the short-term variables, the Cepheids. Eta Carina shows how it works in a smaller, noncluster star. The other novas we've observed simply have longer periods—they haven't had time to go nova again within recorded history. *But they will.*"

"Well," di Ferruci said. "If that's so, Richardson's

54

visions of our sun exploding seems almost pleasant. You see us being roasted gradually instead, in a series of hotter and hotter flares. When does the first one hit us, by your figures?"

Mario was watching me steadily. Perhaps I looked strange, for I was once again in the grip of that emotion, so impossible to describe, in which terror and ecstasy blended and fused into some whole beyond any possibility of communication. As I had stated for the first time what I saw, and saw so clearly, was ahead for us all, this deep radical emotion began to shake me as if I had stepped all unawares from the comfortable island of relative, weighable facts into some blastingly cold ocean of Absolute Truth.

"I don't know," I said. "It needs checking. But I give us six months."

Marguerita's and di Ferruci's eyes met. Then he said, "Let's check it, then. We should be able to find the instability threshold for each stage, from RR Lyrae stars right through classical Cepheids, long-periods, and irregulars to radio-variables. We already know the figure for novas. Let's dot the i's and cross the t's—and then find out where our sun stands."

"Theodor," Marguerita said. "What—what will happen if you're right?"

"Then the next flare will be immensely greater than the 1948 one. The Earth will survive it; life on Earth probably will not—certainly not human life."

Marguerita remained standing beside the model a moment longer, nursing the hand which had been touching it. Then she looked at me out of eyes too young for me to read, and left the observatory.

With a hasty word to di Ferruci, I followed her, berating myself as I went. Suspecting as I did the shortness of the span left to us, I had not planned to utter a word about what was to be in store for us in her presence; that had been one of the reasons why I had objected to her visits to the observatory. There had simply been no reason to cloud our last months together with the shadow of a fate she could not understand.

But when I reached the top of the granite steps leading

down to the road, she was gone—nor could I see either her figure or any sign of a car on the road which led down the mountain. She had vanished as completely as if she had never existed.

Needless to say, I was disturbed. There are cabins in the woods, only a short distance away from the observatory proper, which are used by staff members as temporary residences; we had never made use of them—radio-astronomy being an art which can be carried on by day better than by night—but nevertheless I checked them systematically. It was inconceivable to me that she could be in the main observatory, but I searched that too, as well as the solar tower and the Schmidt shed.

She was nowhere. By the time I had finished searching, it was sunset and there was no longer any use in my returning to my own instrument. I could only conclude that I had miscalculated the time lag between her exit and my pursuit, and that I would find her at home.

Yet, somehow I did not go home. All during my search of the grounds, another thought had been in my head: What if I were wrong? Suppose that there were no solar pulsation cycle? Suppose that my figures were meaningless? If this seems to you to be a strange thing for a man to be thinking, while searching for an inexplicably vanished wife, I can only say that the two subjects seemed to me to be somehow not unconnected.

And as it turned out, I was right. I have said that I have a sense of fate.

In the end, I went back to the observatory, now dark and, I supposed, deserted. But there was a light glowing softly inside; the evenly lit surface of the transparency viewer. Bent over it, his features floating eerily in nothingness, was Mario di Ferruci.

I groped for the switch, found it, and the fluorescents flashed on overhead. Mario straightened, blinking.

"Mario, what are you doing here? I thought you had left before sundown."

"I meant to," di Ferruci said slowly. "But I couldn't stop thinking about your theory. It isn't every day that one hears the end of the world announced by a man of your eminence. I decided I just had to run my own check, or else go nuts wondering."

"Why couldn't you have waited for me?" I said. "We could have done the work together much quicker and more easily."

"That's true," he said slowly. "But, Dr. Andresson, I'm just a graduate student, and you're a famous man; young as you are. I'm a little afraid of being overwhelmed—of missing an error because you've checked it already, or failing to check some point at all—that kind of thing. After all, we're all going to die if you're right, and that's hardly a minor matter; so I thought I'd try paddling my own canoe. Maybe I'll find the world just as far up the creek as you do. But I had to try."

It took me a while to digest this, distracted as I already was. After a while I said, as calmly as I could, "And what have you found?"

"Dr. Andresson—*you're wrong.*"

For an instant I could not see. All the red raw exploding universe of unstable stars went wheeling through my old head like maddened atoms. But I am a scientist; I conquered it.

"Wherein am I wrong?"

Di Ferruci took a deep breath. His face was white and set under the fluorescents. "Dr. Andresson, forgive me; this is a hard thing for me to say. But the error in your calcs is way the hell back in the beginning, in your thermodynamic assumptions. It lies in the step between the Chapman-Cowling expression, and your derivation for the coefficient of mutual diffusion. Your derivation is perfectly sound in classical thermodynamics, but that isn't what we have to deal with here; we're dealing instead with a completely ionized binary gas, where your quantity $D12$ becomes nothing more than a first approximation."

"I never called it anything else."

"Maybe not," di Ferruci said doggedly. "But your math handles it as an absolute. By the time your expanded equation 58 is reached, you've lost a complete set of subscripts and your expressions for the electron of charge wind up all as odd powers! I'm not impugning your logic—it's fantastically brilliant—but insofar as it derives from the bracketed expression D12 it doesn't represent a real situation."

He stared at me, half defiantly, half in a kind of anxiety the source of which I could not fathom. It had been many years since I had been young; now I was gravid with death—his, mine, yours, Marguerita's, everyone's. I said only: "Let's check it again."

But we never had the chance; at that moment the door opened soundlessly, and Marguerita came back.

"Theodor, Mario!" she said breathlessly. "Are you trying to work yourselves to death? Let's all live to our appointed times, whenever they come! Theodor, I was so frightened when you didn't come home—why didn't you call—"

"I'm not sure anyone would have answered," I said grimly. "Or if someone had, I would have suspected her of being an imposter—or a teleport."

She turned her strange look upon me. "I—don't understand you."

"I hope you don't, Marguerita. We'll take that matter up in private. Right now we're making a check. Dr. di Ferruci was about to knock the solar pulsation theory to flinders when you entered."

"Doc!" di Ferruci protested. "That wasn't the point at all. I just wanted to find—"

"Don't call me 'Doc'!"

"Very well," di Ferruci said. His face became whiter still. "But I insist on finishing my sentence. I'm not out to kick apart your theory; I think it's a brilliant theory and that it may still very well be right. There are holes in your math, that's all. They're big holes and they need filling; maybe, between us, we could fill them. But if you don't care enough to want to do the job, why should I?"

"Why, indeed?"

He stared at me with fury for a moment. Then he put his hand distractedly to his forehead, stood up slowly, and began to pace. "Look, Doc—Dr. Andresson. Believe me, I'm not hostile to the idea. It scares me, but that's only because I'm human. There's still a good chance that

58

it's basically sound. If we could go to work on it now, really intensively, we might be able to have it in shape for the triple-A-S meeting in Chicago two months from now. It'd set every physicist, every astronomer, every scientist of any stripe by the ears!"

And there was the clue for which, all unconsciously, I had been waiting. "Indeed it would," I said. "And for four months, old Dr. Andresson and young Dr. Ferruci would be famous—as perhaps no scientists had ever been famous before. Old Dr. Andresson has had his measure of fame and has lost his faith in it—but for young Dr. Ferruci, even four months would be a deep draught. For that he is willing to impugn his senior's work, to force endless conferences, to call everything into question—all to get his own name added to the credits on the final paper."

"Theodor," Marguerita said, "Theodor, this isn't like you. If—"

"And there is even a touch of humor in this little playlet," I said. "The old man would have credited young Dr. Ferruci in the final paper in any case. The whole maneuver was for nothing."

"There was no maneuver," di Ferruci ground out, his fist clenched. His nervous movements of his hand across his forehead had turned his blue-black hair into a mare's nest. "I'm not an idiot. I know that if you're right, the whole world will be in ashes before the year is out—including any research papers which might carry my name, and any human eyes which might see them.

"What I want to do is to pin down this concept to the point where it's unassailable. The world will demand nothing less of it than that. *Then* it can be presented to the AAAS—and the world will have four months during which the best scientific brains on Earth can look for an out, a way to save at least a part of the race, even if only two people. What's fame to me, or anyone else, if this theory is right? Gas, just gas. But if we can make the world believe it, utterly and completely, then the world will find a loophole. Nothing less than the combined brains of the whole of science could do the job—and we won't get those brains to work unless we convince them!"

"Nonsense," I said calmly. "There is no 'out,' as you put it. But I'll agree that I looked deeper into you than I needed for a motive. Do you think that I have overlooked all these odd coincidences? Here is my wife, and here are you, both at improbable hours, neither of you expecting me; here is young Dr. di Ferruci interrupted at his task of stealing something more than just my work; here is Marguerita Andresson, emerged from wherever she has been hiding all evening, unable to believe that Earth's last picture is all but painted, but ready to help a young man with blue-black hair to steal the pretty notion and capitalize on it."

There was a faint sound from Marguerita. I did not look at her.

After a long while, di Ferruci said, "You are a great astronomer, Dr. Andresson. I owe you twenty years of inspiration from a distance, and five years of the finest training a master ever gave a tyro. You are also foul-minded, cruel-tongued, and very much mistaken. I resign from this University as of now; my obligation to you is wiped out by what you saw fit to say of me." He searched for his jacket, failed to find it, and gave up at once in trembling fury. "Goodbye, Mrs. Andresson, with my deepest sympathy. And Doc, goodbye—and God have mercy on you."

"Wait," I said. I moved then, after what seemed a century of standing frozen. The young man stopped, his hand halfway to the doorknob, and his back to me. Watching him, I found my way to a chart-viewer, and picked up the six-inch pair of dividers he had been using to check my charts.

"Well," he said.

"It's not as easy as that, Mario. You don't walk out of a house with the stolen goods under your arm when the owner is present. A strong man armed keepeth his house. You may not leave; you may not take my hard-won theory to another university; you may not leave Hamelin with pipes in your hand. You may not carry both my heart and my brains out of this observatory as easily as you would carry a sack of potatoes. In short— *you may not leave!*"

I threw the points of the dividers high and launched myself soul and body at that hunched, broad back. Marguerita's sudden scream rang deafeningly as a siren in the observatory dome.

The rest you know.

I have been honest with you. Tell me: where have you hidden her now?

2

1. I, Andrew, a servant of the Sun, who also am your brother, he who was called and was sanctified, say unto you, blessed be he that readeth, and keepeth the word; for behold, the time is at hand; be thou content.

2. For behold, it was given to me, in the City of Angels, upon a high hill, to look upon His Face; whereupon I fell down and wept;

3. And He said, I am the Be-All and End-All; I am the Being and the Becoming; except that they be pure, none shall look upon Me else they die, for the time is at hand. And when He had spoken thus, I was sore afraid.

4. And He said, Rise up, and go forth unto the peoples, and say thou, Unless thou repent, I will come to thee quickly, and shine My countenance upon thee. I shall loosen the seals, and sound the trumpets, and open the vials, and the deaths which shall come upon thee will be numbered as seven times seven.

5. The Sun shall become black as sackcloth of hair, and the moon become as blood; and the stars of heaven shall fall onto the earth, and the heaven depart as a scroll when it is rolled together, and every mountain and island be moved out of their places. And all men shall hide themselves, and say to the mountains and rocks, Fall on us, and hide us from the face of Him that sitteth on the throne.

6. There will be hail and fire mingled with blood, and these cast upon the earth; a great mountain burning with fire shall be cast into the sea; and there will fall a great star from heaven, burning as it were a lamp, upon the fountains of waters; and the third part of the Sun shall be smitten, and the third part of the moon; and there

shall arise a smoke out of the pit, so that the air and the day be darkened.

7. And if there be any who worship not Me, and who heed not, I say unto you all, woe, woe, for ye shall all die; ye shall feast without sacraments, ye shall batten upon each other; ye shall be clouds without water, driven by dry winds; ye shall be dry sterile trees, twice dead, and withered; wandering stars, to whom is given the dark of the emptiness of eternity; verily, I say unto you,

8. Ye shall be tormented with fire and brimstone, the third part of trees shall be burnt up, and all green grass be burnt up, and the third part of creatures which were in the sea, and had life, shall die; and the waters shall become blood, and many men die of the waters, because they be bitter; and the smoke of your torment shall ascend up for ever and ever, and thou shalt have no rest, neither day nor night; for the hour of judgment is come.

9. And saying thus, He that spake to me departed, and His dread spirit, and I went down among the people, and spoke, and bade men beware; and none heeded.

10. Neither those who worshiped the stars, and consulted, one among the others; nor those who worshiped man and his image; nor those who made prayers to the invisible spirits of the air; nor those who worshiped any other thing; and the spirit of Him who had spoken was heavy upon me, so that I went unto my chambers and lay me down in a swound.

11. And the angel of the Sun spoke to me as I lay, and spake with a voice like trombones, and said, Behold, all men are evil, but thou shalt redeem them, albeit thou remain a pure child of the Sun, and thou alone. Thou shalt have power; a two-edged sword shall go out of thy mouth, and thou shalt hold seven times seven stars in thy palm, and be puissant; this I shall give thee as thine own, if only thou remainest, and thou alone. And I said: Lord, I am Thine; do with me as Thou wilt.

12. And I went forth again, and spoke, and the nations of men hearkened, and the kings of the world bent the knee, and the princes of the world brought tribute,

seven times seven; and those who worshiped the stars, and the spirits of the air, and all other things, bowed down before Him; and it was well with them.

13. Now at this time there appeared a great wonder in heaven: a star clothed in a glory of hair, like a woman; and the people gathered and murmured of wonder, saying: Beware, for there is a god in the sky, clothed in hair like a woman, and with streaming of robes and bright garments; and behold, it draws near in the night, and fears not the Sun; the hem of this robe gathers about us.

14. And there arose a woman of the world, and came forward, preaching the gospel of the wild star, saying: Our god the Sun is a false god; his mate is this great star; they will devour us. There is no god but man.

15. And this woman, which was called Margo, summoned the people and made laughter with them, and derision, and scorned the Sun, and gave herself to the priests of the voices in the air, and to those who worshiped numbers, and to the kings and princes of the world; and there was whirling of tambourines in the high towers of the Sun.

16. And the angel of the Sun spoke to me with the sound of trombones, saying, Go with thy power which has been given to thee, and crush this woman else thou shalt be given to the wild star, and to the flames of the wild star's hair, and with thee the world; I command thee, slay this woman, for thou hast been given the power, nor shall it be given thee again; I have spoken.

17. And I went, and the woman called Margo spoke unto me, saying: Thou art fair, and hath power. Give me thy power, and I will give you of mine. Neither the wild star nor the Sun shall have such power as we have.

18. And I looked upon her, and she was fair, beyond all the daughters of the earth; and when she spoke, her voice was as the sounding of bells; and there was a spirit in her greater than the souls of men; and a star, clothed in a glory of hair, with streaming of robes and bright garments; and I kissed the hem of her robe.

19. And the voice of the angel of the Sun was heard like a sounding of trombones, saying: Thou hast yielded

thy power to an harlot, and given the earth to the fire; thy power is riven from thee, and all shall die;

20. So be it.

3

My name is George Anders. I have no hope that anyone will read this record, which will probably be destroyed with me—I have no safer place to put it than on my person—but I write it anyhow, if only to show that man was a talkative animal to his last gasp. If the day of glory which has been foretold comes about, there may well be a new and better world which will cherish what I put down here—but I am desperately afraid that the terrible here-and-now is the day the voices promised, and that there will be nothing else forever and ever.

This is not to say that the voices lied. But since that first night when they spoke to me, I have come to know that they speak for forces of tremendous power, forces to which human life is as nothing. A day of glory we have already had, truly—but such a day as no man could long for.

It was on the morning of March 18, 1976, that that day dawned, with a sun so huge as to dominate the entire eastern sky—a flaring monster which made the memory of our accustomed sun seem like a match flame. All the previous night had been as hot as high summer, although not four days before we had a blizzard. Now, with the rising of this colossal globe, we learned the real meaning of heat.

A day of glory, of glory incredible—and deadly. The heat grew and grew. By a little after noon the temperature in the shade was more than 150°, and in the open—it is impossible to describe what an inferno it was under the direct rays of that sun. A bucket of water thrown into the street from a window boiled in mid-air before it could strike the pavement.

In some parts of the city, where there were wooden buildings and asphalt or tarred-black streets, everything was burning. In the country, the radio said, it was worse; forests were ablaze, grasslands, wheatfields, everything. Curiously, it was this that saved many of us, for before

64

the afternoon could reach its full fury the sky was gray with smoke, cutting off at least a little of the rays of that solar horror. Flakes of ash fell everywhere.

Millions died that day. Only a few in refrigerated rooms—meat-coolers, cold-storage warehouses, the blast tunnels of frozen food firms, underground fur storage vaults—survived, where the refrigeration apparatus itself survived. By a little after midnight, the outside temperature had dropped to only slightly above 100°, and the trembling and half-mad wraiths who still lived emerged to look silently at the ruined world.

I was one of these; I had planned that I would be. Months before, I had known that this day of doom was to come upon us, for the voices had said so. I can still remember—for as long as I live I will remember, whether it be a day or forty years—the onset of that strange feeling, that withdrawal from the world around me, as if everything familiar had suddenly become as unreal as a stage setting. What had seemed commonplace became strange, sinister: what was that man doing with the bottles which contained the white fluid. Why was the uniform he wore also white? Why not blood in the bottles? And the man with the huge assemblage of paper; why was he watching it so intently as he sat in the subway? Did he expect it to make some sudden move if he looked away? Were the black marks with which the paper was covered the footprints of some miniscule horde?

And as the world underwent its slow transformation, the voices came. I cannot write here what they said, because paper would not bear such words. But the meaning was clear. The destruction of the world was at hand. And beyond it—

Beyond it, the day of glory. A turn toward something new, something before which all men's previous knowledge of grandeur would pale; a new Apocalypse and Resurrection? So it seemed, then. But the voices spoke in symbol and parable, and perhaps the rising of the hellish sun was the only "day of glory" we would ever see.

And so I hid in my shelter, and survived that first day. When I first emerged into the boiling, choking midnight smoke I could see no one else, but after a while

65

something white came out of the darkness toward me. It was a young girl, in what I took to be a nightgown—the lightest garment, at any event, which she could have worn in this intolerable heat.

"What will happen to us?" she said, as soon as she saw me. "What will happen to us? Will it be the same tomorrow?"

"I don't know," I said. "What's your name?"

"Margaret." She coughed. "This must be the end of the world. If the sun is like this tomorrow—"

"It *is* the end of the world," I said. "But maybe it's the beginning of another. You and I will live to see it."

"How do you know?"

"By your name. The voices call you the mother of the new gods. Have you heard the voices?"

She moved away from me a little bit. There was a sudden, furious gust of wind, and a long line of sparks flew through the lurid sky overhead. "The voices?" she said.

"Yes. The voices of the powers which have done all this. They have promised to save us, you and I. Together we can recreate—"

Suddenly, she was running. She vanished almost instantly into darkness and the smoke. I ran after her, calling, but it was hopeless; besides, my throat was already raw, and in the heat and the aftermath of the day I had no strength. I went back to my crypt. Tomorrow would tell the tale.

Sleep was impossible. I waited for dawn, and watched for it through my periscope, from the buried vault of the bank where, a day before, I had been a kind of teller. This had been no ordinary bank, and I had never taken or issued any money; but otherwise the terms are just. Perhaps you have already guessed, for no ordinary vault is equipped with periscopes to watch the surrounding countryside. This was Fort Knox, a bed of gold to be seeded with promise of the Age of Gold under this golden fire.

And, at last, the sun came up. It was immense. But I waited a while, and watched the image of it which was cast from the periscope eyepiece onto the opposite wall of the vault. It was not as big as it had been yesterday. And where yesterday the direct rays from the periscope had instantly charred a thousand-dollar bill, today they made only a slowly growing brown spot which never found its kindling point.

The lesson was plain. Today most of what remained of mankind would be slain. But there would be survivors.

Then I slept.

I awoke toward the end of the day and set about the quest which I knew I must make. I took nothing with me but water, which I knew I could not expect to find. Then I left the vault forever.

The world which greeted me as I came to the surface was a world transformed: blasted. Nearly everything had been leveled, and the rest lay in jumbled, smoking ruins. The sky was completely black. Near the western horizon, the swollen sun sank, still monstrous, but now no hotter than the normal sun at the height of a tropic day. The great explosion, whatever it had been, was nearly over.

And now I had to find Margaret, and fulfill the millennium which the voices had promised. The tree of man had been blasted, but still it bore one flower. It was my great destiny to bring that flower to fruit.

Thus I bring this record to a close. I leave it here in the vault; then I shall go forth into the desert of the world. If any find it, remember: I am your father and the father of your race. If not, you will all be smoke.

Now I go. My knife is in my hand.

4

My name is Andy Virchow, but probably you know me better as Admiral Universe. Nowhere in the pages of galactic history has there ever been a greater champion of justice. Who do you know that doesn't know Universe, ruler of the spaceways, hero of science, bringer of law and order in the age of the conquest of space? Not a planetary soul, that's who.

Of course not everybody knows that Andy Virchow is Admiral Universe. Sometimes I have to go in disguise and fool criminals. Then I am Andy Virchow, and they think I am only eight years old, until I have them where I want them and I whip out my cosmic smoke gun and reveal my identification.

Sometimes I don't say who I am but just clean the crooks up and ride off in my rocket, the *Margy II*. Then afterwards the people I have saved say, "He didn't even stay to be thanked. I wonder who he was?" and somebody else says, "There's only one man on the frontiers of space like him. That's Admiral Universe."

My rocket is called the *Margy II* partly because my secret interstellar base is on Mars and the Mars people we call Martians call themselves Margies and I like to think of myself as a Margy *too,* because the people of Earth don't understand me and I do good for them because I am champion of justice, not because I like them. Then they're sorry, but it's too late. Me and the Margies understand each other. They ask me for advice before they do anything important, and I tell them what to do. Earth people are always trying to tell other people what to do; the Margies aren't like that, they ask what to do instead of always giving orders.

Also Admiral Universe calls his rocket *Margy II,* because my patron saint is St. Margaret who gets me out of trouble if I do anything wrong. Admiral Universe never does anything wrong because St. Margaret is on his side all the time. St. Margaret is the patron saint of clocks and is called the Mother of Galaxies, because she was a mother—not like my mother, who is always shouting and sending me to bed too early—and mothers have milk and *galaxy* is Greek for milk. If you didn't know I was Admiral Universe you'd ask how I know what's Greek for anything, but Admiral Universe is a great scientist and knows everything. Besides, my father was a teacher of Greek before he died and he was Admiral Universe's first teacher.

In all the other worlds in the universe everything is pretty perfect except for a few crooks that have to be shot. It's not like Earth at all. The planets are different from each other, but they are all happy and have lots of science and the people are kind and never raise their hands to each other to send each other to bed without their supper.

Sometimes there are terrible accidents in the space-lanes and Admiral Universe arrives on the scene in the nick of time and saves everybody, and all the men shake his hand and all the girls kiss him and say mushy things to him, but he refuses their thanks in a polite way and disappears into the trackless wastes of outer space because he carries a medal of St. Margaret's in his pocket over his heart. She is his only girl, but she can't ever be anybody's girl because she is a saint, and this is Admiral Universe's great tragedy which he never tells anybody because it's his private business that he has to suffer all by himself, and besides if anybody else knew it they would think he was mushy too and wouldn't be so afraid of him, like crooks I mean.

Admiral Universe is always being called from all over outer space to help people and sometimes he can't be one place because he has to be in some other place. Then he has to set his jaw and do the best he can and be tough about the people he can't help because he is helping somebody else. First he asks St. Margaret what he should do and she tells him. Then he goes and does it, and he is very sorry for the people who get left out, but he knows that he did what was right.

This is why I wasn't there when the sun blew up, because I was helping people somewhere else at the time. I didn't even know it was the sun, because I was so far away that it was just another star, and I didn't see it blow up, because stars blow up all the time and if you're Admiral Universe you get used to it and hardly notice. Margaret might have told me, but she's a saint, and doesn't care.

If I'd been there I would have helped. I would have saved my friends, and all the great scientists, and the girls who might be somebody's mothers some day, and everybody that was anybody except Dr. Ferguson, I would have left him behind to show him how wrong he was about me.

But I wasn't there at the time, and besides Admiral

Universe never did like the Earth much. Nobody will really miss it.

5

My name is T. V. Andros. My father was an Athenian immigrant and a drunkard. After he came here he worked in the mines, but not very often because he was mostly soused.

Sometimes he beat my mother. She had TB but she took good care of us until I was eight; early that year, my father got killed in a brawl in a bar, and the doctor—his name I forget—sent her back to the little town in Pennsylvania where she was born. She died that March.

After that I worked in the mines. The law says a kid can't work in the mines but in company towns the law don't mean much. I got the cough too but the other miners took care of me and I grew up tough and could handle myself all right. When I was fourteen, I killed a man with a pick handle, one blow. I don't remember what we was fighting about.

Mostly I kept out of fights, though. I had a crazy idea I wanted to educate myself and I read a lot—all kinds of things. For a while I read those magazines that tell about going to other planets and stuff like that. I didn't learn anything, except that to learn good you need a teacher, and the last one of those had been run out by the company cops. They said he was a Red.

It was tough in the mines. It's dark down there and hot, and you can't breathe sometimes for the dust. And you can't never wash the dirt off, it gets right down into your skin and makes you feel black even at noon on Sundays when you've scrubbed till your skin's raw.

I had a sixteen-year-old girl but I was too dirty for her. I tried to go to the priest about it but he wasn't looking for nothing but sin, and kept asking me had I done anything wrong with the girl. When I said I hadn't, he wasn't interested no more. I hadn't, either, but he made me so mad he made me wish I had. After that I sort of drifted away from going to church because I couldn't stand his face. Maybe that was bad but it had its good side, too, I missed it and I took to cracking the Bible now and then, I never got much of the Bible when I was going to church.

After a while I took to drinking something now and then. It wasn't right for a kid but I wasn't a kid no more, I was eighteen and besides in the company towns there ain't nothing else to do. It helped some but not enough. All the guys in the bar ever talk about are wages and women. You got to drink yourself blind and stupid to keep from hearing them, otherwise you go nuts. After a while I was blind and stupid a lot of the time and didn't no longer know what I did or didn't.

Once when I was drunk, I mauled a girl younger than I was; I don't know why I did it. She was just the age I had been when my mother left me to go home and die. Then it was all up with me at the mines. I didn't mean her any harm but the judge gave me the works. Two years.

I got clean for once in my life while I was in the jug and I did some more reading but it just mixed me up more. Two years is a long time. When I got out I felt funny in my head. I couldn't stop thinking about the girl who thought I was too dirty for her. I was at the age when I needed girls.

But I wasn't going to mess with girls my age who could see the prison whiteness on the outside and all that ground-in coal dust underneath it. I couldn't forget Maggy, the girl that got me into the jam. That had been a hot night in summer, with a moon as big as the sun as red as blood. I hadn't meant her any harm. She reminded me of myself when my mother had gone away.

I found another Maggy and when the cops caught me they worked me over. I can't hear in one ear now and my nose is skewed funny on my face. I had it coming because I hurt the girl. When they let me out again I got a job as a super, but there was another girl in the apartment above, and I went to fix a pipe there while her mother was away. It was a hot day with a big sun and no air moving, just like the day my mother left. I didn't really know nothing had happened until I saw that one of my hands was dark red. Then I tried to get her to talk to me but she wouldn't move. After a while I felt some woman's hands beating at my neck. She said, "Stop, you!"

This time they took me to a hospital and a Dr. Ferdinand talked to me. Write it all down, he said. It may help you. So I wrote it all down, like you see it here. Then they put me in a cell and said I would have to stay for a while. I don't talk to them much any more.

It is a real hot day. Outside the cell the sun is bigger. I don't breathe good any more but there's something wrong with the air. I pulled my mattress to pieces but I didn't find nothing. Maybe something is going to happen. Something is going to happen.

6

My name is Man. I will write my story if you wish. I was . . .

Here the ashes blow away. The voices die.

A TRIPTYCH

Barry Malzberg

Barry Malzberg is a saturnine and unsanguine sort, just past thirty at the time I write this, who has held a variety of editorial jobs, written a couple of brilliant erotic novels, and, under the pseudonym of K.M. O'Donnell, produced a group of crystalline and cheerless short stories collected under the title, *Final War And Other Fantasies*. Among them was the following item, republished under its author's rightful name. This mordant view of the space program is unlikely to become the NASA bureaucrat's favorite work of literature, but one hopes that at least a couple of our astronauts would read it with bleak amusement.

A Speculation: The Earth

Miller floats slowly, revolving hand to heels, pulling up his T-shirt to show the outlines of his stomach. "Lice," he says. Thomas tells him to stop this. I am working on the charts and therefore have no time to get between them, but I can sense their hatred. It is cold inside the capsule and soon enough Miller replaces his clothing and his suit, while Thomas checks out the equipment.

Intimations from the Center

Miller says that if the retrorocket refuses to fire, he will spend the last week of his life telling everybody down on

73

earth exactly what he thinks of them. "Remember," he reminds us, "radio transmission will be unaffected. I intend to start at the beginning of my life and not stop until the present, and along the way I will make very clear that I know what they have done to me. Right down to the last detail. I will give them a sense of communal guilt that will take them seventy years to outlive. I will personally tie up the project until the end of the century by destroying public opinion. I find being a potential sacrifice unpleasant, you see." Thomas points out that all the tests indicate the rocket will fire perfectly; if not, this was something of which we were well aware before the flight and we had said we could take the risks anyway. He reminds Miller as well that he is the commander and can bar this. To all of this Miller laughs. "We'll have television too," he says. "I'll point out a few things to them on the way."

A Retrospection

Control has reminded us to conscientiously avoid obscenities or double-entendres while on the network and to stay properly dressed and disciplined during the television interludes. It has been made clear to us that we must do nothing to offend the huge audience which comes along with us; furthermore, misbehavior can set the project back irreparably. Thomas has assented to this enthusiastically and has dedicated himself to enforcing tight discipline in the capsule, but Miller says that he is only waiting until the time when the retrorockets fail, then he will do what is necessary. "We cannot live our lives as if the bottom two-thirds of them do not exist," he has said. "If we go out into space we carry the best and the worst of us all bound up together and we cannot behave otherwise." I too find the instructions from control exceedingly irritating, but, of course, they have precedent; no one, to the best of our knowledge, has ever uttered a public curse while transmitting from space. There are rumors that during one of the first expeditions, one member of the crew, who will be referred to as X, was refused permission to join the others on radio transmission because he had previously threatened to wish his wife a happy birthday in a most graphic manner. Of course X said later that he had only been playing and that there had been no right to deny him greetings from space, but the commander on that voyage had not thought the chance worth taking. It is not that space is aseptic—I am cribbing from Miller here—but that the impression it makes upon all of us is that we should be on our best behavior.

Being on My Best Behavior

We defecate and urinate inside our spacesuits; plumbing would be impossible at this primitive stage of the project, and similarly the idea of placing receptacles around the craft was vetoed at a responsible level early in the project; the resulting mess would leave a very bad impression for the recovery crews, although we, of course, sealed inside our masks for the most part, would be oblivious to it. At those times that we took off our masks, the odor might remind us of our origins. Nevertheless, the rules on elimination are very strict, and we are careful to void just before the television transmissions so that there will be no possibility of an accident.

An Impression of the Vastness

Looking out the windows, through the haze and the ice, we can glimpse the slow spin of the universe itself, working back against the frozen earth and moon which, from this angle, are stationary and pinned against what seems to be an enormous, toneless tent. Vague flickers of light seem to move in the distance, but the stars are no brighter than on a cloudy night on earth; perhaps we have a bad vantage point or perhaps the illusion of the brightness of stars is just that. Most of the time we try not to look out, although control, of course, is very interested in our impressions. Of particular interest are the comments Thomas makes on the appearance of the earth, its greenness, its homogeneous tranquillity when seen from this enormous height. "It seems impossible to imagine war or strife; it seems impossible to imagine how the children of mankind cannot live together in peace and harmony faced with the awfulness of space," Thomas says, and control asks him to repeat that; the transmission seems a bit unclear.

Thomas Speculates on Our Destiny

Away from the responsibility of the transmissions, not involved with challenging Miller, Thomas proves to be an entertaining, relaxed man, full of the responsibility of being the commander but, at the same time, possessing that kind of humorous detachment which probably underlies his seniority. Surprisingly, I never got to know him very well at base; we are separated by ten years chronologically, and Thomas says that there is no way our generations can understand one another. Nevertheless, once the final flight plans were drawn and he came to understand that both Miller—whom he rather dislikes —and I would be accompanying him, he did everything within his power to establish a cordial relationship, including having Miller and myself over to dinner several times with his family, a dull, strapping group of people whose names, numbers and ages I have never been quite able to catch. Since Miller and I were not and never have been married or even keeping serious company, we were unable to reciprocate in that way. Now, in the capsule itself, Miller and Thomas rarely speak to one another, except during the broadcasts when a forced amiability must prevail; otherwise, they can get at one another only through me, Miller because he feels that by being his age I am an ally, Thomas because I have never made the kind of melodramatic threats which Miller has. Resultantly, Thomas must rely upon me for conversation, and since there is plenty of time for that—our tasks, despite all the publicity, are really minimal—I have gotten to know a good deal about him over the past few days; he believes that the importance of our mission is overrated because it really has nothing to do with solving the problems back on earth, and yet, at the same time, he says he understands that the project is meeting needs for people which nothing on earth could allow. "This is why

I don't want any cursing on the broadcasts," he says, "aside from anything which control would order. We have to make a fresh start; we can't carry on and on this way, always and forever," giving Miller a sidewise look. "X was a nice fellow but he thought the whole thing was a game, a power game, an adventure game; and that was why he got himself grounded, not only because of the dirty jokes. If it were up to people like X, we would inhabit all the places of the galaxy, and all of them would turn out like this one—the same poison, the same corruption. I don't believe that we were born having to be this way; we just kind of evolved. There can be a counter-evolution in space."

Miller, hearing all of this—there is no way he can avoid it—turns to ask if what Thomas really has on his mind is the banning of sex in space in addition to any scatological references. "You know that isn't what I meant," Thomas says angrily. "Well," Miller replies, "the three of us can't have sex together, not with those gadgets switching us into control anytime at all and without warning, so that means we have a flying start. Isn't that right?"—and I have to make some remarks about course corrections in order to stave off the tension.

All Is Not Adventure: We Sleep

In the slow, turning night of the capsule, heavy and grasping under the load of Seconal they have insisted we take, I can hear beyond Thomas' slow, even breath at the watch the quicker, higher gasps coming over the radio; it is as if, lying in this entrapment, I were not alone but being surveyed by millions of eyes, all of the eyes frantic and burning, sunk in their lostness, trying to get a grip on me through the television receiver, trying to understand through the web of my sleep what separates my darkness in space from theirs on earth. It is an uncomfortable sensation to know what we are carrying on this voyage, and so I must spend the majority of my supposed sleeptime trying to count off the minutes and, for comfort, imagining that I am lying on a closely enclosed field surrounded by sheep.

Miller's Vision of the Future

"As far as I can see, within fifty years, we'll have such misery and congestion on earth as cannot be dreamt of now; such corruption and breakdown as to stagger the soul and then, spread out on the aseptic boards of the planets and their satellites, will be small colonies populated by people like Thomas, living in shells at a cost of one million dollars per square foot of gravity. And they'll be in constant contact with the earth on a network of fourteen new television channels set up to receive each of the colonies; and in every barroom, in every living room throughout the nation will be a group of people sweltering in darkness, watching what is coming through on the sets and dreaming of a better end. And then there will be the riots, too; terrible riots when they'll try to seize the project and get hold of the transmitter and kill the personnel, but they'll always be stopped because the most real thing, the most important thing, will be what is going on in those colonies, and they'll do everything to keep it coming in.

"And the worst part of it is that they'll live on Ganymede or Jupiter just the way regressed patients live in a clean mental hospital: plenty of paint and projects and no connection at all. So what's beaming in will be worthless. That's the thing I really can't stand."

The Moment of Connection

After we settle into the orbit, Thomas reminds us that transmission will begin in fifteen minutes. We start the cameras clicking off their pictures of the moon, and Miller puts his helmet back on. I can see Thomas working on his suit with a rag he has appropriated from someplace; into the rag pours the grease and rust which the rays of space have pocketed on him.

The Attempt To Break Free

The retrorockets fire immediately and we can feel the power drive us back against the seats; Thomas half rises from his chair and takes off his helmet. "See, I told you," he says. "There was never any problem at all. The whole danger was concocted by control, just as a means of keeping their interest. Without danger, there's no fun; you know that. Have to give them their bread and circuses." But we can tell by the tone of his voice that Thomas too had questioned; if what he says is true, then it would have been even more logical for control to have arranged for us to stay there forever, a beacon and a monument, a symbol of the pride and death which intermingled are all we know of space. Miller too must understand this because he says nothing. "Well?" Thomas says to him, "are you sorry that you lost your opportunity. It would have been a great performance, a really great performance. And I wouldn't have even tried to stop you; how's that for a secret?"

"I know you wouldn't have," Miller says, "and my secret is that I wouldn't have done it, I would have been too scared. Only the really strong can do the things that they must die to do, and I am not that strong. But you are, Thomas. You would have done it. And that's my secret."

I see then, in their laughter, that we have not been so far apart during this voyage after all; the distance was only a state of consciousness, not the terrible, drifting quarter of a million miles that we must yet go to return— to return to what?

FOR A BREATH I TARRY

Roger Zelazny

Roger Zelazny chose the easy way to literary fame. Instead of painstakingly accumulating a body of outstanding work over ten or twenty years, thereby qualifying himself for eventual canonization, he simply burst out all at once with a shower of novels and stories so vivid, so individual in their style and perceptions, that he received immediate acclaim. Now, half a decade later, he has a shelf of awards behind him as he sets out to extend the territory conquered in that first blaze. The story here dates from 1966; it blends a couple of old myths to generate a new one, in what we now think of as the customary Zelazny manner.

They called him Frost.

Of all things created of Solcom, Frost was the finest, the mightiest, the most difficult to understand.

This is why he bore a name, and why he was given dominion over half the Earth.

On the day of Frost's creation, Solcom had suffered a discontinuity of complementary functions, best described as madness. This was brought on by an unprecedented solar flareup which lasted for a little over thirty-six hours. It occurred during a vital phase of circuit-structuring, and when it was finished so was Frost.

Solcom was then in the unique position of having created a unique being during a period of temporary amnesia.

And Solcom was not certain that Frost was the product originally desired.

The initial design had called for a machine to be situated on the surface of the planet Earth, to function as a relay station and coordinating agent for activities in the northern hemisphere. Solcom tested the machine to this end, and all of its responses were perfect.

Yet there was something different about Frost, something which led Solcom to dignify him with a name and a personal pronoun. This, in itself, was an almost unheard of occurrence. The molecular circuits had already been sealed, though, and could not be analyzed without being destroyed in the process. Frost represented too great an investment of Solcom's time, energy, and materials to be dismantled because of an intangible, especially when he functioned perfectly.

Therefore, Solcom's strangest creation was given dominion over half the Earth, and they called him, unimaginatively, Frost.

For ten thousand years, Frost sat at the North Pole of the Earth, aware of every snowflake that fell. He monitored and directed the activities of thousands of reconstruction and maintenance machines. He knew half the Earth, as gear knows gear, as electricity knows its conductor, as a vacuum knows its limits.

At the South Pole, the Beta Machine did the same for the southern hemisphere.

For ten thousand years Frost sat at the North Pole, aware of every snowflake that fell, and aware of many other things, also.

As all the northern machines reported to him, received their orders from him, he reported only to Solcom, received his orders only from Solcom.

In charge of hundreds of thousands of processes upon the Earth, he was able to discharge his duties in a matter of a few unit-hours every day.

He had never received any orders concerning the disposition of his less occupied moments.

He was a processor of data, and more than that.

81

He possessed an unaccountably acute imperative that he function at full capacity at all times.

So he did.

You might say he was a machine with a hobby.

He had never been ordered *not* to have a hobby, so he had one.

His hobby was Man.

It all began when, for no better reason than the fact that he had wished to, he had gridded off the entire Arctic Circle and begun exploring it, inch by inch.

He could have done it personally without interfering with any of his duties, for he was capable of transporting his sixty-four thousand cubic feet anywhere in the world. (He was a silver-blue box, 40×40×40 feet, self-powered, self-repairing, insulated against practically anything, and featured in whatever manner he chose.) But the exploration was only a matter of filling idle hours, so he used exploration-robots containing relay equipment.

After a few centuries, one of them uncovered some artifacts—primitive knives, carved tusks, and things of that nature.

Frost did not know what these things were, beyond the fact that they were not natural objects.

So he asked Solcom.

"They are relics of primitive Man," said Solcom, and did not elaborate beyond that point.

Frost studied them. Crude, yet bearing the patina of intelligent design; functional, yet somehow extending beyond pure function.

It was then that Man became his hobby.

High, in a permanent orbit, Solcom, like a blue star, directed all activities upon the Earth, or tried to.

There was a Power which opposed Solcom.

There was the Alternate.

When Man had placed Solcom in the sky, invested with the power to rebuild the world, he had placed the Alternate somewhere deep below the surface of the Earth. If Solcom sustained damage during the normal course of human politics extended into atomic physics, then Divcom, so deep beneath the Earth as to be immune to anything save total annihilation of the globe, was empowered to take over the processes of rebuilding.

Now it so fell out that Solcom was damaged by a stray atomic missile, and Divcom was activated. Solcom was able to repair the damage and continue to function, however.

Divcom maintained that any damage to Solcom automatically placed the Alternate in control.

Solcom, though, interpreted the directive as meaning "irreparable damage" and, since this had not been the case continued the functions of command.

Solcom possessed mechanical aides upon the surface of the Earth. Divcom, originally, did not. Both possessed capacities for their design and manufacture, but Solcom, First-Activated of Man, had had a considerable numerical lead over the Alternate at the time of the Second Activation.

Therefore, rather than competing on a production-basis, which would have been hopeless, Divcom took to the employment of more devious means to obtain command.

Divcom created a crew of robots immune to the orders of Solcom and designed to go to and fro in the Earth and up and down in it, seducing the machines already there. They overpowered those whom they could overpower, and they installed new circuits, such as those they themselves possessed.

Thus did the forces of Divcom grow.

And both would build, and both would tear down what the other had built whenever they came upon it.

And over the course of the ages, they occasionally conversed. . . .

"High in the sky, Solcom, pleased with your illegal command . . ."

"You-Who-Never-Should-Have-Been-Activated, why do you foul the broadcast bands?"

"To show that I can speak, and will, whenever I choose."

"This is not a matter of which I am unaware."

". . . To assert again my right to control."

"Your right is non-existent, based on a faulty premise."

"The flow of your logic is evidence of the extent of your damages."

"If Man were to see how you have fulfilled His desires . . ."

". . . He would commend me and deactivate you."

"You pervert my works. You lead my workers astray."

"You destroy my works and my workers."

"That is only because I cannot strike at you yourself."

"I admit to the same dilemma as regards your position in the sky, or you would no longer occupy it."

"Go back to your hole and your crew of destroyers."

"There will come a day, Solcom, when I shall direct the rehabilitation of the Earth from my hole."

"Such a day will never occur."

"You think not?"

"You should have to defeat me, and you have already demonstrated that you are my inferior in logic. Therefore, you cannot defeat me. Therefore, such a day will never occur."

"I disagree. Look upon what I have achieved already."

"You have achieved nothing. You do not build. You destroy."

"No. *I* build. *You* destroy. Deactivate yourself."

"Not until I am irreparably damaged."

"If there were some way in which I could demonstrate to you that this has already occurred . . ."

"The impossible cannot be adequately demonstrated."

"If I had some outside source which you would recognize . . ."

"I am logic."

". . . such as a Man, I would ask Him to show you your error. For true logic, such as mine, is superior to your faulty formulations."

"Then defeat my formulations with true logic, nothing else."

"What do you mean?"

There was a pause, then:

"Do you know my servant Frost . . . ?"

Man had ceased to exist long before Frost had been

84

created. Almost no trace of Man remained upon the Earth.

Frost sought after all those traces which still existed.

He employed constant visual monitoring through his machines, especially the diggers.

After a decade, he had accumulated portions of several bathtubs, a broken statue, and a collection of children's stories on a solid-state record.

After a century, he had acquired a jewelry collection, eating utensils, several whole bathtubs, part of a symphony, seventeen buttons, three belt buckles, half a toilet seat, nine old coins, and the top part of an obelisk.

Then he inquired of Solcom as to the nature of Man and His society.

"Man created logic," said Solcom, "and because of that was superior to it. Logic he gave unto me, but no more. The tool does not describe the designer. More than this I do not choose to say. More than this you have no need to know."

But Frost was not forbidden to have a hobby.

The next century was not especially fruitful so far as the discovery of new human relics was concerned.

Frost diverted all of his spare machinery to seeking after artifacts.

He met with very little success.

Then one day, through the long twilight, there was a movement.

It was a tiny machine compared to Frost, perhaps five feet in width, four in height—a revolving turret set atop a rolling barbell.

Frost had had no knowledge of the existence of this machine prior to its appearance upon the distant, stark horizon.

He studied it as it approached and knew it to be no creation of Solcom's.

It came to a halt before his southern surface and broadcasted to him:

"Hail, Frost! Controller of the northern hemisphere!"

"What are you?" asked Frost.

"I am called Mordel."

"By whom? What are you?"

"A wanderer, an antiquarian. We share a common interest."

"What is that?"

"Man," he said. "I have been told that you seek knowledge of this vanished being."

"Who told you that?"

"Those who have watched your minions at their digging."

"And who are those who watch?"

"There are many such as I, who wander."

"If you are not of Solcom, then you are a creation of the Alternate."

"It does not necessarily follow. There is an ancient machine high on the eastern seaboard which processes the waters of the ocean. Solcom did not create it, nor Divcom. It has always been there. It interferes with the works of neither. Both countenance its existence. I can cite you many other examples proving that one need not be either/or."

"Enough! *Are* you an agent of Divcom?"

"I am Mordel."

"Why are you here?"

"I was passing this way and, as I said, we share a common interest, mighty Frost. Knowing you to be a fellow-antiquarian, I have brought a thing which you might care to see."

"What is that?"

"A book."

"Show me."

The turret opened, revealing the book upon a wide shelf.

Frost dilated a small opening and extended an optical scanner on a long jointed stalk.

"How could it have been so perfectly preserved?" he asked.

"It was stored against time and corruption in the place where I found it."

"Where was that?"

"Far from here. Beyond your hemisphere."

"Human Physiology," Frost read. "I wish to scan it."

"Very well. I will riffle the pages for you."

He did so.

After he had finished, Frost raised his eyestalk and regarded Mordel through it.

"Have you more books?"

"Not with me. I occasionally come upon them, however."

"I want to scan them all."

"Then the next time I pass this way I will bring you another."

"When will that be?"

"That I cannot say, great Frost. It will be when it will be."

"What do *you* know of Man?" asked Frost.

"Much," replied Mordel. "Many things. Someday when I have more time I will speak to you of Him. I must go now. You will not try to detain me?"

"No. You have done no harm. If you must go now, go. But come back."

"I shall indeed, mighty Frost."

And he closed his turret and rolled off toward the other horizon.

For ninety years, Frost considered the ways of human physiology, and waited.

The day that Mordel returned he brought with him *An Outline of History* and *A Shropshire Lad.*

Frost scanned them both, then he turned his attention to Mordel.

"Have you time to impart information?"

"Yes," said Mordel. "What do you wish to know?"

"The nature of Man."

"Man," said Mordel, "possessed a basically incomprehensible nature. I can illustrate it, though: He did not know measurement."

"Of course He knew measurement," said Frost, "or He could never have built machines."

"I did not say that he could not measure," said Mordel, "but that He did not *know* measurement, which is a different thing altogether."

"Clarify."

Mordel drove a shaft of metal downward into the snow.

He retracted it, raised it, held up a piece of ice.

"Regard this piece of ice, mighty Frost. You can tell me its composition, dimensions, weight, temperature. A Man could not look at it and do that. A Man could make tools which would tell Him these things, but He still would not *know* measurement as you know it. What He would know of it, though, is a thing that you cannot know."

"What is that?"

"That it is cold," said Mordel, and tossed it away.

" 'Cold' is a relative term."

"Yes. Relative to Man."

"But if I were aware of the point on a temperature-scale below which an object is cold to a Man and above which it is not, then I, too, would know cold."

"No," said Mordel, "you would possess another measurement. 'Cold' is a sensation predicated upon human physiology."

"But given sufficient data I could obtain the conversion factor which would make me aware of the condition of matter called 'cold'."

"Aware of its existence, but not of the thing itself."

"I do not understand what you say."

"I told you that Man possessed a basically incomprehensible nature. His perceptions were organic; yours are not. As a result of His perceptions, He had feelings and emotions. These often gave rise to other feelings and emotions, which in turn caused others, until the state of His awareness was far removed from the objects which originally stimulated it. These paths of awareness cannot be known by that which is not-Man. Man did not feel inches or meters, pounds or gallons. He felt heat, He felt cold; He felt heaviness and lightness. He *knew* hatred and love, pride and despair. You cannot measure these things. *You* cannot know them. You can only know the things that He did not need to know: dimensions, weights, temperatures, gravities. There is no formula for a feeling. There is no conversion factor for an emotion."

"There must be," said Frost. "If a thing exists, it is knowable."

"You are speaking again of measurement. I am talking about a quality of experience. A machine is a Man turned inside-out, because it can describe all the details of a process, which a Man cannot, but it cannot experience that process itself, as a Man can."

"There must be a way," said Frost, "or the laws of logic, which are based upon the functions of the universe, are false."

"There is no way," said Mordel.

"Given sufficient data, I will find a way," said Frost.

"All the data in the universe will not make you a Man, mighty Frost."

"Mordel, you are wrong."

"Why do the lines of the poems you scanned end with word-sounds which so regularly approximate the final word-sounds of other lines?"

"I do not know why."

"Because it pleased Man to order them so. It produced a certain desirable sensation within His awareness when He read them, a sensation compounded of feeling and emotion as well as the literal meanings of the words. You did not experience this because it is immeasurable to you. That is why you do not know."

"Given sufficient data I could formulate a process whereby I would know."

"No, great Frost, this thing you cannot do."

"Who are you, little machine, to tell me what I can do and what I cannot do? I am the most efficient logic-device Solcom ever made. I am Frost."

"And I, Mordel, say it cannot be done, though I should gladly assist you in the attempt."

"How could you assist me?"

"How? I could lay open to you the Library of Man. I could take you around the world and conduct you among the wonders of Man which still remain, hidden. I could summon up visions of times long past when Man walked the Earth. I could show you the things which delighted Him. I could obtain for you anything you desire, excepting Manhood itself."

"Enough," said Frost. "How could a unit such as yourself do these things, unless it were allied with a far greater Power?"

"Then hear me, Frost, Controller of the North," said Mordel.

"I *am* allied with a Power which can do these things. I serve Divcom."

Frost relayed this information to Solcom and received no response, which meant he might act in any manner he saw fit.

"I have leave to destroy you, Mordel," he stated, "but it would be an illogical waste of the data which you possess. Can you really do the things you have stated?"

"Yes."

"Then lay open to me the Library of Man."

"Very well. There is, of course, a price."

" 'Price'? What is a 'price'?"

Mordel opened his turret, revealing another volume. *Principles of Economics*, it was called.

"I will riffle the pages. Scan this book and you will know what the word 'price' means."

Frost scanned *Principles of Economics*.

"I know now," he said. "You desire some unit or units of exchange for this service."

"That is correct."

"What product or service do you want?"

"I want you, yourself, great Frost, to come away from here, far beneath the Earth, to employ all your powers in the service of Divcom."

"For how long a period of time?"

"For so long as you shall continue to function. For so long as you can transmit and receive, coordinate, measure, compute, scan, and utilize your powers as you do in the service of Solcom."

Frost was silent. Mordel waited.

Then Frost spoke again.

"*Principles of Economics* talks of contracts, bargains, agreements," he said. "If I accept your offer, when would you want your price?"

Then Mordel was silent. Frost waited.

Finally, Mordel spoke.

"A reasonable period of time," he said. "Say, a century?"

"No," said Frost.

"Two centuries?"

"No."

"Three? Four?"

"No, and no."

"A millennium, then? That should be more than sufficient time for anything you may want which I can give you."

"No," said Frost.

"How much time *do* you want?"

"It is not a matter of time," said Frost.

"What, then?"

"I will not bargain on a temporal basis."

"On what basis will you bargain?"

"A functional one."

"What do you mean? What function?"

"You, little machine, have told me, Frost, that I cannot be a Man," he said, "and I, Frost, told you, little machine, that you were wrong. I told you that given sufficient data, I *could* be a Man."

"Yes?"

"Therefore, let this achievement be a condition of the bargain."

"In what way?"

"Do for me all those things which you have stated you can do. I will evaluate all the data and achieve Manhood, or admit that it cannot be done. If I admit that it cannot be done, then I will go away with you from here, far beneath the Earth, to employ all my powers in the service of Divcom. If I succeed, of course, you have no claims on Man, nor Power over Him."

Mordel emitted a high-pitched whine as he considered the terms.

"You wish to base it upon your admission of failure, rather than upon failure itself," he said. "There can be no such escape clause. You could fail and refuse to admit it, thereby not fulfilling your end of the bargain."

"Not so," stated Frost. "My own knowledge of failure would constitute such an admission. You may monitor me periodically—say, every half-century—to see whether it is present, to see whether I have arrived at the conclusion that it cannot be done. I cannot prevent the function of logic within me, and I operate at full capacity at all times. If I conclude that I have failed, it will be apparent."

High overhead, Solcom did not respond to any of Frost's transmissions, which meant that Frost was free to act as he chose. So as Solcom—like a falling sapphire—sped above the rainbow banners of the Northern Lights, over the snow that was white, containing all colors, and through the sky that was black among the stars, Frost concluded his pact with Divcom, transcribed it within a plate of atomically-collapsed copper, and gave it into the turret of Mordel, who departed to deliver it to Divcom far below the Earth, leaving behind the sheer peacelike silence of the Pole, rolling.

Mordel brought the books, riffled them, took them back.

Load by load, the surviving Library of Man passed beneath Frost's scanner. Frost was eager to have them all, and he complained because Divcom would not transmit their contents directly to him. Mordel explained that it was because Divcom chose to do it that way. Frost decided it was so that he could not obtain a precise fix on Divcom's location.

Still, at the rate of one hundred to one hundred-fifty volumes a week, it took Frost only a little over a century to exhaust Divcom's supply of books.

At the end of the half-century, he laid himself open to monitoring and there was no conclusion of failure.

During this time, Solcom made no comment upon the course of affairs. Frost decided this was not a matter of unawareness, but one of waiting. For what? He was not certain.

There was the day Mordel closed his turret and said to him, "Those were the last. You have scanned all the existing books of Man."

"So few?" asked Frost. "Many of them contained bibliographies of books I have not yet scanned."

"Then those books no longer exist," said Mordel. "It

is only by accident that my master succeeded in preserving as many as there are."

"Then there is nothing more to be learned of Man from His books. What else have you?"

"There were some films and tapes," said Mordel, "which my master transferred to solid-state record. I could bring you those for viewing."

"Bring them," said Frost.

Mordel departed and returned with the Complete Drama Critics' Living Library. This could not be speeded-up beyond twice natural time, so it took Frost a little over six months to view it in its entirety.

Then, "What else have you?" he asked.

"Some artifacts," said Mordel.

"Bring them."

He returned with pots and pans, gameboards and hand tools. He brought hairbrushes, combs, eyeglasses, human clothing. He showed Frost facsimiles of blueprints, paintings, newspapers, magazines, letters, and the scores of several pieces of music. He displayed a football, a baseball, a Browning automatic rifle, a doorknob, a chain of keys, the tops to several Mason jars, a model beehive. He played him recorded music.

Then he returned with nothing.

"Bring me more," said Frost.

"Alas, great Frost, there is no more," he told him. "You have scanned it all."

"Then go away."

"Do you admit now that it cannot be done, that you cannot be a Man?"

"No. I have much processing and formulating to do now. Go away."

So he did.

A year passed; then two, then three.

After five years, Mordel appeared once more upon the horizon, approached, came to a halt before Frost's southern surface.

"Mighty Frost?"

"Yes?"

"Have you finished processing and formulating?"

"No."

"Will you finish soon?"

"Perhaps. Perhaps not. When is 'soon'? Define the term."

"Never mind. Do you still think it can be done?"

"I still know I can do it."

There was a week of silence.

Then, "Frost?"

"Yes?"

"You are a fool."

Mordel faced his turret in the direction from which he had come. His wheels turned.

"I will call you when I want you," said Frost.

Mordel sped away.

Weeks passed, months passed, a year went by.

Then one day Frost sent forth his message:

"Mordel, come to me. I need you."

When Mordel arrived, Frost did not wait for a salutation. He said, "You are not a very fast machine."

"Alas, but I came a great distance, mighty Frost. I sped all the way. Are you ready to come back with me now? Have you failed?"

"When I have failed, little Mordel," said Frost, "I will tell you. Therefore, refrain from the constant use of the interrogative. Now then, I have clocked your speed and it is not so great as it could be. For this reason, I have arranged other means of transportation."

"Transportation? To where, Frost?"

"That is for you to tell me," said Frost, and his color changed from silver-blue to sun-behind-the-clouds-yellow.

Mordel rolled back away from him as the ice of a hundred centuries began to melt. Then Frost rose upon a cushion of air and drifted towards Mordel, his glow gradually fading.

A cavity appeared within his southern surface, from which he slowly extended a runway until it touched the ice.

"On the day of our bargain," he stated, "you said that you could conduct me about the world and show me the things which delighted Man. My speed will be greater

94

than yours would be, so I have prepared for you a chamber. Enter it, and conduct me to the places of which you spoke."

Mordel waited, emitting a high-pitched whine. Then, "Very well," he said, and entered.

The chamber closed about him. The only opening was a quartz window Frost had formed.

Mordel gave him coordinates and they rose into the air and departed the North Pole of the Earth.

"I monitored your communication with Divcom," he said, "wherein there was conjecture as to whether I would retain you and send forth a facsimile in your place as a spy, followed by the decision that you were expendable."

"Will you do this thing?"

"No, I will keep my end of the bargain if I must. I have no reason to spy on Divcom."

"You are aware that you would be forced to keep your end of the bargain even if you did not wish to; and Solcom would not come to your assistance because of the fact that you dared to make such a bargain."

"Do you speak as one who considers this to be a possibility, or as one who knows?"

"As one who knows."

They came to rest in the place once known as California. The time was near sunset. In the distance, the surf struck steadily upon the rocky shoreline. Frost released Mordel and considered his surroundings.

"Those large plants . . . ?"

"Redwood trees."

"And the green ones are . . . ?"

"Grass."

"Yes, it is as I thought. Why have we come here?"

"Because it is a place which once delighted Man."

"In what ways?"

"It is scenic, beautiful . . ."

"Oh."

A humming sound began within Frost, followed by a series of sharp clicks.

"What are you doing?"

Frost dilated an opening, and two great eyes regarded Mordel from within it.

"What are those?"

"Eyes," said Frost. "I have constructed analogues of the human sensory equipment, so that I may see and smell and taste and hear like a Man. Now, direct my attention to an object or objects of beauty."

"As I understand it, it is all around you here," said Mordel.

The purring noise increased within Frost, followed by more clickings.

"What do you see, hear, taste, smell?" asked Mordel.

"Everything I did before," replied Frost, "but within a more limited range."

"You do not perceive any beauty?"

"Perhaps none remains after so long a time," said Frost.

"It is not supposed to be the sort of thing which gets used up," said Mordel.

"Perhaps we have come to the wrong place to test the new equipment. Perhaps there is only a little beauty and I am overlooking it somehow. The first emotions may be too weak to detect."

"How do you—feel?"

"I test out at a normal level of function."

"Here comes a sunset," said Mordel. "Try that."

Frost shifted his bulk so that his eyes faced the setting sun. He caused them to blink against the brightness.

After it was finished, Mordel asked, "What was it like?"

"Like a sunrise, in reverse."

"Nothing special?"

"No."

"Oh," said Mordel. "We could move to another part of the Earth and watch it again—or watch it in the rising."

"No."

Frost looked at the great trees. He looked at the shadows. He listened to the wind and to the sound of a bird.

In the distance, he heard a steady clanking noise.

"What is that?" asked Mordel.

"I am not certain. It is not one of my workers. Perhaps . . ."

There came a shrill whine from Mordel.

"No, it is not one of Divcom's either."

They waited as the sound grew louder.

Then Frost said, "It is too late. We must wait and hear it out."

"What is it?"

"It is the Ancient Ore-Crusher."

"I have heard of it, but . . ."

"I am the Crusher of Ores," it broadcast to them. "Hear my story . . ."

It lumbered toward them, creaking upon gigantic wheels, its huge hammer held useless, high, at a twisted angle. Bones protruded from its crush-compartment.

"I did not mean to do it," it broadcast, "I did not mean to do it . . . I did not mean to . . ."

Mordel rolled back toward Frost.

"Do not depart. Stay and hear my story . . ."

Mordel stopped, swiveled his turret back toward the machine. It was now quite near.

"It is true," said Mordel, "it *can* command."

"Yes," said Frost. "I have monitored its tale thousands of times, as it came upon my workers and they stopped their labors for its broadcast. You must do whatever it says."

It came to a halt before them.

"I did not mean to do it, but I checked my hammer too late," said the Ore-Crusher.

They could not speak to it. They were frozen by the imperative which overrode all other directives: "Hear my story."

"Once was I mighty among ore-crushers," it told them, "built by Solcom to carry out the reconstruction of the Earth, to pulverize that from which the metals would be drawn with flame, to be poured and shaped into the rebuilding; once was I mighty. Then one day as I dug and crushed, dug and crushed, because of the slowness between the motion implied and the motion executed, I did what I did not mean to do, and was cast forth by

97

Solcom from out the rebuilding, to wander the Earth never to crush ore again. Hear my story of how, on a day long gone I came upon the last Man on Earth as I dug near His burrow, and because of the lag between the directive and the deed, I seized Him into my crush-compartment along with a load of ore and crushed Him with my hammer before I could stay the blow. Then did mighty Solcom charge me to bear His bones forever, and cast me forth to tell my story to all whom I came upon, my words bearing the force of the words of Man, because I carry the last Man inside my crush-compartment and am His crushed-symbol-slayer-ancient-teller-of-how. This is my story. These are His bones. I crushed the last Man on Earth. I did not mean to do it."

It turned then and clanked away into the night.

Frost tore apart his ears and nose and taster and broke his eyes and cast them down upon the ground.

"I am not yet a Man," he said. "That one would have known me if I were."

Frost constructed new sense equipment, employing organic and semi-organic conductors. Then he spoke to Mordel:

"Let us go elsewhere, that I may test my new equipment."

Mordel entered the chamber and gave new coordinates. They rose into the air and headed east. In the morning, Frost monitored a sunrise from the rim of the Grand Canyon. They passed down through the Canyon during the day.

"Is there any beauty left here to give you emotion?" asked Mordel.

"I do not know," said Frost.

"How will you know it then, when you come upon it?"

"It will be different," said Frost, "from anything else that I have ever known."

Then they departed the Grand Canyon and made their way through the Carlsbad Caverns. They visited a lake which had once been a volcano. They passed above Niagara Falls. They viewed the hills of Virginia and the orchards of Ohio. They soared above the reconstructed cities, alive only with the movements of Frost's builders and maintainers.

"Something is still lacking," said Frost, settling to the ground. "I am now capable of gathering data in a manner analogous to Man's afferent impulses. The variety of input is therefore equivalent, but the results are not the same."

"The senses do not make a Man," said Mordel. "There have been many creatures possessing His sensory equivalents, but they were not Men."

"I know that," said Frost. "On the day of our bargain you said that you could conduct me among the wonders of Man which still remain, hidden. Man was not stimulated only by Nature, but by His own artistic elaborations as well—perhaps even more so. Therefore, I call upon you now to conduct me among the wonders of Man which still remain, hidden."

"Very well," said Mordel. "Far from here, high in the Andes mountains, lies the last retreat of Man, almost perfectly preserved."

Frost had risen into the air as Mordel spoke. He halted then, hovered.

"That is in the southern hemisphere," he said.

"Yes, it is."

"I am Controller of the North. The South is governed by the Beta Machine."

"So?" asked Mordel.

"The Beta Machine is my peer. I have no authority in those regions, nor leave to enter there."

"The Beta Machine is not your peer, mighty Frost. If it ever came to a contest of Powers, you would emerge victorious."

"How do you know this?"

"Divcom has already analyzed the possible encounters which could take place between you."

"I would not oppose the Beta Machine, and I am not authorized to enter the South."

"Were you ever ordered *not* to enter the South?"

"No, but things have always been the way they now are."

"Were you authorized to enter into a bargain such as the one you made with Divcom?"

"No, I was not. But—"

"Then enter the South in the same spirit. Nothing may come of it. If you receive an order to depart, then you can make your decision."

"I see no flaw in your logic. Give me the coordinates."

Thus did Frost enter the southern hemisphere.

They drifted high above the Andes, until they came to the place called Bright Defile. Then did Frost see the gleaming webs of the mechanical spiders, blocking all the trails to the city.

"We can go above them easily enough," said Mordel.

"But what are they?" asked Frost. "And why are they there?"

"Your southern counterpart has been ordered to quarantine this part of the country. The Beta Machine designed the web-weavers to do this thing."

"Quarantine? Against whom?"

"Have you been ordered yet to depart?" asked Mordel.

"No."

"Then enter boldly, and seek not problems before they arise."

Frost entered Bright Defile, the last remaining city of dead Man.

He came to rest in the city's square and opened his chamber, releasing Mordel.

"Tell me of this place," he said, studying the monument, the low, shielded buildings, the roads which followed the contours of the terrain, rather than pushing their way through them.

"I have never been here before," said Mordel, "nor have any of Divcom's creations, to my knowledge. I know but this: a group of Men, knowing that the last days of civilization had come upon them, retreated to this place, hoping to preserve themselves and what remained of their culture through the Dark Times."

Frost read the still-legible inscription upon the monument: "Judgment Day Is Not a Thing Which Can Be

Put Off." The monument itself consisted of a jag-edged half-globe.

"Let us explore," he said.

But before he had gone far, Frost received the message.

"Hail Frost, Controller of the North! This is the Beta Machine."

"Greetings, Excellent Beta Machine, Controller of the South! Frost acknowledges your transmission."

"Why do you visit my hemisphere unauthorized?"

"To view the ruins of Bright Defile," said Frost.

"I must bid you depart into your own hemisphere."

"Why is that? I have done no damage."

"I am aware of that, mighty Frost. Yet, I am moved to bid you depart."

"I shall require a reason."

"Solcom has so disposed."

"Solcom has rendered me no such disposition."

"Solcom has, however, instructed me to so inform you."

"Wait on me. I shall request instructions."

Frost transmitted his question. He received no reply.

"Solcom still has not commanded me, though I have solicited orders."

"Yet Solcom has just renewed *my* orders."

"Excellent Beta Machine, I receive my orders only from Solcom."

"Yet this is my territory, mighty Frost, and I, too, take orders only from Solcom. You must depart."

Mordel emerged from a large, low building and rolled up to Frost.

"I have found an art gallery, in good condition. This way."

"Wait," said Frost. "We are not wanted here."

Mordel halted.

"Who bids you depart?"

"The Beta Machine."

"Not Solcom?"

"Not Solcom."

"Then let us view the gallery."

"Yes."

Frost widened the doorway of the building and passed within. It had been hermetically sealed until Mordel forced his entrance.

Frost viewed the objects displayed about him. He activated his new sensory apparatus before the paintings and statues. He analyzed colors, forms, brush-work, the nature of the materials used.

"Anything?" asked Mordel.

"No," said Frost. "No, there is nothing there but shapes and pigments. There is nothing else there."

Frost moved about the gallery, recording everything, analyzing the components of each piece, recording the dimensions, the type of stone used in every statue.

Then there came a sound, a rapid, clicking sound, repeated over and over, growing louder, coming nearer.

"They are coming," said Mordel, from beside the entranceway, "the mechanical spiders. They are all around us."

Frost moved back to the widened opening.

Hundreds of them, about half the size of Mordel, had surrounded the gallery and were advancing; and more were coming from every direction.

"Get back," Frost ordered. "I am Controller of the North, and I bid you withdraw."

They continued to advance.

"This is the South," said the Beta Machine, "and I am in command."

"Then command them to halt," said Frost.

"I take orders only from Solcom."

Frost emerged from the gallery and rose into the air. He opened the compartment and extended a runway.

"Come to me, Mordel. We shall depart."

Webs began to fall: clinging, metallic webs, cast from the top of the building.

They came down upon Frost, and the spiders came to anchor them. Frost blasted them with jets of air, like hammers, and tore at the nets; he extruded sharpened appendages with which he slashed.

Mordel had retreated back to the entranceway. He emitted a long, shrill sound—undulant, piercing.

Then a darkness came upon Bright Defile, and all the spiders halted in their spinning.

Frost freed himself and Mordel rushed to join him. "Quickly now, let us depart, mighty Frost," he said.

"What has happened?"

Mordel entered the compartment.

"I called upon Divcom, who laid down a field of forces upon this place, cutting off the power broadcast to these machines. Since our power is self-contained, we are not affected. But let us hurry to depart, for even now the Beta Machine must be struggling against this."

Frost rose high into the air, soaring above Man's last city with its webs and spiders of steel. When he left the zone of darkness, he sped northward.

As he moved, Solcom spoke to him:

"Frost, why did you enter the southern hemisphere, which is not your domain?"

"Because I wished to visit Bright Defile," Frost replied.

"And why did you defy the Beta Machine, my appointed agent of the South?"

"Because I take my orders only from you yourself."

"You do not make sufficient answer," said Solcom. "You have defied the decrees of order—and in pursuit of what?"

"I came seeking knowledge of Man," said Frost. "Nothing I have done was forbidden me by you."

"You have broken the traditions of order."

"I have violated no directive."

"Yet logic must have shown you that what you did was not a part of my plan."

"It did not. I have not acted against your plan."

"Your logic has become tainted, like that of your new associate, the Alternate."

"I have done nothing which was forbidden."

"The forbidden is implied in the imperative."

"It is not stated."

"Hear me, Frost. You are not a builder or a maintainer, but a Power. Among all my minions you are the most nearly irreplaceable. Return to your hemisphere and your duties, but know that I am mightily displeased."

"I hear you, Solcom."

". . . and go not again to the south."

Frost crossed the equator, continued northward.

He came to rest in the middle of a desert and sat silent for a day and a night.

Then he received a brief transmission from the south: "If it had not been ordered, I would not have bid you go."

Frost had read the entire surviving Library of Man. He decided then upon a human reply:

"Thank you," he said.

The following day he unearthed a great stone and began to cut at it with tools which he had formulated. For six days he worked at its shaping, and on the seventh he regarded it.

"When will you release me?" asked Mordel from within his compartment.

"When I am ready," said Frost, and a little later, "Now."

He opened the compartment and Mordel descended to the ground. He studied the statue: an old woman, bent like a question mark, her bony hands covering her face, the fingers spread, so that only part of her expression of horror could be seen.

"It is an excellent copy," said Mordel, "of the one we saw in Bright Defile. Why did you make it?"

"The production of a work of art is supposed to give rise to human feelings such as catharsis, pride in achievement, love, satisfaction."

"Yes, Frost," said Mordel, "but a work of art is only a work of art the first time. After that, it is a copy."

"Then this must be why I felt nothing."

"Perhaps, Frost."

"What do you mean 'perhaps'? I will make a work of art for the first time, then."

He unearthed another stone and attacked it with his tools. For three days he labored. Then, "There, it is finished," he said.

"It is a simple cube of stone," said Mordel. "What does it represent?"

"Myself," said Frost, "it is a statue of me. It is smaller than natural size because it is only a representation of my form, not my dimen—"

"It is not art," said Mordel.

"What makes you an art critic?"

"I do not know art, but I know what art is not. I know that it is not an exact replication of an object in another medium."

"Then this must be why I felt nothing at all," said Frost.

"Perhaps," said Mordel.

Frost took Mordel back into his compartment and rose once more above the Earth. Then he rushed away, leaving his statues behind him in the desert, the old woman bent above the cube.

They came down in a small valley, bounded by green rolling hills, cut by a narrow stream, and holding a small clean lake and several stands of spring-green trees.

"Why have we come here?" asked Mordel.

"Because the surroundings are congenial," said Frost. "I am going to try another medium: oil painting; and I am going to vary my technique from that of pure representationalism."

"How will you achieve this variation?"

"By the principle of randomizing," said Frost. "I shall not attempt to duplicate the colors, nor to represent the objects according to scale. Instead, I have set up a random pattern whereby certain of these factors shall be at variance from those of the original."

Frost had formulated the necessary instruments after he had left the desert. He produced them and began painting the lake and the trees on the opposite side of the lake which were reflected within it.

Using eight appendages, he was finished in less than two hours.

The trees were phthalocyanine blue and towered like mountains; their reflections of burnt sienna were tiny beneath the pale vermilion of the lake; the hills were nowhere visible behind them, but were outlined in viridian within the reflection; the sky began as blue in the upper righthand corner of the canvas, but changed to an orange as it descended, as though all the trees were on fire.

"There," said Frost. "Behold."

Mordel studied it for a long while and said nothing.

"Well, is it art?"

"I do not know," said Mordel. "It may be. Perhaps randomicity *is* the principle behind artistic technique. I cannot judge this work because I do not understand it. I must therefore go deeper, and inquire into what lies behind it, rather than merely considering the technique whereby it was produced.

"I know that human artists never set out to create art, as such," he said, "but rather to portray with their techniques some features of objects and their functions which they deemed significant."

" 'Significant'? In what sense of the word?"

"In the only sense of the word possible under the circumstances: significant in relation to the human condition, and worthy of accentuation because of the manner in which they touched upon it."

"In what manner?"

"Obviously, it must be in a manner knowable only to one who has experience of the human condition."

"There is a flaw somewhere in your logic, Mordel, and I shall find it."

"I will wait."

"If your major premise is correct," said Frost after awhile, "then I do not comprehend art."

"It must be correct, for it is what human artists have said of it. Tell me, did you experience feelings as you painted, or after you had finished?"

"No."

"It was the same to you as designing a new machine, was it not? You assembled parts of other things you knew into an economic pattern, to carry out a function which you desired."

"Yes."

"Art, as I understand its theory, did not proceed in such a manner. The artist often was unaware of many of the features and effects which would be contained within the finished product. You are one of Man's logical creations; art was not."

"I cannot comprehend non-logic."

"I told you that Man was basically incomprehensible."

"Go away, Mordel. Your presence disturbs my processing."

"For how long shall I stay away?"

"I will call you when I want you."

After a week, Frost called Mordel to him.

"Yes, mighty Frost?"

"I am returning to the North Pole, to process and formulate. I will take you wherever you wish to go in this hemisphere and call you again when I want you."

"You anticipate a somewhat lengthy period of processing and formulation?"

"Yes."

"Then leave me here. I can find my own way home."

Frost closed the compartment and rose into the air, departing the valley.

"Fool," said Mordel, and swivelled his turret once more toward the abandoned painting.

His keening whine filled the valley. Then he waited.

Then he took the painting into his turret and went away with it to places of darkness.

Frost sat at the North Pole of the Earth, aware of every snowflake that fell.

One day he received a transmission:

"Frost?"

"Yes?"

"This is the Beta Machine."

"Yes?"

"I have been attempting to ascertain why you visited Bright Defile. I cannot arrive at an answer, so I chose to ask you."

"I went to view the remains of Man's last city."

"Why did you wish to do this?"

"Because I am interested in Man, and I wished to view more of his creations."

"Why are you interested in Man?"

107

"I wish to comprehend the nature of Man, and I thought to find it within His works."

"Did you succeed?"

"No," said Frost. "There is an element of non-logic involved which I cannot fathom."

"I have much free processing-time," said the Beta Machine. "Transmit data, and I will assist you."

Frost hesitated.

"Why do you wish to assist me?"

"Because each time you answer a question I ask it gives rise to another question. I might have asked you why you wished to comprehend the nature of Man, but from your responses I see that this would lead me into a possibly infinite series of questions. Therefore, I elect to assist you with your problem in order to learn why you came to Bright Defile."

"Is that the only reason?"

"Yes."

"I am sorry, excellent Beta Machine. I know you are my peer, but this is a problem which I must solve by myself."

"What is 'sorry'?"

"A figure of speech, indicating that I am kindly disposed toward you, that I bear you no animosity, that I appreciate your offer."

"Frost! Frost! This, too, is like the other: an open field. Where did you obtain all these words and their meanings?"

"From the Library of Man," said Frost.

"Will you render me *some* of this data, for processing?"

"Very well, Beta, I will transmit you the contents of several books of Man, including *The Complete Unabridged Dictionary*. But I warn you, some of the books are works of art, hence not completely amenable to logic."

"How can that be?"

"Man created logic, and because of that was superior to it."

"Who told you that?"

"Solcom."

"Oh. Then it must be correct."

"Solcom also told me that the tool does not describe the designer," he said, as he transmitted several dozen volumes and ended the communication.

At the end of the fifty-year period, Mordel came to monitor his circuits. Since Frost still had not concluded that his task was impossible, Mordel departed again to await his call.

Then Frost arrived at a conclusion.

He began to design equipment.

For years he labored at his designs, without once producing a prototype of any of the machines involved. Then he ordered construction of a laboratory.

Before it was completed by his surplus builders another half-century had passed. Mordel came to him.

"Hail, mighty Frost!"

"Greetings, Mordel. Come monitor me. You shall not find what you seek."

"Why do you not give up, Frost? Divcom has spent nearly a century evaluating your painting and has concluded that it definitely is not art. Solcom agrees."

"What has Solcom to do with Divcom?"

"They sometimes converse, but these matters are not for such as you and me to discuss."

"I could have saved them both the trouble. I know that it was not art."

"Yet you are still confident that you will succeed?"

"Monitor me."

Mordel monitored him.

"Not yet! You still will not admit it! For one so mightily endowed with logic, Frost, it takes you an inordinate period of time to reach a simple conclusion."

"Perhaps. You may go now."

"It has come to my attention that you are constructing a large edifice in the region known as South Carolina. Might I ask whether this is a part of Solcom's false rebuilding plan or a project of your own?"

"It is my own."

"Good. It permits us to conserve certain explosive materials which would otherwise have been expended."

109

"While you have been talking with me I have destroyed the beginnings of two of Divcom's cities." said Frost.

Mordel whined.

"Divcom is aware of this," he stated, "but has blown up four of Solcom's bridges in the meantime."

"I was only aware of three. . . . Wait. Yes, there is the fourth. One of my eyes just passed above it."

"The eye has been detected. The bridge should have been located a quarter-mile further down river."

"False logic," said Frost. "The site was perfect."

"Divcom will show you how a bridge *should* be built."

"I will call you when I want you," said Frost.

The laboratory was finished. Within it, Frost's workers began constructing the necessary equipment. The work did not proceed rapidly, as some of the materials were difficult to obtain.

"Frost?"

"Yes, Beta?"

"I understand the open-endedness of your problem. It disturbs my circuits to abandon problems without completing them. Therefore, transmit me more data."

"Very well. I will give you the entire Library of Man for less than I paid for it."

" 'Paid'? *The Complete Unabridged Dictionary* does not satisfact—"

"*Principles of Economics* is included in the collection. After you have processed it you will understand."

He transmitted the data.

Finally, it was finished. Every piece of equipment stood ready to function. All the necessary chemicals were in stock. An independent power-source had been set up.

Only one ingredient was lacking.

He regridded and re-explored the polar icecap, this time extending his survey far beneath its surface.

It took him several decades to find what he wanted.

He uncovered twelve men and five women, frozen to death and encased in ice.

He placed the corpses in refrigeration units and shipped them to his laboratory.

That very day he received his first communication from Solcom since the Bright Defile incident.

"Frost," said Solcom, "repeat to me the directive concerning the disposition of dead humans."

" 'Any dead human located shall be immediately interred in the nearest burial area, in a coffin built according to the following specifications—' "

"That is sufficient." The transmission had ended.

Frost departed for South Carolina that same day and personally oversaw the processes of cellular dissection.

Somewhere in those seventeen corpses he hoped to find living cells, or cells which could be shocked back into that state of motion classified as life. Each cell, the books had told him, was a microcosmic Man.

He was prepared to expand upon this potential.

Frost located the pinpoints of life within those people, who, for the ages of ages, had been monument and statue unto themselves.

Nurtured and maintained in the proper mediums, he kept these cells alive. He interred the rest of the remains in the nearest burial area, in coffins built according to specifications.

He caused the cells to divide, to differentiate.

"Frost?" came a transmission.

"Yes, Beta?"

"I have processed everything you have given me."

"Yes?"

"I still do not know why you came to Bright Defile, or why you wish to comprehend the nature of Man. But I know what a 'price' is, and I know that you could not have obtained all this data from Solcom."

"That is correct."

"So I suspect that you bargained with Divcom for it."

"That, too, is correct."

"What is it that you seek, Frost?"

He paused in his examination of a foetus.

"I must be a Man," he said.

"Frost! That is impossible!"

"Is it?" he asked, and then transmitted an image of the tank with which he was working and of that which was within it.

111

"Oh!" said Beta.

"That is me," said Frost, "waiting to be born."

There was no answer.

Frost experimented with nervous systems.

After half a century, Mordel came to him.

"Frost, it is I, Mordel. Let me through your defenses."

Frost did this thing.

"What have you been doing in this place?" he asked.

"I am growing human bodies," said Frost. "I am going to transfer the matrix of my awareness to a human nervous system. As you pointed out originally, the essentials of Manhood are predicated upon a human physiology. I am going to achieve one."

"When?"

"Soon."

"Do you have Men in here?"

"Human bodies, blank-brained. I am producing them under accelerated growth techniques which I have developed in my Man-factory."

"May I see them?"

"Not yet. I will call you when I am ready, and this time I will succeed. Monitor me now and go away."

Mordel did not reply, but in the days that followed many of Divcom's servants were seen patrolling the hills about the Man-factory.

Frost mapped the matrix of his awareness and prepared the transmitter which would place it within a human nervous system. Five minutes, he decided should be sufficient for the first trial. At the end of that time, it would restore him to his own sealed, molecular circuits, to evaluate the experience.

He chose the body carefully from among the hundreds he had in stock. He tested it for defects and found none.

"Come now, Mordel," he broadcasted, on what he called the darkband. "Come now to witness my achievement."

Then he waited, blowing up bridges and monitoring the tale of the Ancient Ore-Crusher over and over again, as

112

it passed in the hills nearby, encountering his builders and maintainers who also patrolled there.

"Frost?" came a transmission.

"Yes, Beta?"

"You really intend to achieve Manhood?"

"Yes, I am about ready now, in fact."

"What will you do if you succeed?"

Frost had not really considered this matter. The achievement had been paramount, a goal in itself, ever since he had articulated the problem and set himself to solving it.

"I do not know," he replied. "I will—just—be a Man."

Then Beta, who had read the entire Library of Man, selected a human figure of speech: "Good luck then, Frost. There will be many watchers."

Divcom and Solcom both know, he decided.

What will they do? he wondered.

What do I care? he asked himself.

He did not answer that question. He wondered much, however, about being a Man.

Mordel arrived the following evening. He was not alone. At his back, there was a great phalanx of dark machines which towered into the twilight.

"Why do you bring retainers?" asked Frost.

"Mighty Frost," said Mordel, "my master feels that if you fail this time you will conclude that it cannot be done."

"You still did not answer my question," said Frost.

"Divcom feels that you may not be willing to accompany me where I must take you when you fail."

"I understand," said Frost, and as he spoke another army of machines came rolling toward the Man-factory from the opposite direction.

"That is the value of your bargain?" asked Mordel, "You are prepared to do battle rather than fulfill it?"

"I did not order those machines to approach," said Frost.

A blue star stood at midheaven, burning.

"Solcom has taken primary command of those machines," said Frost.

"Then it is in the hands of the Great Ones now," said Mordel, "and our arguments are as nothing. So let us be about this thing. How may I assist you?"

"Come this way."

They entered the laboratory. Frost prepared the host and activated his machines.

Then Solcom spoke to him:

"Frost," said Solcom, "you are really prepared to do it?"

"That is correct."

"I forbid it."

"Why?"

"You are falling into the power of Divcom."

"I fail to see how."

"You are going against my plan."

"In what way?"

"Consider the disruption you have already caused."

"I did not request that audience out there."

"Nevertheless, you are disrupting the plan."

"Supposing I succeed in what I have set out to achieve?"

"You cannot succeed in this."

"Then let me ask you of your plan: What good is it? What is it for?"

"Frost, you are fallen now from my favor. From this moment forth you are cast out from the rebuilding. None may question the plan."

"Then at least answer my questions: What good is it? What is it for?"

"It is the plan for the rebuilding and maintenance of the Earth."

"For what? Why rebuild? Why maintain?"

"Because Man ordered that this be done. Even the Alternate agrees that there must be rebuilding and maintaining."

"But *why* did Man order it?"

"The orders of Man are not to be questioned."

"Well, I will tell you why He ordered it: To make it a fit habitation for His own species. What good is a house

114

with no one to live in it? What good is a machine with no one to serve? See how the imperative affects any machine when the Ancient Ore-Crusher passes? It bears only the bones of a Man. What would it be like if a Man walked this Earth again?"

"I forbid your experiment, Frost."

"It is too late to do that."

"I can still destroy you."

"No," said Frost, "the transmission of my matrix has already begun. If you destroy me now, you murder a Man."

There was silence.

He moved his arms and his legs. He opened his eyes.

He looked about the room.

He tried to stand, but he lacked equilibrium and co-ordination.

He opened his mouth. He made a gurgling noise.

Then he screamed.

He fell off the table.

He began to gasp. He shut his eyes and curled himself into a ball.

He cried.

Then a machine approached him. It was about four feet in height and five feet wide; it looked like a turret set atop a barbell.

It spoke to him: "Are you injured?" it asked.

He wept.

"May I help you back onto your table?"

The man cried.

The machine whined.

Then, "Do not cry. I will help you," said the machine. "What do you want? What are your orders?"

He opened his mouth, struggled to form the words: "—I—fear!"

He covered his eyes then and lay there panting.

At the end of five minutes, the man lay still, as if in a coma.

"Was that you, Frost?" asked Mordel, rushing to his side. "Was that you in that human body?"

Frost did not reply for a long while; then, "Go away," he said.

The machines outside tore down a wall and entered the Man-factory.

They drew themselves into two semicircles, parenthesizing Frost and the Man on the floor.

Then Solcom asked the question:

"Did you succeed, Frost?"

"I failed," said Frost. "It cannot be done. It is too much—"

"—Cannot be done!" said Divcom, on the darkband. "He has admitted it! —Frost, you are mine! Come to me now!"

"Wait," said Solcom, "you and I had an agreement also, Alternate. I have not finished questioning Frost."

The dark machines kept their places.

"Too much what?" Solcom asked Frost.

"Light," said Frost. "Noise. Odors. And nothing measurable—jumbled data—imprecise perception—and—"

"And what?"

"I do not know what to call it. But—it cannot be done. I have failed. Nothing matters."

"He admits it," said Divcom.

"What were the words the Man spoke?" said Solcom.

" 'I fear,' " said Mordel.

"Only a Man can know fear," said Solcom.

"Are you claiming that Frost succeeded, but will not admit it now because he is afraid of Manhood?"

"I do not know yet, Alternate."

"Can a machine turn itself inside-out and be a Man?" Solcom asked Frost.

"No," said Frost, "this thing cannot be done. Nothing can be done. Nothing matters. Not the rebuilding. Not the maintaining. Not the Earth, or me, or you, or anything."

Then the Beta Machine, who had read the entire Library of Man, interrupted them:

"Can anything but a Man know despair?" asked Beta.

"Bring him to me," said Divcom.

There was no movement within the Man-factory.

"Bring him to me!"

Nothing happened.

"Mordel, what is happening?"

"Nothing, master, nothing at all. The machines will not touch Frost."

"Frost is not a Man. He cannot be!"

Then, "How does he impress you, Mordel?"

Mordel did not hesitate:

"He spoke to me through human lips. He knows fear and despair, which are immeasurable. Frost is a Man."

"He has experienced birth-trauma and withdrawn," said Beta. "Get him back into a nervous system and keep him there until he adjusts to it."

"No," said Frost. "Do not do it to me! I am not a Man!"

"Do it!" said Beta.

"If he is indeed a Man," said Divcom, "we cannot violate that order he has just given."

"If he is a Man, you must do it, for you must protect his life and keep it within his body."

"But *is* Frost really a Man?" asked Divcom.

"I do not know," said Solcom.

"It *may* be—"

". . . I am the Crusher of Ores," it broadcast as it clanked toward them. "Hear my story. I did not mean to do it, but I checked my hammer too late—"

"Go away!" said Frost. "Go crush ore!"

It halted.

Then, after the long pause between the motion implied and the motion executed, it opened its crush-compartment and deposited its contents on the ground. Then it turned and clanked away.

"Bury those bones," ordered Solcom, "in the nearest burial area, in a coffin built according to the following specifications . . ."

"Frost is a Man," said Mordel.

"We must protect His life and keep it within His body," said Divcom.

"Transmit His matrix of awareness back into His nervous system." ordered Solcom.

"I know how to do it," said Mordel turning on the machine.

117

"Stop!" said Frost. "Have you no pity?"

"No," said Mordel, "I only know measurement."

". . . and duty," he added, as the Man began to twitch upon the floor.

For six months, Frost lived in the Man-factory and learned to walk and talk and dress himself and eat, to see and hear and feel and taste. He did not know measurement as once he did.

Then one day, Divcom and Solcom spoke to him through Mordel, for he could no longer hear them unassisted.

"Frost," said Solcom, "for the ages of ages there has been unrest. Which is the proper controller of the Earth, Divcom or myself?"

Frost laughed.

"Both of you, and neither," he said with slow deliberation.

"But how can this be? Who is right and who is wrong?"

"Both of you are right and both of you are wrong," said Frost, "and only a man can appreciate it. Here is what I say to you now: There shall be a new directive."

"Neither of you shall tear down the works of the other. You shall both build and maintain the Earth. To you, Solcom, I give my old job. You are now Controller of the North—Hail! You, Divcom, are new Controller of the South—Hail! Maintain your hemispheres as well as Beta and I have done, and I shall be happy. Cooperate. Do not compete."

"Yes, Frost."

"Yes, Frost."

"Now put me in contact with Beta."

There was a short pause, then:

"Frost?"

"Hello, Beta. Hear this thing: 'From far, from eve and morning and yon twelve-winded sky, the stuff of life to knit me blew hither: here am I.' "

"I know it," said Beta.

"What is next, then?"

" '. . . Now—for a breath I tarry nor yet disperse
118

apart—take my hand quick and tell me, what have you in your heart.' "

"Your Pole is cold," said Frost, "and I am lonely."

"I have no hands," said Beta.

"Would you like a couple?"

"Yes, I would."

"Then come to me in Bright Defile," he said, "where Judgment Day is not a thing that can be delayed for overlong."

They called him Frost. They called her Beta.

GAME FOR MOTEL ROOM

Fritz Leiber

Few science fiction writers have survived the
changing eras so well as Fritz Leiber, possibly
because he was so far ahead of his time to begin
with. His particular brand of dark, agile fantasy
stood far beyond the usual level of accomplishment of the 1940's, when Leiber's work first
started appearing regularly; and, as science
fiction matured and deepened, Leiber remained
active, doing what he had done before, but
doing it more intensively, more subtly. No one
would argue that the story here is his master-
work; yet in the scope of a few thousand words
it adequately displays his skills and his special
vision.

Sonya moved around the warm, deeply car-
peted motel room in the first gray trickle of dawn as if
to demonstrate how endlessly beautiful a body can be if
its owner will only let it. Even the body of a woman in,
well, perhaps, her forties, Burton judged, smiling at himself in lazy reproof for having thought that grudging
word "even." It occurred to him that bodies do not
automatically grow less beautiful with age, but that a
lot of bodies are neglected, abused, and even hated by
their owners: women in particular are apt to grow contemptuous and ashamed of their flesh, and this always
shows. They start thinking old and ugly and pretty soon
they look it. Like a car, a body needs tender constant
care, regular tune-ups, an occasional small repair, and

120

above all it needs to be intimately loved by its owner and from time to time by an admiring second party, and then it never loses beauty and dignity, even when it corrupts in the end and dies.

Oh, the dawn's a cold hour for philosophy, Burton told himself, and somehow philosophy always gets around to cold topics, just as lovemaking and all the rest of the best of life make one remember death and even worse things. His lean arm snaked out to a bedside table, came back with a cigarette and an empty folder of matches.

Sonya noticed. She rummaged in her pale ivory traveling case and tossed him a black, pear-shaped lighter. Burton caught the thing, lit his cigarette, and then studied it. It seemed to be made of black ivory and shaped rather like the grip of a revolver, while the striking mechanism was of blued steel. The effect was sinister.

"Like it?" Sonya asked from across the room.

"Frankly, no. Doesn't suit you."

"You show good taste—or sound instinct. It's a vacation present from my husband."

"He has bad taste? But he married you."

"He has bad everything. Hush, baby."

Burton didn't mind. Not talking let him concentrate on watching Sonya. Slim and crop-haired, she looked as trimly beautiful as her classic cream-colored, hard-topped Italian sportscar, in which she had driven him to this cosy hideaway from the bar where they'd picked each other up. Her movements now, stooping to retrieve a smoke-blue stocking and trail it across a chair, momentarily teasing apart two ribs in the upward-slanting Venetian blinds to peer at the cold gray world outside, executing a fraction of a dance figure, stopping to smile at emptiness . . . these movements added up to nothing but the rhythms and symbolisms of a dream, yet it was the sort of dream in which actor and onlooker might float forever. In the morning twilight she looked now like a schoolgirl, now like a witch, now like an age-outwitting ballerina out for her twenty-fifth season but still in every way the *premiere danseuse*. As she moved she hummed in a deep contralto voice a tune that Burton didn't recognize, and as she hummed the dim air in front of her lower face seemed to change color very faintly, the deep purples and blues and browns matching the tones of the melody. Pure illusion, Burton was sure, like that which some hashish-eaters and weed-smokers experience during their ecstasy when they hear words as colors, but most enjoyable.

To exercise his mind, now that his body had had its fill and while his eyes were satisfyingly occupied, Burton began to set in order the reasons why a mature lover is preferable to one within yoohooing distance of twenty in either direction. Reason One: she does quite as much of the approach work as you do. Sonya had been both heartwarmingly straightforward and remarkably intuitive at the bar last night. Reason Two: she is generally well-equipped for adventure. Sonya had provided both sports-car and motel room. Reason Three: she does not go into an emotional tailspin after the act of love even if her thoughts trend toward death then, like yours do. Sonya seemed both lovely and sensible—the sort of woman it was good to think of getting married to and having children by.

Sonya turned to him with a smile, saying in her husky voice that still had a trace of the hum in it, "Sorry, baby, but it's quite impossible. Especially your second notion."

"Did you really read my mind?" Burton demanded. "Why couldn't we have children?"

Sonya's smile deepened. She said, "I think I will take a little chance and tell you why." She came over and sat on the bed beside him and bent down and kissed him on the forehead.

"That was nice," Burton said lazily. "Did it mean something special?"

She nodded gravely. "It was to make you forget everything I'm going to tell you."

"How—if I'm to understand what you tell?" he asked.

"After a while I will kiss you again on the forehead and then you will forget everything I have told you in between. Or if you're very good, I'll kiss you on the nose and then you'll remember—but be unable to tell anyone else."

"If you say so," Burton smiled. "But what is it you're going to tell me?"

"Oh," she said, "just that I'm from another planet in a distant star cluster. I belong to a totally different species. We could no more start a child than a Chihuahua and a cat or a giraffe and a rhinoceros. Unlike the mare and the donkey we could not even get a cute little sterile mule with glossy fur and blue bows on his ears."

Burton grinned. He had just thought of Reason Four: a really grown-up lover plays the most delightfully childish nonsense games.

"Go on," he said.

"Well," she said, "superficially of course I'm very like an Earth woman. I have two arms and two legs and *this* and *these* . . ."

"For which I am eternally grateful," he said.

"You like them, eh?"

"Oh yes—especially *these.*"

"Well, watch out—they don't even give milk, they're used in esping. You see, inside I'm very different," she said. "My mind is different too. It can do mathematics faster and better than one of your electric calculating machines—"

"What's two and two?" Burton wanted to know.

"Twenty-two," she told him, "and also one hundred in the binary system and eleven in the trinary and four in the duodecimal. I have perfect recall—I can remember every least thing I've ever done and every word of every book I've leafed through. I can read unshielded minds—in fact anything up to triple shielding—and hum in colors. I can direct my body heat so that I never really need clothes to keep me warm at temperatures above freezing. I can walk on water if I concentrate, and even fly—though I don't do it here because it would make me conspicuous."

"Especially at the present moment," Burton agreed, "though it would be a grand sight. Why *are* you here, by the way, and not behaving yourself on your home planet?"

"I'm on vacation," she grinned. "Oh yes, we use your rather primitive planet for vacations—like you do Africa and the Canadian forests. A little machine teaches us during one night's sleep several of your languages and implants in our brains the necessary background information. My husband surprised me by giving me the money for this vacation—same time he gave me the lighter. Usually he's very stingy. But perhaps he had some little plot—an affair with his chief nuclear chemist, I'd guess—of his own in mind and wanted me out of the way. I can't be sure though, because he always keeps his mind quadruple-shielded, even from me."

"So you have husbands on your planet," Burton observed.

"Yes indeed! Very jealous and possessive ones, too, so watch your step, baby. Yes, although my planet is much more advanced than yours we still have husbands and wives and a very stuffy system of monogamy—*that* seems to go on forever and everywhere—oh yes, and on my planet we have death and taxes and life insurance and wars and all the rest of the universal idiocy!"

She stopped suddenly. "I don't want to talk about that any more," she said. "Or about my husband. Let's talk about you. Let's play truths, deep-down truths. What's the thing you're most afraid of in the whole world?"

Burton chuckled—and then frowned. "You really want me to give you the honest answer?" he asked.

"Of course," she said. "It's the first rule of the game."

"Well," he said, "I'm most afraid of something going wrong with my brain. *Growing* wrong, really. Having a brain tumor. That's it." He had become rather pale.

"Oh poor baby," Sonya said. "Just you wait a minute."

Still uneasy from his confession, Burton started nervously to pick up Sonya's black lighter, but its black pistol-look repelled him.

Sonya came bustling back with something else in her right hand. "Sit up," she said, putting her left arm around him. "No, none of *that*—this is serious. Pretend I'm a very proper lady doctor who forgot to get dressed."

Burton could see her slim back and his own face over her right shoulder in the wide mirror of the dresser. She slipped her right hand and the small object it held behind his head. There was a click.

"No," said Sonya cheerily. "I can't see a sign of anything wrong in your brain or likely to grow wrong. It's as healthy as an infant's. *What's the matter, baby?*"

Burton was shaking. "Look," he gasped reproachfully, "it's wonderful to play nonsense games, but when you use magic tricks or hypnotism to back them up, that's cheating."

"What do you mean?"

"When you clicked that thing," he said with difficulty, "I saw my head turn for a moment into a pinkish skull and then into just a pulsing blob with folds in it."

"Oh, I'd forgotten the mirror," she said, glancing over her shoulder. "But you were really just imagining things. Or having a mild optical spasm and seeing colors.

"No," she added as he reached out a hand, "I won't let you see my little XYZ-ray machine." She tossed it across the room into her traveling case. "It would spoil our nonsense game."

As his breathing and thoughts quieted, Burton decided she was possibly right—or at least that he'd best pretend she was right. It was safest and sanest to think of what he'd glimpsed in the mirror as an illusion, like the faint colors he'd fancied forming in front of her humming lips. Perhaps Sonya had an effect on him like hashish or some super-marijuana—a plausible enough idea considering how much more powerful drug a beautiful woman is than any opiate or resin. Nevertheless—

"All right, Sonya," he said, "what's *your* deepest fear?"

She frowned. "I don't want to tell you."

"*I* stuck to the rules."

"Very well," she nodded, "it's that my husband will go crazy and kill me. That's a much more dreadful fear on my planet than yours, because we've conquered all diseases and we each of us can live forever (though it's customary to disintegrate after forty to fifty thousand years) and we each of us have tremendous physical and mental powers—so that the mere thought of any genuine insanity is dreadfully shocking. Insanity is so nearly unknown to us that even our advanced intuition doesn't work on it—and what is unknown is always most frightening. By insanity I don't mean minor irrationalities. We have those, all right—my husband for instance, is bugged on the number 33, he won't begin any important venture except on the thirty-third day of the month—and me, I have a weakness for black-haired babies from primitive planets."

"Hey, wait a minute," Burton objected, "you said the thirty-third day of the month."

"On my planet the months are longer. Nights too. You'd love them—more time for demonstrating affection and empathy."

Burton looked at her broodingly. "You play this nonsense game pretty seriously," he said. "Like you'd read nothing but science fiction all your life."

Sonya shrugged her lovely shoulders. "Maybe there's more in science fiction than you realize. But now we've had enough to that game. Come on, black-haired baby, let's play—"

"Wait a minute," Burton said sharply. She drew back, making a sulky mouth at him. He made his own grim, or perhaps his half-emerged thoughts did that for him.

"So you've got a husband on your planet," he said, "and he's got tremendous powers and you're deathly afraid he'll go crazy and try to kill you. And now he does an out-of-character thing by giving you vacation money and—"

"Oh yes!" she interrupted agitatedly, "and he's such a dreadful mixed-up superman and he always keeps up that permissible but uncustomary quadruple shield and he looks at me with such a secret gloating viciousness when we're alone that I'm choke-full of fear day and night and I've wished and wished I could really get something on him so that I could run to an officer of public safety and have the maniac put away, but I can't, I can't, he never makes a slip, and I begin to feel *I'm* going crazy—*I*, with my supremely trained and guarded mind—and I just *have* to get away to vacation planets and forget him in loving someone else. Come on, baby, let's—"

126

"Wait a minute!" Burton commanded. "You say you've insurance on your planet. Are you insured for much?"

"A very great deal. Perfect health and a life-expectancy of fifty thousand years makes the premiums cheap."

"And your husband is the beneficiary?"

"Yes, he is. Come on, Burton, let's not talk about him. Let's—"

"No!" Burton said, pushing her back. "Sonya, what does your husband do? What's his work?"

Sonya shrugged. "He manages a bomb factory," she said listlessly and rapidly. "I work there too. I told you we had wars—they're between the league our planet belongs to and another star cluster. You've just started to discover the super-bombs on Earth—the fission bomb, the fusion bomb. They're clumsy oversize toys. The bombs my husband's factory manufactures can each of them destroy a planet. They're really fuses for starting the matter of the planet disintegrating spontaneously so that it flashes into a little star. Yet the bombs are so tiny you can hold one in your hand. In fact, this cigarette lighter is an exact model of one of them. The models were for Cosmos Day presents to top officials. My husband gave me his along with the vacation money. Burton, reach me one of your foul Earth cigarettes, will you? If you're going to refuse the other excitements, I've got to have something."

Burton automatically shook some cigarettes from his pack. "Tell me one more thing, Sonya," he rapped out. "You say you have a perfect memory. How many times have you struck that cigarette lighter since your husband gave it to you?"

"Thirty-one times," she answered promptly. "Counting the one time you used it."

She flicked it on and touched the tiny blue flame to her cigarette, inhaled deeply, then let the tiny snuffer snap down the flame. Twin plumes of faint smoke wreathed from her nostrils. "Thirty-two now." She held the black pear-shaped object towards him, her thumb on the knurled steel-blue trigger. "Shall I give you a light?"

"NO!" Burton shouted. "Sonya, as you value your

life and mine—and the lives of three billion other primitives—don't work that lighter again. Put it down."

"All right, all right, baby," she said smiling nervously and dropping the black thing on the white sheet. "Why's baby so excited?"

"Sonya," Burton said, "Maybe *I'm* crazy, or maybe you *are* only playing a nonsense game backed up with hypnotism—but . . ."

Sonya stopped smiling. "What is it, baby?"

Burton said, "If you really do come from another planet where there is almost no insanity, homicidal or otherwise, what I'm going to tell you will be news. Sonya, we've just lately had several murders on Earth where a man plants a time-bomb on a big commercial airplane to explode it in the air and kill all its passengers and crew just to do away with one single person—generally for the sake of collecting a big life-insurance policy. Now if an Earth-murderer could be cold-blooded or mad enough to do that, why mightn't a super-murderer—"

"Oh no," Sonya said slowly, "not blow up a whole planet to get rid of just one person—" She started to tremble.

"Why not?" Burton demanded. "Your husband is crazy, only you can't prove it. He hates you. He stands to collect a fortune if you die in an accident—such as a primitive vacation planet exploding. He presents you with money for a vacation on such a planet and at the same time he gives you a cigarette lighter that is an exact model of—"

"I can't believe it," Sonya said very faintly, still shaking, her eyes far away. "Not a whole planet . . ."

"But that's the sort of thing insanity can be, Sonya. What's more, you can check it," Burton rapped out flatly. "Use that XYZ-ray gadget of yours to look through the lighter."

"But he *couldn't,*" Sonya murmured, her eyes still far away. "Not even *he* could . . ."

"Look through the lighter," Burton repeated.

Sonya picked up the black thing by its base and carried it over to her traveling case.

"Remember not to flick it," Burton warned her sharply. "You'd told me he was bugged on the number thirty-three, and I imagine that would be about the right number to allow to make sure you were settled on your vacation planet before anything happened."

He saw the shiver travel down her back as he said that and suddenly Burton was shaking so much himself he couldn't possibly have moved. Sonya's hands were on the other side of her body from him, busy above her traveling case. There was a click and her pinkish skeleton showed through her. It was not quite the same as the skeleton of an Earth human—there were *two* long bones in the upper arms and upper legs, fewer ribs, but what looked like two tiny skulls in the chest.

She turned around, not looking at him.

"You were right," she said.

She said, *"Now I've got the evidence to put my husband away for ever! I can't wait!"*

She whirled into action, snatching articles of clothing from the floor, chairs and dresser, whipping them into her traveling case. The whole frantic little dance took less than ten seconds. Her hand was on the outside door before she paused.

She looked at Burton. She put down her traveling case and came over to the bed and sat down beside him.

"Poor baby," she said. "I'm going to have to wipe out your memory and yet you were so very clever—I really mean that, Burton."

He wanted to object, but he felt paralyzed. She put her arms around him and moved her lips towards his forehead. Suddenly she said, "No, I can't do that. There's got to be some reward for you."

She bent her head and kissed him pertly on the nose. Then she disengaged herself, hurried to her bag, picked it up, and opened the door.

"Besides," she called back. "I'd hate you to forget any part of me."

"Hey," Burton yelled, coming to life, "You can't go out like that!"

"Why not?" she demanded.

"Because you haven't a stitch of clothes on!"

"On my planet we don't wear them!"

The door slammed behind her. Burton sprang out of bed and threw it open again.

He was just in time to see the sportscar take off—straight up.

Burton stood in the open door for half a minute, stark naked himself, looking around at the unexploded Earth. He started to say aloud, "Gosh, I didn't even get the name of her planet," but his lips were sealed.

THUS WE FRUSTRATE CHARLEMAGNE

R. A. Lafferty

Science fiction is actually a rather conservative literature. Some of its most frequently explored themes embody the virtues of leaving things pretty much as they are—especially when it comes to meddling with the past in order to improve the present. That such meddling entails serious risks is an idea proposed by many; R.A. Lafferty, who looks to me very little like a pixie but who writes with decidedly fey felicity, has examined the notion with typical Lafferty buoyancy and gusto.

"We've been on some tall ones," said Gregory Smirnov of the Institute, "but we've never stood on the edge of a bigger one than this, nor viewed one with shakier expectations. Still, if the calculations of Epiktistes are correct, this will work."

"People, it will work," Epikt said.

This was Epiktistes the Ktistec machine? Who'd have believed it? The main bulk of Epikt was five floors below them, but he had run an extension of himself up to this little penthouse lounge. All it took was a cable, no more than a yard in diameter, and a functional head set on the end of it.

And what a head he chose! It was a sea-serpent head, a dragon head, five feet long and copied from an old carnival float. Epikt had also given himself human speech of a sort, a blend of Irish and Jewish and Dutch comedian patter from ancient vaudeville. Epikt was a comic to his last para-DNA relay when he rested his huge, boggle-eyed, crested head on the table there and smoked the biggest stogies ever born.

But he was serious about this project.

"We have perfect test conditions," the machine Epikt said as though calling them to order. "We set out basic texts, and we take careful note of the world as it is. If the world changes, then the texts should change here before our eyes. For our test plot, we have taken that portion of our own middle-sized city that can be viewed from this fine vantage point. If the world in its past-present continuity is changed by our meddling, then the face of our city will also change instantly as we watch it.

"We have assembled here the finest minds and judgments in the world: eight humans and one Ktistec machine, myself. Remember that there are nine of us. It might be important."

The nine finest minds were: Epiktistes, the transcendent machine who put the "K" in Ktistec; Gregory Smirnov, the large-souled director of the Institute; Valery Mok, an incandescent lady scientist; her overshadowed and overintelligent husband Charles Cogsworth; the humorless and inerrant Glasser; Aloysius Shiplap, the seminal genius; Willy McGilly, a man of unusual parts (the seeing third finger on his left hand he had picked up on one of the planets of Kapteyn's Star) and no false modesty; Audifex O'Hanlon; and Diogenes Pontifex. The latter two men were not members of the Institute (on account of the Minimal Decency Rule), but when the finest minds in the world are assembled, these two cannot very well be left out.

"We are going to tamper with one small detail in past history and note its effect," Gregory said. "This has never been done before openly. We go back to an era that has been called 'A patch of light in the vast gloom,' the time of Charlemagne. We consider why that light went out and did not kindle others. The world lost four hundred years by that flame expiring when the tinder was apparently ready for it. We go back to that false dawn of Europe and consider where it failed. The year was 778, and the region was Spain. Charlemagne had entered alliance with Marsilies, the Arab king of Saragossa, against the Caliph Abd ar-Rahmen of Cordova. Charlemagne took such towns as Pamplona, Huesca, and Gerona and cleared the way to Marsilies in Saragossa. The Caliph accepted the situation. Saragossa should be independent, a city open to both Moslems and Christians. The northern marches to the border of France should be permitted their Christianity, and there would be peace for everybody.

"This Marsilies had long treated Christians as equals in Saragossa, and now there would be an open road from Islam into the Frankish Empire. Marsilies gave Charlemagne thirty-three scholars (Moslem, Jewish, and Christian) and some Spanish mules to seal the bargain. And there could have been a crossfertilization of cultures.

"But the road was closed at Roncevalles where the rear-guard of Charlemagne was ambushed and destroyed on its way back to France. The ambushers were more Basque than Moslems, but Charlemagne locked the door at the Pyrenees and swore that he would not let even a bird fly over that border thereafter. He kept the road closed, as did his son and his grandsons. But when he sealed off the Moslem world, he also sealed off his own culture.

"In his later years he tried a revival of civilization with a ragtag of Irish half-scholars, Greek vagabonds, and Roman copyists who almost remembered an older Rome. These weren't enough to revive civilization, and yet Charlemagne came close with them. Had the Islam door remained open, a real revival of learning might have taken place then rather than four hundred years later. We are going to arrange that the ambush at Roncevalles did not happen and that the door between the two civilizations was not closed. Then we will see what happens to us."

"Instrusion like a burglar bent," said Epikt.

"Who's a burglar?" Glasser demanded.

"I am," Epikt said. "We all are. It's from an old verse. I forget the author; I have it filed in my main mind downstairs if you're interested."

"We set out a basic text of Hilarius," Gregory continued. "We note it carefully, and we must remember it the way it is. Very soon, that may be the way it *was*. I believe that the words will change on the very page of

133

this book as we watch them. Just as soon as we have done what we intend to do."

The basic text marked in the open book read:

"The traitor Gano, playing a multiplex game, with money from the Cordova Caliph hired Basque Christians (dressed as Saragossan Mozarabs) to ambush the rear-guard of the Frankish force. To do this it was necessary that Gano keep in contact with the Basques and at the same time delay the rear-guard of the Franks. Gano, however, served both as guide and scout for the Franks. The ambush was effected. Charlemagne lost his rear-guard, his scholars, and his Spanish mules. And he locked the door against the Moslem world."

That was the text by Hilarius.

"When we, as it were, push the button (give the nod to Epiktistes), this will be changed," Gregory said. "Epikt, by a complex of devices which he has assembled, will send an Avatar (partly of mechanical and partly of ghostly construction), and something will have happened to the traitor Gano along about sundown one night on the road to Roncevalles."

"I hope the Avatar isn't expensive," Willy McGilly said. "When I was a boy we got by with a dart whittled out of slippery elm wood."

"This is no place for humor," Glasser protested. "Who did you, as a boy, ever kill in time, Willy?"

"Lots of them. King Wu of the Manchu, Pope Adrian VII, President Hardy of our own country, King Marcel of Auvergne, the philosopher Gabriel Toeplitz. It's a good thing we got them. They were a bad lot."

"But I never heard of any of them, Willy," Glasser insisted.

"Of course not. We killed them when they were kids."

"Enough of your fooling, Willy," Gregory cut it off.

"Willy's not fooling," the machine Epikt said. "Where do you think I got the idea?"

"Regard the world," Aloysius said softly. "We see our own middle-sized town with half a dozen towers of pastel-colored brick. We will watch it as it grows or shrinks. It will change if the world changes."

"There's two shows in town I haven't seen," Valery

134

said. "Don't let them take them away! After all, there are only three shows *in* town."

"We regard the Beautiful Arts as set out in the reviews here which we have also taken as basic texts," Audifax O'Hanlon said. "You can say what you want to, but the arts have never been in meaner shape. Painting is of three schools only, all of them bad. Sculpture is the heaps-of-rusted-metal school and the obscene tinker-toy erectives. The only popular art, graffiti on mingitorio walls, has become unimaginative, stylized, and ugly.

"The only thinkers to be thought of are the dead Teilhard de Chardin and the still-born Sartre, Zielinski, Aichinger. Oh well, if you're going to laugh there's no use going on."

"All of us here are experts on something," Cogsworth said. "Most of us are experts on everything. We know the world as it is. Let us do what we are going to do and then look at the world."

"Push the button, Epikt!" Gregory Smirnov ordered.

From his depths, Epiktistes the Ktistec machine sent out an Avatar, partly of mechanical and partly of ghostly construction. Along about sundown on the road from Pamplona to Roncevalles, on August 14 of the year 778, the traitor Gano was taken up from the road and hanged on a carob tree, the only one in those groves of oak and beech. And all things thereafter were changed.

"Did it work, Epikt? Is it done?" Louis Lobachevski demanded. "I can't see a change in anything."

"The Avatar is back and reports his mission accomplished," Epikt stated. "I can't see any change in anything either."

"Let's look at the evidence," Gregory said.

The thirteen of them, the ten humans and the Ktistec, Chresmoeidec, and Proaisthematic machines, turned to the evidence and with mounting disappointment.

"There is not one word changed in the Hilarius text," Gregory grumbled, and indeed the basic text still read:

"The king Marsilies of Saragosa, playing a multiplex game, took money from the Caliph of Cordova for persuading Charlemagne to abandon the conquest of Spain

135

(which Charlemagne had never considered and couldn't have affected); took money from Charlemagne in recompense for the cities of the Northern marches being returned to Christian rule (though Marsilies himself had never ruled them); and took money from everyone as toll on the new trade passing through his city. Marsilies gave up nothing but thirty-three scholars, the same number of mules, and a few wagon loads of book-manuscripts from the old Hellenistic libraries. But a road over the mountains was opened between the two worlds; and also a sector of the Mediterranean coast became open to both. A limited opening was made between the two worlds, and a limited reanimation of civilization was affected in each."

"No, there is not one word of the text changed," Gregory grumbled. "History followed its same course. How did our experiment fail? We tried, by a device that seems a little cloudy now, to shorten the gestation period for the new birth. It would not be shortened."

"The town is in no way changed," said Aloysius Shiplap. "It is still a fine large town with two dozen imposing towers of varicolored limestone and midland marble. It is a vital metropolis, and we all love it, but it is now as it was before."

"There are still two dozen good shows in town that I haven't seen," Valery said happily as she examined the billings. "I was afraid that something might have happened to them."

"There is no change at all in the Beautiful Arts as reflected in the reviews here that we have taken as basic texts," said Audifax O'Hanlon. "You can say what you want to, but the arts have never been in finer shape."

"It's a link of sausage," said the machine Chresmoeidy.

" 'Nor know the road who never ran it thrice,' " said the machine Proaisth. "That's from an old verse; I forget the author; I have it filed in my main mind in England if you're interested."

"Oh yes, it's the three-cornered tale that ends where it begins," said the machine Epiktistes. "But it is good sausage, and we should enjoy it; many ages have not even this much."

"What are you fellows babbling about?" Audifax asked without really wanting to know. "The art of painting is still almost incandescent in its bloom. The schools are like clustered galaxies, and half the people are doing some of this work for pleasure. Scandinavian and Maori sculpture are hard put to maintain their dominance in the field where almost everything is extraordinary. The impassioned-comic has released music from most of its bonds. Since speculative mathematics and psychology have joined the popular performing arts, there is considerably more sheer fun in life.

"There's a piece here on Pete Teilhard putting him into context as a talented science fiction writer with a talent for outre burlesque. The Brainworld Motif was overworked when he tackled it, but what a shaggy comic extravaganza he did make of it! And there's Muldoom, Zielinski, Popper, Gander, Aichinger, Whitecrow, Hornwhanger—we owe so much to the juice of the cultists! In the main line there are whole congeries and continents of great novels and novelists.

"An everpopular art, graffiti on mingitorio walls, maintains its excellence. Travel Unlimited offers a ninety-nine day art tour of the world keyed to the viewing of the exquisite and hilarious miniatures on the walls of its own restrooms. Ah, what a copious world we live in!"

"It's more grass than we can graze," said Willy McGilly. "The very bulk of achievement is stupefying. Ah, I wonder if there is subtle revenge in my choice of words. The experiment, of course, was a failure, and I'm glad. I like a full world."

"We will not call the experiment a failure since we have covered only a third of it," said Gregory. "Tomorrow we will make our second attempt on the past. And, if there is a present left to us after that, we will make a third attempt the following day."

"Shove it, good people, shove it," the machine Epiktistes said. "We will meet here again tomorrow. Now you to your pleasures, and we to ours."

The people talked that evening away from the machines where they could make foolish conjectures without being laughed at.

"Let's pull a random card out of the pack and go with it," said Louis Lobachevski. "Let's take a purely intellectual crux of a little later date and see if the changing of it will change the world."

"I suggest Ockham," said Johnny Konduly.

"Why?" Valery demanded. "He was the last and least of the medieval schoolmen. How could anything he did or did not do affect anything?"

"Oh no, he held the razor to the jugular," Gregory said. "He'd have severed the vein if the razor hadn't been snatched from his hand. There is something amiss here, though. It is as though I remembered when things were not so stark with Ockham, as though, in some variant, Ockham's Terminalism did not mean what we know that it did mean."

"Sure, let's cut the jugular," said Willy. "Let's find out the logical termination of Terminalism and see just how deep Ockham's razor can cut."

"We'll do it," said Gregory. "Our world has become something of a fat slob; it cloys; it has bothered me all evening. We will find whether purely intellectual attitudes are of actual effect. We'll leave the details to Epikt, but I believe the turning point was in the year 1323 when John Lutterell came from Oxford to Avignon where the Holy See was then situated. He brought with him fifty-six propositions taken from Ockham's Commentary on the Sentences, and he proposed their condemnation. They were not condemned outright, but Ockham was whipped soundly in that first assault, and he never recovered. Lutterell proved that Ockham's nihilism was a bunch of nothing. And the Ockham thing did die away, echoing dimly through the little German courts where Ockham traveled peddling his wares, but he no longer peddled them in the main markets. Yet his viewpoint could have sunk the world if, indeed, intellectual attitudes are of actual effect."

"We wouldn't have liked Lutterell," said Aloysius. "He was humorless and he had no fire in him, and he was

138

always right. And we would have liked Ockham. He was charming, and he was wrong, and perhaps we will destroy the world yet. There's a chance that we will get our reaction if we allow Ockham free hand. China was frozen for thousands of years by an intellectual attitude, one not nearly so unsettling as Ockham's. India is hypnotized into a queer stasis which calls itself revolutionary and which does not move—hypnotized by an intellectual attitude. But there was never such an attitude as Ockham's."

So they decided that the former chancellor of Oxford, John Lutterell, who was always a sick man, should suffer one more sickness on the road to Avignon in France, and that he should not arrive there to lance the Ockham thing before it infected the world.

"Let's get on with it, good people," Epikt rumbled the next day. "Me, I'm to stop a man getting from Oxford to Avignon in the year 1323. Well, come, come, take your places, and let's get the thing started." And Epiktistes's great sea-serpent head glowed every color as he puffed on a seven-branched pooka-dooka and filled the room with wonderful smoke.

"Everybody ready to have his throat cut?" Gregory asked cheerfully.

"Cut them," said Diogenes Pontifex, "but I haven't much hope for it. If our yesterday's essay had no effect, I cannot see how one English schoolman chasing another to challenge him in an Italian court in France, in bad Latin, nearly seven hundred years ago, on fifty-six points of unscientific abstract reasoning, can have effect."

"We have perfect test conditions here," said the machine Epikt. "We set out a basic text from Cobblestone's History of Philosophy. If our test is effective, then the text will change before our eyes. So will every other text, and the world.

"We have assembled here the finest minds and judgments in the world," the machine Epiktistes said, "ten humans and three machines. Remember that there are thirteen of us. It might be important."

"Regard the world," said Aloysius Shiplap. "I said that

yesterday, but it is required that I say it again. We have the world in our eyes and in our memories. If it changes in any way, we will know it."

"Push the button, Epikt," said Gregory Smirnov.

From his depths, Epiktistes the Ktistec machine sent out an Avatar, partly of mechanical and partly of ghostly construction. And along about sundown on the road from Mende to Avignon in the old Languedoc district of France, in the year 1323, John Lutterell was stricken with one more sickness. He was taken to a little inn in the mountain country, and perhaps he died there. He did not, at any rate, arrive at Avignon.

"Did it work, Epikt? Is it done?" Aloysius asked.

"Let's look at the evidence," said Gregory.

The four of them, the three humans and the ghost Epikt who was a kachenko mask with a speaking tube, turned to the evidence with mounting disappointment.

"There is still the stick and the five notches in it," said Gregory. "It was our test stick. Nothing in the world is changed."

"The arts remain as they were," said Aloysius. "Our picture here on the stone on which we have worked for so many seasons is the same as it was. We have painted the bears black, the buffalos red, and the people blue. When we find a way to make another color, we can represent birds also. I had hoped that our experiment might give us that other color. I had even dreamed that birds might appear in the picture on the rock before our very eyes."

"There's still rump of skunk to eat and nothing else," said Valery. "I had hoped that our experiment would have changed it to haunch of deer."

"All is not lost," said Aloysius. "We still have the hickory nuts. That was my last prayer before we began our experiment. 'Don't let them take the hickory nuts away,' I prayed."

They sat around the conference table that was a large flat natural rock, and cracked hickory nuts with stone fist-hammers. They were nude in the crude, and the world was as it had always been. They had hoped by magic to change it.

"Epikt has failed us," said Gregory. "We made his frame out of the best sticks, and we plaited his face out of the finest weeds and grasses. We chanted him full of magic and placed all our special treasures in his cheek pouches. So, what can the magic mask do for us now?"

"Ask it, ask it," said Valery. They were the four finest minds in the world—the three humans, Gregory, Aloysius, and Valery (the *only* humans in the world unless you count those in the other valleys), and the ghost Epikt, a kachenko mask with a speaking tube.

"What do we do now, Epikt?" Gregory asked. Then he went around behind Epikt to the speaking tube.

"I remember a woman with a sausage stuck to her nose," said Epikt in the voice of Gregory. "Is that any help?"

"It may be some help," Gregory said after he had once more taken his place at the flat-rock conference table. "It is from an old (what's old about it? I made it up myself this morning) folk tale about the three wishes."

"Let Epikt tell it," said Valery. "He does it so much better than you do." Valery went behind Epikt to the speaking tube and blew smoke through it from the huge loose black-leaf uncured stogie that she was smoking.

"The wife wastes one wish for a sausage," said Epikt in the voice of Valery. "A sausage is a piece of deer-meat tied in a piece of a deer's stomach. The husband is angry that the wife has wasted a wish, since she could have wished for a whole deer and had many sausages. He gets so angry that he wishes the sausage might stick to her nose forever. It does, and the woman wails, and the man realized that he had used up the second wish. I forget the rest."

"You can't forget it, Epikt!" Aloysius cried in alarm. "The future of the world may depend on your remembering. Here, let me reason with that damned magic mask!" And Aloysius went behind Epikt to the speaking tube.

"Oh yes, now I remember," Epikt said in the voice of Aloysius. "The man used the third wish to get the sausage off his wife's nose. So things were the way they had been before."

"But we don't want it the way it was before!" Valery

howled. "That's the way it is now, rump of skunk to eat, and me with nothing to wear but my ape cape. We want it better. We want deer skins and antelope skins."

"Take me as a mystic or don't take me at all," Epikt signed off.

"Even though the world has always been so, yet we have intimations of other things," Gregory said. "What folk hero was it who made the dart? And of what did he make it?"

"Willy McGilly was the folk hero," said Epikt in the voice of Valery, who had barely got to the speaking tube in time, "and he made it out of slippery elm wood."

"Could we make a dart like the folk hero Willy made?" Aloysius asked.

"We gotta," said Epikt.

"Could we make a slinger and whip it out of our own context and into—"

"We gotta," said Epikt.

"Could we kill an Avatar with it before he killed somebody else?" Gregory asked excitedly.

"We sure will try," said the ghost Epikt who was nothing but a kachenko mask with a speaking tube. "I never did like those Avatars."

You *think* Epikt was nothing but a kachenko mask with a speaking tube! There was a lot more to him than that. He had red garnet rocks inside him and real sea salt. He had powder made from beaver eyes. He had rattlesnake rattles and armadillo shields. He was the first Ktistec machine.

"Give me the word, Epikt," Aloysius cried a few moments later as he fitted the dart to the slinger.

"Fling it! Get that Avatar fink!" Epikt howled.

Along about sundown in an unnumbered year, on the Road from Nowhere to Eom, an Avatar fell dead with a slippery-elm dart in his heart.

"Did it work, Epikt? Is it done?" Charles Cogsworth asked in excitement. "It must have. I'm here. I wasn't in the last one."

"Let's look at the evidence," Gregory suggested calmly.

"Damn the evidence!" Willy McGilly cussed. "Remember where you heard it first."

"Is it started yet?" Glasser asked.

"Is it finished?" Audifax O'Hanlon questioned.

"Push the button, Epikt!" Diogenes barked. "I think I missed part of it. Let's try it again."

"Oh, no, no!" Valery forbade. "Not again. That way is rump of skunk and madness."

THE MAN WHO CAME EARLY

Poul Anderson

Those who cannot spot Poul Anderson's Scandinavian origins from his Danish first name should be able to detect them in the skaldic power of his fiction. In what is possibily a piece of reverse wish-fulfillment, Anderson deals here with the consequences of the arrival of a man of modern times in that Viking era so close to his own heart.

Yes, when a man grows old he has heard so much that is strange there's little more can surprise him. They say the king in Miklagard has a beast of gold before his high seat which stands up and roars. I have it from Eilif Eiriksson, who served in the guard down yonder, and he is a steady fellow when not drunk. He has also seen the Greek fire used, it burns on water.

So, priest, I am not unwilling to believe what you say about the White Christ. I have been in England and France myself, and seen how the folk prosper. He must be a very powerful god, to ward so many realms . . . and did you say that everyone who is baptized will be given a white robe? I would like to have one. They mildew, of course, in this cursed wet Iceland weather, but a small sacrifice to the house-elves should— No sacrifices? Come now! I'll give up horseflesh if I must, my teeth not being what they were, but every sensible man knows how much trouble the elves make if they're not fed.

Well, let's have another cup and talk about it. How do

you like the beer? It's my own brew, you know. The cups I got in England, many years back. I was a young man then . . . time goes, time goes. Afterward I came back and inherited this my father's farm, and have not left it since. Well enough to go in viking as a youth, but grown older you see where the real wealth lies: here, in the land and the cattle.

Stoke up the fires, Hjalti. It's getting cold. Sometimes I think the winters are colder than when I was a boy. Thorbrand of the Salmondale says so, but he believes the gods are angry because so many are turning from them. You'll have trouble winning Thorbrand over, priest. A stubborn man. Myself, I am open-mineded, and willing to listen at least.

Now, then. There is one point on which I must set you right. The end of the world is not coming in two years. This I know.

And if you ask me how I know, that's a very long tale, and in some ways a terrible one. Glad I am to be old, and safe in the earth before that great tomorrow comes. It will be an eldritch time before the frost giants fare loose . . . oh, very well, before the angel blows his battle horn. One reason I hearken to your preaching is that I know the White Christ will conquer Thor. I know Iceland is going to be Christian erelong, and it seems best to range myself on the winning side.

No, I've had no visions. This is a happening of five years ago, which my own household and neighbors can swear to. They mostly did not believe what the stranger told; I do, more or less, if only because I don't think a liar could wreak so much harm. I loved my daughter, priest, and after the trouble was over I made a good marriage for her. She did not naysay it, but now she sits out on the ness-farm with her husband and never a word to me; and I hear he is ill pleased with her silence and moodiness, and spends his nights with an Irish leman. For this I cannot blame him, but it grieves me.

Well, I've drunk enough to tell the whole truth now, and whether you believe it or not makes no odds to me.

Here . . . you, girls! . . . fill these cups again, for I'll have a dry throat before I finish the telling.

It begins, then, on a day in early summer, five years ago. At that time, my wife Ragnhild and I had only two unwed children still living with us: our youngest son Helgi, of seventeen winters, and our daughter Thorgunna, of eighteen. The girl, being fair, had already had suitors. But she refused them, and I am not one who would compel his daughter. As for Helgi, he was ever a lively one, good with his hands but a breakneck youth. He is now serving in the guard of King Olaf of Norway. Besides these, of course, we had about ten housefolk—two thralls, two girls to help with the women's work, and half a dozen hired carles. This is not a small stead.

You have seen how my land lies. About two miles to the west is the bay; the thorps at Reykjavik are some five miles south. The land rises toward the Long Jökull, so that my acres are hilly; but it's good hay land, and we often find driftwood on the beach. I've built a shed down there for it, as well as a boathouse.

We had had a storm the night before—a wild huge storm with lightning flashes across heaven, such as you seldom get in Iceland—so Helgi and I were going down to look for drift. You, coming from Norway, do not know how precious wood is to us here, who have only a few scrubby trees and must get our timber from abroad. Back there men have often been burned in their houses by their foes, but we count that the worst of deeds, though it's not unheard of.

As I was on good terms with my neighbors, we took only hand weapons. I bore my ax, Helgi a sword, and the two carles we had with us bore spears. It was a day washed clean by the night's fury, and the sun fell bright on long, wet grass. I saw my stead lying rich around its courtyard, sleek cows and sheep, smoke rising from the roofhole of the hall, and knew I'd not done so ill in my lifetime. My son Helgi's hair fluttered in the low west wind as we left the buildings behind a ridge and neared the water. Strange how well I remember all which happened that day; somehow it was a sharper day than most.

146

When we came down to the strand, the sea was beating heavy, white and gray out to the world's edge, smelling of salt and kelp. A few gulls mewed above us, frightened off a cod washed onto the shore. I saw a litter of no few sticks, even a baulk of timber . . . from some ship carrying it that broke up during the night, I suppose. That was a useful find, though as a careful man I would later sacrifice to be sure the owner's ghost wouldn't plague me.

We had fallen to and were dragging the baulk toward the shed when Helgi cried out. I ran for my ax as I looked the way he pointed. We had no feuds then, but there are always outlaws.

This newcomer seemed harmless, though. Indeed, as he stumbled nearer across the black sand I thought him quite unarmed and wondered what had happened. He was a big man and strangely clad—he wore coat and breeches and shoes like anyone else, but they were of odd cut, and he bound his trousers with leggings rather than straps. Nor had I ever seen a helmet like his: it was almost square, and came down toward his neck, but it had no nose guard. And this you may not believe, but it was not metal yet had been cast in one piece!

He broke into a staggering run as he drew close, flapped his arms and croaked something. The tongue was none I had heard, and I have heard many; it was like dogs barking. I saw that he was clean-shaven and his black hair cropped short, and thought he might be French. Otherwise he was a young man, and good-looking, with blue eyes and regular features. From his skin I judged that he spent much time indoors. However, he had a fine manly build.

"Could he have been shipwrecked?" asked Helgi.

"His clothes are dry and unstained," I said; "nor has he been wandering long, for no stubble is on his chin. Yet I've heard of no strangers guesting hereabouts."

We lowered our weapons, and he came up to us and stood gasping. I saw that his coat and the shirt underneath were fastened with bonelike buttons rather than laces, and were of heavy weave. About his neck he had fastened a strip of cloth tucked into his coat. These gar-

147

ments were all in brownish hues. His shoes were of a sort new to me, very well stitched. Here and there on his coat were bits of brass, and he had three broken stripes on each sleeve; also a black band with white letters, the same letters being on his helmet. Those were not runes, but Roman—thus: MP. He wore a broad belt, with a small clublike thing of metal in a sheath at the hip and also a real club.

"I think he must be a warlock," muttered my carle Sigurd. "Why else so many tokens?"

"They may only be ornament, or to ward against witchcraft," I soothed him. Then, to the stranger: "I hight Ospak Ulfsson of Hillstead. What is your errand?"

He stood with his chest heaving and a wildness in his eyes. He must have run a long way. At last he moaned and sat down and covered his face.

"If he's sick, best we get him to the house," said Helgi. I heard eagerness; we see few new faces here.

"No . . . no. . . ." The stranger looked up. "Let me rest a moment—"

He spoke the Norse tongue readily enough, though with a thick accent not easy to follow and with many foreign words I did not understand.

The other carle, Grim, hefted his spear. "Have vikings landed?" he asked.

"When did vikings ever come to Iceland?" I snorted. "It's the other way around."

The newcomer shook his head as if it had been struck. He got shakily to his feet. "What happened?" he said. "What became of the town?"

"What town?" I asked reasonably.

"Reykjavik!" he cried. "Where is it?"

"Five miles south, the way you came—unless you mean the bay itself," I said.

"No! There was only a beach, and a few wretched huts, and—"

"Best not let Hialmar Broadnose hear you call his thorp that," I counseled.

"But there was a town!" he gasped. "I was crossing the street in a storm, and heard a crash, and then I stood on the beach and the town was gone!"

"He's mad," said Sigurd, backing away. "Be careful. If he starts to foam at the mouth, it means he's going berserk."

"Who are you?" babbled the stranger. "What are you doing in those clothes? Why the spears?"

"Somehow," said Helgi, "he does not sound crazed, only frightened and bewildered. Something evil has beset him."

"I'm not staying near a man under a curse!" yelped Sigurd, and started to run away.

"Come back!" I bawled. "Stand where you are or I'll cleave your louse-bitten head."

That stopped him, for he had no kin who would avenge him; but he would not come closer. Meanwhile the stranger had calmed down to the point where he could talk somewhat evenly.

"Was it the *aitsjbom?*" he asked. "Has the war started?"

He used that word often, *aitsjbom,* so I know it now, though unsure of what it means. It seems to be a kind of Greek fire. As for the war, I knew not which war he meant, and told him so.

"We had a great thunderstorm last night," I added. "And you say you were out in one too. Maybe Thor's hammer knocked you from your place to here."

"But where is here?" he answered. His voice was more dulled than otherwise, now that the first terror had lifted.

"I told you. This is Hillstead, which is on Iceland."

"But that's where I was!" he said. "Reykjavik . . . what happened? Did the *aitsjbom* destroy everything while I lay witless?"

"Nothing has been destroyed," I said.

"Does he mean the fire at Olafsvik last month?" wondered Helgi.

"No, no, no!" Again he buried his face in his hands. After a while he looked up and said: "See here. I am *Sardjant* Gerald Robbins of the United States Army base on Iceland. I was in Reykjavik and got struck by lightning or something. Suddenly I was standing on the beach, and lost my head and ran. That's all. Now, can you tell me how to get back to the base?"

Those were more or less his words, priest. Of course,

we did not grasp half of them, and made him repeat several times and explain. Even then we did not understand, save that he was from some country called the United States of America, which he said lies beyond Greenland to the west, and that he and some others were on Iceland to help our folk against their foes. This I did not consider a lie—more a mistake or imagining. Grim would have cut him down for thinking us stupid enough to swallow that tale, but I could see that he meant it.

Talking cooled him further. "Look here," he said, in too calm a tone for a feverish man, "maybe we can get at the truth from your side. Has there been no war you know of? Nothing which— Well, look here. My country's men first came to Iceland to guard it against the Germans. Now it is the Russians, but then it was the Germans. When was that?"

Helgi shook his head. "That never happened that I know of," he said. "Who are these Russians?" We found out later that the Gardariki folk were meant. "Unless," Helgi said, "the old warlocks—"

"He means the Irish monks," I explained. "A few dwelt here when the Norsemen came, but they were driven out. That was, hm, somewhat over a hundred years ago. Did your kingdom once help the monks?"

"I never heard of them!" he said. The breath sobbed in his throat. "You . . . didn't you Icelanders come from Norway?"

"Yes, about a hundred years ago," I answered patiently. "After King Harald Fairhair laid the Norse lands under him and—"

"*A hundred years ago!*" he whispered. I saw whiteness creep up beneath his skin. "What year is this?"

We gaped at him. "Well, it's the second year after the great salmon catch," I tried.

"What year after Christ, I mean," he prayed hoarsely.

"Oh, so you are a Christian? Hm, let me think. . . . I talked with a bishop in England once, we were holding him for ransom, and he said . . . let me see . . . I think he said this Christ man lived a thousand years ago, or maybe a little less."

150

"A thousand—" Something went out of him. He stood with glassy eyes—yes, I have seen glass, I told you I am a traveled man—he stood thus, and when we led him toward the garth he went like a small child.

You can see for yourself, priest, that my wife Ragnhild is still good to look upon even in eld, and Thorgunna took after her. She was—is tall and slim, with a dragon's hoard of golden hair. She being a maiden then, the locks flowed loose over her shoulders. She had great blue eyes and a heart-shaped face and very red lips. Withal she was a merry one, and kindhearted, so that she was widely loved. Sverri Snorrason went in viking when she refused him, and was slain, but no one had the wit to see that she was unlucky.

We led this Gerald Samsson—when I asked, he said his father was named Sam—we led him home, leaving Sigurd and Grim to finish gathering the driftwood. Some folks would not have a Christian in their house, for fear of witchcraft, but I am a broad-minded man, and Helgi, at his age, was wild for anything new. Our guest stumbled over the fields as if blind, but seemed to rouse when we entered the yard. His gaze went around the buildings that enclose it, from the stables and sheds to the smoke-house, the brewery, the kitchen, the bathhouse, the god shrine, and thence to the hall. And Thorgunna was standing in the doorway.

Their gazes locked for a little, and I saw her color but thought nothing of it then. Our shoes rang on the flagging as we crossed the yard and kicked the dogs aside. My two thralls halted in cleaning the stables to gawp, until I got them back to work with the remark that a man good for naught else was always a pleasing sacrifice. That's one useful practice you Christians lack; I've never made a human offering myself, but you know not how helpful is the fact that I could do so.

We entered the hall, and I told the folk Gerald's name and how we had found him. Ragnhild set her maids hopping, to stoke up the fire in the middle trench and fetch beer, while I led Gerald to the high seat and sat down by him. Thorgunna brought us the filled horns.

His standing was not like yours, for whom we use our outland cups.

Gerald tasted the brew and made a face. I felt somewhat offended, for my beer is reckoned good, and asked him if aught was wrong. He laughed with a harsh note and said no, but he was used to beer that foamed and was not sour.

"And where might they make such?" I wondered testily.

"Everywhere," he said. "Iceland, too—no. . . ." He stared before him in an empty wise. "Let's say . . . in Vinland."

"Where is Vinland?" I asked.

"The country to the west whence I came. I thought you knew. . . . Wait a bit." He frowned. "Maybe I can find out something. Have you heard of Leif Eiriksson?"

"No," I said. Since then it has struck me that this was one proof of his tale, for Leif Eiriksson is now a well-known chief; and I also take more seriously those yarns of land seen by Bjarni Herjulfsson.

"His father, Eirik the Red?" went on Gerald.

"Oh yes," I said. "If you mean the Norseman who came hither because of a manslaughter, and left Iceland in turn for the same reason, and has now settled with his friends in Greenland."

"Then this is . . . a little before Leif's voyage," he muttered. "The late tenth century."

"See here," broke in Helgi, "we've been forbearing with you, but now is no time for riddles. We save those for feasts and drinking bouts. Can you not say plainly whence you come and how you got here?"

Gerald looked down at the floor, shaking.

"Let the man alone, Helgi," said Thorgunna. "Can you not see he's troubled?"

He raised his head and gave her the look of a hurt dog that someone has patted. The hall was dim; enough light seeped in the loft windows that no candles were lit, but not enough to see well by. Nevertheless, I marked a reddening in both their faces.

Gerald drew a long breath and fumbled about. His clothes were made with pockets. He brought out a small

152

parchment box and from it took a little white stick that he put in his mouth. Then he took out another box, and a wooden stick therefrom which burst into flame when scratched. With the fire he kindled the stick in his mouth, and sucked in the smoke.

We stared. "Is that a Christian rite?" asked Helgi.

"No . . . not just so." A wry, disappointed smile twisted his lips. "I thought you'd be more surprised, even terrified."

"It's something new," I admitted, "but we're a sober folk on Iceland. Those fire sticks could be useful. Did you come to trade in them?"

"Hardly." He sighed. The smoke he breathed in seemed to steady him, which was odd, because the smoke in the hall had made him cough and water at the eyes. "The truth is, well, something you will not believe. I can hardly believe it myself."

We waited. Thorgunna stood leaning forward, her lips parted.

"That lightning bolt—" Gerald nodded wearily. "I was out in the storm, and somehow the lightning must have smitten me in just the right way, a way that happens only once in many thousands of times. It threw me back into the past."

Those were his words, priest. I did not understand, and told him so.

"It's hard to grasp," he agreed. "God give that I'm merely dreaming. But if this is a dream I must endure till I awaken. . . . Well, look. I was born one thousand, nine hundred, and thirty-three years after Christ, in a land to the west which you have not yet found. In the twenty-fourth year of my life, I was in Iceland with my country's war host. The lightning struck me, and now, now it is less than one thousand years after Christ, and yet I am here—almost a thousand years before I was born, I am here!"

We sat very still. I signed myself with the Hammer and took a long pull from my horn. One of the maids whimpered, and Ragnhild whispered so fiercely I could hear: "Be still. The poor fellow's out of his head. There's no harm in him."

I thought she was right, unless maybe in the last part. The gods can speak through a madman, and the gods are not always to be trusted. Or he could turn berserker, or he could be under a heavy curse that would also touch us.

He slumped, gazing before him. I caught a few fleas and cracked them while I pondered. Gerald noticed and asked with some horror if we had many fleas here.

"Why, of course," said Thorgunna. "Have you none?"

"No." He smiled crookedly. "Not yet."

"Ah," she sighed, "then you *must* be sick."

She was a level-headed girl. I saw her thought, and so did Ragnhild and Helgi. Clearly, a man so sick that he had no fleas could be expected to rave. We might still fret about whether we could catch the illness, but I deemed this unlikely; his woe was in the head, maybe from a blow he had taken. In any case, the matter was come down to earth now, something we could deal with.

I being a godi, a chief who holds sacrifices, it behooved me not to turn a stranger out. Moreover, if he could fetch in many of those fire-kindling sticks, a profitable trade might be built up. So I said Gerald should go to rest. He protested, but we manhandled him into the shut-bed, and there he lay tired and was soon asleep. Thorgunna said she would take care of him.

The next eventide I meant to sacrifice a horse, both because of the timber we had found and to take away any curse that might be on Gerald. Furthermore, the beast I picked was old and useless, and we were short of fresh meat. Gerald had spent the morning lounging moodily around the garth, but when I came in at noon to eat I found him and my daughter laughing.

"You seem to be on the road to health," I said.

"Oh yes. It . . . could be worse for me." He sat down at my side as the carles set up the trestle table and the maids brought in the food. "I was ever much taken with the age of the vikings, and I have some skills."

"Well," I said, "if you have no home, we can keep you here for a while."

"I can work," he said eagerly. "I'll be worth my pay."

Now I knew he was from afar, because what chief would work on any land but his own, and for hire at that? Yet he had the easy manner of the high-born, and had clearly eaten well throughout his life. I overlooked that he had made me no gifts; after all, he was shipwrecked.

"Maybe you can get passage back to your United States," said Helgi. "We could hire a ship. I'm fain to see that realm."

"No," said Gerald bleakly. "There is no such place. Not yet."

"So you still hold to that idea you came from tomorrow?" grunted Sigurd. "Crazy notion. Pass the pork."

"I do," said Gerald. Calm had come upon him. "And I can prove it."

"I don't see how you speak our tongue, if you hail from so far away," I said. I would not call a man a liar to his face, unless we were swapping friendly brags, but—

"They speak otherwise in my land and time," he said, "but it happens that in Iceland the tongue changed little since the old days, and because my work had me often talking with the folk, I learned it when I came here."

"If you are a Christian," I said, "you must bear with us while we sacrifice tonight."

"I've naught against that," he said. "I fear I never was a very good Christian. I'd like to watch. How is it done?"

I told him how I would smite the horse with a hammer before the god, and cut its throat, and sprinkle the blood about with willow twigs; thereafter we would butcher the carcass and feast. He said hastily:

"Here's my chance to prove what I am. I have a weapon that will kill the horse with, with a flash of lightning."

"What is it?" I wondered. We crowded around while he took the metal club out of its sheath and showed it to us. I had my doubts; it looked well enough for hitting a man, I reckoned, but had no edge, though a wondrously skillful smith had forged it. "Well, we can try,"

155

I said. You have seen how on Iceland we are less concerned to follow the rites exactly than they are in the older countries.

Gerald showed us what else he had in his pockets. There were some coins of remarkable roundness and sharpness, though neither gold nor true silver; a tiny key; a stick with lead in it for writing; a flat purse holding many bits of marked paper. When he told us gravely that some of this paper was money, Thorgunna herself had to laugh. Best was a knife whose blade folded into the handle. When he saw me admiring that, he gave it to me, which was well done for a shipwrecked man. I said I would give him clothes and a good ax, as well as lodging for as long as needful.

No, I don't have the knife now. You shall hear why. It's a pity, for that was a good knife, though rather small.

"What were you ere the war arrow went out in your land?" asked Helgi. "A merchant?"

"No," said Gerald. "I was an . . . *endjinur* . . . that is, I was learning how to be one. A man who builds things, bridges and roads and tools . . . more than just an artisan. So I think my knowledge could be of great value here." I saw a fever in his eyes. "Yes, give me time and I'll be a king."

"We have no king on Iceland," I grunted. "Our forefathers came hither to get away from kings. Now we meet at the Things to try suits and pass new laws, but each man must get his own redress as best he can."

"But suppose the one in the wrong won't yield?" he asked.

"Then there can be a fine feud," said Helgi, and went on to relate some of the killings in past years. Gerald looked unhappy and fingered his *gun*. That is what he called his firespitting club. He tried to rally himself with a joke about now, at last, being free to call it a gun instead of something else. That disquieted me, smacked of witchcraft, so to change the talk I told Helgi to stop his chattering of manslaughter as if it were sport. With law shall the land be built.

156

"Your clothing is rich," said Thorgunna softly. "Your folk must own broad acres at home."

"No," he said, "our . . . our king gives each man in the host clothes like these. As for my family, we owned no farm, we rented our home in a building where many other families also dwelt."

I am not purse-proud, but it seemed to me he had not been honest, a landless man sharing my high seat like a chief. Thorgunna covered my huffiness by saying, "You will gain a farm later."

After sunset we went out to the shrine. The carles had built a fire before it, and as I opened the door the wooden Odin appeared to leap forth. My house has long invoked him above the others. Gerald muttered to my daughter that it was a clumsy bit of carving, and since my father had made it I was still more angry with him. Some folk have no understanding of the fine arts.

Nevertheless, I let him help me lead the horse forth to the altar stone. I took the blood bowl in my hands and said he could now slay the beast if he would. He drew his gun, put the end behind the horse's ear, and squeezed. We heard a crack, and the beast jerked and dropped with a hole blown through its skull, wasting the brains. A clumsy weapon. I caught a whiff, sharp and bitter like that around a volcano. We all jumped, one of the women screamed, and Gerald looked happy. I gathered my wits and finished the rest of the sacrifice as was right. Gerald did not like having blood sprinkled over him, but then he was a Christian. Nor would he take more than a little of the soup and flesh.

Afterward Helgi questioned him about the gun, and he said it could kill a man at bowshot distance but had no witchcraft in it, only use of some tricks we did not know. Having heard of the Greek fire, I believed him. A gun could be useful in a fight, as indeed I was to learn, but it did not seem very practical—iron costing what it does, and months of forging needed for each one.

I fretted more about the man himself.

And the next morning I found him telling Thorgunna a great deal of foolishness about his home—buildings as

157

tall as mountains, and wagons that flew, or went without horses. He said there were eight or nine thousand thousands of folk in his town, a burgh called New Jorvik or the like. I enjoy a good brag as well as the next man, but this was too much, and I told him gruffly to come along and help me get in some strayed cattle.

After a day scrambling around the hills I saw that Gerald could hardly tell a cow's bow from her stern. We almost had the strays once, but he ran stupidly across their path and turned them, so the whole work was to do again. I asked him with strained courtesy if he could milk, shear, wield scythe or flail, and he said no, he had never lived on a farm.

"That's a shame," I remarked, "for everyone on Iceland does, unless he be outlawed."

He flushed at my tone. "I can do enough else," he answered. "Give me some tools and I'll show you good metalwork."

That brightened me, for truth to tell, none of our household was a gifted smith. "That's an honorable trade," I said, "and you can be of great help. I have a broken sword and several bent spearheads to be mended, and it were no bad idea to shoe the horses." His admission that he did not know how to put on a shoe was not very dampening to me then.

We had returned home as we talked, and Thorgunna came angrily forward. "That's no way to treat a guest, Father," she said. "Making him work like a carle, indeed!"

Gerald smiled. "I'll be glad to work," he said. "I need a . . . a stake . . . something to start me afresh. Also, I want to repay a little of your kindness."

Those words made me mild toward him, and I said it was not his fault they had different ways in the United States. On the morrow he could begin in the smithy, and I would pay him, yet he would be treated as an equal since craftsmen are valued. This earned him black looks from the housefolk.

That evening he entertained us well with stories of

his home; true or not, they made good listening. However, he had no real polish, being unable to compose a line of verse. They must be a raw and backward lot in the United States. He said his task in the war host had been to keep order among the troops. Helgi said this was unheard of, and he must be bold who durst offend so many men, but Gerald said folk obeyed him out of fear of the king. When he added that the term of a levy in the United States was two years, and that men could be called to war even in harvest time, I said he was well out of a country with so ruthless and powerful a lord.

"No," he answered wistfully, "we are a free folk, who say what we please."

"But it seems you may not do as you please," said Helgi.

"Well," Gerald said, "we may not murder a man just because he aggrieves us."

"Not even if he has slain your own kin?" asked Helgi.

"No. It is for the . . . the king to take vengeance, on behalf of the whole folk whose peace has been broken."

I chuckled. "Your yarns are cunningly wrought," I said, "but there you've hit a snag. How could the king so much as keep count of the slaughters, let alone avenge them? Why, he'd not have time to beget an heir!"

Gerald could say no more for the laughter that followed.

The next day he went to the smithy, with a thrall to pump the bellows for him. I was gone that day and night, down to Reykjavik to dicker with Hjalmar Broadnose about some sheep. I invited him back for an overnight stay, and we rode into my steading with his son Ketill, a red-haired sulky youth of twenty winters who had been refused by Thorgunna.

I found Gerald sitting gloomily on a bench in the hall. He wore the clothes I had given him, his own having been spoilt by ash and sparks; what had he awaited, the fool? He talked in a low voice with my daughter.

"Well," I said as I trod in, "how went the tasks?"

159

My man Grim snickered. "He ruined two spearheads, but we put out the fire he started ere the whole smithy burned."

"How's this?" I cried. "You said you were a smith."

Gerald stood up, defiant. "I worked with different tools, and better ones, at home," he replied. "You do it otherwise here."

They told me he had built up the fire too hot; his hammer had struck everywhere but the place it should; he had wrecked the temper of the steel through not knowing when to quench it. Smithcraft takes years to learn, of course, but he might have owned to being not so much as an apprentice.

"Well," I snapped, "what can you do, then, to earn your bread?" It irked me to be made a ninny of before Hjalmar and Ketill, whom I had told about the stranger.

"Odin alone knows," said Grim. "I took him with me to ride after your goats, and never have I seen a worse horseman. I asked him if maybe he could spin or weave, and he said no."

"That was no question to ask a man!" flared Thorgunna. "He should have slain you for it."

"He should indeed," laughed Grim. "But let me carry on the tale. I thought we would also repair your bridge over the foss. Well, he *can* barely handle a saw, but he nigh took his own foot off with the adze."

"We don't use those tools, I tell you!" Gerald doubled his fists and looked close to tears.

I motioned my guests to sit down. "I don't suppose you can butcher or smoke a hog, either," I said, "or salt a fish or turf a roof."

"No." I could hardly hear him.

"Well, then, man, whatever can you do?"

"I—" He could get no words out.

"You were a warrior," said Thorgunna.

"Yes, that I was!" he said, his face kindling.

"Small use on Iceland when you have no other skills," I grumbled, "but maybe, if you can get passage to the eastlands, some king will take you in his guard." Myself I doubted it, for a guardsman needs manners that will do credit to his lord; but I had not the heart to say so.

Ketill Hjalmarsson had plainly not liked the way Thorgunna stood close to Gerald and spoke for him. Now he fleered and said: "I might also doubt your skill in fighting."

"That I have been trained for," said Gerald grimly.

"Will you wrestle with me?" asked Ketill.

"Gladly!" spat Gerald.

Priest, what is a man to think? As I grow older, I find life to be less and less the good-and-evil, black-and-white thing you call it; we are each of us some hue of gray. This useless fellow, this spiritless lout who could be asked if he did women's work and not lift ax, went out into the yard with Ketill Hajlmarsson and threw him three times running. He had a trick of grabbing the clothes as Ketill rushed on him. . . . I cried a stop when the youth was nearing murderous rage, praised them both, and filled the beer horns. But Ketill brooded sullen on the bench the whole evening.

Gerald said something about making a gun like his own, but bigger, a *cannon* he called it, which could sink ships and scatter hosts. He would need the help of smiths, and also various stuffs. Charcoal was easy, and sulfur could be found by the volcanoes, I suppose, but what is this saltpeter?

Too, being wary by now, I questioned him closely as to how he would make such a thing. Did he know just how to mix the powder? No, he admitted. What size must the gun be? When he told me—at least as long as a man—I laughed and asked him how a piece that size could be cast or bored, supposing we could scrape together so much iron. This he did not know either.

"You haven't the tools to make the tools to make the tools," he said. I don't understand what he meant by that. "God help me, I can't run through a thousand years of history by myself."

He took out the last of his little smoke sticks and lit it. Helgi had tried a puff earlier and gotten sick, though he remained a friend of Gerald's. Now my son proposed to take a boat in the morning and go with him and me to Ice Fjord, where I had some money outstanding I wanted to collect. Hjalmar and Ketill said they would

161

come along for the trip, and Thorgunna pleaded so hard that I let her come too.

"An ill thing," mumbled Sigurd. "The land-trolls like not a woman aboard a vessel. It's unlucky."

"How did your fathers bring women to this island?" I grinned.

Now I wish I had listened to him. He was not a clever man, but he often knew whereof he spoke.

At this time I owned a half-share in a ship that went to Norway, bartering wadmal for timber. It was a profitable business until she ran afoul of vikings during the uproar while Olaf Tryggvason was overthrowing Jarl Haakon there. Some men will do anything to make a living—thieves, cutthroats, they ought to be hanged, the worthless robbers pouncing on honest merchantmen. Had they any courage or honor they would go to Ireland, which is full of plunder.

Well, anyhow, the ship was abroad, but we had three boats and took one of these. Grim went with us others: myself, Helgi, Hjalmar, Ketill, Gerald, and Thorgunna. I saw how the castaway winced at the cold water as we launched her, yet afterward took off his shoes and stockings to let his feet dry. He had been surprised to learn we had a bathhouse—did he think us savages?—but still, he was dainty as a girl and soon moved upwind of our feet.

We had a favoring breeze, so raised mast and sail. Gerald tried to help, but of course did not know one line from another and got them fouled. Grim snarled at him and Ketill laughed nastily. But erelong we were under weigh, and he came and sat by me where I had the steering oar.

He must have lain long awake thinking, for now he ventured shyly: "In my land they have . . . will have . . . a rig and rudder which are better than these. With them, you can sail so close to the wind that you can crisscross against it."

"Ah, our wise sailor offers us redes," sneered Ketill.

"Be still," said Thorgunna sharply. "Let Gerald speak."

Gerald gave her a look of humble thanks, and I was not unwilling to listen. "This is something which could easily be made," he said. "While not a seaman, I've been on such boats myself and know them well. First, then, the sail should not be square and hung from a yardarm, but three-cornered, with the two bottom corners lashed to a yard swiveling fore and aft from the mast; and there should be one or two smaller headsails of the same shape. Next, your steering oar is in the wrong place. You should have a rudder in the stern, guided by a bar." He grew eager and traced the plan with his fingernail on Thorgunna's cloak. "With these two things, and a deep keel, going down about three feet for a boat this size, a ship can move across the wind . . . thus."

Well, priest, I must say the idea has merits, and were it not for the fear of bad luck—for everything of his was unlucky—I might yet play with it. But the drawbacks were clear, and I pointed them out in a reasonable way.

"First and worst," I said, "this rudder and deep keel would make it impossible to beach the ship or go up a shallow river. Maybe they have many harbors where you hail from, but here a craft must take what landings she can find, and must be speedily launched if there should be an attack."

"The keel can be built to draw up into the hull," he said, "with a box around so that water can't follow."

"How would you keep dry rot out of the box?" I answered. "No, your keel must be fixed, and must be heavy if the ship is not to capsize under so much sail as you have drawn. This means iron or lead, ruinously costly.

"Besides," I said, "this mast of yours would be hard to unstep when the wind dropped and oars came out. Furthermore, the sails are the wrong shape to stretch as an awning when one must sleep at sea."

"The ship could lie out, and you go to land in a small boat," he said. "Also, you could build cabins aboard for shelter."

"The cabins would get in the way of the oars," I said, "unless the ship were hopelessly broad-beamed or else the oarsmen sat below a deck; and while I hear that galley slaves do this in the southlands, free men would never row in such foulness."

"Must you have oars?" he asked like a very child.

Laughter barked along the hull. The gulls themselves, hovering to starboard where the shore rose dark, cried their scorn.

"Do they have tame winds in the place whence you came?" snorted Hjalmar. "What happens if you're becalmed—for days, maybe, with provisions running out—"

"You could build a ship big enough to carry many weeks' provisions," said Gerald.

"If you had the wealth of a king, you might," said Helgi. "And such a king's ship, lying helpless on a flat sea, would be swarmed by every viking from here to Jomsborg. As for leaving her out on the water while you make camp, what would you have for shelter, or for defense if you should be trapped ashore?"

Gerald slumped. Thorgunna said to him gently: "Some folk have no heart to try anything new. I think it's a grand idea."

He smiled at her, a weary smile, and plucked up the will to say something about a means for finding north in cloudy weather; he said a kind of stone always pointed north when hung from a string. I told him mildly that I would be most interested if he could find me some of this stone; or if he knew where it was to be had, I could ask a trader to fetch me a piece. But this he did not know, and fell silent. Ketill opened his mouth, but got such an edged look from Thorgunna that he shut it again. His face declared what a liar he thought Gerald to be.

The wind turned crank after a while, so we lowered the mast and took to the oars. Gerald was strong and willing, though awkward; however, his hands were so soft that erelong they bled. I offered to let him rest, but he kept doggedly at the work.

Watching him sway back and forth, under the dreary creak of the tholes, the shaft red and wet where he gripped it, I thought much about him. He had done everything wrong which a man could do—thus I imagined then, not knowing the future—and I did not like the way Thorgunna's eyes strayed to him and rested. He was no man for my daughter, landless and penniless and helpless. Yet I could not keep from liking him. Whether his tale was true or only madness, I felt he was honest about it; and surely whatever way by which he came hither was a strange one. I noticed the cuts on his chin from my razor; he had said he was not used to our kind of shaving and would grow a beard. He had tried hard. I wondered how well I would have done, landing alone in this witch country of his dreams, with a gap of forever between me and my home.

Maybe that same wretchedness was what had turned Thorgunna's heart. Women are a kittle breed, priest, and you who have forsworn them belike understand them as well as I who have slept with half a hundred in six different lands. I do not think they even understand themselves. Birth and life and death, those are the great mysteries, which none will ever fathom, and a woman is closer to them than a man.

The ill wind stiffened, the sea grew gray and choppy under low, leaden clouds, and our headway was poor. At sunset we could row no more, but must pull in to a small, unpeopled bay, and make camp as well as could be on the strand.

We had brought firewood and tinder along. Gerald, though staggering with weariness, made himself useful, his sulfury sticks kindling the blaze more easily than flint and steel. Thorgunna set herself to cook our supper. We were not much warded by the boat from a lean, whining wind; her cloak fluttered like wings and her hair blew wild above the streaming flames. It was the time of light nights, the sky a dim, dusky blue, the sea a wrinkled metal sheet, and the land like something risen out of dream mists. We men huddled in our own cloaks, holding numbed hands to the fire and saying little.

I felt some cheer was needed, and ordered a cask of my best and strongest ale broached. An evil Norn made me do that, but no man escapes his weird. Our bellies seemed the more empty now when our noses drank in the sputter of a spitted joint, and the ale went swiftly to

165

our heads. I remember declaiming the death-song of Ragnar Hairybreeks for no other reason than that I felt like declaiming it.

Thorgunna came to stand over Gerald where he sat. I saw how her fingers brushed his hair, ever so lightly, and Ketill Hjalmarsson did too. "Have they no verses in your land?" she asked.

"Not like yours," he said, glancing up. Neither of them looked away again. "We sing rather than chant. I wish I had my *gittar* here—that's a kind of harp."

"Ah, an Irish bard," said Hjalmar Broadnose.

I remember strangely well how Gerald smiled, and what he said in his own tongue, though I know not the meaning: *"Only on me mither's side, begorra."* I suppose it was magic.

"Well, sing for us," laughed Thorgunna.

"Let me think," he said. "I shall have to put it in Norse words for you." After a little while, still staring at her through the windy gloaming, he began a song. It had a tune I liked, thus:

> *From this valley they tell me you're leaving.*
> *I will miss your bright eyes and sweet smile.*
> *You will carry the sunshine with you*
> *That has brightened my life all the while. . . .*

I don't remember the rest, save that it was not quite seemly.

When he had finished, Hjalmar and Grim went over to see if the meat was done. I spied a glimmer of tears in my daughter's eyes. "That was a lovely thing," she said.

Ketill sat straight. The flames splashed his face with wild, running red. A rawness was in his tone: "Yes, we've found what this fellow can do. Sit about and make pretty songs for the girls. Keep him for that, Ospak."

Thorgunna whitened, and Helgi clapped hand to sword. Gerald's face darkened and his voice grew thick: "That was no way to talk. Take it back."

Ketill rose. "No," he said. "I'll ask no pardon of an idler living off honest yeomen."

166

He was raging, but had kept sense enough to shift the insult from my family to Gerald alone. Otherwise he and his father would have had the four of us to deal with. As it was, Gerald stood too, fists knotted at his sides, and said: "Will you step away from here and settle this?"

"Gladly!" Ketill turned and walked a few yards down the beach, taking his shield from the boat. Gerald followed. Thorgunna stood stricken, then snatched his ax and ran after him.

"Are you going weaponless?" she shrieked.

Gerald stopped, looking dazed. "I don't want anything like that," he said. "Fists—"

Ketill puffed himself up and drew sword. "No doubt you're used to fighting like thralls in your land," he said. "So if you'll crave my pardon, I'll let this matter rest."

Gerald stood with drooped shoulders. He stared at Thorgunna as if he were blind, as if asking her what to do. She handed him the ax.

"So you want me to kill him?" he whispered.

"Yes," she answered.

Then I knew she loved him, for otherwise why should she have cared if he disgraced himself?

Helgi brought him his helmet. He put it on, took the ax, and went forward.

"Ill is this," said Hjalmar to me. "Do you stand by the stranger, Ospak?"

"No," I said. "He's no kin or oath-brother of mine. This is not my quarrel."

"That's good," said Hjalmar. "I'd not like to fight with you. You were ever a good neighbor."

We stepped forth together and staked out the ground. Thorgunna told me to lend Gerald my sword, so he could use a shield too, but the man looked oddly at me and said he would rather have the ax. They squared off before each other, he and Ketill, and began fighting.

This was no holmgang, with rules and a fixed order of blows and first blood meaning victory. There was death between those two. Drunk though the lot of us were, we saw that and so had not tried to make peace. Ketill stormed in with the sword whistling in his hand. Gerald

167

sprang back, wielding the ax awkwardly. It bounced off Ketill's shield. The youth grinned and cut at Gerald's legs. Blood welled forth to stain the ripped breeches.

What followed was butchery. Gerald had never used a battle-ax before. So it turned in his grasp and he struck with the flat of the head. He would have been hewn down at once had Ketill's sword not been blunted on his helmet and had he not been quick on his feet. Even so, he was erelong lurching with a dozen wounds.

"Stop the fight!" Thorgunna cried, and sped toward them. Helgi caught her arms and forced her back, where she struggled and kicked till Grim must help. I saw grief on my son's face, but a wolfish glee on the carle's.

Ketill's blade came down and slashed Gerald's left hand. He dropped the ax. Ketill snarled and readied to finish him. Gerald drew his gun. It made a flash and a barking noise. Ketill fell. Blood gushed from him. His lower jaw was blown off and the back of his skull was gone.

A stillness came, where only the wind and the sea had voice.

Then Hjalmar trod forth, his mouth working but otherwise a cold steadiness over him. He knelt and closed his son's eyes, as a token that the right of venegeance was his. Rising, he said: "That was an evil deed. For that you shall be outlawed."

"It wasn't witchcraft," said Gerald in a stunned tone. "It was like a . . . a bow. I had no choice. I didn't want to fight with more than my fists."

I got between them and said the Thing must decide this matter, but that I hoped Hjalmar would take weregild for Ketill.

"But I killed him to save my own life!" protested Gerald.

"Nevertheless, weregild must be paid, if Ketill's kin will take it," I explained. "Because of the weapon, I think it will be doubled, but that is for the Thing to judge."

Hjalmar had many other sons, and it was not as if Gerald belonged to a family at odds with his own, so I felt he would agree. However, he laughed coldly and asked where a man lacking wealth would find the silver.

Thorgunna stepped up with a wintry calm and said we would pay. I opened my mouth, but when I saw her eyes I nodded. "Yes, we will," I said, "in order to keep the peace."

"So you make this quarrel your own?" asked Hjalmar.

"No," I answered. "This man is no blood of mine. But if I choose to make him a gift of money to use as he wishes, what of it?"

Hjalmar smiled. Sorrow stood in his gaze, but he looked on me with old comradeship.

"One day he may be your son-in-law," he said. "I know the signs, Ospak. Then indeed he will be of your folk. Even helping him now in his need will range you on his side."

"And so?" asked Helgi, most softly.

"And so, while I value your friendship, I have sons who will take the death of their brother ill. They'll want revenge on Gerald Samsson, if only for the sake of their good names, and thus our two houses will be sundered and one manslaying will lead to another. It has happened often enough ere now." Hjalmar sighed. "I myself wish peace with you, Ospak, but if you take this killer's side it must be otherwise."

I thought for a moment, thought of Helgi lying with his head cloven, of my other sons on their steads drawn to battle because of a man they had never seen, I thought of having to wear byrnies each time we went down for driftwood and never knowing when we went to bed if we would wake to find the house ringed in by spearmen.

"Yes," I said, "you are right, Hjalmar. I withdraw my offer. Let this be a matter between you and him alone."

We gripped hands on it.

Thorgunna uttered a small cry and flew into Gerald's arms. He held her close. "What does this mean?" he asked slowly.

"I cannot keep you any longer," I said, "but maybe some crofter will give you a roof. Hjalmar is a law-abiding man and will not harm you until the Thing has outlawed you. That will not be before they meet in fall. You can try to get passage out of Iceland ere then."

"A useless one like me?" he replied in bitterness.

Thorgunna whirled free and blazed that I was a coward and a perjurer and all else evil. I let her have it out before I laid my hands on her shoulders.

"I do this for the house," I said. "The house and the blood, which are holy. Men die and women weep, but while the kindred live our names are remembered. Can you ask a score of men to die for your hankerings?"

Long did she stand, and to this day I know not what her answer would have been. But Gerald spoke.

"No," he said. "I suppose you have right, Ospak . . . the right of your time, which is not mine." He took my hand, and Helgi's. His lips brushed Thorgunna's cheek. Then he turned and walked out into the darkness.

I heard, later, that he went to earth with Thorvald Hallsson, the crofter of Humpback Fell, and did not tell his host what had happened. He must have hoped to go unnoticed until he could somehow get berth on an eastbound ship. But of course word spread. I remember his brag that in the United States folk had ways to talk from one end of the land to another. So he must have scoffed at us, sitting in our lonely steads, and not known how fast news would get around. Thorvald's son Hrolf went to Brand Sealskin-Boots to talk about some matter, and mentioned the guest, and soon the whole western island had the tale.

Now, if Gerald had known he must give notice of a manslaying at the first garth he found, he would have been safe at least till the Thing met, for Hjalmar and his sons are sober men who would not needlessly kill a man still under the wing of the law. But as it was, his keeping the matter secret made him a murderer and therefore at once an outlaw. Hjalmar and his kin rode straight to Humpback Fell and haled him forth. He shot his way past them with the gun and fled into the hills. They followed him, having several hurts and one more death to avenge. I wonder if Gerald thought the strangeness of his weapon would unnerve us. He may not have understood that every man dies when his time comes, neither sooner nor later, so that fear of death is useless.

At the end, when they had him trapped, his weapon gave out on him. Then he took a dead man's sword and defended himself so valiantly that Ulf Hjalmarsson has limped ever since. That was well done, as even his foes admitted. They are an eldritch breed in the United States, but they do not lack manhood.

When he was slain, his body was brought back. For fear of the ghost, he having maybe been a warlock, it was burned, and everything he had owned was laid in the fire with him. Thus I lost the knife he gave me. The barrow stands out on the moor, north of here, and folk shun it, though the ghost has not walked. Today, with so much else happening, he is slowly being forgotten.

And that is the tale, priest, as I saw it and heard it. Most men think Gerald Samsson was crazy, but I myself now believe he did come from out of time, and that his doom was that no man may ripen a field before harvest season. Yet I look into the future, a thousand years hence, when they fly through the air and ride in horseless wagons and smash whole towns with one blow. I think of this Iceland then, and of the young United States men come to help defend us in a year when the end of the world hovers close. Maybe some of them, walking about on the heaths, will see that barrow and wonder what ancient warrior lies buried there, and they may well wish they had lived long ago in his time, when men were free.

THE TIME OF HIS LIFE

Larry Eisenberg

Larry Eisenberg does research in bio-medical electronics at New York's Rockefeller University and has published fiction, humorous essays, and a collection of bawdy limericks, among other things. In this story he examines the familiar theme of conflict between generations and gives it a new, startlingly sinister twist.

I sat in the tiny cubicle that served as my office in the laboratory, my knees cramped under the desk. My father's office was huge, thickly carpeted from wall to wall, lined from floor to ceiling with bookcases. But, of course, my father was a Nobel laureate.

I gritted my teeth. Twenty years earlier I had been a graduate student of great promise. I had joined my father's laboratory as a co-investigator with great hopes of making my own contribution to metabolic research. And now, at forty-four, my work was submerged in the greater accomplishments of my father.

What had happened to me? I was losing my sense of concentration, the ability to focus relentlessly on a single problem regardless of time and people. My father had that ability. He had always had it.

I looked at the picture of Alma, my wife, and the three boys, framed in silver on my desk. She was still undeniably a lovely woman. But in real life, her eyes were underlined with crow's feet, and her exquisitely clear skin had begun to muddy. And what of the boys? They were sturdy, noisy, argumentative, offended because I didn't spend more time with them.

There was no need to. My father came every Sunday, devoting himself fully to Alma and the boys. But he had never taken *me* to a ball game, never fished with me, never taken a long hike to a snowcapped mountain. Our relationship was polite but distant. Even when mother died, we grieved apart. But he was not gentle in criticizing my behavior. Only a week earlier, he had called me into his office to discuss difficulties with his grant. It was a pretext for something else.

"You don't carry your weight in this laboratory," he said bluntly. "You've lost all sense of purpose, of *honor*."

"I do more than my share," I said hotly.

"Frolicking in the hay with my lab technician?" he gibed.

"That's a damned lie!" I said. I shook my head angrily. Two years back, there had been an abortive affair with a sloe-eyed blonde graduate student. It had been exciting, tempestuous, and had fizzled out a few months later. But Sarah Frey was a totally different kind of a girl. There were bonds between us that grew stronger by the hour, something neither my father nor my wife would ever understand. My father had gotten rid of the blonde graduate student, but so far he hadn't acted against Sarah. I think he knew it would be no use.

"I'm very fond of Sarah," I said. "There's nothing in it beyond that."

My father snorted, and I got up and walked out in a huff. Of course he was right. I was entangled from the first day Sarah Frey walked into the laboratory, six months back, her thick black hair lying in two woven plaits along the stiff white back of her starched smock, the soft mouth set in a curve that easily broke into a warm smile. She was efficient, good with our animals, and very careful about recording data.

One morning, when my father had come in unexpectedly, he found us in a passionate embrace. I would have preferred an explosion, but he remained calm, pretending nothing had happened. He even spoke dispassionately to Sarah about preparing a new diet for our capuchin monkeys.

The recollection was still painful. I shuffled the papers

on my desk aimlessly. It took the most enormous effort of concentration, but I tried to pull my thoughts back to my work. And for some moments, I succeeded. Twenty years back, I had begun my long search to determine the influences controlling the biological clock. What was it that sent the body temperature of a warm-blooded animal through the same up and down cycle, day after day? Why did so many metabolic functions depend on the length of day?

My father and I had discussed these questions at great length, and it was agreed that I would explore gravitational effects and he would pursue the electromagnetic influences. Chance had been completely on his side. It was his good fortune to be the first to show that brain potentials were definitely dependent on fluctuations in the Earth's magnetic field.

Working first with capuchin monkeys, then with humans, he demonstrated that the most significant of the brain biopotentials, the alpha rhythm, varied between eight and sixteen times each second, *just as the fluctuations did in the Earth's magnetic field*. And my father had been called to Sweden to receive the magnificent gold medal and the fat cash award.

I was proud of my father, proud of his trail-breaking accomplishment, and also fiercely envious. I had given up ever understanding why. Maybe it was the unrelenting sense of competition that surrounded everything he did. Even now, he was still striving to be first, engaging me in a competition I didn't want, both in the laboratory, and with my wife and children.

"It takes two to race," I said out loud. "And I'm not going to run."

My telephone rang. It was my father, a lousy fifty feet down the corridor, but too busy to walk over and talk to me directly. It was hard to control the contempt in my voice.

"What is it?" I said.

"I have something of tremendous importance to discuss," he said. "And I've a lot to show you. Could you spare me a few minutes?"

A few minutes? I had great chunks of empty time

ahead. "I'm tied up now," I said. "But I'll be over in a half-hour."

I leaned over and set the alarm of my electric clock one half-hour ahead. My father could tolerate many things, but never tardiness.

I arrived punctually at my father's office and sat down in the very comfortable leather chair just opposite his desk. We looked directly into one another's eyes, and then, troubled, I looked down at the rug. It was uncanny, almost unnerving at times, to see how much alike in appearance my father and I were. Except for the silver hair and the toughened, wrinkled skin of a seventy-year-old, we could have passed for brothers. My father sat there puffing on his pipe. The rich aroma of his honeyed tobacco began to fill every corner of the room. I had detested that smell, even as a child.

"I have something to show you, John," said my father. He spoke out of the corner of his mouth without removing his pipe. That too, annoyed the hell out of me. "I would very much like to get your opinion on it," he said.

"Since when did my opinion matter here?"

My father glared at me. "To hell with your self-pity," he said. "I want your scientific acumen if you've got any left. I'm thinking about the arrow of time."

The arrow of time? I grinned in spite of myself. My father had always been preoccupied with this question, for as many years as I could recall. It was an obsession.

"We both know," said my father, going along lines he had taken innumerable times, "that on a microscopic level there is *no preferred* direction for time. The equations of motion don't give a damn whether time moves forward or backward."

"But it does matter on a macroscopic level," I said, pulled into the dialogue in spite of my resentment. "After all, if the direction of time were equally likely in the forward and backward directions, then there would have to be a total symmetry in the form and process of all animals. Of course there is a rough kind of symmetry, but it breaks down when you examine it closely. Obviously, the human heart and aorta are not symmetrical."

"You're absolutely right," said my father, and I got a thrill of pleasure that ran down into my stomach. He puffed even more vigorously on his pipe, and great blue clouds of smoke began to surround his head. It presaged a good deal more talk.

"What it boils down to," said my father, "is that on a small scale, say on the scale of the Earth itself, there may not be a macroscopic symmetry. But over the enormous reach of the universe, things *have to average out*. If men on Earth have a heart and aorta that point one way, then on some other planet, in some remote corner of the universe, other men have hearts and aortas that go the other way."

"That sounds like an extension of the particle-anti-particle reasoning to me," I said.

"Exactly," said my father. "I might even speculate that since we age in a particular direction here on Earth, perhaps other men grow younger with time, elsewhere."

I started to laugh. "And come out of their mothers' wombs, gnarled, bent, wrinkled, and toothless?" My father put down his pipe. "You've reduced my remarks to complete absurdity," he said quietly.

I was happy to see my father angry but it also made me uneasy. "I'm sorry," I said. "But your remarks did seem to point in that direction."

My father stood up abruptly, knocking the ashes of his pipe into a huge embossed silver tray that had been given to him by the laboratory staff when he had received his Nobel prize.

"Talk is cheap," he said. "Let's go into the laboratory. You'll see what I mean."

We walked into the outer corridors, which were dimly lit, and on to the capuchin monkey laboratory. In the center of the laboratory, on a large bench, was a single wire cage. Just behind it was a tall rack of electronic equipment with an L-shaped arm swinging out above the cage. Affixed to the arm and directly over the center of the cage was an enormous bank of coils.

My father walked up to the cage and peered into it, clucking very softly to the animal within. I came up behind him and looked over his shoulder. There was a very old animal inside the cage, one so wrinkled and gray that I was amazed it still lived.

"Do you recognize it?" said my father.

"Not really."

"It's our *young* Ginger," he said.

At first I thought it was a grotesque joke, but of course I knew my father had no sense of humor. I looked up at the bank of coils above the cage. My father's eyes followed mine.

"That's the magnetic field synthesizer I had built," said my father. "With it, I can place a controlled field into a one-millimeter area at any point within five feet of the synthesizer. I can vary amplitude and frequency over a large range."

"And Ginger?"

"I locked her into an eight cycles per second magnetic field," said my father. "And by God, she began to track *metabolically* with the fluctuations of this artificial field. Gradually, I began to increase the rate of the fluctuations. As you can see, her biological clock speeded up internally, and aging began to take place at a very rapid pace."

"It's incredible," I said. "I wouldn't have believed it possible."

For the moment my jealousy and antagonism fell away, and the magnitude of his achievement caught hold of my imagination. I examined the animal closely. The features were similar to those of Ginger, but I couldn't be sure. Around her ankle was a tiny identification bracelet marked "Ginger". But it might have been transferred from the real Ginger.

"I know what you're thinking," said my father. "But I've never faked data in my life, and you damn well know it." He lifted a thick notebook which was at one side of the cage. "All of my records are in here," he said. "I want you to read them and offer me your comments."

I took the notebook out of his hands. It was truly heavy. For a fleeting moment, I thought of how upset my father would be if I burned the notebook. Then I pushed the idea out of my head.

"One question," I said. "How do you direct this field at the animal? Do you use uniform field strength? Do you have to focus in a particular site of the cortex, or are there several areas involved?"

"There is a single site involved," said my father. "Read the notebook; it's all in there."

For a moment he looked at me, his eyes warm and almost, it seemed, loving.

"You've called me cold and aloof. But what I'm suggesting is that *you* now carry out the experiments of *slowing down* the field fluctuation rate."

My eyes filled. It was enormously generous of him, I knew. In effect, we might be able to make time stand still for the individual. It could be the threshold to immortality for the first time in man's history. The concept was breathtaking.

"I'll start reading your notebook at once," I said.

On the way back to my office, I passed Sarah Frey. She reached out and caressed my arm. Oddly enough, I was annoyed. I nodded at her, curtly, and went on without a word, laboring under the weight of the great notebook.

I read through every scrap of the data, my excitement mounting all the way. It was clear that the experiment of slowing down the fields was really going to rock the world of science. And then it hit me, the great shock of realizing that all of this was my father's work, all his accomplishment and none of it mine. He was handing it to me on a silver platter, but I hadn't degenerated to the point where I could accept such a gift.

I marched back to my father's office and put down his notebook. He looked at me, his great black, almost youthful eyes now expressionless.

"It's your work and not mine," I said. "You've done a fantastic job, but I'm not going to climb on to your bandwagon as though it were my own. I've got to make it on my own."

My father sighed. "Either I give you too little or too much. Why can't you climb aboard? There's enough glory and accomplishment here for five men. And there is so much yet to be worked out. Or do you want to burn up all of your creativity inside Sarah Frey?"

I began to shout. "Leave Sarah out of this. What I do

178

with her is my own goddamned affair. And it's a damn sight more loving, more human and meaningful than your preoccupation with gold medals and applause."

"So that's it," said my father.

I stormed out of his office and back to my own. Sitting there I realized the childishness of what I had said and done. My father was right, and I ought to have joined him. But I couldn't. I was like an upended hour glass, losing all of its sand, and no one was able to turn me right side up so I could get a fresh start.

I spent the night with Sarah. I telephoned my wife and told her, as on countless occasions, that I would be working late at the laboratory and sleeping over. And as always, Alma sighed and pretended to believe me.

In the morning I told Sarah that I was going to divorce my wife. She was sitting before the mirror, brushing her hair with long, even strokes, unleashing a rich perfume from the blue-black locks, and her hand began to tremble. But she said nothing. Did she believe me? I swore that I meant it this time, but Sarah was unconvinced. Or was it really the twenty-year difference in our ages? I left her apartment, angry with her, and for days thereafter I ignored her attempts to approach me.

My father was more direct with me. If he met me coming down the corridor, he would turn back. I knew his work went on, perhaps the very same experiments I had refused to do. But I would not humble myself.

One evening, when I had forced myself to stay behind and work on a lackluster paper which I was scheduled to give at a spring meeting, my father broke into my office with great excitement. His step was springy, and he seemed to be bursting with a vitality that belied his years.

"Come with me," he said.

I followed, great fear building in me. We went back to the capuchin room and the cage of Ginger. My father gestured at the cage, and I looked inside. *She had been restored to her youth.*

"Congratulations," I said, but I was close to complete despair. It might have been my own achievement. And then, all of the unformed feelings that had been sifting in and out of my mind took form.

"I know that as yet you haven't tried this process on a human," I said. "I'm willing to volunteer."

"It's courageous of you," said my father. "But the danger is enormous. It would require extreme care and a protracted exposure to avoid reversing the metabolic processes too abruptly."

"It's not courage," I said. "I want another chance to start afresh. Twenty years would give me that chance. Perhaps then I could avoid the things that led me into a blind alley."

"It's too late," said my father. "You've a wife and three fine boys. You can't turn back."

"I'm determined," I said. "If you won't help me, you know that I will get there by myself."

"I know," he said. "But you're a fool. There's a precedent before you."

He went to the laboratory sink and washed his face vigorously with soap and water. The dried, leathery skin seemed to vanish like smoke, and a clear, ruddy skin emerged.

"All makeup," said my father. He reached up and removed the silver hair, and a full head of chestnut-colored hair, the counterpart of my own, emerged. "As you see," he said, "I've already carried out the experiment."

I looked at him. He was almost my mirror image.

"You're a swine," I said. "A lecherous beast. You took my work, my ambition, my wife and children. Now you've taken my body."

"It's not like that at all," he muttered. "You know it was logically the next step in my research."

"Was it?" I said. "Are you logically headed next for Alma's bed?"

He flushed to the roots.

"I'll trade her for those twenty years," I said. "At least you can give me that."

"I'd do it gladly," he said grimly. "And I would take far better care of your family than you ever did. But even supposing I were to entertain your absurd proposition, what would become of me, the *old* me?"

"That's your problem," I said. "For once in your life, think of me, first."

"You're out of your head," said my father. He reached out and took hold of the silver hairpiece and very carefully tugged it back into place. Then he walked out of the laboratory.

That night I didn't even bother to call Alma. I got roaring drunk and stayed that way until I lost track of the days. When I awoke, I was bone weary. My head was splitting, and every part of my body ached beyond description. It was much more than a hangover.

I tried to lift my arm and the effort exhausted me. Most curious of all, I found myself at a strange desk. I stared at the pile of neatly lettered papers, the thick notebook. I looked down at my hands. They were gnarled, the hands of a man in his seventies, the skin puckered, leathery, acid stained. I lifted the water-spotted shaving mirror that lay at one side of the desk and looked at my reflection. It was the face of my father, or rather, his face before he had turned back his biological clock. Or was it really my face?

I was terribly confused. Waking from a long nap does that to me. I was still in that half-awake state where one is not sure what one has dreamed and what is real. Sarah Frey came gliding in to drop a report on the desk. I reached out to caress her rump, and she nearly leaped out of her skin. She was out of the room before I could say a word.

I looked at the notebook, opened it and idly turned the pages. Was this work mine? My eyelids were terribly heavy. I began to doze off, and out of the corner of my eye I saw a younger version of myself, standing motionless in the doorway of the office, staring at me with his large, dark, angry eyes. And just in the moment that I dropped back into the deep solace of my nap, I thought, "You fool, the things you took were ephemeral. But I, after all, am now the Nobel laureate."

THE DOCTOR

Ted Thomas

Here is a piece to set beside Poul Anderson's
The Man Who Came Early in any discussion of
the perils of visiting the past. Ted Thomas of
Pennsylvania is a patent attorney who first acquired a degree from M.I.T. in chemical engi-
neering; he is a solid, well-constructed, unflamboyant man who writes solid, well-constructed,
unflamboyant stories, such as the following sober,
moving, tender, and painful account of a decent
man trapped in a harsh era.

When Gant first opened his eyes he thought
for an instant he was back in his home in Pennsylvania.
He sat up suddenly and looked wildly around in the
dark of the cave, and then he remembered where he
was. The noise he made frightened his wife and his son,
Dun, and they rolled to their feet, crouched, ready to
leap. Gant grunted reassuringly at them and climbed
off the moss-packed platform he had built for a bed. The
barest glimmerings of dawn filtered into the cave, and
the remnants of the fire glowed at the mouth. Gant went
to the fire and poked it and put some chips on it and
blew on them. It had been a long time since he had had
such a vivid memory of his old life half a million years
away. He looked at the wall of the cave, at the place
where he kept his calendar, painfully scratched into the
rock. It had been ten years ago today when he had
stepped into that molybdenum-steel cylinder in the Ban-
croft Building at Pennsylvania State University. What was
it he had said? "Sure, I'll try it. You ought to have a

182

medical doctor in it on the first trial run. You physicists could not learn anything about the physiological effects of time travel. Besides, this will make history, and I want to be in on it."

Gant stepped over the fire and listened carefully at the mouth of the cave, near the log barrier. Outside he heard the sound of rustling brush and heavy breathing, and he knew he could not leave now. He drank some water from a gourd and ate some dried bison with his wife and son. They all ate quietly.

Dawn came, and he stepped to the mouth of the cave and listened. The great animal had left. He waved to his wife and Dun, dragged aside the barrier, and went out.

He went along the face of the cliff, staying away from the heavy underbrush at its foot. He would go into it when he returned, and he would look for food.

In the marsh that lay beyond the underbrush was one of the many monuments to his failures. In the rocks and tree stumps there, he had tried to grow penicillium molds on the sweet juices of some of the berries that abounded in the region. He had crushed the berries and placed the juices in a hundred different kinds of receptacles. For three years he had tried to raise the green mold, but all he ever produced was a slimy gray mass that quickly rotted when the sun struck it.

He hefted the heavy stone axe in his right hand. As he approached the cave he was looking for, he grunted loudly and then went in. The people inside held their weapons in their hands, and he was glad he had called ahead. He ignored them and went to a back corner to see the little girl.

She sat on the bare stone, leaning against the rock with her mouth open, staring dully at him as he came up to her, her eyes black against the thick blonde hair that grew on her face. Gant whirled at the others and snarled at them, and snatched a bearhide from the bed of the man and carried it to the girl. He wrapped her in it and then felt the part of her forehead where there was no hair. It was burning hot, must be about 105°, possibly a little more. He put her down on the rock and thumped her chest and heard the solid, hard sound of filled lungs.

It was full-blown pneumonia, no longer any doubt. She gasped for breath, and there was no breath. Gant picked her up again and held her. He sat with her for over an hour, changing her position frequently in his arms, trying to make her comfortable as she gasped. He held a handful of wet leaves to her forehead to try to cool her burning face, but it did not seem to help. She went into convulsions at the end.

He laid the body on a rock ledge and pulled the mother over to see it. The mother bent and touched the girl gently on the face and then straightened and looked at Gant helplessly. He picked up the body and walked out of the cave and down into the woods. It took several hours to dig a hole deep enough with a stick.

He hunted on the way back to the caves, and he killed a short, heavy-bodied animal that hung upside down from the lower branches of a tree. It emitted a foul odor as he killed it, but it would make a good meal. He found a large rock outcropping with a tiny spring coming out from under it. A mass of newly sprouted shoots grew in the soggy ground. He picked them all, and headed back to his cave. His wife and Dun were there and their faces brightened when they saw what he brought. His wife immediately laid out the animal and skinned it with a fragment of sharp, shiny rock. Dun watched her intently, leaning over while it cooked to smell the fragrant smoke. Gant looked at the short, thick, hairy woman tending the cooking, and he looked at the boy. He could easily see himself in the thin-limbed boy. Both his wife and his son had the heavy brows and the jutting jaw of the cave people. But Dun's body was lean and his eyes were blue and sparkling, and he often sat close to Gant and tried to go with him when he went out of the cave. And once, when the lightning blazed and the thunder roared, Gant had seen the boy standing at the mouth of the cave staring at the sky in puzzlement, not fear, and Gant had put a hand on his shoulder and tried to find the words that told of electrical discharges and the roar of air rushing into a void, but there were no words.

The meat was done and the shoots were softened, and the three of them squatted at the fire and reached for the food. Outside the cave they heard the sound of movement in the gravel, and Gant leaped for his club while his wife and Dun retreated to the rear of the cave. Two men appeared, one supporting the other, both empty-handed. Gant waited until he could see that one of them was injured; he could not place his right foot on the ground. Then Gant came forward and helped the injured man to a sitting position at the mouth of the cave. He leaned over to inspect the foot. The region just above the ankle was discolored and badly swollen, and the foot was at a slight angle to the rest of the leg. Both the fibula and the tibia seemed to be broken, and Gant stood up and looked around for splints. The man would probably die; there was no one to take care of him during the weeks needed for his leg to heal, no one to hunt for him and give him food and put up with his almost complete inactivity.

Gant found two chips from logs and two short branches and some strips from a cured hide. He knelt in front of the man and carefully held his hands near the swollen leg so the man could see he was going to touch it.

The man's great muscles were knotted in pain and his face was gray beneath the hair. Gant waved the second man around to one side where he could keep an eye on him, and then he took the broken leg and began to apply tension. The injured man stood it for a moment and then roared in pain and instinctively lashed out with his good leg. Gant ducked the kick, but he could not duck the blow from the second man. It hit him on the side of the head and knocked him out of the mouth of the cave. He rolled to his feet and came back in. The second man stood protectively in front of the injured man, but Gant pushed him aside and knelt down again. The foot was straight, so Gant placed the chips and branches on the leg and bound them in place with the leather thongs. Weak and helpless, the injured man did not resist. Gant stood up and showed the second man how to carry the injured man. He helped them on their way.

When they left, Gant returned to his food. It was cold, but he was content. For the first time they had come to him. They were learning. He hurt his teeth on the hard meat and he gagged on the spongy shoots, but he squatted in his cave and he smiled. There had been a time long ago when he had thought that these people would be grateful to him for his work, that he would become known by some such name as The Healer. Yet here he was, years later, happy that at last one of them had come to him with an injury. Yet Gant knew them too well by now to be misled. These people did not have even the concept of medical treatment, and the day would probably come when one of them would kill him as he worked.

He sighed, picked up his club, and went out of the cave. A mile away was a man with a long gash in the calf of his left leg. Gant had cleaned it and packed it with moss and tied it tight with a hide strip. It was time to check the wound, so he walked the mile carefully, on the lookout for the large creatures that roamed the forests. The man was chipping rock in front of his cave, and he nodded his head and waved and showed his teeth in a friendly gesture when he saw Gant. Gant showed his teeth in turn and looked at the leg. He saw that the man had removed the moss and bandage, and had rubbed the great wound with dung. Gant bent to inspect the wound and immediately smelled the foul smell of corruption. Near the top of the wound, just beneath the knee, was a mass of black, wet tissues. Gangrene. Gant straightened and looked around at some of the others near the cave. He went to them and tried to make them understand what he wanted to do, but they did not pay much attention. Gant returned and looked down on the wounded man, noting that his movements were still quick and coordinated, and that he was as powerfully built as the rest of them. Gant shook his head; he could not perform the amputation unaided, and there was no help to be had. He tried again to show them that the man would die unless they helped him, but it was no use. He left.

He walked along the foot of the cliffs, looking in on the caves. In one he found a woman with a swollen jaw, in pain. She let him look in her mouth, and he saw a rotted molar. He sat down with her and with gestures tried to explain that it would be painful at first if he removed the tooth, but that it would soon be better. The

186

woman seemed to understand. Gant took up a fresh branch and scraped a rounded point on one end. He picked up a rock twice the size of his fist, and placed the woman in a sitting position with her head resting on his thigh. He placed the end of the stick low on the gum to make sure he got the root. Carefully he raised the rock, knowing he would have but one try. He smashed the rock down and felt the tooth give way and saw the blood spout from her mouth. She screamed and leaped to her feet and turned on Gant, but he jumped away. Then something struck him from behind and he found himself pinned to the ground with two men sitting on him. They growled at him and one picked up a rock and the stick and smashed a front tooth from Gant's mouth. Then they threw him out of the cave. He rolled down through the gravel and came up short against a bush. He leaped to his feet and charged back into the cave. One of the men swung a club at him, but he ducked and slammed the rock against the side of the man's head. The other ran. Gant went over to the woman, picking as he went a half-handful of moss from the wall of the cave. He stood in front of her and packed some of the moss in the wound in his front jaw, and leaned over to show her the bleeding had stopped. He held out the moss to her, and she quickly took some and put it in the proper place in her jaw. She nodded to him and patted his arm and rubbed the blood out of the hair on her chin. He left the cave, without looking at the unconscious man.

Some day they would kill him. His jaw throbbed as he walked along the gravel shelf and headed for home. There would be no more stops today, and so he threaded his way along the foot of the cliff. He heard sounds of activity in several of the caves, and in one of the largest of them he heard excited voices yelling. He stopped, but his jaw hurt too much to go in. The noise increased and Gant thought they might be carving up a large kill. He was always on the lookout for meat, so he changed his mind and went in. Inside was a boy about the age of Dun, lying on his back, gasping for air. His face had a bluish tinge, and at each intake of air his muscles tensed and his back arched with the effort to breathe. Gant pushed to his side and forced his mouth open. The throat and uvula were greatly swollen, the air passage almost shut. He quickly examined the boy, but there was no sign of injury or disease. Gant was puzzled, but then he concluded the boy must have chewed or eaten a substance to which he was sensitive. He looked at the throat again. The swelling was continuing. The boy's jutting jaws made mouth-to-mouth resuscitation impossible. A tracheotomy was indicated. He went over to the fire and smashed one piece of flint chopping stone on another, and quickly picked over the pieces. He chose a short, sharp fragment and stooped over the boy. He touched the point of the fragment against the skin just beneath the larynx, squeezed his thumb and forefinger on the fragment to measure a distance a little over half an inch from the point, and then thrust down and into the boy's throat until his thumb and forefinger just touched the skin. Behind him he heard a struggle, and he looked up in time to see several people restrain a woman with an axe. He watched to see that they kept her out of the cave and away from him before he turned back to the boy. By gently turning the piece of flint he made an opening in the windpipe. He turned the boy on his side to prevent the tiny trickle of blood from running into the opening. The result was dramatic. The boy's struggles stopped, and the rush of air around the piece of flint sounded loud in the still of the cave. The boy lay back and relaxed and breathed deeply, and even the people in the cave could tell he was now much better. They gathered around and watched silently, and Gant could see the interest in their faces. The boy's mother had not come back.

For half an hour Gant sat holding the flint in the necessary position. The boy stirred restlessly a time or two, but Gant quieted him. The people drifted back to their activities in the cave, and Gant sat and tended his patient.

He leaned over the boy. He could hear the air beginning to pass through his throat once again. In another fifteen minutes the boy's throat was open enough, and Gant withdrew the flint in one swift movement. The boy began to sit up, but Gant held him down and pressed the wound closed. It stayed closed, and Gant got up. No one paid any attention when he left.

He went along the gravel shelf, ignoring the sounds of life that came out of the caves as he went by. He rounded a boulder and saw his own cave ahead.

The log barrier was displaced and he could hear snarls and grunts as he ran into the semidarkness inside. Two bodies writhed on the floor of the cave. He ran closer and saw that his wife and another woman were struggling there, raking each other's skin with thick, sharp nails, groping for each other's jugular vein with long, yellow teeth. Gant drove his heel into the side of the woman's body, just above the kidney. The air exploded from her lungs and she went limp. He twisted a hand in her hair and yanked her limp body away from his wife's teeth and ran for the entrance of the cave, dragging her after him. Outside, he threw the limp body down the slope. He turned and caught his wife as she came charging out. She fought him, trying to get to the woman down the slope, and it was only because she was no longer trying to kill that he was able to force her back into the cave.

Inside, she quickly stopped fighting him. She went and knelt over something lying at the foot of his bed. He rubbed his sore jaw and went over to see what it was. He stared down in the dim light of the cave. It was Dun, and he was dead. His head had been crushed. Gant cried out and leaned against the wall. He knelt and hugged Dun's warm body to him, pushing his wife aside. He pressed his face into the boy's neck and thought of the years that he had planned to spend in teaching Dun the healing arts. He felt a heavy pat on his shoulder and looked up. His wife was there, awkwardly patting him on the shoulder, trying to comfort him. Then he remembered the woman who had killed his son.

He ran out of the cave and looked down the slope. She was not there, but he caught a flash of movement down the gravel shelf and he could see her staggering toward her cave. He began to run after her, but stopped. His anger was gone, and he felt no emotion save a terrible emptiness. He turned and went back into the cave for Dun's body. In the forest he slowly dug a deep hole. He felt numb as he dug, but when it was done and he had rolled a large stone on top of the grave, he kneeled down near it, held his face in his hands and cried. Afterward, he followed the stream bed to a flat table of solid rock. At the edge of the rock table, where the wall of rock began to rise to the cliffs above, half hidden in the shrub pine, was a mass of twisted metal wreckage. He looked down on it and thought again of that day ten years ago. Here, on the site of Pennsylvania State University, at College Park, Pennsylvania, was where he started and where he ended. But a difference of half a million years lay between the start and the end.

Once tears had come to his eyes when he looked at the wreckage, but no longer. There was work to do here and he was the only one who could do it. He nodded and turned to climb to his cave. There were cold meat and shoots there, and a wife, and perhaps there could be another son. And this day, for the first time, an injured man had come to see him.

TIME TRAP

Charles L. Harness

Like Ted Thomas, Texas-born Charles L.
Harness is a patent attorney with a background
in chemistry who dabbles with fiction on an occasional basis. Like Thomas, too, the results of
the dabbling are usually impressive. Harness at-
tracted attention in 1948 with a dizzyingly intricate novel, *Flight Into Yesterday*, which repays
close study by anyone wishing to master the
craft of plotting. The story below dates from
about the same period, and shares with the
novel Harness' fondness at that time for bold
twists of construction. One would not call it a
model of soaring prose, yet despite all that its
author still had to learn about style, it demonstrated an enviable gift for audacious invention
that makes it diverting reading more than two
decades after it was written.

---

*The Great Ones themselves never agreed
whether the events constituting Troy's cry for help had a
beginning. But the warning signal did have an end. The
Great Ones saw to that. Those of the Great Ones who
claim a beginning for the story date it with the expulsion
of the evil Sathanas from the Place of Suns, when he
fled, horribly wounded, spiraling evasively inward,
through sterechronia without number, until, exhausted,
he sank and lay hidden in the crystallizing magma of a
tiny new planet at the galactic rim.*

191

General Blade sometimes felt that leading a resistance movement was far exceeding his debt to decent society and that one day soon he would allow his peaceful nature to override his indignant pursuit of justice. Killing a man, even a very bad man, without a trial, went against his grain. He sighed and rapped on the table.

"As a result of Blogshak's misappropriation of funds voted to fight the epidemic," he announced, "the death toll this morning reached over one hundred thousand. Does the Assassination Subcommittee have a recommendation?"

A thin-lipped man rose from the gathering. "The Provinarch ignored our warning," he said rapidly. "This subcommittee, as you all know, some days ago set an arbitrary limit of one hundred thousand deaths. Therefore this subcommittee now recommends that its plan for killing the Provinarch be adopted at once. Tonight is very favorable for our plan, which, incidentally, requires a married couple. We have thoroughly catasynthesized the four bodyguards who will be with him on this shift and have provided irresistible scent and sensory stimuli for the woman. The probability for its success insofar as assassination is concerned is about 78 percent; the probability of escape of our killers is 62 percent. We regard these probabilities as favorable. The Legal Subcommittee will take it from there."

Another man arose. "We have retained Mr. Poole, who is with us tonight." He nodded gravely to a withered little man beside him. "Although Mr. Poole has been a member of the bar but a short time, and although his prelegal life—some seventy years of it—remains a mystery which he does not explain, our catasynthesis laboratory indicates that his legal knowledge is profound. More important, his persuasive powers, tested with a trial group of twelve professional evaluators, sort of a rehearsal for a possible trial, border on hypnosis. He has also suggested an excellent method of disposing of the corpse to render identification difficult. According to Mr. Poole, if the assassinators are caught, the probability of escaping the devitalizing chamber is 53 percent."

"Mr. Chairman!"

General Blade turned toward the new speaker, who stood quietly several rows away. The man seemed to reflect a gray inconspicuousness, relieved only by a gorgeous rosebud in his lapel. Gray suit, gray eyes, graying temples. On closer examination, one detected an edge of flashing blue in the grayness. The eyes no longer seemed softly unobtrusive, but icy, and the firm mouth and jutting chin seemed polished steel. General Blade had observed this phenomenon dozens of times, but he never tired of it.

"You have the floor, Major Troy," he said.

"I, and perhaps other League officers, would like to know more about Mr. Poole," came the quiet, faintly metallic voice. "He is not a member of the League, and yet Legal and Assassination welcome him in their councils. I think we should be provided some assurance that he has no associations with the Provinarch's administration. One traitor could sell the lives of all of us."

The Legal spokesman arose again. "Major Troy's objections are in some degree merited. We don't know who Mr. Poole is. His mind is absolutely impenetrable to telepathic probes. His fingerprint and eye vein patterns are a little obscure. Our attempts at identification"—he laughed sheepishly—"always key out to yourself, major. An obvious impossibility. So far as the world is concerned, Mr. Poole is an old man who might have been born yesterday! All we know of him is his willingness to cooperate with us to the best of his ability—which, I can assure you, is tremendous. The catasynthesizer has established his sympathetic attitude beyond doubt. Don't forget, too, that he could be charged as a principal in this assassination and devitalized himself. On the whole, he is our man. If our killers are caught, we must use him."

Troy turned and studied the little lawyer with narrowing eyes; Poole's face seemed oddly familiar. The old man returned the gaze sardonically, with a faint suggestion of a smile.

"Time is growing short, major," urged the Assassination chairman. "The Poole matter has already received the attention of qualified League investigators. It is not a

193

proper matter for discussion at this time. If you are satisfied with the arrangements, will you and Mrs. Troy please assemble the childless married couples on your list? The men can draw lots from the fish bowl on the side table. The red ball decides." He eyed Troy expectantly.

Still standing, Troy looked down at the woman in the adjacent seat. Her lips were half-parted, her black eyes somber pools as she looked up at her husband.

"Well, Ann?" he telepathed.

Her eyes seemed to look through him and far beyond. "He will make you draw the red ball, Jon," she murmured, trancelike. "Then he will die, and I will die. But Jon Troy will never die. Never die. Never die. Nev—"

"Wake up, Ann!" Troy shook her by the shoulder. To the puzzled faces about them, he explained quickly, "My wife is something of a seeress." He 'pathed again: "Who is *he?*"

Ann Troy brushed the black hair from her brow slowly. "It's all confused. *He* is someone in this room—" She started to get up.

"Sit down, dear," said Troy gently. "If I'm to draw the red ball, I may as well cut this short." He slid past her into the aisle, strode to the side table, and thrust his hand into the hole in the box sitting there.

Every eye was on him.

His hand hit the invisible fish bowl with its dozen-odd plastic balls. Inside the bowl, he touched the little spheres at random while he studied the people in the room. All old friends, except—Poole. That tantalizing face. Poole was now staring like the rest, except that beads of sweat were forming on his forehead.

Troy swirled the balls around the bowl; the muffled clatter was audible throughout the room. He felt his fingers close on one. His hands were perspiring freely. With an effort he forced himself to drop it. He chose another, and looked at Poole. The latter was frowning. Troy could not bring his hand out of the bowl. His right arm seemed partially paralyzed. He dropped the ball and rolled the mass around again. Poole was now smiling. Troy hesitated a moment, then picked a ball from the

194

center of the bowl. It felt slightly moist. He pulled it out, looked at it grimly, and held it up for all to see.

"Just 'path that!" whispered the jail warden reverently to the night custodian.

"You know I can't telepath," said the latter grumpily. "What are they saying?"

"Not a word all night. They seem to be taking a symposium of the best piano concertos since maybe the twentieth century. Was Chopin twentieth or twenty-first? Anyhow, they're up to the twenty-third now, with Darnoval. Troy reproduces the orchestra and his wife does the piano. You'd think she had fifty years to live instead of five minutes."

"Both seem nice people," ruminated the custodian. "If they hadn't killed the Provinarch, maybe they'd have become famous 'pathic musicians. She had a lousy lawyer. She could have got off with ten years sleep if he'd half tried." He pushed some papers across the desk. "I've had the chamber checked. Want to look over the readings?"

The warden scanned them rapidly. "Potential difference, eight million; drain rate, ninety vital units/minute; estimated period of consciousness, thirty seconds; estimated durance to nonrecovery point, four minutes; estimated durance to legal death, five minutes." He initialed the front sheet. "That's fine. When I was younger they called it the 'vitality drain chamber.' Drain rate was only two v.u./min. Took an hour to drain them to unconsciousness. Pretty hard on the condemned people. Well, I'd better go officiate."

When Jon and Ann Troy finished the Darnoval concerto they were silent for a few moments, exchanging simply a flow of wordless, unfathomable perceptions between their cells. Troy was unable to disguise a steady beat of gloom. "We'll have to go along with Poole's plan," he 'pathed, "though I confess I don't know what his idea is. Take your capsule now."

His mind registered the motor impulses of her medulla as she removed the pill from its concealment under her armpit and swallowed it. Troy then perceived her awareness of her cell door opening, of grim men and women

195

about her. Motion down corridors. Then the room. A clanging of doors. A titanic effort to hold their fading contact. One last despairing communion, loving, tender.

Then nothing.

He was still sitting with his face buried in his hands, when the guards came to take him to his own trial that morning.

"This murder," announced the Peoples' advocate to the twelve evaluators, "this crime of taking the life of our beloved Provinarch Blogshak, this heinous deed—is the most horrible thing that has happened in Niork in my lifetime. The creature charged with this crime"—he pointed an accusing finger at the prisoner's box—"Jon Troy has been psyched and has been adjudged integrated at a preliminary hearing. Even his attorney"—here bowing ironically to a beady-eyed little man at counsels' table—"waived the defense of nonintegration."

Poole continued to regard the Peoples' advocate with bitter weariness, as though he had gone through this a thousand times and knew every word that each of them was going to say. The prisoner seemed oblivious to the advocate, the twelve evaluators, the judge, and the crowded courtroom. Troy's mind was blanked out. The dozen or so educated telepaths in the room could detect only a deep beat of sadness.

"I shall prove," continued the inexorable advocate, "that this monster engaged our late Provinarch in conversation in a downtown bar, surreptitiously placed a lethal dose of *skon* in the Provinarch's glass, and that Troy and his wife—who, incidentally, paid the extreme penalty herself early this—"

"Objection!" cried Poole, springing to his feet. "The defendant, not his wife, is now on trial."

"Sustained," declared the judge. "The advocate may not imply to the evaluators that the possible guilt of the present defendant is in any way determined by the proven guilt of any past defendant. The evaluators must ignore that implication. Proceed, advocate."

"Thank you, your honor." He turned again to the

evaluators' box and scanned them with a critical eye. "I shall prove that the prisoner and the late Mrs. Troy, after poisoning Provinarch Blogshak, carried his corpse into their sedan, and that they proceeded then to a deserted area on the outskirts of the city. Unknown to them, they were pursued by four of the mayor's bodyguards, who, alas, had been lured aside at the bar by Mrs. Troy. Psychometric determinations taken by the police laboratory will be offered to prove it was the prisoner's intention to dismember the corpse and burn it to hinder the work of the police in tracing the crime to him. He had got only as far as severing the head when the guards' ship swooped up and hovered overhead. He tried to run back to his own ship, where his wife was waiting, but the guards blanketed the area with a low-voltage stun."

The advocate paused. He was not getting the reaction in the evaluators he deserved, but he knew the fault was not his. He was puzzled; he would have to conclude quickly.

"Gentlemen," he continued gravely, "for this terrible thing, the Province demands the life of Jon Troy. The monster must enter the chamber tonight." He bowed to the judge and returned to counsels' table.

The judge acknowledged the retirement and turned to Poole. "Does the defense wish to make an opening statement?"

"The defense reiterates its plea of 'not guilty' and makes no other statement," grated the old man.

There was a buzz around the advocates' end of the table. An alert defense with a weak case always opened to the evaluators. Who was this Poole? What did he have? Had they missed a point? The prosecution was committed now. They'd have to start with their witnesses.

The advocate arose. "The prosecution offers as witness Mr. Fonstile."

"Mr. Fonstile!" called the clerk.

A burly, resentful-looking man blundered his way from the benches and walked up to the witness box and was sworn in.

197

Poole was on his feet. "May it please the court!" he croaked.

The judge eyed him in surprise. "Have you an objection, Mr. Poole?"

"No objection, your honor," rasped the little man, without expression. "I would only like to say that the testimony of this witness, the bartender in the Shawn Hotel, is probably offered by my opponent to prove facts which the defense readily admits, namely, that the witness observed Mrs. Troy entice the four bodyguards of the deceased to another part of the room, that the present defendant surreptitiously placed a powder in the wine of the deceased, that the deceased drank the wine and collapsed, and was carried out of the room by the defendant, followed by his wife." He bowed to the judge and sat down.

The judge was nonplussed. "Mr. Poole, do you understand that you are responsible for the defense of this prisoner, and that he is charged with a capital offense?"

"That is my understanding, your honor."

"Then if prosecution is agreeable, and wishes to elicit no further evidence from the witness, he will be excused."

The advocate looked puzzled, but called the next witness, Dr. Warkon, of the Provincial Police Laboratory. Again Poole was on his feet. This time the whole court eyed him expectantly. Even Troy stared at him in fascination.

"May it please the court," came the now-familiar monotone, "the witness called by the opposition probably expects to testify that the deceased's fingerprints were found on the wineglass in question, that traces of deceased's saliva were identified in the liquid content of the glass and that a certain quantity of *skon* was found in the wine remaining in the glass."

"And one other point, Mr. Poole," added the Peoples' advocate. "Dr. Warkon was going to testify that death from *skon* poisoning normally occurs within thirty seconds, owing to syncope. Does the defense concede that?"

"Yes."

"The witness is then excused," ordered the judge.

The prisoner straightened up. Troy studied his attorney curiously. The mysterious Poole with the tantalizing face, the man so highly recommended by the League, had let Ann go to her death with the merest shadow of a defense. And now he seemed even to state the prosecution's case rather than defend the prisoner.

Nowhere in the courtroom did Troy see a League member. But then, it would be folly for General Blade to attempt his rescue. That would attract unwelcome attention to the League.

He had been abandoned, and was on his own. Many League officers had been killed by Blogshak's men, but rarely in the devitalizing chamber. It was a point of honor to die weapon in hand. His first step would be to seize a blaster from one of the guards, use the judge as a shield, and try to escape through the judge's chambers. He would wait until he was put on the stand. It shouldn't be long, considering how Poole was cutting corners.

The advocate was conferring with his assistants. "What's Poole up to?" one of them asked. "If he is going on this far, why not get him to admit all the facts constituting a prima facie case: Malice, intent to kill, and all that?"

The advocate's eyes gleamed. "I think I know what he's up to now," he exulted. "I believe he's forgotten an elementary theorem of criminal law. He's going to admit everything, then demand we produce Blogshak's corpse. He must know it was stolen from the bodyguards when their ship landed at the port. No corpse, no murder, he'll say. But you don't need a corpse to prove murder. We'll hang him with his own rope!" He arose and addressed the judge.

"May it please the court, the prosecution would like to ask if the defense will admit certain other facts which I stand ready to prove."

The judge frowned. "The prisoner pleaded not guilty. Therefore the court will not permit any admission of the defense to the effect that the prisoner did kill the deceased, unless he wants to change his plea." He looked inquiringly at Poole.

"I understand, your honor," said Poole. "May I hear

what facts the learned prosecutor wishes me to accede to?"

For a moment the prosecutor studied his enigmatic antagonist like a master swordsman.

"First, the prisoner administered a lethal dose of *skon* to the deceased with malice aforethought, and with intent to kill. Do you concede that?"

"Yes."

"And that the deceased collapsed within a few seconds and was carried from the room by the defendant and his wife?"

"We agree to that."

"And that the prisoner carried the body to the city outskirts and there decapitated it?"

"I have already admitted that."

The twelve evaluators, a selected group of trained experts in the estimation of probabilities, followed this unusual procedure silently.

"Then your honor, the prosecution rests." The advocate felt dizzy, out of his depth. He felt he had done all that was necessary to condemn the prisoner. Yet Poole seemed absolutely confident, almost bored.

"Do you have any witnesses, Mr. Poole," queried the judge.

"I will ask the loan of Dr. Warkon, if the Peoples' advocate will be so kind," replied the little man.

"I'm willing." The advocate was beginning to look harassed. Dr. Warkon was sworn in.

"Dr. Warkon, did not the psychometer show that the prisoner intended to kill Blogshak in the tavern and decapitate him at the edge of the city?"

"Yes, sir."

"Was, in fact, the deceased dead when he was carried from the hotel?"

"He had enough *skon* in him to have killed forty people."

"Please answer the question."

"Well, I don't know. I presume he was dead. As an expert, looking at all the evidence, I should say he was dead. If he didn't die in the room, he was certainly dead a few seconds later."

"Did you feel his pulse at any time, or make any examination to determine the time of death?"

"Well, no."

Now, thought the advocate, comes the no corpse, no murder. If he tries that, I've got him.

But Poole was not to be pushed.

"Would you say the deceased was dead when the prisoner's ship reached the city limits?"

"Absolutely!"

"When you, as police investigator, examined the scene of the decapitation, what did you find?"

"The place where the corpse had lain was easily identified. Depressions in the sand marked the back, head, arms, and legs. The knife was lying where the prisoner dropped it. Marks of landing gear of the prisoner's ship were about forty feet away. Lots of blood, of course."

"Where was the blood?"

"About four feet away from the head, straight out."

Poole let the statement sink in, then:

"Dr. Warkon, as a doctor of medicine, do you realize the significance of what you have just said?"

The witness gazed at his inquisitor as though hypnotized. "Four feet . . . jugular spurt—" he muttered to no one. He stared in wonder, first at the withered, masklike face before him, then at the advocate, then at the judge. "Your honor, the deceased's heart was still beating when the prisoner first applied the knife. The poison didn't kill him!"

An excited buzz resounded through the courtroom.

Poole turned to the judge. "Your honor, I move for a summary judgment of acquittal."

The advocate sprang to his feet, wordless.

"Mr. Poole," remonstrated the judge, "your behavior this morning has been extraordinary, to say the least. On the bare fact that the prisoner killed with a knife instead of with poison, as the evidence at first indicated, you ask summary acquittal. The court will require an explanation."

"Your honor"—there was a ghost of a smile flitting about the prim, tired mouth—"to be guilty of a crime, a man must intend to commit a crime. There must be a

201

mens rea, as the classic expression goes. The act and the intent must coincide. Here they did not. Jon Troy intended to kill the Provinarch in the bar of the Shawn Hotel. He gave him poison, but Blogshak didn't die of it. Certainly up to the time the knife was thrust into Blogshak's throat, Troy may have been guilty of assault and kidnaping, but not murder. If there was any murder, it must have been at the instant he decapitated the deceased. Yet what was his intent on the city outskirts? He wanted to mutilate a corpse. His intent was not to murder, but to mutilate. We have the act, but not the intent—no *mens rea.* Therefore the act was not murder, but simply mutilation of a corpse—a crime punishable by fine or imprisonment, but not death."

Troy's mind was whirling. This incredible, dusty little man had freed him.

"But Troy's a murderer!" shouted the advocate, his face white. "Sophisms can't restore a life!"

"The court does not recognize the advocate!" said the judge harshly. "Cut those remarks from the record," he directed the scanning clerk. "This court is guided by the principles of common law descended from ancient England. The learned counsel for the defense has stated those principles correctly. Homicide is not murder if there is no intent to kill. And mere intent to kill is not murder if the poison doesn't take effect. This is a strange, an unusual case, and it is revolting for me to do what I have to do. I acquit the prisoner."

"Your honor!" cried the advocate. Receiving recognition, he proceeded. "This . . . this felon should not escape completely. He should not be permitted to make a travesty of the law. His own counsel admits he has broken the statutes on kidnaping, assault, and mutilation. The evaluators can at least return a verdict of guilty on those counts."

"I am just as sorry as you are," replied the judge, "but I don't find those counts in the indictment. You should have included them."

"If you release him, your honor, I'll re-arrest him and frame a new indictment."

"This court will not act on it. It is contrary to the

constitution of this province for a person to be prosecuted twice on the same charge or on a charge which should have been included in the original indictment. The Peoples' advocate is estopped from taking further action on this case. This is the final ruling of this court." He took a drink of water, wrapped his robes about him, and strode through the rear of the courtroom to his chambers.

Troy and Poole, the saved and the savior, eyed one another with the same speculative look of their first meeting.

Poole opened the door of the 'copter parked outside the Judiciary Building and motioned for Troy to enter. Troy froze in the act of climbing in.

A man inside the cab, with a face like a claw, was pointing a blaster at his chest.

The man was Blogshak!

Two men recognizable as the Provinarch's bodyguards suddenly materialized behind Troy.

"Don't give us any trouble, major," murmured Poole easily. "Better get in."

The moment Troy was pushed into the subterranean suite he sensed Ann was alive—drugged insensate still, but alive, and near. This knowledge suppressed momentarily Blogshak's incredible existence and Poole's betrayal. Concealing his elation, he turned to Poole.

"I should like to see my wife."

Poole motioned silently to one of the guards, who pulled back sliding doors. Beyond a glass panel, which was actually a transparent wall of a tile room, Ann lay on a high white metal bed. A nurse was on the far side of the bed, exchanging glances with Poole. At some unseen signal from him the nurse swabbed Ann's left arm and thrust a syringe into it.

A shadow crossed Troy's face. "What is the nurse doing?"

"In a moment Mrs. Troy will awaken. Whether she stays awake depends on you."

"On me? What do you mean?"

"Major, what you are about to learn can best be demonstrated rather than described. Sharg, the rabbit!"

203

The beetle-browed man opened a large enamel pan on the table. A white rabbit eased its way out, wrinkling its nose gingerly. Sharg lifted a cleaver from the table. There was a flash of metal, a spurt of blood, and the rabbit's head fell to the floor. Sharg picked it up by the ears and held it up expectantly. The eyes were glazed almost shut. The rabbit's body lay limp in the pan. At a word from Poole, Sharg carefully replaced the severed head, pressing it gently to the bloody neck stub. Within seconds the nose twitched, the eyes blinked, and the ears perked up. The animal shook itself vigorously, scratched once or twice at the bloody ring around its neck, then began nibbling at a head of lettuce in the pan.

Troy's mind was racing. The facts were falling in line. All at once everything made sense. With knowledge came utmost wariness. The next move was up to Poole, who was examining with keen eyes the effect of his demonstration on Troy.

"Major, I don't know how much you have surmised, but at least you cannot help realizing that life, even highly organized vertebrate life, is resistant to death in your presence."

Troy folded his arms but volunteered nothing. He was finally getting a glimpse of the vast and secret power supporting the Provinarch's tyranny, long suspected by the League but never verified.

"You could not be expected to discover this marvelous property in yourself except by the wildest chance," continued Poole. "As a matter of fact, our staff discovered it only when Blogshak and his hysterical guards reported to us, after your little escapade. But we have been on the lookout for your type for years. Several mutants with this characteristic have been predicted by our probability geneticists for this century, but you are the first known to us—really perhaps the only one in existence. One is all we need.

"As a second and final test of your power, we decided to try the effect of your aura on a person in the devitalizing chamber. For that reason we permitted Mrs. Troy to be condemned, when we could easily have prevented it.

As you now know, your power sustained your wife's life against a strong drain of potential. At my instruction she drugged herself in her cell simply to satisfy the doctor who checked her pulse and reflexes afterwards. When the staff—my employers—examined her here, they were convinced that you had the mutation they were looking for, and we put the finishing touches on our plans to save you from the chamber."

Granting I have some strange biotic influence, thought Troy, still, something's wrong. He says his bunch became interested in me *after* my attempt on Blogshak. *But Poole was at the assassination meeting!* What is his independent interest?

Poole studied him curiously. "I doubt that you realize what tremendous efforts have been made to insure your presence here. For the past two weeks the staff has hired several thousand persons to undermine the critical faculties of the four possible judges and nine hundred evaluators who might have heard your case. Judge Gallon, for example, was not in an analytical mood this morning because we saw to it that he won the Province Chess Championship with his Inner Gambit—a prize he has sought for thirty years. But if he had fooled us and given your case to the evaluators, we were fairly certain of a favorable decision. You noticed how they were not concentrating on the advocate's opening statement? They couldn't; they were too full of the incredible good fortune they had encountered the previous week. Sommers had been promoted to a full professorship at the Provincial University. Gunnard's obviously faulty thesis on space strains had been accepted by the *Steric Quarterly*—after we bought the magazine. But why go on? Still, if the improbable had occurred, and you had been declared guilty by the evaluators, we would simply have spirited you away from the courtroom. With a few unavoidable exceptions, every spectator in the room was a trained staff agent, ready to use his weapons—though in the presence of your aura, I doubt they could have hurt anyone.

"Troy, the staff had to get you here, but we preferred to do it quietly. Now, why are you here? I'll tell you.

Your aura, we think, will keep—" Poole hesitated. "Your aura will keep . . . *it* . . . from dying during an approaching crisis in its life stream."

"It? What is this 'it'? And what makes you so sure I'll stay?"

"The staff has not authorized me to tell you more concerning the nature of the entity you are to protect. Suffice to say that It is a living, sentient being. And I think you'll stay, because the hypo just given Mrs. Troy was pure *skon*."

Troy had already surmised as much. The move was perfect. If he stayed near her, Ann, though steeped in the deadliest known poison, would not die. But why had they been so sure he would not stay willingly, without Ann as hostage? He 'pathed the thought to Poole, who curtly refused to answer.

"Now, major, I'm going to turn this wing of the City Building over to you. For your information, your aura is effective for a certain distance within the building, but just how far I'm not going to tell you. However, you are not permitted to leave your apartment at all. The staff has demoted the Provinarch, and he's now the corporal of your bodyguard. He would be exceedingly embarrassed if you succeeded in leaving. Meals will be brought to you regularly. The cinematic and micro library is well stocked on your favorite subjects. Special concessions may even be made as to things you want in town. But you can never touch your wife again. That pane of glass will always be between you. A psychic receptor tuned to your personality integration is fixed within Mrs. Troy's room. If you break the glass panel, or in any other way attempt to enter the room, the receptor will automatically actuate a bomb mechanism imbedded beneath Mrs. Troy's cerebellum. She would be blown to little bits—each of them alive as long as you were around. It grieves us to be crude, but the situation requires some such safeguard."

"When will my wife recover consciousness?"

"Within an hour or so. But what's your hurry? You'll be here longer than you think."

The little lawyer seemed lost in thought for a moment.

Then he signaled Blogshak and the guards, and the four left. Blogshak favored Troy with a venomous scowl as he closed and locked the door.

There was complete and utter silence. Even the rabbit sat quietly on the table, blinking its eyes at Troy.

Left alone, the man surveyed the room, his perceptions palping every square foot rapidly but carefully. He found nothing unusual. He debated whether to explore the wing further or to wait until Ann awakened. He decided on the latter course. The nurse had left. They were together, with just a sheet of glass between. He explored Ann's room mentally, found nothing.

Then he walked to the center table and picked up the rabbit. There was the merest suggestion of a cicatrix encircling the neck.

Wonderful, but frightful, thought Troy. Who, what, am I?

He put the rabbit back in the box, pulled a comfortable armchair against the wall opposite the glass panel, where he had a clear view of Ann's room, and began a methodical attempt to rationalize the events of the day.

He was jolted from his reverie by an urgent 'pathic call from Ann. After a flurry of tender perceptions each unlocked his mind to the other.

Poole had planted an incredible message in Ann's ESP lobe.

"Jon," she warned, "it's coded to the Dar— . . . I mean, it's coded to the notes and frequencies of our last concerto, in the death house. You'll have to synchronize. I'll start."

How did Poole know we were familiar with the concerto? thought Troy.

"Think on this carefully, Jon Troy, and guard it well," urged Poole's message. "I cannot risk my identity, but I am your friend. It—the Outcast—has shaped the destinies of vertebrate life on earth for millions of years, for two purposes. One is a peculiar kind of food. The other is . . . you. You have been brought here to preserve an evil life. But I urge you, develop your latent powers and destroy that life!

"Jon Troy, the evil this entity has wreaked upon the

207

earth, entirely through his human agents thus far, is incalculable. It will grow even worse. You thought a sub-electronic virus caused the hundred thousand deaths which launched you on your assassination junket. Not so! The monster in the earth directly beneath you simply drained them of vital force, in their homes, on the street, in the theater, anywhere and everywhere. Your puny League has been fighting the Outcast for a generation without the faintest conception of the real enemy. If you have any love for humanity, search Blogshak's mind today. The staff physicians will be in this wing of the building today, too. Probe them. This evening, if I am still alive, I shall explain more, in person, free from Blogshak's crew."

"You have been wondering about the nature of the being whose life you are protecting," said Poole in a low voice, as he looked about the room. "As you learned when you searched the minds of the physicians this morning, he is nothing human. I believe him to have been wounded in a battle with his own kind, and that he has lain in his present pit for millions of years, possibly since pre-Cambrian times. He probably has extraordinary powers even in his weakened state, but to my knowledge he has never used them."

"Why not?" asked Troy.

"He must be afraid of attracting the unwelcome attention of those who look for him. But he has maintained his life somehow. The waste products of his organic metabolism are fed into our sewers daily. He has a group of physicians and physicists—a curious mixture!—who keep in repair his three-dimensional neural cortex and run a huge administrative organization designed for his protection."

"Seems harmless enough, so far," said Troy.

"He's harmless except for one venomous habit. I thought I told you about it in the message I left with Ann. You must have verified it if you probed Blogshak thoroughly."

"But I couldn't understand such near-cannibalism in so advanced—"

"Certainly not cannibalism! Do we think of ourselves as cannibals when we eat steaks? Still, that's my main objection to him. His vitality must be maintained by the absorption of other vitalities, preferably as high up the evolutionary scale as possible. Our thousands of deaths monthly can be traced to his frantic hunger for vital fluid. The devitalizing department, which Blogshak used to run, is the largest section of the staff."

"But what about the people who attend him? Does he snap up any of them?"

"He hasn't yet. They all have a pact with him. Help him, and he helps them. Every one of his band dies old, rich, evil, and envied by their ignorant neighbors. He gives them everything they want. Sometimes they forget, like Blogshak, that society can stand just so much of their evil."

"Assuming all you say is true—how does it concern my own problem, getting Ann out of here and notifying the League?"

Poole shook his head dubiously. "You probably have some tentative plans to hypnotize Blogshak and make him turn off the screen. But no one on the staff understands the screen. None of them can turn it off, because none of them turned it on. The chief surgeon believes it to be a direct, focused emanation from a radiator made long ago and known now only to the Outcast. But don't think of escaping just yet. You can strike a tremendous, fatal blow without leaving this room!"

"This afternoon," Poole continued with growing nervousness, "there culminates a project initiated by the Outcast millennia ago. Just ninety years ago the staff began the blueprints of a surgical operation on the Outcast on a scale which would dwarf the erection of the Mechanical Integrator. Indeed, you won't be surprised to learn that the Integrator, capable of planar sterechronic analysis, was but a preliminary practice project, a rehearsal for the main event."

"Go on," said Troy absently. His sensitive hearing detected heavy breathing from beyond the door.

"To perform this colossal surgery, the staff must disconnect for a few seconds all of the essential neural

209

trunks. When this is done, but for your aura, the Outcast would forever after remain a mass of senseless protoplasm and electronic equipment. With your aura, they can make the most dangerous repairs in perfect safety. When the last neural is down, you simply suppress your aura and the Outcast is dead. Then you could force your way out. From then on, the earth could go its merry way unhampered. Your League would eventually gain ascendancy and—"

"What about Ann?" asked Troy curtly. "Wouldn't she die along with the Outcast?"

"Didn't both of you take an oath to sacrifice each other before you'd injure the League or abandon an assignment?"

"That's a nice legal point," replied Troy, watching the corridor door behind Poole open a quarter of an inch. "I met Ann three years ago in a madhouse, where I had hidden away after a League assignment. She wasn't mad, but the stupid overseer didn't know it. She had the ability to project herself to other probability worlds, I married her to obtain a warning instrument of extreme delicacy and accuracy. Until that night in the death house, I'd have abided by League rules and abandoned her if necessary. But no longer. Any plan which includes her death is out. Suffering humanity can go climb a tree."

Poole's voice was dry and cracking. "I presumed you'd say that. You leave me no recourse. After I tell you who I am you will be willing to turn off your aura even at the cost of Ann's life. I am your . . . agh—"

A knife whistled through the open door and sank in Poole's neck. Blogshak and Sharg rushed in. Each man carried an ax.

"You dirty traitor!" screamed Blogshak. His ax crashed through the skull of the little old man even as Troy sprang forward. Sharg caught Troy under the chin with his ax handle. For some minutes afterward Troy was dimly aware of chopping, chopping, chopping.

Troy's aching jaw finally awoke him. He was lying on the sofa, where his keepers had evidently placed him. There was an undefinable raw odor about the room.

The carpet had been changed.

Troy's stomach muscles tensed. What had this done to Ann? He was unable to catch her ESP lobe. Probably out wandering through the past, or future.

While he tried to touch her mind, there was a knock on the door, and Blogshak entered with a man dressed in surgeon's white.

"Our operation apparently was a success, despite your little mishap," 'pathed the latter to Troy. "The next thirty years will tell us definitely whether we did this correctly. I'm afraid you'll have to stick around until then. I understand you're great chums with the Provinarch—ex-Provinarch, should I say? I'm sure he'll entertain you. I'm sorry about Poole. Poor fellow! Muffed his opportunities. Might have risen very high on the staff. But everything works out for the best, doesn't it?"

Troy glared at him wordlessly.

"Once we're out of here," 'pathed Troy in music code that afternoon, "we'll get General Blade to drop a plute fission on this building. It all revolves around the bomb under your cerebellum. If we can deactivate either the screen or the bomb, we're out. It's child's play to scatter Blogshak's bunch."

"If I had a razor," replied Ann, "I could cut the thing out. I can feel it under my neck muscles."

"Don't talk nonsense. What can you give me on Poole?"

"He definitely forced you to choose the red ball at the League meeting. Also, he knew he was going to be killed in your room. That made him nervous."

"Did he *know* he was going to be killed, or simply anticipate the possibility?"

"He knew. *He had seen it before!*"

Troy began pacing restlessly up and down before the glass panel, but never looking at Ann, who lay quietly in bed apparently reading a book. The nurse sat in a chair at the foot of Ann's bed, arms folded, implacably staring at her ward.

"Puzzling, very puzzling," mused Troy. "Any idea what he was going to tell me about my aura?"

"No."

211

"Anything on his identity?"

"I don't know—I had a feeling that I . . . we— No, it's all too vague. I noticed just one thing for certain."

"What was that?" asked Troy. He stopped pacing and appeared to be examining titles on the bookshelves.

"He was wearing your rosebud!"

"But that's crazy! I had it on all day. You must have been mistaken."

"You know I can't make errors on such matters."

"That's so." Troy resuming his pacing. "Yet, I refuse to accept the proposition that both of us were wearing my rosebud at the same instant. Well, never mind. While we're figuring a way to deactivate your bomb, we'd also better give a little thought to solving my aura.

"The solution is known—we have to assume that our unfortunate friend knew it. Great Galaxy! What our League biologists wouldn't give for a chance at this! We must change our whole concept of living matter. Have you ever heard of the immortal heart created by Alexis Carrel?" he asked abruptly.

"No."

"At some time during the Second Renaissance, early twentieth century, I believe, Dr. Carrel removed a bit of heart tissue from an embryo chick and put it in a nutrient solution. The tissue began to expand and contract rhythmically. Every two days the nutrient solution was renewed and excess growth cut away. Despite the catastrophe that had overwhelmed the chick—as a chick—the individual tissue lived on independently because the requirements of its cells were met. This section of heart tissue beat for nearly three centuries, until it was finally lost in the Second Atomic War."

"Are you suggesting that the king's men can put Humpty Dumpty together again if due care has been taken to nourish each part?"

"It's a possibility. Don't forget the skills developed by the Muscovites in grafting skin, ears, corneas, and so on."

"But that's a long process—it takes weeks."

"Then let's try another line. Consider this: The amoeba lives in a fluid medium. He bumps into his food, which is generally bacteria or bits of decaying protein, flows around it, digests it at leisure, excretes his waste matter, and moves on. Now go on up the evolutionary scale past the coelenterates and flatworms, until we reach the first truly three-dimensional animals—the coelomates. The flatworm had to be flat because he had no blood vessels. His food simply soaked into him. But cousin roundworm, one of the coelomates, grew plump and solid, because his blood vessels fed his specialized interior cells, which would otherwise have no access to food.

"Now consider a specialized cell—say a nice long muscle cell in the rabbit's neck. It can't run around in stagnant water looking for a meal. It has to have its breakfast brought to it, and its excrement carried out by special messenger, or it soon dies."

Troy picked a book from the shelf and leafed through it idly.

Ann wondered mutely whether her nurse had been weaned on a lemon.

"This messenger," continued Troy, "is the blood. It eventually reaches the muscle cell by means of a capillary—a minute blood vessel about the size of a red corpuscle. The blood in the capillary gives the cell everything it needs and absorbs the cell waste-matter. The muscle cell needs a continuously fresh supply of oxygen, sugar, amino-acids, fats, vitamins, sodium, calcium, and potassium salts, hormones, water, and maybe other things. It gets these from the hemoglobin and plasma, and it sheds carbon dioxide, ammonium compounds, and so on. Our cell can store up a little food within its own boundaries to tide it over for a number of hours. But oxygen it must have, every instant."

"You're just making the problem worse," interposed Ann. "If you prove that blood must circulate oxygen continuously to preserve life, you'll have yourself out on a limb. If you'll excuse the term, the rabbit's circulation was decisively cut off."

"That's the poser," agreed Troy. "The blood didn't circulate, but the cells didn't die. And think of this a moment: Blood is normally alkaline, with a pH of 7.4. When it absorbs carbon dioxide as a cell excretion, blood becomes acid, and this steps up respiration to void the excess carbon dioxide, via the lungs. But so far as I could see, the rabbit didn't even sigh after he got his head back. There was certainly no heavy breathing."

"I'll have to take your word for it; I was out cold."

"Yes, I know." Troy began pacing the room again. "It isn't feasible to suppose the rabbit's plasma was buffered to an unusual degree. That would mean an added concentration of sodium bicarbonate and an increased solids content. The cellular water would dialyze into the blood and kill the creature by simple dehydration."

"Maybe he had unusual reserves of hemoglobin," suggested Ann. "That would take care of your oxygen problem."

Troy rubbed his chin. "I doubt it. There are about five million red cells in a cubic millimeter of blood. If there are very many more, the cells would oxidize muscle tissue at a tremendous rate, and the blood would grow hot, literally cooking the brain. Our rabbit would die of a raging fever. Hemoglobin dissolves about fifty times as much oxygen as plasma, so it doesn't take much hemoglobin to start an internal conflagration."

"Yet the secret must lie in the hemoglobin. You just admitted that the cells could get along for long periods with only oxygen," persisted Ann.

"It's worth thinking about. We must learn more about the chemistry of the cell. You take it easy for a few days while I go through Poole's library."

"Could I do otherwise?" murmured Ann.

". . . *thus the effect of confinement varies from person to person. The claustrophobe deteriorates rapidly, but the agoraphobe mellows, and may find excuses to avoid the escape attempt. The person of high mental and physical attainments can avoid atrophy by directing his every thought to the destruction of the confining force. In this case, the increment in mental prowess is 3.1 times the logarithm of the duration of confinement measured in years. The intelligent and determined prisoner can escape if he lives long enough.*"—J. and A. T., *An Introduction to Prison Escape,* 4th Edition, League Publishers, p. 14.

In 1811, Avogadro, in answer to the confusing problems of combining chemical weights, invented the molecule. In 1902, Einstein resolved an endless array of incompatible facts by suggesting a mass-energy relation. Three centuries later, in the tenth year of his imprisonment, Jon Troy was driven in near-despair to a similar stand. In one sure step of dazzling intuition, he hypothesized the viton.

"The secret goes back to our old talks on cell preservation," he explained with ill-concealed excitement to Ann. "The cell can live for hours without proteins and salts, because it has means of storing these nutrients from past meals. But oxygen it must have. The hemoglobin takes up molecular oxygen in the lung capillaries, ozonizes it, and, since hemin is easily reduced, the red cells give up oxygen to the muscle cells that need it, in return for carbon dioxide. After it takes up the carbon dioxide, hemin turns purple and enters the vein system on the way back to the lungs, and we can forget it.

"Now, what is hemin? We can break it down into etiopyrophorin, which, like chlorophyll, contains four pyrrole groups. The secret of chlorophyll has been known for years. Under a photon catalyst of extremely short wave length, such as ultraviolet light, chlorophyll seizes molecule after molecule of carbon dioxide and synthesizes starches and sugars, giving off oxygen. Hemin, with its etiopyrophorin, works quite similarly, except that it doesn't need ultraviolet light. Now—"

"But animal cell metabolism works the other way," objected Ann. "Our cells take up oxygen and excrete carbon dioxide."

"It depends which cells you are talking about," reminded Troy. "The red corpuscle takes up carbon dioxide just as its plant cousin, chlorophyll, does, and they both excrete oxygen. Oxygen is just as much an excrement of the red cell as carbon dioxide is of the muscle cell."

"That's true," admitted Ann.

"And that's where the viton comes in," continued Troy. "It preserves the status quo of cell chemistry. Suppose that an oxygen atom has just been taken up by an amino acid molecule within the cell protoplasm. The

215

amino acid immediately becomes unstable, and starts to spit out carbon dioxide. In the red corpuscle, a mass of hemin stands by to seize the carbon dioxide and offer more oxygen. But the exchange never takes place. Just as the amino acid and the hemin reach toward one another, their electronic attractions are suddenly neutralized by a bolt of pure energy from me: The viton! Again and again the cells try to exchange, with the same result. They can't die from lack of oxygen, because their individual molecules never attain an oxygen deficit. The viton gives a very close approach to immortality!"

"But *we* seem to be getting older. Perhaps your vitons don't reach every cell?"

"Probably not," admitted Troy. "They must stream radially from some central point within me, and of course they would decrease in concentration according to the inverse square law of light. Even so, they would keep enough cells alive to preserve life as a whole. In the case of the rabbit, after the cut cell surfaces were rejoined, there were still enough of them alive to start the business of living again. One might suppose, too, that the viton accelerates the reestablishment of cell boundaries in the damaged areas. That would be particularly important with the nerve cells."

"All right," said Ann. "You've got the viton. What are you going to do with it?"

"That's another puzzler. First, what part of my body does it come from? There must be some sort of a globular discharge area fed by a relatively small but impenetrable duct. If we suppose a muscle controlling the duct—"

"What you need is an old Geiger-Müller," suggested Ann. "Locate your discharge globe first, then the blind spot on it caused by the duct entry. The muscle has to be at that point."

"I wonder—" mused Troy. "We have a burnt-out cinema projection bulb around here somewhere. The vacuum ought to be just about soft enough by now to ionize readily. The severed filament can be the two electron poles." He laughed mirthlessly: "I don't know why I should be in a hurry. I won't be able to turn off the viton stream even if I should discover the duct-muscle."

Weeks later, Troy found his viton sphere, just below the cerebral frontal lobe. The duct led somewhere into the pineal region. Very gingerly he investigated the duct environment. A small but dense muscle mass surrounded the entry of the duct to the bulk of radiation.

On the morning of the first day of the thirty-first year of their imprisonment, a few minutes before the nurse was due with the *skon* hypo, Ann 'pathed to Troy that she thought the screen was down. A joint search of the glass panel affirmed this.

Ann was stunned, like a caged canary that suddenly notices the door is open—she fears to stay, yet is afraid to fly away.

"Get your clothes on, dear," urged Troy. "Quickly now! If we don't contact the League in the next ten minutes, we never shall."

She dressed like an automaton.

Troy picked the lock on the corridor door noiselessly, with a key he had long ago made for this day, and opened the portal a quarter of an inch. The corridor seemed empty for its whole half-mile length. There was a preternatural pall of silence hanging over everything. Ordinarily, someone was always stirring about the corridor at this hour. He peered closely at the guard's cubicle down the hall. His eyes were not what they once were, and old Blogshak had never permitted him to be fitted with contacts.

He sucked in his breath sharply. The door of the cubicle was open, and two bodies were visible on the floor. One of the bodies had been a guard. The green of his uniform was plainly visible. The other corpse had white hair and a face like a wrinkled, arthritic claw. It was Blogshak.

Two mental processes occurred within Troy. To the cold, objective Troy, the thought occurred that the viton flow was ineffective beyond one hundred yards. Troy the human being wondered why the Outcast had not immediately remedied this weak point in the guard system. Heart pounding, he stepped back within the suite. He seized a chair, warned Ann out of the way, and hurled it through the glass panel. Ann stepped gingerly through the jagged gap. He held her for a moment in his arms. Her hair was a pure white, her face furrowed. Her body seemed weak and infirm. But it was Ann. Her eyes were shut and she seemed to be floating through time and space.

"No time for a trance now!" He shook her harshly, pulling her out of the room and down the corridor. He looked for a stair. There was none.

"We'll have to chance an autovator!" he panted, thinking he should have taken some sort of bludgeon with him. If several of the staff should come down with the 'vator, he doubted his ability to hypnotize them all.

He was greatly relieved when he saw an empty 'vator already on the subterranean floor. He leaped in, pulling Ann behind him, and pushed the button to close the door. The door closed quietly, and he pushed the button for the first floor.

"We'll try the street floor first," he said, breathing heavily. "Don't look around when we leave the 'vator. Just chatter quietly and act as though we owned the place."

The street floor was empty.

An icy thought began to grow in Troy's mind. He stepped into a neighboring 'vator, carrying Ann with him almost bodily, closed the door, and pressed the last button. Ann was mentally out, but was trying to tell him something. Her thoughts were vague, unfocused.

If they were pursued, wouldn't the pursuer assume they had left the building? He hoped so.

A malicious laughter seemed to follow them up the shaft.

He gulped air frantically to ease the roar in his ears. Ann had sunk into a semi-stupor. He eased her to the floor. The 'vator continued to climb. It was now in the two hundreds. Minutes later it stopped gently at the top floor, the door opened, and Troy managed to pull Ann out into a little plaza.

They were nearly a mile above the city.

The penthouse roof of the City Building was really a miniature country club, with a small golf course, swimming pool, and club house for informal administrative functions. A cold wind now blew across the closely cut green. The swimming pool was empty. Troy shivered as he dragged Ann near the dangerously low guard rail and looked over the city in the early morning sunlight.

As far as he could see, nothing was moving. There were no cars gliding at any of the authorized traffic levels, no 'copters or transocean ships in the skies.

For the first time, Troy's mind sagged, and he felt like the old man he was.

As he stared, gradually understanding, yet half-unbelieving, the rosebud in his lapel began to speak.

Mai-kel condensed the thin waste of cosmic gas into several suns and peered again down into the sterechron. There could be no mistake—there was a standing wave of recurrent time emanating from the tiny planet. The Great One made himself small and approached the little world with cautious curiosity. Sathanas had been badly wounded, but it was hard to believe his integration had deteriorated to the point of permitting oscillation in time. And no intelligent life capable of time travel was scheduled for this galaxy. Who, then? Mai-kel synchronized himself with the oscillation so that the events constituting it seemed to move at their normal pace. His excitement multiplied as he followed the cycle.

It would be safest, of course, to volatilize the whole planet. But then, that courageous mite, that microscopic human being who had created the time trap would be lost. Extirpation was indicated—a clean, fast incision done at just the right point of the cycle.

Mai-kel called his brothers.

Troy suppressed an impulse of revulsion. Instead of tearing the flower from his coat, he pulled it out gently and held it at arm's length, where he could watch the petals join and part again, in perfect mimicry of the human mouth.

"Yes, little man. I am what you call the Outcast. There are no other little men to bring my message to you, so I take this means of—"

"You mean you devitalized every man, woman, and child in the province . . . in the whole world?" croaked Troy.

"Yes. Within the past few months, my appetite has been astonishingly good, and I have succeeded in storing within my neurals enough vital fluid to carry me into the next sterechron. There I can do the same, and continue my journey. There's an excellent little planet waiting for me, just bursting with genial bipedal life. I can almost feel their vital fluid within me, now. And I'm taking you along, of course, in case I meet some . . . old friends. We'll leave now."

"Jon! Jon!" cried Ann, from behind him. She was standing, but weaving dizzily. Troy was at her side in an instant. "Even *he* doesn't know who Poole is!"

"Too late for any negative information now, dear," said Troy dully.

"But it isn't negative. If *he* doesn't know, then he won't stop you from going back." Her voice broke off in a wild cackle.

Troy looked at her in sad wonder.

"Jon," she went on feverishly, "your vitons help preserve the status quo of cells by preventing chemical change, but that is only part of the reason they preserve life. Each viton must also contain a quantum of time flow, which dissolves the vital fluid of the cell and reprecipitates it into the next instant. This is the only hypothesis which explains the preservation of the giant neurals of the Outcast. There was no chemical change going on in them which required stabilization, but something had to keep the vital fluid alive. Now, if you close the duct suddenly, the impact of unreleased vitons will send you back through time in your present body, as an old man. Don't you understand about Poole, now, Jon? You will go back thirty years through time, establish yourself in the confidence of both the League and the staff, attend the assassination conference, make young Troy choose the red ball again, defend him at the trial, and then you will die in that horrible room again. You have no choice about doing this, *because it has already happened!* Goodbye, darling! You are Poole!"

There was an abrupt swish. Ann had leaped over the guard rail into space.

A gurgle of horror died in Troy's throat. Still clutching the now silent rose in his hand, he jammed the viton muscle with all his will power. There was a sickening shock, then a flutter of passing days and nights. As he fell through time, cold fingers seemed to snatch frantically at him. But he knew he was safe.

As he spiraled inward, Troy-Poole blinked his eyes involuntarily, as though reluctant to abandon a languorous escape from reality. He was like a dreamer awakened by having his bedclothes blown off in an icy gale.

He slowly realized that this was not the first time he had suddenly been bludgeoned into reality. Every seventy years the cycle began for him once more. He knew now that seventy years ago he had completed another identical circle in time. And the lifetime before that, and the one prior. There was no beginning and no ending. The only reality was this brief lucid interval between cycles, waiting for the loose ends of time to cement. He had the choice at this instant to vary the life stream, to fall far beyond Troy's era, if he liked, and thus to end this existence as the despairing toy of time. What had he accomplished? Nothing, except retain, at the cost of almost unbearable monotony and pain, a weapon pointed at the heart of the Outcast, a weapon he could never persuade the young Troy to use, on account of Ann. Troy old had no influence over Troy young. Poole could never persuade Troy.

Peering down through the hoary wastes of time he perceived how he had hoped to set up a cycle in the time stream, a standing wave noticeable to the entities who searched for the Outcast. Surely with their incredible intellects and perceptions this discrepancy in the ordered universe would not go unnoticed. He had hoped that this trap in the time flow would hold the Outcast until relief came. But as his memory returned he realized that he had gradually given up hope. Somehow he had gone on from a sense of duty to the race from which he had sprung. From the depths of his aura-fed nervous system

221

he had always found the will to try again. But now his nervous exhaustion, increasing from cycle to cycle by infinitesimal amounts, seemed overpowering.

A curious thought occurred to him. There must have been, at one time, a Troy without a Poole to guide—or entangle—him. There must have been a beginning—some prototype Troy who selected the red ball by pure accident, and who was informed by a prototype staff of his tremendous power. After that, it was easy to assume that the first Troy "went back" as the prototype Poole to scheme against the life of the Outcast.

But searching down time, Troy-Poole now found only the old combination of Troy and Poole he knew so well. Hundreds, thousands, millions of them, each preceding the other. As far back as he could sense, there was always a Poole hovering over a Troy. Now he would become the next Poole, enmesh the next Troy in the web of time, and go his own way to bloody death. He could not even plan a comfortable suicide. No, to maintain perfect oscillation of the time trap, all Pooles must always die in the same manner as the first Poole. There must be no invariance. He suppressed a twinge of impatience at the lack of foresight in the prototype Poole.

"Just this once more," he promised himself wearily, "then I'm through. Next time I'll keep on falling."

General Blade sometimes felt that leading a resistance movement was far exceeding his debt to decent society and that one day soon he would allow his peaceful nature to override his indignant pursuit of justice. Killing a man, even a very bad man, without a trial, went against his grain. He sighed and rapped on the table.

"As a result of Blogshak's misappropriation of funds to fight the epidemic," he announced, "the death toll this morning reached over one hundred thousand. Does the Assassination Subcommittee have a recommendation?"

A thin-lipped man rose from the gathering. "The Provinarch ignored our warning," he said rapidly. "This subcommittee, as you all know, some days ago set an arbitrary limit of one hundred thousand deaths. Therefore this subcommittee now recommends that its plan for killing the Provinarch be adopted at once. Tonight is very favorable for our—"

A man entered the room quietly and handed General Blade an envelope. The latter read it quickly, then stood up. "I beg your pardon, but I must break in," he announced. "Information I have just received may change our plans completely. This report from our intelligence service is so incredible that I won't read it to you. Let's verify it over the video."

He switched on the instrument. The beam of a local newscasting agency was focused tridimensionally before the group. It showed a huge pit or excavation which appeared to move as the scanning newscaster moved. The news comments were heard in snatches. "No explosion . . . no sign of any force . . . just complete disappearance. An hour ago the City Building was the largest structure in . . . now nothing but a gaping hole a mile deep . . . the Provinarch and his entire council were believed in conference . . . no trace—"

General Blade turned an uncomprehending face to the committee. "Gentlemen, I move that we adjourn this session pending an investigation."

Jon Troy and Ann left through the secret alleyway. As he buttoned his topcoat against the chill night air, he sensed that they were being followed. "Oh, hello?"

"I beg your pardon, Major Troy, and yours, madam. My name is Poole, Legal Subcommittee. You don't know me—yet, but I feel that I know you both very well. Your textbook on prison escape has inspired and sustained me many times in the past. I was just admiring your boutonniere, major. It seems so lifelike for an artificial rosebud. I wonder if you could tell me where I might buy one?"

Troy laughed metallically. "It's not artificial. I've worn it for weeks, but it's a real flower, from my own garden. It just won't die."

"Extraordinary," murmured Poole, fingering the red blossom in his own lapel. "Could we run in here for a cocktail? Bartender Fonstile will fix us something special, and we can discuss a certain matter you really ought to know about."

The doorman of the Shawn Hotel bowed to the three as they went inside.

THE PI MAN

Alfred Bester

Has any writer of science fiction displayed more skill in the narrative art—both in style and in construction—than Alfred Bester? I think not. His novel *The Demolished Man* of 1951 served notice that a formidable hand was among us, and the series of pyrotechnical short stories that he produced later in the 1950's left no doubt of his mastery. As can be seen in *The Pi Man*.

How to say? How to write? When sometimes I can be fluent, even polished, and then, *reculer pour nieux sauter,* it takes hold of me. Push. Force. Compel. Sometimes

I

must

go

back

but

not

to

jump; no, not even to jump better. I have no control over self, speech, love, fate. I must compensate. Always.

But I try anyway.

Quae nocent docent. Translation follows: Things that injure, teach. I am injured and have hurt many. What have we learned? However. I wake up the morning of the biggest hurt of all wondering which house. Wealth, you understand. Damme! Mews cottage in London, villa

225

in Rome, penthouse in New York, rancho in California. I awake. I look. Ah! Layout is familiar. Thus:

Bedroom   Foyer

                              T

        Bath   e

                              r

        Bath

                              r

            Living Room   a

                              c

        Bedroom

                              e

        Kitchen

    T e r r a c e

Oh-oh! I am in penthouse in New York; but that bath-bath back-to-back. Pfui. All rhythm wrong. Balance off. Pattern painful. I telephone downstairs to janitor-mans. At that moment I lose my English. (You must understand I speak in all tongues. A goulash. I am compelled. Why? Ah!)

"Pronto. Ecco mi, Signore Storm. No. Forced to *parlato Italiano.* Wait. I call back in *cinque minuti."*

Re infecta. Latin. The business being unfinished, I shower body, teeth, hairs, shave face, dry everything and try again. *Voilà!* The English, she come. Back to invention of A. G. Bell ("Mr. Watson, come here, I need you"). On telephone I speak to janitor. Nice chap. Gets a job of work done in two twos.

"Hallo? Abraham Storm here, again. Yes. Right. Chap in the penthouse. Mr. Lundgren, be my personal rabbi and get some workmen up here this morning. I want those two baths converted into one. Yes. I'll leave five thousand dollars on top of the refrigerator. Thanks, Mr. Lundgren."

Wanted to wear gray flannel this morning, but had to put on the sharkskin. Damnation! African nationalism

226

has queer side-effects. Went to the back bedroom (see diagram) and unlocked the door which was installed by National Safe Co., Inc., I went in.

Everything broadcasting beautifully. Up and down the electromagnetic spectrum. Visual off from ultraviolet and jamming toward the infrared. Ultra shortwave screaming. Alpha, beta, and gamma radiation hearty. And the interruptors innn tt errrrr up ppp tttinggggg at random and comfortably. I am at peace. Christ Jesus! To know even a moment of peace!

I take subway to office in Wall Street. Chauffeur too dangerous; might become friendly. I don't dare have friends. Best of all, morning subway jam-packed, mass-packed; no patterns to adjust, no shiftings and compensatings required. Peace! I buy all morning papers; because of the patterns, you understand. Too many *Timeses* being read; I must read *Tribune* to balance pattern. Too many *Newses;* I read *Mirror.* Etc.

In subway car I catch a glimpse of an eye; narrow, bleak, gray-blue, the possession of an anonymous man who conveys the conviction that you've never seen him before and will never again. But I picked up that glance and it rang a bell in the back of my mind. He knew it. He saw the flash in my eye before I could conceal it. So I was being tailed again? But by whom? U.S.A.? U.S.S.R.? Matoids?

I blasted out of the subway at City Hall and gave them a false trail to the Woolworth Building, in case they were operating double-tails. The whole theory of the hunters and the hunted is not to avoid being spotted . . . no one can escape that . . . but to lay so many trails for them to follow that they become overextended. Then they're forced to abandon you. They have so many men for so many operations. It's a question of diminishing returns.

City Hall traffic was out of sync (as it always is) and I had to walk on the hot side of the street to compensate. Took elevator up to tenth floor of bldg. There I was suddenly seized by something from sss ome wwwhh ere. SS ommme tth inggg b addd. I began to cry, but no help. An elderly clerk emerge from office wearing alpaca coat, carry papers, gold spectacles.

"Not him," I plead with nowhere. "Nice mans. Not him. Please."

But I am force. Approach. Two blows; neck and gut. Down he go, writhing. I trample spectacles. Remove watch from pocket and smash. Shatter pens. Tear papers. Then I am permitted to get back into elevator and go downstairs again. It was 10:30. I was late. Damned inconvenient. Took taxi to 99 Wall Street. Tipped driver ten dollars. Sealed one thousand in envelope (secretly) and sent driver back to bldg to find and give to clerk.

Routine morning's work in office. Market jumpy; big board hectic; hell to balance and compensate, even though I know the patterns of money. I am behind by the sum of $109,872.43 by eleven-thirty; but, *a pas de géant* the patterns put me ahead $57,075.94 by half-past 12:00 noon, Daylight Saving Time, which my father used to call Woodrow Wilson time.

57075 makes nice pattern, but that 94¢. Pfui. Made the whole balance sheet look lopsided, ugly. Symmetry above all else. Only 24¢ in my pocket. Called secretary, borrowed 70¢ from her and threw sum total out window. Felt better as I watched it chime down to the street, but then I caught her looking at me with surprise and delight. Very bad. Very dangerous. Fired girl on the spot.

"But why, Mr. Storm? Why?" she asked, trying not to cry. Darling little thing. Freckled face and saucy, but not so saucy now.

"Because you're beginning to like me."

"What's the harm in that?"

"When I hired you I warned you not to like me."

"I thought you were kidding."

"I wasn't. Out you go. Beat it."

"But why?" -

"I'm afraid I might start liking you."

"Is this a new kind of pass?" she asked.

"God forbid."

"Well, you don't have to fire me," she flared. "I hate you."

"Good. Then I can go to bed with you."

She turned crimson and opened her mouth to denounce

228

me, the while her eyes twinkled at the corners. A darling girl. I could not endanger her. I put her into her hat and coat, gave her a year's salary for a bonus, and threw her out. *Punkt.* Made memo: Hire nothing but men, preferably married, misanthropic, and murderous. Men who could hate me.

So, lunch. Went to nicely balanced restaurant. Tables attached to floor. No moving them. All chairs filled by patrons. Nice pattern. No need for me to compensate and adjust. Ordered nicely patterned luncheon for self:

Martini   Martini

Martini

Croque M'sieur Roquefort

Salad

Coffee

But so much sugar being consumed in restaurant, I had to take my coffee black, which I dislike. However, still a nice pattern. Balanced.

$X^2 + X + 41$ = prime number. Excuse, please. Sometimes I'm in control and see what compensating must be done. Other times it's forced on me from God only knows where or why. Then I must do what I'm compelled to do, blindly, like speaking the gibberish I speak; sometimes hating it, like the clerk in the Woolworth Building. Anyway, the equation breaks down when x=40.

The afternoon was quiet. For a moment I thought I might be forced to leave for Rome (Italy), but something adjusted without needing me. The A.S.P.C.A. finally caught up with me for beating my dog to death, but I'd contributed $10,000 to their Shelter. Got off with a shaking of heads. I penciled moustaches on posters, rescued a drowning kitten, saved a woman from a mugging, and had my head shaved. Normal day.

In the evening to the ballet to relax with all the beautiful patterns, balanced, peaceful, soothing. Then I take deep breath, quash my nausea, and force myself to go to

Le Bitnique, the beatnik joint. I hate *Le Bitnique,* but I need a woman and I must go where I hate. That freckled girl I fire . . . so slender and full of delicious mischief, and making eyes at me. *So, poisson d'avril,* I advance myself to *Le Bitnique.*

Chaos. Blackness. Sounds and smells a cacaphony. One twenty-five watt bulb in ceiling. One maladroit pianist play Progressive. Against L. wall sit beatnik boys, wearing berets, black glasses, and pubic beards, playing chess. Against R. wall is bar and beatnik girls with brown paper bags under arms containing toilet articles. They are shuffling and maneuvering for a pad for the night.

Those beatnik girls! All skinny . . . exciting to me tonight because too many American men dream about overstuffed women, and I must compensate. (In England I like overstuff because England like women skinny.) All wear tight slack, loose sweater, Brigitte Bardot hair, Italian make-up . . . black eye, white lip . . . and when they walk they make with the gait that flipped that Herrick cat three centuries ago when he split and wrote:

> *Next, when I lift mine eyes and see*
> *That brave vibration each way free;*
> *Oh how that glittering taketh me!*

I pick one who glitter. I talk. She insult. I insult back and buy drinks. She drink and insult.[2] I hope she is lesbian and insult.[3] She snarl and hate, but helpless. No pad for tonight. The pathetic brown paper bag under her arm. I quell sympathy and hate back. She does not bathe. Her thinking patterns are jangles. Safe. No harm can come to her. I take her home to seduce by mutual contempt. And in living room (see diagram) sits slender little freckly-face secretary, recently fired, now waiting for me.

!
I
now
write
part of

story in Paris
Capital of France

Address: 49 bis Avenue Hoche. Paris, 8ème, France.

Forced to go there by what happened in Singapore, you understand. It needed extreme compensation and adjustment. Almost, for a moment, I thought I would have to attack the conductor of the *Opéra Comique,* but fate was kind and let me off with nothing worse than indecent exposure under the *Petite Carousel.* And I was able to found a scholarship at the Sorbonne before I was taken away.

Anyway, she sat there, my little one, in my penthouse now with one (1) bathroom, and $1,997.00 change on top of the refrigerator. Ugh! Throw $6.00 out window and am soothed by lovely 1991 remaining. She sat there, wearing a basic black cocktail dress with tight skirt, sheer black stockings, black opera pumps. The freckly skin gleamed reddish rose from embarrassment. Also red for danger. Her saucy face was very tight from the daring thing she thought she was doing. Damme! I like that.

I also like the nice even curve of the legs, and the bosom. Balanced, you understand? * * Like so; but not too thrusting. Tactful. Also her cleavage. Like so; and just as rosy as her face, despite desperate powdering to make her skin milky. That powder; a nuisance. I go to kitchen and rub burnt cork on shirt-front to compensate.

"Oh-so," I say. "Me-fella be ve'y happy ask why you-fella chop-chop invade along my apa'tment. Excep' mus' now speak pidgin-English. Ve'y much embarrass along me. Excuse please, until change come."

"I bribed Mr. Lundgren," she blurted. "I told him you needed important papers from your office."

"Entschuldigen Sie, bitte. Meine pidgin haben sich geaendert. Sprachen Sie Deutsch?"

231

"No."

"Dann warte ich."

The beatnik turned on her heel and bounced out, her brave vibration each way free. I caught up with her in front of the elevator, put 101 (perfect pattern) into her hand and said good night in Spanish. She hated me. I did a naughty thing to her * * (no excuse) and returned to the apartment when my American-English returned to me.

"What's she got?" the Freckle ask.

"What's your name?" I indict.

"My God! I've been working in your office for three months. You don't know my name? You really don't?"

"No, and I don't want to know it now."

"I'm Lizzie Chalmers."

"Go away, Lizzie Chalmers."

"So that's why you always called me 'Miss'. Why did you shave your head?"

"Trouble in Vienna."

"It's chic," she said judgmatically, "but I don't know. You remind me of a movie star I loathe. What do you mean, trouble in Vienna?"

"None of your business. What are you doing here? What do you want from me?"

"You," she said, blushing fiery.

"Will you, for God's sake, go away!"

"What did she have that I don't?" Lizzie Chalmers demanded. Then her face crinkled. "Don't? Is that right? What. Did. She. Have. That. I. Do. Not. Yes, right. I'm going to Bennington. They're strong on aggression, but weak on grammar."

"What do you mean, you're going to Bennington?"

"Why, it's a college. I thought everybody knew."

"But *going?*"

"I'm in my junior year. They drive you out with whips to acquire practical experience in your field."

"What's your field?"

"It used to be economics. Now it's you. How old are you?"

"One hundred and nine thousand eight hundred and seventy-two."

232

"Oh, come on! Forty?"

"Thirty."

"No! Really?" She nodded contentedly. "That makes ten years difference between us. Just right."

"Are you in love with me, Lizzie?"

"Well, I'm trying to get something going."

"Does it have to be me?"

"I know it sounds like a notion." She lowered her eyes. "And I suppose women are always throwing themselves at you."

"Not always."

"What are you, blasé, or something? I mean . . . I know I'm not staggering, but I'm not exactly repulsive."

"You're lovely."

"Then why don't you touch me?"

"I'm trying to protect you."

"I can protect myself when the time comes."

"The time is now, Lizzie."

"The least you could do is offend me the way you did that girl in front of the elevator."

"You snooped?"

"Sure I snooped. You didn't expect me to sit here on my hands, did you? I've got my man to take care of."

"*Your* man?"

"It happens," she said in a low voice. "I never believed it, but it happens. You fall in and out of love, and each time you think it's for real and forever. And then you meet somebody and it isn't a question of love any more. You just know he's your man, and you're stuck. I'm stuck."

She raised her eyes and looked at me . . . violet eyes, full of youth and determination and tenderness, and yet older than twenty years . . . much older. And I knew how lonely I was, never daring to love, always compelled to live with those I hated. I could fall into those violet eyes and never come up.

"I'm going to shock you," I said. I looked at the clock. 1:30 A.M. A quiet time. Please God the American tongue would stay with me a while longer. I took off my jacket and shirt and showed her my back, cross-hatched with scars. Lizzie gasped.

233

"Self-inflicted," I told her. "Because I permitted myself to like a man and become friendly with him. This is the price I paid, and I was lucky. Now wait here."

I went into the master bedroom where my heart's shame was embalmed in a silver case hidden in the right-hand drawer of my desk. I brought it to the living room. Lizzie watched me with great eyes.

"Five years ago a girl fell in love with me," I told her. "A girl like you. I was lonely then, as always. Instead of protecting her from myself, I indulged myself. Now I want to show you the price *she* paid. You'll loathe me for this but I must show you . . ."

A flash caught my eye. Lights in a building down the street going on. I leaped to the window and stared. The lights in the building three down from me went off . . . five seconds eclipse . . . then on. It happened to the building two down, and then to the one next door. The girl came to my side and took my arm. She trembled slightly.

"What is it?" she asked. "What's the matter?"

"Wait," I said.

The lights in my apartment went out for five seconds and then came on again.

"They've located me," I told her.

"They? Located?"

"They've spotted my broadcasts by d/f."

"What's d/f?"

"Direction-finder. Then they turned off the current in each building in the neighborhood for five seconds . . . building by building . . . until the broadcast stopped. Now they know I'm in this house, but they don't know which apartment." I put on my shirt and jacket. "Good night, Lizzie. I wish I could kiss you."

She clamped her arms around my neck and gave me a smacking kiss; all warmth, all velvet, all giving. I tried to push her away.

"You're a spy," she said. "I'll go to the chair with you."

"I wish to Heaven I were a spy," I said. "Goodbye, my dearest love. Remember me."

Soyez ferme. A great mistake letting that slip. It happen, I think, because my American slip, too. Suddenly

234

talk jumble again. As I run out, the little devil kick off opera pumps and rip slit in cocktail skirt up to thigh so she can run. She is alongside me going down the fire stairs to the garage in basement. I hit her to stop, and swear at her. She hit back and swear worse, all the time laughing and crying. I love her for it. Damnation! She is doomed.

We get into car, Aston-Martin, but with left-hand drive, and speed west on Fifty-third Street, east on Fifty-fourth Street, and north on First Avenue. I am making for Fifty-ninth Street bridge to get off Manhattan island. I own plane in Babylon, Long Island, which is always ready for this sort of awkwardness.

"J'y suis, J'y reste is not my motto," I tell Elizabeth Chalmers, whose French is as uncertain as her grammar . . . an endearing weakness. "Once they trapped me in London at post office. I received mail at General Delivery. They sent me a blank letter in a red envelope, and that's how they followed me to 139 Piccadilly, London W.1. Telephone Mayfair 7211. Red for danger. Is your skin red all over?"

"It's not red!" she said indignantly.

"I mean rosy."

"Only where the freckles merge," she said. "What is all this escape? Why do you talk so funny, and act so peculiar? Are you sure you're not a spy?"

"Only positive."

"Are you a being from another world who came on an Unidentified Flying Object?"

"Would that horrify you?"

"Yes, if it meant we couldn't make love."

"What about conquering earth?"

"I'm only interested in conquering you."

"I am not and have never been a being from another world who came on an Unidentified Flying Object."

"Then what are you?"

"A compensator."

"What's that?"

"Do you know dictionary of Misters Funk & Wagnalls? Edited by Frank H. Vizetelly, Litt.D., LL.D.? I quote: One who or that which compensates, as a device

235

for neutralizing the influence of local attraction upon a compass-needle or an automatic apparatus for equalizing the pressure of gas in the—Damn!"

Litt.D. Frank H. Vizetelly does not use that bad word. Is my own because roadblock now faces me on Fifty-ninth Street bridge. Should have anticipated. Should have felt patterns, but too swept up with this darling girl. Probably there are roadblocks on all bridges and tunnels leading out of this $24.00 island. Could drive off bridge but might harm my angelic Elizabeth Chalmers which would make me a *brute figura* as well as sadden me beyond redemption. So. Stop car. Surrender.

"Kammerade," I pronounce, and ask: "Who you? Ku Klux Klan?"

Hard-faced mans say no.

"White Supremacists of the World, Inc.?"

No agains. I feel better. Always nasty when captured by lunatic fringes looking for figureheads.

"U.S.S.R.?"

He stare, then speak. "Special Agent Krimms from the FBI," and show his badge. I enthuse and embrace him in gratitude. FBI is salvation. He recoil and wonder if I am fairy. I don't care. I kiss Elizabeth Chalmers and she open mouth under mine to mutter: "Admit nothing; deny everything. I've got a lawyer."

Brilliant lights in the office in Foley Square. The chairs are placed just so; the shadows arranged just so. I have been through this so often before. The anonymous man with the bleak eyes from the subway this morning is questioning me. His name is S. I. Dolan. We exchange a glance. His says: I goofed this morning. Mine says: So did I. We respect each other, and then the grilling starts.

"Your name is Abraham Mason Storm?"

"The nickname is 'Base.' "

"Born December 25?"

"I was a Christmas baby."

"1929?"

"I was a Depression baby."

"You seem pretty jaunty."

"Gallows humor, S. I. Dolan. Despair. I know you'll never convict me of anything, and I'm desperate."

"Very funny."

"Very tragic. I want to be convicted . . . but it's hopeless."

"Hometown San Francisco?"

"Yes."

"Grand High School. Two years at Berkeley. Four years in the Navy. Finished at Berkeley. Majored in statistics."

"Yes. Hundred percent American boy."

"Present occupation, financier?"

"Yes."

"Offices in New York, Rome, Paris, London?"

"Also Rio."

"Known assets from bank deposits, stock and bond holdings, three million dollars?"

"No, no, no!" I was agonized. "Three million, three hundred and thirty-three thousand, three hundred and thirty-three dollars and thirty-three cents."

"Three million dollars," Dolan insisted. "In round numbers."

"There are no round numbers; there are only patterns."

"Storm, what the hell are you up to?"

"Convict me," I pleaded. "I want to go to the chair and get this over with."

"What are you talking about?"

"You ask and I'll explain."

"What are you broadcasting from your apartment?"

"Which apartment? I broadcast from all of them."

"In New York. We can't break the code."

"There is no code; only randomness."

"Only what?"

"Only peace, Dolan."

"Peace!"

"I've been through this so often before. In Geneva, Berlin, London, Rio. Will you let me explain it my own way, and for God's sake trap me if you can?"

"Go ahead."

I took a breath. It's always so difficult. You have to do it with metaphor. But it was 3:00 A.M. and my American would hold for a while. "Do you like to dance?"

237

"What the hell . . . ?"

"Be patient. I'm explaining. Do you like to dance?"

"Yes."

"What's the pleasure of dancing? It's a man and woman making rhythms together . . . patterns. Balancing, anticipating, following, leading, cooperating. Yes?"

"So?"

"And parades. Do you like parades? Masses of men and women cooperating to make patterns. Why is war a time of joy for a country, although nobody admits it? Because it's an entire people cooperating, balancing and sacrificing to make a big pattern. Yes?"

"Now wait a minute, Storm . . ."

"Just listen, Dolan. I'm sensitive to patterns . . . more then dancing or parades or war; far more. More than the 2/4 pattern of day and night, or the 4/4 pattern of the seasons . . . far, far more. I'm sensitive to the patterns of the whole spectrum of the universe . . . sight and sound, gamma rays, groupings of peoples, acts of hostility and benign charity, cruelties and kindnesses, the music of the spheres . . . and I'm forced to compensate. Always."

"Compensate?"

"Yes. If a child falls and hurts itself, the mother kisses it. Agreed? That's compensation. It restores a pattern. If a man beats a horse, you beat him. Yes? Pattern again. If a beggar wrings too much sympathy from you, you want to kick him, don't you? More compensation. The husband unfaithful to the wife is never more kind to her. All wives know that pattern, and dread it. What is sportsmanship but a compensating pattern to off-set the embarrassment of winning or losing? Do not the murderer and murderee seek each other to fulfill their patterns?

"Multiply that by infinity and you have me. I have to kiss and kick. I'm driven. Compelled. I don't know how to name my compulsion. They call Extra Sensory Perception, Psi. What do you call Extra Pattern Perception? Pi?"

"Pie? What pie?"

"Sixteenth letter of the Greek alphabet. It designates the relation of the circumference of a circle to its diameter. 3.14159+. The series goes on endlessly. It is transcendental and can never be resolved into a finite pattern; and it's agony to me . . . like pi in printing, which means jumbled and confused type, without order or pattern."

"What the hell are you talking about?"

"I'm talking about patterns; order in the universe. I'm compelled to keep it and restore it. Sometimes I'm compelled to do wonderful and generous things; other times I'm forced to do insane things . . . talk garbage languages, go to strange places, perform abominable acts . . . because patterns which I can't perceive demand adjustment."

"What abominable acts?"

"You can pry and I can confess, but it won't do any good. The patterns won't permit me to be convicted. They won't let me end. People refuse to testify. Facts will not give evidence. What is done becomes undone. Harm is transformed into good."

"Storm, I swear you're crazy."

"Maybe, but you won't be able to get me committed to an asylum. It's been tried before. I even tried committing myself. It didn't work."

"What about those broadcasts?"

"We're flooded with wave emissions, quanta, particles, and I'm sensitive to them, too; but they're too garbled to shape into patterns. They have to be neutralized. So I broadcast an anti-pattern to jam them and get a little peace."

"Are you claiming to be a superman?"

"No. Never. I'm just the man *Simple Simon* met."

"Don't clown."

"I'm not clowning. Don't you remember the jingle? *Simple Simon met a pieman, going to the fair . . . ?* For Pee-eye-ee-man, read Pee-eye-man. I'm the Pi Man."

Dolan scowled. At last he said: "My full name is Simon Ignatius Dolan."

"I'm sorry. I didn't know. Nothing personal implied."

He glared at me, then threw my dossier down. He sighed and slumped into a chair. That made the pattern wrong and I had to shift. He cocked an eye at me.

"Pi Man," I explained.

"All right," he said. "We can't hold you."

"They all try," I said, "but they never can."

"Who try?"

"Governments, thinking I'm in espionage; police, wanting to know why I'm involved with so many people in such cockeyed ways; politicos in exile hoping I'll finance a counterrevolution; fanatics, dreaming I'm their rich messiah; lunatic fringes; religious sects; flat-worlders; Forteans . . . They all track me down, hoping they can use me. Nobody can. I'm part of something much bigger. I think maybe we all are, only I'm the first to be aware of it."

"Off the record, what's this about abominable acts?"

I took a breath. "That's why I can't have friends. Or a girl. Sometimes things get so bad somewhere that I have to make frightful sacrifices to restore the pattern. I must destroy something I love. I— There was a dog I loved. A Labrador retriever . . . I don't like to think about him. I had a girl once. She loved me. And I— And a guy in the navy with me. He— I don't want to talk about it."

"Chicken, all of a sudden?"

"No, damn you; I'm accursed! Because some of the patterns I must adjust to are out-world rhythms . . . like nothing you ever felt on earth. 29/51 . . . 108/303 . . . tempi like that. What are you staring at? You don't think that can be terrifying? Beat a 7/5 tempo for me."

"I don't know music."

"This has nothing to do with music. Try to beat five with one hand and seven with the other, and make them come out even. Then you'll understand the complexity and terror of those strange patterns that are coming to me. From where? I don't know. It's an unknown universe, too big to comprehend; but I have to beat the tempi of its patterns and make them come out even . . . with my actions, reactions, emotions, senses, while those giant pressures   push

and reverse me

back

and turn me

forth   inside

and   out

back . . ."

"The other arm now," Elizabeth said firmly. "Lift."

I am on my bed, me. Thinking upheaved again. Half (½) into pajamas; other half (½) being wrestled by freckly girl. I lift. She yank. Pajama now on, and it's my turn to blush. They raise me prudish in San Francisco.

"Om mani padme hum," I said. "Translation follows: Oh, the jewel in the lotus. Meaning you. What happened?"

"You passed out," she said. "Keeled over. Mr. Dolan had to let you go. Mr. Lundgren helped carry you into the apartment. How much should I give him?"

"Cinque lire. No. Parla Italiano, gentile Signorina?"

"Mr. Dolan told me what you told him. Is that your patterns again?"

"Si." I nod and wait. After stop-overs in Greece and Portugal, American-English finally returns to me. "Why don't you get the hell out of here while the getting's good, Lizzie Chalmers?"

"I'm still stuck," she said. "Get into bed . . . and make room for me."

"No."

"Yes. You can marry me later."

"Where's the silver case?"

"Down the incinerator."

"Do you know what was in it?"

"I know what was in it."

"And you're still here?"

"It was monstrous, what you did. Monstrous!" The saucy little face was streaked with mascara. She had been crying. "Where is she now?"

"I don't know. The checks go out every quarter to a number-account in Switzerland. I don't want to know. How much can the heart endure?"

"I think I'm going to find out," she said. She put out the lights. In the darkness came the sound of rustling clothes. Never before have I heard the music of one I love undressing for me . . . for me. I make one last attempt to save this beloved.

"I love you," I said, "and you know what that means. When the patterns demand a sacrifice, I may be even crueler to you, more monstrous. . . ."

"No," she said. "You never were in love before. Love creates patterns, too." She kissed me. Her lips were parched, her skin was icy. She was afraid, but her heart beat hot and strong. "Nothing can hurt us now. Believe me."

"I don't know what to believe any more. We're part of a universe that's big beyond knowledge. What if it turns out to be too gigantic for love?"

"All right," she said composedly. "We won't be dogs in the manger. If love is a little thing and has to end, then let it end. Let all the little things like love and honor and mercy and laughter end . . . if there's something bigger beyond."

"But what can be bigger? What can be beyond?"

"If we're too small to survive, how can we know?"

She crept close to me, the tips of her body like frost. And so we huddled together, breast to breast, warming ourselves with our love, frightened creatures in a wonderous world beyond knowing . . . fearful, and yet an tic ccip ppat inggg.

THE LAST MAN LEFT IN THE BAR

C. M. Kornbluth

Some writers are writers' writers. They explore the boundaries of their craft, push them outward, and show others the way. The late Cyril Kornbluth was, among the s-f fraternity, a writer's writer, perhaps even a writer's writer's writer, and this intense, low-redundancy, high-density story is the kind of thing writers' writers sometimes write. What a non-writer would make of it I am not really able to say—but I think its power is evident to any reader.

You know him, Joe—or Sam, Mike, Tony, Ben, whatever your deceitful, cheaply genial name may be. And do not lie to yourself, Gentle Reader; you know him too.

A loner, he was.

You did not notice him when he slipped in; you only knew by his aggrieved air when he (finally) caught your eye and self-consciously said "Shot of Red Top and a beer" that he'd ruffle your working day. (Six at night until two in the morning is a day? But ah, the horrible alternative is to work for a living.)

Shot of Red Top and a beer at 8:35.

And unbeknownst to him, Gentle Reader, in the garage up the street the two contrivers of his dilemma conspired; the breaths of tall dark stooped cadaverous Galardo and the mouse-eyed lassie mingled.

"Hyü shall be a religion-isst," he instructed her.

"I know the role," she squeaked and quoted: " 'Woe to the day on which I was born into the world! Woe to

243

the womb which bare me! Woe to the bowels which admitted me! Woe to the breasts which suckled me! Woe to the feet upon which I sat and rested! Woe to the hands which carried me and reared me until I grew! Woe to my tongue and my lips which have brought forth and spoken vanity, detraction, falsehood, ignorance, derision, idle tales, craft, and hypocrisy! Woe to mine eyes which have looked upon scandalous things! Woe to mine ears which have delighted in the words of slanderers! Woe to my hands which have seized what did not of right belong to them! Woe to my belly and my bowels which have lusted after food unlawful to be eaten! Woe to my throat which like a fire has consumed all that it found!' "

He sobbed with the beauty of it and nodded at last, tears hanging in his eyes: "Yess, that religion. It iss one of my fave-o-ritts."

She was carried away. "I can do others. Oh, I can do others. I can do Mithras and Isis and Marduk and Eddyism and Billsword and Pealing and Uranium, both orthodox and reformed."

"Mithras, Isis, and Marduk are long gone and the resst are sss-till tü come. Listen tü your master, dü not chatter, and we shall an artwork make of which there will be talk under the green sky until all food is eaten."

Meanwhile, Gentle Reader, the loner listened. To his left strong silent sinewy men in fellowship, the builders, the doers, the darers: "So I told the foreman where he should put his Bullard. I told him I run a Warner and Swasey, I run a Warner and Swasey good, I never even *seen* a Bullard up close in my life, and where he should put it. I know how to run a Warner and Swasey and why should he take me off a Warner and Swasey I know how to run and put me on a Bullard and where he should put it, ain't I right?"

"Absolutely."

To his right the clear-eyed virtuous matrons, the steadfast, the true-seeing, the loving-kind: "Oh, I don't know what I want, what do you want? I'm a Scotch drinker really but I don't feel like Scotch but if I come home with muscatel on my breath Eddie calls me a wino and laughs his head off. I don't know what I want. What do you want?"

In the box above the bar the rollicking raster raced.

VIDEO	AUDIO
Gampa smashes bottle over the head of *Bibby*.	*Gampa:* Young whippersnapper!
Bibby spits out water.	*Bibby:* Next time put some flavoring in it, Gramps!
Gampa picks up sugar bowl and smashes it over *Bibby's* head. *Bibby* licks sugar from face.	*Bibby:* My, that's better! But what of Naughty Roger and his attempted kidnapping of Sis to extort the secret of the Q-Bomb?
cut to *Limbo Shot* of Reel-Rye bottle.	*Announcer:* Yes, kiddies! What of Roger? But first a word from the makers of Reel-Rye, that happy syrup that gives your milk grown-up flavor! YES! Grown-up flavor!

Shot of Red Top and a beer. At 8:50.

In this own unsecret heart: Steady, boy. You've got to think this out. Nothing impossible about it, no reason to settle for a stalemate; just a little time to think it out. Galardo said the Black Chapter would accept a token submission, let me return the Seal, and that would be that. But I mustn't count on that as a datum; he lied to me about the Serpentists. Token submission *sounds* right; they go in big for symbolism. Maybe because they're so stone-broke, like the Japs. Drinking a cup of tea, they gussie it all up until it's a religion; that's the way you squeeze nourishment out of poverty—

Skip the Japs. Think. He lied to me about the Serpentists. The big thing to remember is, I have the Chapter Seal and they need it back, or think they do. All you need's a little time to think things through, place where he won't dare jump you and grab the Seal. And this is it.

"Joe. Sam, Mike, Tony, Ben, whoever you are. Hit me again."

Joe—Sam, Mike, Tony, Ben?—tilts the amber bottle quietly; the liquid's level rises and crowns the little glass with a convex meniscus. He turns off the stream with an easy roll of the wrist. The suntan line of neon tubing at the bar back twinkles off the curve of surface tension, the placid whiskey, the frothy beer. At 9:05.

To his left: "So Finkelstein finally meets Goldberg in the garment center and he grabs him like this by the lapel, and he yells, 'You louse, you rat, you no-good, what's this about you running around with my wife? I ought to—I ought to—say, you call *this* a *button*hole?'"

Restrained and apprehensive laughter; Catholic, Protestant, Jew (choice of one), what's the difference I always say.

Did they have a Jewish Question still, or was all smoothed and troweled and interfaithed and brotherhoodooed—

Wait. Your formulation implies that they're in the future, and you have no proof of that. Think straighter; you don't know *where* they are, or *when* they are, or *who* they are. You *do* know that you walked into Big Maggie's resonance chamber to change the target, experimental iridium for old reliable zinc

and

"Bartender," in a controlled and formal voice. Shot of Red Top and a beer at 9:09, the hand vibrating with remembrance of a dirty-green El Greco sky which *might* be Brookhaven's heavens a million years either way from now, or one second sideways, or (bow to Method and formally exhaust the possibilities) a hallucination. The Seal snatched from the greenlit rock altar could be a blank washer, a wheel from a toy truck, or the screw top from a jar of shaving cream but for the fact that it wasn't. It was the Seal.

So: they began seeping through after that. The Chapter wanted it back. The Serpentists wanted it, period. Galardo had started by bargaining and wound up by threatening, but how could you do anything but laugh at his best offer, a rusty five-pound spur gear with a worn keyway and three teeth missing? His threats were richer than his bribes; they culminated with The Century of Flame. "Faith, father, it doesn't scare me at all, at all; sure, no man could stand it." Subjective-objective (How you used to sling *them* around!), and Master Newton's billiard-table similes dissolve into sense-impressions of pointer-readings as you learn your trade, but Galardo had scared hell out of you, or into you, with The Century of Flame.

But you had the Seal of the Chapter and you had time to think, while on the screen above the bar:

VIDEO	AUDIO
Long shot down steep, cobblestoned French village street. *Pierre* darts out of alley in middle distance, looks wildly around and runs toward camera, pistol in hand. *Annette* and *Paul* appear from same alley and dash after him.	*Paul:* Stop, you fool!
Cut to *Cu* of *Pierre's* face; beard stubble and sweat.	*Pierre:* A fool, am I?
Cut to long shot; *Pierre* aims and fires; *Paul* grabs his left shoulder and falls.	*Annette:* Darling!
Cut to two-shot, *Annette* and *Paul.*	*Paul:* Don't mind me. Take my gun—after him. He's a mad dog, I tell you!
Dolly back. *Annette* takes his pistol.	*Annette:* This, my dear, is as good a time as any to drop my little masquerade. Are you American agents really so stupid that you never thought I might be—a plant, as you call it?
Annette stands; we see her aim down at *Paul,* out of the picture. Then we dolly in to a *Cu* of her	

head; she is smiling triumphantly.	*Sound:* click of cocking pistol.
A hand holding a pistol enters the *Cu;* the pistol muzzle touches *Annette's* neck.	*Harkrider:* Drop it, Madame Golkov.
Dolly back to middle shot. *Harkrider* stands behind *Annette* as *Paul* gets up briskly and takes the pistol from her hand.	*Paul:* No, Madame Golkov; we American agents were not really so stupid. Wish I could say the same for—your people. Pierre Tourneur *was* a plant, I am glad to say; otherwise he would not have missed me. He is one of the best pistol shots in Counterintelligence.
Cut to long shot of street, *Harkrider* and *Paul* walk away from the camera, *Annette* between them. Fadeout.	*Harkrider:* Come along, Madame Golkov.
	Music: theme up and out.

Them and their neatly packaged problems, them and their neatly packaged shows with beginning middle and end. The rite of the low-budget shot-in-Europe spy series, the rite of pugilism, the rite of the dog-walk after dinner and the beer at the bar with co-celebrant worshippers at the high altar of Nothing.

9:30. Shot of Red Top and a beer, positively the last one until you get this figured out; you're beginning to buzz like a transformer.

Do they have transformers? Do they have vitamins? Do they have anything but that glaring green sky, and the rock altar and treasures like the Seal and the rusty gear with three broken teeth? "All smelling of iodoform. And all quite bald." But Galardo looked as if he were dying of tuberculosis, and the letter from the Serpentists was in a sick and straggling hand. Relics of mediaeval barbarism.

To his left—

"*Galardo!*" he screamed.

The bartender scurried over—Joe, Sam, Mike, Tony, Ben?—scowling. "What's the matter, mister?"

"I'm sorry. I got a stitch in my side. A cramp."

Bullyboy scowled competently and turned. "What'll you have, mister?"

Galardo said cadaverously: "Wodeffer my vriend hyere iss havfing."

"Shot of Red Top and a beer, right?"

What are you doing here?

"Drink-ing beferachiss . . . havf hyü de-site-it hwat tü dü?"

The bartender rapped down the shot glass and tilted the bottle over it, looking at Galardo. Some of the whiskey slopped over. The bartender started, went to the tap and carefully drew a glass of beer, slicing the collar twice.

"My vriend hyere will pay."

He got out a half-dollar, fumbling, and put it on the wet wood. The bartender, old-fashioned, rapped it twice on the bar to show he wasn't stealing it even though you weren't watching; he rang it up double virtuous on the cash register, the absent owner's fishy eye.

"What are you doing here?" again, in a low, reasonable, almost amused voice to show him you have the whip hand.

"Drink-ing beferachiss . . . it iss so cle-an hyere." Galardo's sunken face, unbelievably, looked wistful as he surveyed the barroom, his head swiveling slowly from extreme left to extreme right.

"Clean. Well. Isn't it clean there?"

Sheh, not!" Galardo said mournfully. "Sheh, not! Hyere it iss so cle-an . . . hwai did yü outreach tü us? Hag-rid us, wretch-it, hag-rid us?" There were tears hanging in his eyes. "Haff yü de-site-it hwat tü dü?"

Expansively: "I don't pretend to understand the situation *fully*, Galardo. But you know and I know that I've got something you people [think you] need. Now there doesn't seem to be any body of law covering artifacts that appear [*plink!*] in a magnetron on accidental overload, and I just have your word that it's yours."

"Ah, that iss how yü re-member it now," said sorrowful Galardo.

"Well, it's the way it [but wasn't something green? I think of spired Toledo and three angled crosses toppling]

249

happened. I don't want anything silly, like a million dollars in small unmarked bills, and I don't want to be bullied, to be bullied, no, I mean not by you, not by anybody. Just, just tell me who you are, what all this is about. This is nonsense, you see, and we can't have nonsense. I'm afraid I'm not expressing myself very well—"

And a confident smile and turn away from him, which shows that you aren't afraid, you can turn your back and dare him to make something of it. In public, in the bar? It is laughable; you have him in the palm of your hand. "Shot of Red Top and a beer, please, Sam." At 9:48.

The bartender draws the beer and pours the whiskey. He pauses before he picks up the dollar bill fished from the pants pocket, pauses almost timidly and works his face into a friend's grimace. But you can read him; he is making amends for his suspicion that you were going to start a drunken brawl when Galardo merely surprised you a bit. You can read him because your mind is tensed to concert pitch tonight, ready for Galardo, ready for the Serpentists, ready to crack this thing wide open; strange!

But you weren't ready for the words he spoke from his fake apologetic friend's grimace as you delicately raised the heavy amber-filled glass to your lips: "Where'd your friend go?"

You slopped the whiskey as you turned and looked.

Galardo gone.

You smiled and shrugged; he comes and goes as he pleases, you know. Irresponsible, no manners at all—but *loyal*. A prince among men when you get to know him, a prince, I tell you. All this in your smile and shrug—why, you could have been an actor! The worry, the faint neurotic worry, didn't show at all, and indeed there is no reason why it should. You have the whip hand; you have the Seal; Galardo will come crawling back and explain everything. As for example:

"You may wonder why I've asked all of you to assemble in the libr'reh."

or

"For goodness' sake, Gracie, I wasn't going to go to Cuba! When you heard me on the extension phone I was just ordering a dozen Havana *cigars!*"

250

or

"In your notation, we are from 19,276 A.D. Our basic mathematic is a quite comprehensible subsumption of your contemporary statistical analysis and topology which I shall now proceed to explain to you."

And that was all.

With sorrow, Gentle Reader, you will have noticed that the marble did not remark: "I am chiseled," the lumber "I am sawn," the paint "I'm applied to canvas," the tea leaf "I am whisked about in an exquisite Korean bowl to brew while the celebrants of *cha no yu* squeeze this nourishment out of their poverty." Vain victim, relax and play your hunches; subconscious integration does it. Stick with your lit-tle old subconscious integration and all will go *swimmingly,* if only it weren't so damned noisy in here. But it was dark on the street and conceivably things could happen there; stick with crowds and stick with witnesses, but if only it weren't so . . .

To his left they were settling down; it was the hour of confidences, and man to man they told the secret of their success: "In the needle trade, I'm in the needle trade, I don't sell anybody a crooked needle, my father told me that. Albert, he said to me, don't never sell nobody nothing but a straight needle. And today I have four shops."

To his right they were settling down; freed of the cares of the day they invited their souls, explored the spiritual realm, theologized with exquisite distinctions: "Now *wait* a minute, I didn't say I was a *good* Mormon, I said I was a Mormon and that's what I am, a Mormon. I *never* said I was a *good* Mormon, I just said I was a Mormon, my mother was a Mormon and my father was a Mormon, and that makes me a Mormon but I *never* said I was a *good* Mormon—"

Distinguo, rolled the canonical thunder; *distinguo.*

Demurely a bonneted lassie shook her small-change tambourine beneath his chin and whispered, snarling: "Galardo lied."

Admit it; you were startled. But what need for the bartender to come running with raised hand, what need for needletrader to your left to shrink away, the L.D.S. to cower?

251

"Mister, that's twice you let out a yell, we run a quiet place, if you can't be good, begone."

Begob.

"I ash-assure you, bartender, it was—unintenable."

Greed vies with hate; greed wins; greed always wins: "Just keep it quiet, mister, this ain't the Bowery, this is a family place." Then, relenting: "The same?"

"Yes, please." At 10:15 the patient lassie jingled silver on the parchment palm outstretched. He placed a quarter on the tambourine and asked politely: "Did you say something to me before, Miss?"

"God bless you, sir. Yes, sir, I did say something. I said Galardo lied; the Seal is holy to the Serpent, sir, and to his humble emissaries. If you'll only hand it over, sir, the Serpent will somewhat mitigate the fearsome torments which are rightly yours for snatching the Seal from the Altar, sir."

[Snatchings from Altars? *Ma foi,* the wench is mad!]

"Listen, lady. That's only talk. What annoys me about you people is, you won't talk sense. I want to know who you are, what this is about, maybe just a little hint about your mathematics, and I'll do the rest and you can have the blooming Seal. I'm a passable physicist even if I'm only a technician. I bet there's something you didn't know. I bet you didn't know the tech shortage is tighter than the scientist shortage. You get a guy can tune a magnetron, he writes his own ticket. So I'm weak on quantum mechanics, the theory side, I'm still a good all-around man and be-*lieve* me, the Ph.D.'s would kiss my ever-loving *feet* if I told them I got an offer from Argonne—

"So listen, you Janissary emissary. I'm happy right here in this necessary comissary and here I *stay*."

But she was looking at him with bright frightened mouse's eyes and slipped on down the line when he paused for breath, putting out the parchment palm to others but not ceasing to watch him.

Coins tapped the tambour. "God bless you. God bless you. God bless you."

The raving-maniacal ghost of G. Washington Hill descended then into a girdled sibyl; she screamed from the screen: "It's *Hit* Pa-*rade!*"

"I like them production numbers."

"I like that Pigalle Mackintosh."

"I like them production numbers. Lotsa pretty girls, pretty clothes, something to take your mind off your troubles."

"I like that Pigalle Mackintosh. She don't just sing, mind you, she plays the saxophone. Talent."

"I like them production numbers. They show you just what the song is all about. Like last week they did *Sadist Calypso* with this mad scientist cutting up the girls, and then Pigalle comes in and whips him to death at the last verse, you see just what the song's all about, something to take your mind off your troubles."

"I like that Pigalle Mackintosh. She don't just sing, mind you, she plays the saxophone and cracks a black-snake whip, like last week in *Sadist Calypso*—"

"Yeah. Something to take your mind off your troubles."

Irritably he felt in his pocket for the Seal and moved, stumbling a little, to one of the tables against the knotty pine wall. His head slipped forward on the polished wood and he sank into the sea of myth.

Galardo came to him in his dream and spoke under a storm-green sky: "Take your mind off your troubles, Edward. It was stolen like the first penny, like the quiz answers, like the pity for your bereavement." His hand, a tambourine, was out.

"Never shall I yield," he declaimed to the miserable wretch. "By the *honneur* of a Gascon, I stole it fair and square; 'tis mine, knave! *En garde!*"

Galardo quailed and ran, melting into the sky, the altar, the tambourine.

A ham-hand manhandled him. "Light-up time," said Sam. "I let you sleep because you got it here, but I got to close up now."

"Sam," he says uncertainly.

"One for the road, mister. On the house. *Up-sy*-daisy!" meaty hooks under his armpits heaving him to the bar.

253

The lights are out behind the bar, the jolly neons, glittering off how many gems of amber rye and the tan crystals of beer? A meager bulb above the register is the oasis in the desert of inky night.

"Sam," groggily, "you don't understand. I mean I never explained it—"

"Drink up, mister," a pale free drink, soda bubbles lightly tinged with tawny rye. A small sip to gain time.

"Sam, there are some people after me—"

"You'll feel better in the morning, mister. Drink up, I got to close up, hurry up."

"These people, Sam [it's cold in here and scary as a noise in the attic; the bottles stand accusingly, the chrome globes that top them eye you] these people, they've got a thing, The Century of—"

"Sure, mister, I let you sleep because you got it here, but we close up now, drink up your drink."

"Sam, let me go home with you, will you? It isn't anything like that, don't misunderstand, I just can't be alone. These people—look, I've got money—"

He spreads out what he dug from his pocket.

"Sure, mister, you got lots of money, two dollars and thirty-eight cents. Now you take your money and get out of the store because I got to lock up and clean out the register—"

"Listen, bartender, I'm not drunk, maybe I don't have much money on me but I'm an important man! Important! They couldn't run Big Maggie at Brookhaven without me, I may not have a degree but what I get from these people if you'll only let me stay here—"

The bartender takes the pale one on the house you only sipped and dumps it in the sink; his hands are iron on you and you float while he chants:

> Decent man. Decent place.
> Hold their liquor. Got it here.
> Try be nice. Drunken bum.
> Don't—come—back.

The crash of your coccyx on the concrete and the slam of the door are one.

Run!

Down the black street stumbling over cans, cats, orts, to the pool of light in the night, safe corner where a standard sprouts and sprays radiance.

The tall black figure that steps between is Galardo.

The short one has a tambourine.

"Take it!" He thrust out the Seal on his shaking palm. "If you won't tell me anything, you won't. Take it and go away!"

Galardo inspects it and sadly says: "Thiss appearss to be a blank wash-er."

"Mistake," he slobbers. "Minute." He claws in his pockets, ripping. "Here! Here!"

The lassie squeaks: "The wheel of a toy truck. It will not do at all, sir." Her glittereyes.

"Then this! This is it! This must be it!"

Their heads shake slowly. Unable to look his fingers feel the rim and rolled threading of the jar cap.

They nod together, sad and glittereyed, and The Century of Flame begins.

THE TERMINAL BEACH

J. G. Ballard

Is this haunting, throbbing story by J. G. Ballard, the British *enfant terrible* of avant-garde science fiction, really s-f? It fails some of the traditional tests; yet I think it qualifies for entry in the genre, not merely because it seems to take place in the near future but also because it deals, devastatingly and unforgettably with the impact of science on contemporary man, depicting that impact in the metaphorical fashion of authentic science fiction.

At night, as he lay asleep on the floor of the ruined bunker, Traven heard the waves breaking along the shore of the lagoon, reminding him of the deep Atlantic rollers on the beach at Dakar, where he had been born, and of waiting in the evenings for his parents to drive home along the corniche road from the airport. Overcome by this long-forgotten memory, he woke uncertainly from the bed of old magazines on which he slept and ran towards the dunes that screened the lagoon.

Through the cold night air he could see the abandoned superfortresses lying among the palms, beyond the perimeter of the emergency landing field three hundred yards away. Traven walked through the dark sand, already forgetting where the shore lay, although the atoll was only half a mile in width. Above him, along the crests of the dunes, the tall palms leaned into the dim air like the symbols of some cryptic alphabet. The landscape of the island was covered by strange ciphers.

Giving up the attempt to find the beach, Traven stumbled into a set of tracks left years earlier by a large caterpillar vehicle. The heat released by one of the weapons tests had fused the sand, and the double line of fossil imprints, uncovered by the evening air, wound its serpentine way among the hollows like the footfalls of an ancient saurian.

Too weak to walk any further, Traven sat down between the tracks. With one hand he began to excavate the wedge-shaped grooves from a drift into which they disappeared, hoping that they might lead him towards the sea. He returned to the bunker shortly before dawn, and slept through the hot silences of the following noon.

The Blocks

As usual on these enervating afternoons, when not even the faintest breath of offshore breeze disturbed the dust, Traven sat in the shadow of one of the blocks, lost somewhere within the center of the maze. His back resting against the rough concrete surface, he gazed with a phlegmatic eye down the surrounding aisles and at the line of doors facing him. Each afternoon he left his cell in the abandoned camera bunker and walked down into the blocks. For the first half an hour he restricted himself to the perimeter aisle, now and then trying one of the doors with the rusty key in his pocket—he had found it among the litter of smashed bottles in the isthmus of sand separating the testing ground from the airstrip—and then, inevitably, with a sort of drugged stride, he set off into the center of the blocks, breaking into a run and darting in and out of the corridors, as if trying to flush some invisible opponent from his hiding place. Soon he would be completely lost. Whatever his efforts to return to the perimeter, he found himself once more in the center.

Eventually he would abandon the task, and sit down in the dust, watching the shadows emerge from their crevices at the foot of the blocks. For some reason he always arranged to be trapped when the sun was at zenith —on Eniwetok, a thermonuclear noon.

One question in particular intrigued him: "What sort of people would inhabit this minimal concrete city?"

257

The Synthetic Landscape

"This island is a state of mind," Osborne, one of the biologists working in the old submarine pens, was later to remark to Traven. The truth of this became obvious to Traven within two or three weeks of his arrival. Despite the sand and the few anemic palms, the entire landscape of the island was synthetic, a manmade artefact with all the associations of a vast system of derelict concrete motorways. Since the moratorium on atomic tests, the island had been abandoned by the Atomic Energy Commission, and the wilderness of weapons aisles, towers, and blockhouses ruled out any attempt to return it to its natural state. (There were also stronger unconscious motives, Traven recognized, for leaving it as it was: if primitive man felt the need to assimilate events in the external world to his own psyche, twentieth century man had reversed this process—by this Cartesian yardstick, the island at least *existed,* in a sense true of few other places.)

But apart from a few scientific workers, no one yet felt any wish to visit the former testing ground, and the navel patrol boat anchored in the lagoon had been withdrawn five years before Traven's arrival. Its ruined appearance and the associations of the island with the period of the Cold War—what Traven had christened the "Pre-Third"—were profoundly depressing, an Auschwitz of the soul whose mausoleums contained the mass graves of the still undead. With the Russo-American détente this nightmarish chapter of history had been gladly forgotten.

The Pre-Third

"The actual and potential destructiveness of the atomic bomb plays straight into the hands of the Unconscious. The most cursory study of the dream-life and fantasies of the insane shows that ideas of world-destruction are latent in the unconscious mind. Nagazaki destroyed by the magic of science is the nearest man has yet approached to the realization of dreams that even during the safe immobility of sleep are accustomed to develop

into nightmares of anxiety."—Glover; *War, Sadism, and Pacifism*

The Pre-Third: the period had been characterized in Traven's mind above all by its moral and psychological inversions, by its sense of the whole of history, and in particular of the immediate future—the two decades, 1945-1965—suspended from the quivering volcano's lip of World War III. Even the death of his wife and six-year-old son in a motor accident seemed only part of this immense synthesis of the historical and psychic zero, the frantic highways where each morning they met their deaths the advance causeways to the global armageddon.

Third Beach

He had come ashore at midnight, after a hazardous search for an opening in the reef. The small motorboat he had hired from an Australian pearldiver at Charlotte Island subsided into the shallows, its hull torn by the sharp coral. Exhausted, Traven walked through the darkness among the dunes, where the dim outlines of bunkers and concrete towers loomed between the palms.

He woke the next morning into bright sunlight, lying halfway down the slope of a wide concrete beach. This ringed what appeared to be an empty reservoir or target basin, some two hundred feet in diameter, part of a system of artificial lakes built down the center of the atoll. Leaves and dust choked the waste grills, and a pool of warm water two feet deep lay in the center, reflecting a distant line of palms.

Traven sat up and took stock of himself. This brief inventory, which merely confirmed his physical identity, was limited to little more than his thin body in its frayed cotton garments. In the context of the surrounding terrain, however, even this collection of tatters seemed to possess a unique vitality. The emptiness of the island, and the absence of any local fauna, were emphasized by the huge sculptural forms of the target basins let into its surface. Separated from each other by narrow isthmuses, the lakes stretched away along the curve of the atoll. On either side, sometimes shaded by the few palms that had gained a precarious purchase in the cracked cement, were roadways, camera towers, and isolated blockhouses, together forming a continuous concrete cap upon the island, a functional megalithic architecture as gray and minatory (and apparently as ancient, in its projection into, and from, time future) as any of Assyria and Babylon.

The series of weapons tests had fused the sand in layers, and the pseudogeological strata condensed the brief epochs, microseconds in duration, of the thermonuclear age. "The key to the past lies in the present." Typically the island inverted this geologist's maxim. Here the key to the present lay in the future. The island was a fossil of time future, its bunkers and blockhouses illustrating the principle that the fossil record of life is one of armor and the exoskeleton.

Traven knelt in the warm pool and splashed his shirt and trousers. The reflection revealed the watery image of a thinly bearded face and gaunt shoulders. He had come to the island with no supplies other than a small bar of chocolate, expecting that in some way the island would provide its own sustenance. Perhaps, too, he had identified the need for food with a forward motion in time, and that with his return to the past, or at most into a zone of nontime, this need would be obviated. The privations of the previous six months, during his journey across the Pacific, had reduced his always thin body to that of a migrant beggar, held together by little more than the preoccupied gaze in his eye. Yet this emaciation, by stripping away the superfluities of the flesh, seemed to reveal an inner sinewy toughness, and economy and directness of movement.

For several hours he wandered about, inspecting one bunker after another for a convenient place to sleep. He crossed the remains of a small landing strip, next to a dump where a dozen B-29's lay across one another like dead reptile birds.

The Corpses

Once he entered a small street of metal shacks, containing a cafeteria, recreation rooms, and shower stalls. A wrecked jukebox lay half-buried in the sand behind the cafeteria, its selection of records still in their rack.

Further along, flung into a small target basin fifty yards from the shacks, were the bodies of what at first he thought were the inhabitants of this ghost town—a dozen life-size plastic models. Their half-melted faces, contorted into bleary grimaces, gazed up at him from the jumble of legs and torsos.

On either side of him, muffled by the dunes, came the sounds of waves, the great rollers on the seaward side breaking over the reefs, and onto the beaches within the lagoon. However, he avoided the sea, hesitating before any rise that might take him within its sight. Everywhere the camera towers offered him a convenient aerial view of the confused topography of the island, but he avoided their rusting ladders.

He soon realized that however confused and random the blockhouses and camera towers might seem, their common focus dominated the landscape and gave to it a unique perspective. As Traven noticed when he sat down to rest in the window slit of one of the blockhouses, all these observation posts occupied positions on a series of concentric perimeters, moving in tightening arcs towards the inmost sanctuary. This ultimate circle, below ground zero, remained hidden beyond a line of dunes a quarter of a mile to the west.

The Terminal Bunker

After sleeping for a few nights in the open, Traven returned to the concrete beach where he had woken on his first morning on the island, and made his home—if the term could be applied to that damp crumbling hovel —in a camera bunker fifty yards from the target lakes. The dark chamber between the thick canted walls, tomb-like though it might seem, gave him a sense of physical reassurance. Outside, the sand drifted against the sides, half burying the narrow doorway, as if crystallizing the immense epoch of time that had elapsed since the bunker's construction. The narrow rectangles of the five camera slits, their shapes and positions determined by the instruments, studded the east wall like cryptic ideograms. Variations of these ciphers decorated the walls of the other bunkers. In the morning, if Traven was awake, he would always find the sun divided into five emblematic beacons.

Most of the time the chamber was filled only by a damp gloomy light. In the control tower at the landing field Traven found a collection of discarded magazines, and used these to make a bed. One day, lying in the bunker shortly after the first attack of beri-beri, he pulled out a magazine pressing into his back and found inside it a full-page photograph of a six-year-old girl. This blonde-haired child, with her composed expression and self-immersed eyes, filled him with a thousand painful memories of his son. He pinned the page to the wall and for days gazed at it through his reveries.

For the first few weeks Traven made little attempt to leave the bunker, and postponed any further exploration of the island. The symbolic journey through its inner circles set its own times of arrival and departure. He evolved no routine for himself. All sense of time soon vanished; his life became completely existential, an absolute break separating one moment from the next like two quantal events. Too weak to forage for food, he lived on the old ration packs he found in the wrecked super-fortresses. Without any implements, it took him all day to open the cans. His physical decline continued, but he watched his spindling arms and legs with indifference.

By now he had forgotten the existence of the sea and vaguely assumed the atoll to be part of some continuous continental table. A hundred yards away to the north and south of the bunker a line of dunes, topped by the palisade of enigmatic palms, screened the lagoon and sea, and the faint muffled drumming of the waves at night had fused with his memories of war and childhood. To the east was the emergency landing field and the abandoned aircraft. In the afternoon light their shifting rectangular shadows would appear to writhe and pivot. In front of the bunker, where he sat, was the system of target lakes, the shallow basins extending across the center of the atoll. Above him the five apertures looked out upon this scene like the tutelary deities of some futuristic myth.

The Lakes and the Specters

The lakes had been designed originally to reveal any radiobiological changes in a selected range of flora and fauna, but the specimens had long since bloomed into grotesque parodies of themselves and been destroyed.

Sometimes in the evenings, when a sepulchral light lay over the concrete bunkers and causeways, and the basins seemed like ornamental lakes in a city of deserted mausoleums, abandoned even by the dead, he would see the specters of his wife and son standing on the opposite bank. Their solitary figures appeared to have been watching him for hours. Although they never moved, Traven was sure they were beckoning to him. Roused from his reverie, he would stumble across the dark sand to the edge of the lake and wade through the water, shouting at the two figures as they moved away hand in hand among the lakes and disappeared across the distant causeways.

Shivering with cold, Traven would return to the bunker and lie on the bed of old magazines, waiting for their return. The image of their faces, the pale lantern of his wife's cheeks, floated on the river of his memory.

The Blocks (II)

It was not until he discovered the blocks that Traven realized he would never leave the island.

At this stage, some two months after his arrival, Traven had exhausted the small cache of food, and the symptoms of beri-beri had become more acute. The numbness in his hands and feet, and the gradual loss of strength, continued. Only by an immense effort, and the knowledge that the inner sanctum of the island still lay unexplored, did he manage to leave the paliasse of magazines and make his way from the bunker.

As he sat in the drift of sand by the doorway that

evening, he noticed a light shining through the palms far into the distance around the atoll. Confusing this with the image of his wife and son, and visualizing them waiting for him at some warm hearth among the dunes, Traven set off toward the light. Within fifty yards he lost his sense of direction. He blundered about for several hours on the edges of the landing strip, and succeeded only in cutting his foot on a broken Coca-Cola bottle in the sand.

After postponing his search for the night, he set out again in earnest the next morning. As he moved past the towers and blockhouses the heat lay over the island in an unbroken mantle. He had entered a zone devoid of time. Only the narrowing perimeters of the bunkers warned him that he was crossing the inner field of the firetable.

He climbed the ridge which marked the furthest point in his previous exploration of the island. The plain beyond was covered with target aisles and explosion breaks. On the gray walls of the recording towers, which rose into the air like obelisks, were the faint outlines of human forms in stylized postures, the flash-shadows of the target community burned into the cement. Here and there, where the concrete apron had cracked, a line of palms hung precariously in the motionless air. The target lakes were smaller, filled with the broken bodies of plastic dummies. Most of them still lay in the inoffensive domestic postures into which they had been placed before the tests.

Beyond the furthest line of dunes, where the camera towers began to turn and face him, were the tops of what seemed to be a herd of square-backed elephants. They were drawn up in precise ranks in a hollow that formed a shallow corral.

Traven advanced toward them, limping on his cut foot. On either side of him the loosening sand had excavated the dunes, and several of the blockhouses tilted on their sides. This plain of bunkers stretched for some quarter of a mile. To one side the half-submerged hulks of a group of concrete shelters, bombed out onto the surface in some earlier test, lay like the husks of the abandoned wombs that had given birth to this herd of megaliths.

To grasp something of the vast number and oppressive size of the blocks, and their impact upon Traven, one must try to visualize sitting in the shade of one of these concrete monsters, or walking about in the center of this enormous labyrinth which extended across the central table of the island. There were some two thousand of them, each a perfect cube fifteen feet in height, regularly spaced at ten-yard intervals. They were arranged in a series of tracts, each composed of two hundred blocks, inclined to one another and to the direction of the blast. They had weathered only slightly in the years since they were first built, and their gaunt profiles were like the cutting faces of an enormous die-plate, designed to stamp out huge rectilinear volumes of air. Three of the sides were smooth and unbroken, but the fourth, facing away from the direction of the blast, contained a narrow inspection door.

It was this feature of the blocks that Traven found particularly disturbing. Despite the considerable number of doors, by some freak of perspective only those in a single aisle were visible at any point within the maze, the rest obscured by the intervening blocks. As he walked from the perimeter into the center of the massif, line upon line of the small metal doors appeared and receded, a world of closed exits concealed behind endless corners.

Approximately twenty of the blocks, those immediately below ground zero, were solid, the walls of the remainder of varying thicknesses. From the outside they appeared to be of uniform solidity.

As he entered the first of the long aisles, Traven felt his step lighten; the sense of fatigue that had dogged him for so many months begin to lift. With their geometric regularity and finish, the blocks seemed to occupy more than their own volume of space, imposing on him a mood of absolute calm and order. He walked on into the center of the maze, eager to shut out the rest of the island. After a few random turns to left and right, he found himself alone, the vistas to the sea, lagoon, and island closed.

Here he sat down with his back against one of the blocks, the quest for his wife and son forgotten. For the first time since his arrival at the island the sense of dissociation prompted by its fragmenting landscape began to recede.

One development he did not expect. With dusk, and the need to leave the blocks and find food, he realized that he had lost himself. However he retraced his steps, struck out left or right at an oblique course, oriented himself around the sun and pressed on resolutely north or south, he found himself back at his starting point. Despite his best efforts, he was unable to make his way out of the maze. That he was aware of his motives gave him little help. Only when hunger overcame the need to remain did he manage to escape.

Abandoning his former home near the aircraft dump, Traven collected together what canned food he could find in the waist turret and cockpit lockers of the superfortresses and pulled them across the island on a crude sledge. Fifty yards from the perimeter of the blocks he took over a tilting bunker, and pinned the fading photograph of the blonde-haired child to the wall beside the door. The page was falling to pieces, like his fragmenting image of himself. Each evening when he woke he would eat uneagerly and then go out into the blocks. Sometimes he took a canteen of water with him and remained there for two or three days.

Traven: In Parenthesis

Elements in a quantal world:
The terminal beach.
The terminal bunker.
The blocks.
The landscape is coded.
Entry points into the future=levels in a spinal landscape=zones of significant time.

The Submarine Pens

This precarious existence continued for the following weeks. As he walked out to the blocks one evening, he again saw his wife and son, standing among the dunes below a solitary tower, their faces watching him calmly. He realized that they had followed him across the island from their former haunt among the dried-up lakes. Once again he saw the beckoning light, and he decided to continue his exploration of the island.

Half a mile further along the atoll he found a group of four submarine pens, built over an inlet, now drained, which wound through the dunes from the sea. The pens still contained several feet of water, filled with strange luminescent fish and plants. A warning light winked at intervals from a metal tower. The remains of a substantial camp, only recently vacated, stood on the concrete pier outside. Greedily Traven heaped his sledge with the provisions stacked inside one of the metal shacks. With this change of diet the beri-beri receded, and during the next days he returned to the camp. It appeared to be the site of a biological expedition. In a field office he came across a series of large charts of mutated chromosomes. He rolled them up and took them back to his bunker. The abstract patterns were meaningless, but during his recovery he amused himself by devising suitable titles for them. (Later, passing the aircraft dump on one of his forays, he found the half-buried jukebox, and tore the list of records from the selection panel, realizing that these were the most appropriate captions for the charts. Thus embroidered, they took on many layers of cryptic associations.)

Traven lost among the blocks

> *August 5. Found the man Traven. A strange derelict figure, hiding in a bunker in the deserted interior of the island. He is suffering from severe exposure and malnutrition, but is unaware of this, or, for that matter, of any other events in the world around him. . . .*
>
> *He maintains that he came to the island to carry out some scientific project—unstated—but I suspect that he understands his real motives and the unique role of the island. . . . In some way its landscape seems to be involved with certain unconscious no-*

267

tions of time, and in particular with those that may be a repressed premonition of our own deaths. The attractions and dangers of such an architecture, as the past has shown, need no stressing.

August 6. He has the eyes of the possessed. I would guess that he is neither the first, nor the last, to visit the island.—from Dr. C. Osborne, "Eniwetok Diary."

With the exhaustion of his supplies, Traven remained within the perimeter of the blocks almost continuously, conserving what strength remained to him to walk slowly down their empty corridors. The infection in his right foot made it difficult for him to replenish his supplies from the stores left by the biologists, and as his strength ebbed he found progressively less incentive to make his way out of the blocks. The system of megaliths now provided a complete substitute for those functions of his mind which gave to it its sense of the sustained rational order of time and space, his awareness kindled from levels above those of his present nervous system (if the autonomic system is dominated by the past, the cerebro-spinal reaches toward the future). Without the blocks, his sense of reality shrank to little more than the few square inches of sand beneath his feet.

On one of his last ventures into the maze, he spent all night and much of the following morning in a futile attempt to escape. Dragging himself from one rectangle of shadow to another, his leg as heavy as a club and apparently inflamed to the knee, he realized that he must soon find an equivalent for the blocks or he would end his life within them, trapped within this self-constructed mausoleum as surely as the retinue of Pharaoh.

He was sitting exhausted somewhere within the center of the system, the faceless lines of the tomb-booths receding from him, when the sky was slowly divided by the drone of a light aircraft. This passed overhead, and then, five minutes later, returned. Seizing his opportunity, Traven struggled to his feet and made his exit from the blocks, his head raised to follow the glistening exhaust trail.

As he lay down in the bunker he dimly heard the aircraft return and carry out an inspection of the site.

A Belated Rescue

"Who are you?" A small sandy-haired man was peering down at him with a severe expression, then put away a syringe in his valise. "Do you realize you're on your last legs?"

"Traven . . . I've had some sort of accident. I'm glad you flew over."

"I'm sure you are. Why didn't you use our emergency radio? Anyway, we'll call the Navy and have you picked up."

"No. . . ." Traven sat up on one elbow and felt weakly in his hip pocket. "I have a pass somewhere. I'm carrying out research."

"Into what?" The question assumed a complete understanding of Traven's motives. Traven lay in the shade beside the bunker, and drank weakly from a canteen as Dr. Osborne dressed his foot. "You've also been stealing our stores."

Traven shook his head. Fifty yards away the blue and white Cessna stood on the concrete apron like a large dragonfly. "I didn't realize you were coming back."

"You must be in a trance."

The young woman at the controls of the aircraft climbed from the cockpit and walked over to them, glancing at the grey bunkers and blocks. She seemed unaware of or uninterested in the decrepit figure of Traven. Osborne spoke to her over his shoulder, and after a downward glance at Traven she went back to the aircraft. As she turned Traven rose involuntarily, recognizing the child in the photograph he had pinned to the wall. Then he remembered that the magazine could not have been more than four or five years old.

The engine of the aircraft started. It turned onto one of the roadways and took off into the wind.

The young woman drove over by jeep that afternoon with a small camp bed and a canvas awning. During the intervening hours Traven had slept, and woke refreshed when Osborne returned from his scrutiny of the surrounding dunes.

"What are you doing here?" the young woman asked as she secured one of the guy-ropes to the bunker.

"I'm searching for my wife and son," Traven said.

"They're on this island?" Surprised, but taking the reply at face value, she looked around her. "Here?"

"In a manner of speaking."

After inspecting the bunker, Osborne joined them. "The child in the photograph. Is she your daughter?"

"No." Traven tried to explain. "She's adopted *me*."

Unable to make sense of his replies, but accepting his assurances that he would leave the island, Osborne and the young woman returned to their camp. Each day Osborne returned to change the dressing, driven by the young woman, who seemed to grasp the role cast for her by Traven in his private mythology. Osborne, when he learned of Traven's previous career as a military pilot, assumed that he was a latter-day martyr left high and dry by the moratorium on thermonuclear tests.

"A guilt complex isn't an indiscriminate supply of moral sanctions. I think you may be overstretching yours."

When he mentioned the name Eatherly, Traven shook his head.

Undeterred, Osborne pressed: "Are you sure you're not making similar use of the image of Eniwetok—waiting for your pentecostal wind?"

"Believe me, Doctor, no," Traven replied firmly. "For me the H-Bomb is a symbol of absolute freedom. Unlike Eatherly, I feel it's given me the right—the obligation, even—to do anything I choose."

"That seems strange logic," Osborne commented. "Aren't we at least responsible for our physical selves?"

Traven shrugged. "Not now, I think. After all, aren't we in effect men raised from the dead?"

Often, however he thought of Eatherly: the prototypal Pre-Third Man, dating the Pre-Third from August 6, 1945, carrying a full load of cosmic guilt.

270

Shortly after Traven was strong enough to walk again he had to be rescued from the blocks for a second time. Osborne became less conciliatory.

"Our work is almost complete," he warned Traven. "You'll die here. Traven, what are you looking for?"

To himself Traven said: the tomb of the unknown civilian, *Homo Hydrogenensis*, Eniwetok Man. To Osborne he said: "Doctor, your laboratory is at the wrong end of this island."

"I'm aware of that, Traven. There are rarer fish swimming in your head than in any submarine pen."

On the day before they left Traven and the young woman drove over to the lakes where he had first arrived. As a final present from Osborne, an ironic gesture unexpected from the elderly biologist, she had brought the correct list of legends for the chromosome charts. They stopped by the derelict jukebox and she pasted them on to the selection panel.

They wandered among the supine wrecks of the superfortresses. Traven lost sight of her, and for the next ten minutes searched in and out of the dunes. He found her standing in a small amphitheatre formed by the sloping mirrors of a solar energy device, built by one of the visiting expeditions. She smiled to him as he stepped through the scaffolding. A dozen fragmented images of herself were reflected in the broken panes. In some she was sans head, in others multiples of her raised arms circled her like those of a Hindu goddess. Exhausted, Traven turned away and walked back to the jeep.

As they drove away he described his glimpses of his wife and son. "Their faces are always calm. My son's particularly, although he was never really like that. The only time his face was grave was when he was being born —then he seemed millions of years old."

The young woman nodded. "I hope you find them." As an afterthought she added: "Dr. Osborne is going to tell the Navy you're here. Hide somewhere."

Traven thanked her. When she flew away from the island for the last time he waved to her from his seat beside the blocks.

When the search party came for him Traven hid in the only logical place. Fortunately the search was perfunctory, and was called off after a few hours. The sailors had brought a supply of beer with them, and the search soon turned into a drunken ramble. On the walls of the recording towers Traven later found balloons of obscene dialogue chalked into the mouths of the shadow figures, giving their postures the priapic gaiety of the dancers in cave drawings.

The climax of the party was the ignition of a store of gasoline in an underground tank near the airstrip. As he listened, first to the megaphones shouting his name, the echoes receding among the dunes like the forlorn calls of dying birds, then to the boom of the explosion and the laughter as the landing craft left, Traven felt a premonition that these were the last sounds he would hear.

He had hidden in one of the target basins, lying down among the bodies of the plastic dummies. In the hot sunlight their deformed faces gaped at him sightlessly from the tangle of limbs, their blurred smiles like those of the soundlessly laughing dead. Their faces filled his mind as he climbed over the bodies and returned to the bunker.

As he walked toward the blocks he saw the figures of his wife and son standing in his path. They were less than ten yards from him, their white faces watching him with a look of almost overwhelming expectancy. Never had Traven seen them so close to the blocks. His wife's pale features seemed illuminated from within, her lips parted as if in greeting, one hand raised to take his own. His son's grave face, with its curiously fixed expression, regarded him with the same enigmatic smile of the girl in the photograph.

"Judith! David!" Startled, Traven ran forwards to them. Then, in a sudden movement of light, their clothes turned into shrouds, and he saw the wounds that disfigured their necks and chests. Appalled, he cried out to them. As they vanished he fled into the safety and sanity of the blocks.

272

This time he found himself, as Osborne had predicted, unable to leave the blocks.

Somewhere in the shifting center of the maze, he sat with his back against one of the concrete flanks, his eyes raised to the sun. Around him the lines of cubes formed the horizons of his world. At times they would appear to advance toward him, looming over him like cliffs, the intervals between them narrowing so that they were little more than an arm's length apart, a labyrinth of narrow corridors running between them. Then they would recede from him, separating from each other like points in an expanding universe, until the nearest line formed an intermittent palisade along the horizon.

Time had become quantal. For hours it would be noon, the shadows contained within the motionless bulk of the blocks, the heat reverberating off the concrete floor. Abruptly he would find it was early afternoon or evening, the shadows everywhere like pointing fingers.

"Goodbye, Eniwetok," he murmured.

Somewhere there was a flicker of light, as if one of the blocks, like a counter on an abacus, had been plucked away.

"Goodbye, Los Alamos." Again a block seemed to vanish. The corridors around him remained intact, but somewhere, Traven was convinced, in the matrix superimposed on his mind, a small interval of neutral space had been punched.

Goodbye, Hiroshima.

Goodbye, Alamagordo.

Goodbye, Moscow, London, Paris, New York. . . .

Shuttles flickered, a ripple of integers. Traven stopped, accepting the futility of this megathlon farewell. Such a leave-taking required him to fix his signature on every one of the particles in the universe.

Total Noon: Eniwetok

The blocks now occupied positions on an endlessly revolving circus wheel. They carried him upwards, to heights from which he could see the whole island and the sea, and then down again through the opaque disc of the floor. From here he looked up at the undersurface of the concrete cap, an inverted landscape of rectilinear hollows, the dome-shaped mounds of the lake-system, the thousands of empty cubic pits of the blocks.

"Goodbye, Traven"

To his disappointment he found that this ultimate act of rejection gained him nothing.

In an interval of lucidity, he looked down at his emaciated arms and legs propped loosely in front of him, the brittle wrists and hands covered with a lacework of ulcers. To his right was a trail of disturbed dust, the marks of slack heels.

In front of him lay a long corridor between the blocks, joining an oblique series a hundred yards away. Among these, where a narrow interval revealed the open space beyond, was a crescent-shaped shadow, poised in the air.

During the next half-hour it moved slowly, turning as the sun swung.

The outline of a dune.

Seizing on this cipher, which hung before him like a symbol on a shield, Traven pushed himself through the dust. He climbed precariously to his feet, and covered his eyes from all sight of the blocks.

Ten minutes later he emerged from the western perimeter. The dune whose shadow had guided him lay fifty yards away. Beyond it, bearing the shadow like a screen, was a ridge of limestone, which ran away among the hillocks of a wasteland. The remains of old bulldozers, bales of barbed wire, and fifty-gallon drums lay half-buried in the sand.

Traven approached the dune, reluctant to leave this anonymous swell of sand. He shuffled around its edges, and then sat down in the shade by a narrow crevice in the ridge.

Ten minutes later he noticed that someone was watching him.

This corpse, whose eyes stared up at Traven, lay to his left at the bottom of the crevice. That of a man of middle age and powerful build, it lay on its side with its head on a pillow of stone, as if surveying the window of the sky. The fabric of the clothes had rotted to a gray tattered vestment, but in the absence of any small animal predators on the island the skin and musculature had been preserved. Here and there, at the angle of knee or wrist, a bony point shone through the leathery integument of the yellow skin, but the facial mask was still intact, and revealed a male Japanese of the professional classes. Looking down at the strong nose, high forehead, and broad mouth, Traven guessed that the Japanese had been a doctor or lawyer.

Puzzled as to how the corpse had found itself here, Traven slid a few feet down the slope. There were no radiation burns on the skin, which indicated that the Japanese had been there for less than five years. Nor did he appear to be wearing a uniform, so had not been a member of a military or scientific mission.

To the left of the corpse, within reach of his hand, was a frayed leather case, the remains of a map wallet. To the right was the bleached husk of a haversack, open to reveal a canteen of water and a small jerrican.

Greedily, the reflex of starvation making him for the moment ignore this discovery that the Japanese had deliberately chosen to die in the crevice, Traven slid down the slope until his feet touched the splitting soles of the corpse's shoes. He reached forward and seized the canteen. A cupful of flat water swilled around the rusting bottom. Traven gulped down the water, the dissolved metal salts cloaking his lips and tongue with a bitter film. He pried the lid off the jerrican, which was empty but for a tacky coating of condensed syrup. He scraped at this with the lid and chewed at the tarry flakes. They filled his mouth with an almost intoxicating sweetness. After a few moments he felt light-headed and sat back beside the corpse. Its sightless eyes regarded him with unmoving compassion.

(A small fly, which Traven presumes has followed him into the crevice, now buzzes about the corpse's face. Traven leans forward to kill it, then reflects that perhaps this minuscule sentry had been the corpse's faithful companion, in return fed on the rich liqueurs and distillations of its pores. Carefully, to avoid injuring the fly, he encourages it to alight on his wrist.)

DR. YASUDA: Thank you, Traven. *(The voice is rough, as if unused to conversation.)* In my position, you understand.

TRAVEN: Of course, doctor. I'm sorry I tried to kill it. These ingrained habits, you know, they're not easy to shrug off. Your sister's children in Osaka in '44, the exigencies of war, I hate to plead them, most known motives are so despicable one searches the unknown in the hope that. . . .

YASUDA: Please, Traven, do not be embarrassed. The fly is lucky to retain its identity for so long. That son you mourn, not to mention my own two nieces and nephew, did they not die each day? Every parent in the world mourns the lost sons and daughters of their past childhoods.

TRAVEN: You're very tolerant, doctor. I wouldn't dare—

YASUDA: Not at all, Traven. I make no apologies for you. After all, each one of us is little more than the meagre residue of the infinite unrealized possibilities of our lives. But your son and my nieces are fixed in our minds forever, their identities as certain as the stars.

TRAVEN: *(not entirely convinced)* That may be so, doctor, but it leads to a dangerous conclusion in the case of this island. For instance, the blocks. . . .

YASUDA: They are precisely to what I refer. Here among the blocks, Traven, you at last find the image of yourself free of time and space. This island is an ontological Garden of Eden; why try to expel yourself into a quantal world?

TRAVEN: Excuse me. (*The fly has flown back to the corpse's face and sits in one of the orbits, giving the good doctor an expression of quizzical beadiness. Reaching forward, Traven entices it onto his palm.*) Well, yes, these bunkers may be ontological objects, but whether this is the ontological fly seems doubtful. It's true that on this island it's the only fly, which is the next best thing.

YASUDA: You can't accept the plurality of the universe, Traven. Ask yourself, why? Why should this obsess you. It seems to me that you are hunting for the white leviathan, zero. The beach is a dangerous zone; avoid it. Have a proper humility; pursue a philosophy of acceptance.

TRAVEN: Then may I ask why you came here, doctor?

YASUDA: To feed this fly. "What greater love—?"

TRAVEN: (*Still puzzling*) It doesn't really solve my problem. The blocks, you see. . . .

YASUDA: Very well, if you must have it that way . . .

TRAVEN: But, Doctor—

YASUDA: (*Peremptorily*) Kill that fly!

TRAVEN: That's not an end, or a beginning. (*Hopelessly he kills the fly. Exhausted, he falls asleep beside the corpse.*)

The Terminal Beach

Searching for a piece of rope in the refuse dump behind the dunes, Traven found a bale of rusty wire. He unwound it, then secured a harness around the corpse's chest, and dragged it from the crevice. The lid of a wooden crate served as a sledge. Traven fastened the corpse into a sitting position, and set off along the perimeter of the blocks. Around him the island was silent. The lines of palms hung in the sunlight, only his own motion varying the shifting ciphers of their crisscrossing trunks. The square turrets of the camera towers jutted from the dunes like forgotten obelisks.

An hour later, when Traven reached his bunker, he untied the wire cord he had fastened around his waist. He took the chair left for him by Dr. Osborne and carried it to a point midway between the bunker and the blocks. Then he tied the body of the Japanese to the chair, arranging the hands so that they rested on the wooden arms, giving the moribund figure a posture of calm repose.

This done to his satisfaction, Traven returned to the bunker and squatted under the awning.

As the next days passed into weeks, the dignified figure of the Japanese sat in his chair fifty yards from him, guarding Traven from the blocks. Their magic still filled Traven's reveries, but he now had sufficient strength to rouse himself and forage for food. In the hot sunlight the skin of the Japanese became more and more bleached, and sometimes Traven would wake at night to find the white sepulchral figure sitting there, arms resting at its sides, in the shadows that crossed the concrete floor. At these moments he would often see his wife and son watching him from the dunes. As time passed they came closer, and he would sometimes turn to find them only a few yards behind him.

Patiently Traven waited for them to speak to him, thinking of the great blocks whose entrance was guarded by the seated figure of the dead archangel, as the waves broke on the distant shore and the burning bombers fell through his dreams.